COLLEEN GLEASON

The Vampire Voss

D1636089

MIRA

MIRA

ISBN-13: 978-0-7783-1367-0

THE VAMPIRE VOSS

Recycling programs
for this product may
not exist in your area.

For questions and comments about the quality of this book please contact us at
Customer_eCare@Harlequin.ca.

www.Harlequin.com

Printed in U.S.A.

To my dear Kelly...you're always such a bright spot in my life. Thanks for all your wisdom and guidance.

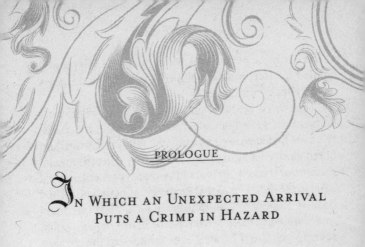

In Which an Unexpected Arrival Puts a Crimp in Hazard

London, 1804

"What in the dark hell is he doing here?" Dimitri, the Earl of Corvindale, set his glass precisely on the table, then adjusted it with great deliberation. He still held his cards but was no longer looking at them.

The man in question—the term "man" being a loose one, of course—had walked through the door of the hidden apartments at White's. These rooms were reserved for Dimitri and those of his ilk, and could only be accessed by someone who knew the right thing to say.

It was more than unfortunate that the man in question knew what to say to gain entrance. It was damned annoying.

The newcomer strode into the chamber and scanned the space, which hosted fewer than a dozen occupants on a good night. He was average in height, with thick hair the color of molasses and a square, dimpled chin—both characteristics that made him very popular with those of the feminine persuasion. More than a bit of swagger colored his step, making Dimitri itch to adjust the glass again. Bloody nuisance.

"I haven't any idea what he's doing here," replied his companion, Giordan Cale, looking up from his cards. His eyes had narrowed as well, and Dimitri saw the hint of red glow emanating from their pupils. He presumed it was due to the new arrival rather than a particularly bad hand. Cale didn't have that large pile of pound notes and coins in front of him simply due to luck. "The last time I saw Voss was…hell. Must have been in Prague—sixty, seventy years ago." Cale's eyes crinkled at the corners. "How time flies when you live forever."

Dimitri didn't respond. There were days when forever was interminable. And days when he found it convenient to know he'd live forever.

Or, at least, for a very long time.

To his great irritation, at that moment, Voss made eye contact with him. Dimitri allowed a warning to flare in his own eyes then banked it. The man wasn't worth the effort.

"I don't believe I've seen the man for years m'self," commented the third at their game of hazard.

"Consider yourself fortunate," Dimitri murmured to Lord Eddersley as the newcomer made his way toward them.

Voss moved with what could only be described as flair and confidence. Despite his long absence, he had the right to be there, in the private, subterranean apartments at the famous White's men's club. The place Dimitri and his ilk considered their own, the place where it didn't matter what they drank or how they found their pleasure. A place where they didn't have to pretend.

Voss lifted an insouciant finger toward the footman in the corner and gestured for his drink to be brought to their table.

His arrogance made Dimitri's grip tighten around the heavy glass, but he kept his expression passive as Voss pulled a chair over to join them. "Corvindale," Voss greeted Dimitri by his title with a nod, then turned to his companion. "Eddersley."

"Cale, recall Voss. Dewhurst's heir." Dimitri kept his tone bored. "Voss, Giordan Cale."

"Of course Cale and I have met," said Voss as he nodded toward the third man at the table. A curl tumbled artfully over one brow and Dimitri's lip curled. "And, incidentally, I'm now Lord Dewhurst. Father passed on a year ago. Or so the story goes." He gave an arch laugh and even Dimitri couldn't resist a wry smile then.

Such was the sort of artifice to which the immortal of the Draculia were consigned. Constant lies, subterfuge and half-truths.

And, naturally, much relocating. One couldn't stay in one place for more than three decades without facing awkward questions.

"No mourning clothing in sight," Dimitri observed. "Tsk, tsk. Of course, one shouldn't be surprised, knowing how that puts off the ladies."

Voss gave him a half smile along with a flash of eyeglow as if to let him know he was fully aware how annoyed Dimitri was. "Deal me in," he said, dropping a stack of notes onto the table.

Satan's stones. Dimitri was about to rise and toss his own cards onto the table when Voss looked over at him. His face had lost that languid expression, the deviltry that so beguiled the ladies—and that got him into so many difficult circumstances—dissolved.

"Sit down, Corvindale," Voss said. This time, he showed a tip of fang. "I've news for you. Consider it a gift."

Dimitri's own fangs extended in automatic reaction to the show of provocation. "The last time you brought me a gift, you did nothing but irritate me and cost me a generation's worth of property, not to mention my heart nearly on a stake." *And helped cause the death of a woman.*

The other man smiled, though it wasn't quite as easy, still showing just a tip of both pointed incisors. "But I thought for certain you would have forgotten that by now. It's been nearly a hundred years since Vienna, two generations past, Corvindale. Surely you haven't been stewing about it for all this time."

Light, light words. But the reality was much darker. And though it had been decades, and Dimitri had come to terms with the fact that it mostly had been an accident, he still wished Voss to hell on a more than occasional basis. Nevertheless, Dimitri didn't rise to the bait. He sheathed his fangs and hooded his eyes, although he wasn't able to resist letting his annoyance glow from them. "Then shall we dispense with hazard and discuss your tidings?" The bored tone had returned to his voice. "Why waste a perfectly good card game."

Voss bowed his head in supercilious acquiescence. "Your command, my lord." He lifted the drink that had appeared a moment earlier and sipped, then nodded at the glass as if in agreement with it. "French. Been running the lines, have you, Corvindale? Or is this not from your private stock?"

The Treaty of Amiens had dissolved more than a year

ago and war between England and France had flared again, making it impossible to fill one's cellar with any French vintage or fashion. Unless one had special arrangements.

Dimitri gave him an arch glance that answered the newcomer's question. Naturally it was from his private stock, acquired through illegal means. Not that legalities or governing bodies meant anything to any of the Draculia.

"I approve, for I drink only for pleasure tonight, Dimitri," Voss was saying. "I fed yesterday. A lovely, very promiscuous young woman and her two best friends. A plump and generous threesome tasting of a hint of rose and coriander." He lifted his square, dimpled chin and smiled knowingly. "Warm and delightful. And *fresh.*"

"Country girls, I presume?" Dimitri said coolly, although his fangs threatened to shoot to full extension. Bastard. "What a shame the bourgeois aren't foolish enough to lift their skirts for you. All those lovely white thighs and blue blood."

Pure red burned in Voss's eyes, making even his dark irises glow. "I can't imagine what it would be like to deny oneself the pleasure of a real feeding for decades. To be resigned only to a bottle of pig's blood, or worse. It would certainly make one cold and empty. Unpleasant, to say the least. Slow. And repulsive."

Dimitri accepted the slur; it was nothing new. The others feared him, keeping their distance, interacting with him only when necessary, pretending to be his comrade whilst whispering behind his back. Within the Draculia—those who bore Lucifer's Mark identifying the crack in their souls—it was common knowledge that Dimitri hadn't fed on a living human for more than two generations. He'd taken up that abstinence not long after the events in Vienna.

The exception to the divide between himself and the wary deference of the others was Voss, who had only this sort of insolence to show, and Cale, whom Dimitri considered his only true friend.

Unlike Dimitri, Voss wore his dissociation from the other Dracule like a mantle of pride—mainly because it was of his own making. Voss, now the very wealthy Viscount Dewhurst, amused himself by seeking and collecting information that could be sold or bartered and, Dimitri suspected, he did so also in order to insulate himself from the others.

Dimitri, on the other hand, didn't care what anyone thought of him and did nothing to challenge long-held perceptions. He simply wanted to be left alone with his studies and occasionally emerge to the gentlemen's clubs for a game of chance or a midnight horse race. Or perhaps a bout of pugilism at Gentleman Jackson's.

"If you have news, I suggest you share it. Sooner rather than later," Dimitri said at last.

Voss's contemptuousness seemed to evaporate as he leaned toward him, as did the anger in his eyes. For a moment, Dimitri sensed a sort of hesitation, perhaps, or doubt, from the younger man. Younger in years on the earth by perhaps a generation, but not in physical appearance. To an ignorant mortal, the two men would appear to be in their thirties instead of well over one century old.

Voss's fingers traced idly over the sides of his cognac glass, giving him the appearance of being relaxed. But his face was intense and his voice pitched low enough for only Dimitri to hear.

"Narcise Moldavi has disappeared."

Next to him, Cale stilled, and Dimitri flickered a glance at his companion. The man's face was passive, his eyes flat and dark as he lifted his glass of wine. He remained silent.

"Cezar Moldavi can't keep control of his own sister. Why is that such great news?" Dimitri's tone was flat and bored. Yet, his attention sharpened. He had a bad feeling about this.

Voss sipped then returned his drink to the table. "You're not a fool. You know Moldavi will eagerly blame no one other than yourself for her disappearance. Regardless of any evidence—or the lack thereof."

"Again, you bring me no information that I don't already possess," Dimitri replied, annoyed at the reminder that Cezar Moldavi continued to disfigure the face of the earth after two centuries. He forced his fingers to release the glass, slowly and deliberately. "You've interrupted my game for naught."

"From the looks of it, Cale is the one with the largest pot. Perhaps you ought to thank me." Voss settled back in his chair, once again looking like the rake he was well-known for being: heavy-eyed, half smiling, relaxed. "But here is the information you likely don't possess."

Dimitri didn't care for the smile twitching the corners of the man's mouth. What the hell had brought Voss back to London anyway? Surely not this sort of dancing, parleying conversation. Probably the women. It had always been the women, the pleasure, the hedonism for Voss and others of the Dracule. And for a time, Dimitri had tried to enjoy it as well, and had even promoted it through his establishment in Vienna. A renewal of annoyance flushed through him, and he pushed it away. It wasn't worth the effort.

Standing, he swiped up the handful of notes and coins he'd won in the game and folded them neatly. "I find myself bored with the company and conversation. Carry on."

As he turned, shoving the winnings into his coat pocket, Voss's parting words came to settle on the back of his neck, as if burned there. "Chas Woodmore was last seen in Paris, with Narcise. He's gone missing, as well."

Woodmore was gone? With Narcise? Bloody damned bones of Satan. Woodmore was supposed to *kill* Moldavi, not run off with his sister. Dimitri didn't pause but his gut tightened. That pronouncement meant a variety of things, but by his personal estimation the worst was what it meant to Dimitri, himself.

It meant that his well-ordered, if monotonous, life was about to turn upside down. It meant that his solitude, his studies, his very existence was about to be invaded by the trio of silly, giggling, frippery-happy Woodmore sisters. Including Miss Maia Woodmore.

Why in the name of the Fates had he ever promised Chas Woodmore he'd watch over them? Why did Woodmore have to do something so blasted foolish? He should have left Cezar Moldavi to Dimitri to handle.

Damn it all to Lucifer.

Dimitri curled his lips and darkly considered his predicament. He had a few days to put things in order before the girls would invade his home. They couldn't stay at their residence, not with Cezar Moldavi coming after their brother. But Dimitri wasn't about to have them under the Corvindale roof until he was prepared to be overrun.

Damn and blast and burning bones.

He'd have to set some guards to watch over the girls until he was ready to have them to Blackmont Hall. *Damn the Fates.* What the hell was it going to be like with three young, *mortal* women in his house? Hell, he'd probably have to have Mirabella come in from the country. And a chaperone to keep it proper.

Grinding his teeth, Dimitri poured another glass of whiskey, then tossed it back with a big swallow. When he glanced up, Voss, the bastard, was watching him with a smirk.

He knew exactly how annoyed Dimitri was. And the man was enjoying every moment of it.

Damn it to Lucifer.

1

WHEREIN MISS WOODMORE'S SERVICES ARE ENGAGED

Voss adjusted the shoulders of his coat, aligning the seams, then smoothed the lapels and hem. Having been alive for more than a hundred forty years, he'd seen his share of fashions come and go—and some of them had been horrific. Thank the Fates that the wigs and long, swinging coats that had been in fashion during all of the upheaval around Charles II had given way to shirts and neckcloths and pantaloons. The tailoring was much more attractive, and showing one's own hair was much preferred after decades of wigs and powder.

But Voss's mind wasn't, for once, wholly on his appearance or how he was going to find a nice plump thigh or two to sample…along with, of course, a bit more intimacy. Instead he was still mulling over the expression on Dimitri's face two nights ago in the back rooms at White's.

Dimitri still hadn't forgiven him for that night in Vienna, and Voss supposed he couldn't wholly blame him. The incident in 1690 that had caused their rift had been a combination of misjudgment and unfortunate happenstance. Voss had long written it off to his inexperience and having only been Dracule for six years at the time. Nevertheless, he should have realized that whatever sense of humor Dimitri had had long been lost after becoming Dracule. Or perhaps he'd never even had one, growing up the son of an English earl during the dark times of Oliver Cromwell and his stark Puritan ways.

But that occasion in Vienna had taken place so long ago that the Plague had still been a threat, and unfortunate as it was, the resulting destruction of Dimitri's property and the death of his mistress had been an accident. Most of the blame was, and rightly should be, laid at the feet of Cezar Moldavi—who'd also been in Vienna.

But however the blame had been distributed, the fact that he'd infuriated Dimitri all those years ago made it more difficult for Voss to get what he needed from him. And the fact was he needed Dimitri's cooperation now that Woodmore was gone. They weren't precisely enemies, Voss and Dimitri—but neither did they fully trust each other. It was more as if they were two dogs circling, eyeing each other balefully. With Dimitri doing most of the baleful eyeing, if one was to be wholly honest.

Voss frowned, adjusting the cuff of his shirt. Even if Chas Woodmore—who was not a member of the Draculia—wasn't dead now, he would be as soon as Cezar Moldavi found him with his sister. It was only a matter of time.

"Bastard's as cold and frigid as a dead mortal," he muttered to himself, thinking of Dimitri and his decades of self-denial of the most basic of needs. Whether it stemmed from the incident with Moldavi and Lerina that night in Vienna, or maybe because of his previous mistress, Meg, he didn't know, but Dimitri's choice was an abstinence worse than chastity. Neither of which were the least bit attractive to Voss.

"Beg pardon, my lord?" said his valet, Kimton, turning from the wardrobe. A variety of rejected neckcloths hung from his fingers and over his arms.

"Nothing," Voss replied, picking up his hat and gloves. He paused one last time to admire the cut of his steel-blue coat and gray, gold and midnight patterned vest. His shirt was crisp and white, and the chosen neckcloth a rich sapphire. He'd chosen to stud it with a black jet pin in the shape of an X.

Or, if looked at from a different angle, a cross. But no one would recognize the irony of that except another Dracule.

He smiled, admired the glint of his fangs as they eased smoothly out to press against his lower lip and flashed a bit of that alluring glow from his pupils. Tonight was going to be a delightful challenge. He wondered which of the Woodmore sisters would fall prey to his charm first. Another game, of course. It didn't really matter which one did, as long as one of them succumbed and he could get the information he needed—namely, which of them had the gift of the Sight.

After that, it would be a simple matter to coax the information he wanted from the chit, and then he could be on his way before Woodmore was any wiser. The biggest concern was, however, whether Moldavi knew yet just how valuable the sisters were. The last thing Voss wanted was for Moldavi to realize he could procure his own information from the girls, for it would decidedly deflate Voss's leverage with him. And it would take all of the amusement out of things.

If nothing else, Voss appreciated pleasure and amusement in his life.

After all, when one lived forever, and one was rich as sin, one had to find entertainment and pleasure in order to keep things from becoming mundane. Unfortunately his attempt at amusement and puzzle-solving was precisely what had driven the wedge between him and Dimitri more than a century ago.

But then again, a simple life without pleasure, diversion and the matching of wits would be tedious. Especially when it stretched on for eternity.

Voss ignored the internal rumble of discontent and reached for the handkerchief that Kimton had neatly folded, tucking it into a pocket, giving himself a last critical once-over in the mirror.

It was a relief to return to civilization after spending the majority of the last generation in the Colonies. The man who'd been installed as his father, Lord Dewhurst, had retired from his post—which was to say, he'd been paid off to live the rest of his years in the mountains of Romania or Switzerland—and Voss had been able to reinstate himself as Dewhurst after a forty-year exile. During that time, he'd managed brief trips to Paris, Vienna, Rome and even London, of course, but he couldn't remain there long and still draw on his accounts.

It was too difficult and certainly impolitic to explain why Viscount Dewhurst never aged, disliked going outside when it was very sunny and preferred the warm rich taste of blood to any vintage or, Luce forbid, the rot they called ale in Boston. And if anyone noticed the extreme resemblance between every other generation of Lord Dewhursts, it was merely written off to a strong family tree.

Voss smiled as he pulled on his own gloves. A strong and quite unique family tree indeed. The fact that he and Dimitri, as well as Cezar Moldavi, sprang from the same widespread branches was merely an irritation in the grand scheme of things. It was fortunate to Voss's way of thinking that *his* Draculian ancestors, as well as those of Dimitri, Cale and a limited number of others, had found their wives among the British and French peerage and thus had conferred upon them their titles and estates throughout Western Europe. Moldavi's roots, on the other hand, were firmly entrenched in the cold, uncivilized mountains of Transylvania and Romania. Drafty castles and mountainous estates located leagues from anything resembling civilization would not be to Voss's liking. Perhaps that was part of the reason Moldavi was so intent on growing his power over mortal and Dracule alike, and why he'd established himself in Paris, trying to create an ally in Bonaparte.

At the bottom of the stairs of his James Park residence, Voss found his butler, Moross (whom he privately called Morose for obvious reasons), waiting at the door.

"Your carriage, my lord," the man intoned. It wasn't time for his once-a-decade smile, so he merely looked down his long bloodhound face.

"Where's Eddersley? And Brickbank?" Voss asked, glancing at the clock in the foyer. Nearly eleven. They'd been expected by half past ten, and he thought he'd heard voices below as he finished dressing. Everyone in the household knew better than to interrupt him in his toilette.

"Here!" trilled a voice. A very happy voice—rather a bit high in pitch to be comfortably masculine—which belonged to Brickbank. From the sound of it, he'd been into Voss's private vintage in the study. Blast. He'd only been back in London for three days and already Brickbank was becoming an annoyance.

Yes, Voss was more than ready to make the rounds in Society and take advantage of any offered—or coaxed—opportunities therein whilst going about his more urgent business, but there was a time for play and a time for business. To quote a book that he was only vaguely familiar with.

In most cases, however, Voss found a way to combine both business and pleasure.

Brickbank cared for little more than charming a few debutantes in a dark corner to see how far down their gloves would slip. Although Voss wasn't averse to those challenges himself, he had a bit more on his mind than that. With Moldavi riding his tongue along Bonaparte's arse crack, the Draculia cartel in London would be well served by preparedness.

And Voss was in the position to accomplish just that.

The door to the study opened and out tottered Brickbank, his eyes bright and his nose tinged red. Behind him strode Eddersley, his mop of thick dark hair a mess as usual and a bemused expression on his face. Voss met his eyes and Eddersley shrugged.

"Shall we?" Voss asked coolly, resisting the urge to look at the condition of his study. Morose would see to any disruption with pleasure. "The ball should be in full crush by now."

"You're certain the Woodmore chits will be there?" asked Brickbank, bumping against him as they both moved toward the front door. "Abhor stuffy crushes."

"By all accounts they will. At least, the two elder ones. Unless Corvindale has locked them away already,"

Voss replied, stepping back so that his clumsy friend could precede him through the front door.

Eddersley gave a short laugh. "Dimitri likely hasn't yet met them. He'd be in no hurry to accept his responsibility as their guardian, temporary or otherwise. That would mean actually speaking to a mortal—and a female one at that—and removing himself from his study."

Voss nodded, smiling to himself. He'd given Corvindale the news only two nights ago; even he wouldn't have moved that quickly to get the girls under his roof and safe from Moldavi. And that was precisely the reason he was taking himself off to the Lundhames' ball tonight.

There were rumors about the Woodmore girls and their abilities, of course—which was why Dimitri had become ensnared in a mess that he surely would prefer to be left out of—but whether those rumors about the sisters and their secrets had yet reached the streets of Paris, and thus the ears of Moldavi, was uncertain. Since the war and the new Emperor Bonaparte's subsequent buildup of brigades ready to invade England, even those who were Dracule had a bit more difficulty with expedient communication.

Chas Woodmore had done his best to keep his sisters and their abilities under wraps while at the same time making himself indispensable to Corvindale and other members of the Draculia. It was too bad Woodmore didn't trust Voss enough to turn the guardianship of his sisters over to *him*, instead of Corvindale. That would have made things much simpler.

The three men climbed into the carriage and Voss settled himself on the green velvet seat. Eddersley and Brickbank found their places across from him, and he rapped on the ceiling. The conveyance started off with nary a jolt and he peered out the window as they drove through St. James. As they rumbled along, the wheels quick and smooth over the cobbles below, Voss found himself less interested in the conversation of his companions than the sights outside the window.

A new moon gave no assistance to the faulty oil lamps illuminating the streets, exposing little but the shadows of random persons making their way along the walkways. The houses and shops, cluttered and clustered together in a jumbled-together fashion so unlike that in the sprawling Colonies, rose like unrelieved black walls on either side of the street. The only texture in that solid dark rise was the occasional alley or mews, just as dark and dangerous.

To mortals, anyway.

Voss felt oddly prickly tonight, as if something irregular were about to happen.

Perhaps it was simply that he'd not been out in London Society for years, although he would never ascribe his unsettled feeling to nerves. A one-hundred-forty-eight-year-old vampire simply didn't have nervous energy…even when he came face-to-face with his own weakness, which, in the case of Voss, was the unassuming hyssop plant.

Each of them, each Dracule, had a personal Asthenia—an Achilles' heel or vulnerability, or whatever one wanted to call it. Other than a wooden stake to the heart, a blade bent on severing head from body or full sunlight, the Asthenia was the only real threat to a member of the Draculia. And even then, the Asthenia caused only pain and great weakness—which often allowed for the stake, sword or sun to do its business.

Not that the Dracule ever discussed or even disclosed this frailty. It was a personal thing, akin to having a flaccid member at the most inopportune moments. Never spoken of, never acknowledged, never dissected. There was, as Giordan Cale had once said, honor among thieves, pirates *and* the Draculia.

Yet, in an attempt to keep his mind occupied and in a bid for personal amusement as well as leverage in the event he needed it, Voss had made a sort of game of it to determine the Asthenias of his Draculian brothers. He considered it nothing more than each man's unique puzzle, and by craft, cunning or mere observation, he had determined the weaknesses of many of his associates.

It was nothing he hadn't been doing for years, for Voss had long been a trained observer. He'd grown up the youngest child and long-awaited heir, and he spent much of his youth eluding tutors and spying on his five elder sisters.

At an early age, he discovered that information was power and that secrets were leverage. His sisters doted on him, spoiled him and easily succumbed to his manipulations, paying him in sweetmeats or playtime when he threatened to divulge who was kissing whose beau, sneaking into the barn with a footman and "borrowing" another sibling's clothing and shoes. The price became even higher when said beau belonged to another sister, or when the gown in question mysteriously reappeared in the owner's wardrobe, torn or stained.

He considered it all in good fun, and as a result, Voss ate plenty of jumballs, candied rosemary and rosewater fritters as well as earned games of chess or backgammon from his sisters or their beaus.

When he turned fifteen and went off to school, Voss realized that his tendency toward observation and manipulation was no longer a simple matter of entertainment, but personal security, as well. The upperclassmen at Eton leeched almost immediately onto the pretty blond boy who tended toward the scrawny side, tossing him into the privy on his second day of school. That shock, after having been petted and fussed over for his young life, caused Voss to look at the world of men quite differently.

Although he spent more than seven hours in the privy that first week, it took Voss no longer than that to skulk around the college, spying and observing and gathering information. He learned that the biggest and most fearsome of the upperclassmen, Barding Delton, had a terrible secret that he could not allow to be divulged. When Voss approached him and indicated that the next time he was thrown into the privy, he would be more than pleased to share with the entire school that Delton couldn't raise his prick to pleasure a woman no matter how hard he tried and how much he boasted about doing so, Delton decided to find someone else to toss into the muck.

And so it went. The mathematics professor who tried to coerce Voss into dropping his breeches for him in a dark corner was deterred by the threat of exposure to his wife and father. The priest who couldn't remember where he'd put the consecrated hosts after a serious drinking bout was induced to give Voss the highe marks in Latin, even when he refused to attend

The most attractive of women fell prey to tion as well, long before he had the abi them with his vampiric eyes. The teacher, the sister of one of hi promised to another—even the mistress of the city's mayor—all found themselves sharing a bed with him.

And that was even before he finished at Eton.

When he became Dracule and realized that each one of his "brothers" had the penultimate secret of a life-threatening Asthenia, Voss found it an amusing pastime to learn what it was for as many of them as possible. He used whatever method it took—deduction, trickery or bribes—and for this reason he found himself all but ostracized by the rest of the Draculia. They simply didn't trust him.

The ostracization was unfair, if not highly amusing to Voss, for he'd rarely sold the information or otherwise utilized it. Nor did he intend to—unless his own life was at stake. The collection of knowledge had become a personal triumph. Some men collected horses or women or wine. Voss collected information.

He was rich, titled, handsome, powerful, could bed any woman he wanted whenever he wanted and he was never going to die. What else was he to do with his infinite amount of time?

What else?

Voss pursed his ⸺s as the carriage trundled along. His comp⸺ ⸺ conversing about some twilight ho⸺ ⸺ had no interest, while he must ⸺ ⸺ore sister out from under the

⸺st another puzzle.

⸺ed as a movement in the ⸺he carriage rolled speed-⸺ into the dark recess of ⸺'s seat as they went by. ⸺figure swooping. His eyes narrowed and he rapped sharply on the vehicle's roof to signal the driver to stop.

Pleasure rushed through him as he sprang from the conveyance before it came to a full stop. Ignoring the exclamations of his companions, Voss was out the door and streaking back down the street toward the long, dark passage between two close-knit buildings.

It was a matter of a breath before he arrived in the engulfing shadows that, nevertheless, appeared to him only like green haze mottled with gray. Although the details were obscured, he could still clearly see shapes and some texture in the dark. His fangs he kept retracted and he knew his eyes glowed faintly, but he didn't allow them to burn very hot. Not yet.

The muffled sounds of struggle filtered through the silence and Voss smiled in anticipation. Just a bit of a diversion before the propriety of the ball.

He moved so silently and quickly that the man had no sense of his presence until Voss closed his fingers over the scruff of his jacket and hoisted him up and away from his prey. Nearly twice his size, the attacker flailed with a meaty arm, attempting to whirl about as Voss propelled him through the air like a child's ball. He landed against a rough brick wall with a satisfying thump as Voss turned to the woman.

Blood scented the air—thick and full and tempting. It had, after all, been two days since he'd fed. Voss drew in a breath of pleasure and looked down at her. In the greenish-glowing dimness, he took note of her wide eyes and her dress—a frock that he could see was of decent quality. The daughter of a tradesman perhaps, or a servant, but certainly not a beggar or even a whore. Her clothing and grooming were much too nice.

She gaped at him, staggering back into the wall behind her as she stumbled away, clearly frightened of everything, including her rescuer.

Voss heard the noise behind him as the heavy man
struggled to his feet, but he ignored it and instead spoke
to the woman. "A bit dark down in here, isn't it, m'dear?"

Her neck and the expanse of her bosom gleamed pale
in the dimness and he saw blood trailing from a cut on
her cheek. It was still fresh; glistening and raw and its
scent teased him. A young woman's blood, cut with fear,
rich and sweet. He could already taste it.

Her mouth moved but nothing came out, yet Voss
stepped closer, reaching for her arm. "Come," he said.
"You don't want to stay here." He turned just as she
gasped in alarm, his arm whipping out to crash solidly
into the other man, who'd lunged at them.

One effortless slash against the attacker's gut, then
an elbow smashing into the side of his head, and this
time the man collapsed like a stone. The aroma of his
blood filled the air, heavy and metallic. And plentiful.

Voss wasn't even tempted.

During this additional altercation, Voss hadn't loosened his grip on the woman's arm, and now he turned
back to coax her. "Come now," he said again, leaning
closer to get a better whiff of her bloodscent. Lovely. "He
won't bother you again. Let's get you somewhere safe."

She made a whimpering sound, and he banked the
glow of his eyes. He'd kept his fangs sheathed all this
time; there was no reason to frighten her any further. He
had other methods, and he preferred an at least some-
what willing partner. Once she understood that pleasure
awaited, she'd be willing and ready.

He'd already stripped off his gloves, and now, with a

bare finger, he reached out and swiped the blood from her cheek. His skin seemed to heat as the liquid touched his flesh, and he brought his finger to his lips. A delicate taste, just there on his mouth…warm, but a bit thin. Not as sweet as he'd expected, or hoped. But pleasant enough. It would do.

She was still gaping up at him with frantic eyes and Voss tugged her closer. "You're safe now," he murmured, and deftly shifted so his foot brushed against hers.

So simple, so easy. He allowed his eyes to shift and beckon, and felt her tension ease as he captured her gaze, just enough to take the edge off her panic. Even in this dim light, he could find the center of a mortal, he could tug and coax and lead.…

She stumbled a bit and he moved closer, still holding the eye contact. "I want to taste you."

Her breath stuttered and she stared at him, her hand trembling against her throat. Her lips parted but nothing came out.

"May I?" he asked, but he was already moving in. Closer. The warmth of her breath puffed against him, buffeting his mouth, the smell of bloodscent filling his nose. He smiled. Then he released and loosened the thrall he had cast upon her so that she knew what he was about to do.

So she would feel the pleasure.

She softened and her eyes fluttered.

His fangs had emerged and he showed them to her. "It won't hurt," he murmured, lifting her arm, smoothing away the sleeve of her frock. Then in a burst of ferocity, he changed his mind and reached for her shoulders. She muttered and shifted, and he pulled away to look at her. A bit of fear leaped there…fear and an edge of curiosity and desire. The glamouring, the thrall, was no longer necessary: he saw only clear need and question. He smiled and bent to her neck.

She stiffened and gasped in shock as his fangs sank in, down into the soft flesh.

Ah. The blood, the sweet flood of it, the smell and taste of iron and fear and naked desire poured through him. His veins surged and filled, his body heated and the familiar throb lifted his cock. She trembled, shuddered, her hands against his shoulders. Whether she were pushing him away or merely steadying herself, he wasn't certain. He didn't care.

When he wanted, he took.

She moaned against him, suddenly soft, suddenly pressing her body all along his. The curve of her breasts and the swell of her arse were tempting and he pulled away from her neck long enough to smother her mouth with his. Heat mixed with the heavy iron of her lifeblood. She shuddered beneath his kiss, her lips opening and the warm sleek thrust of her tongue shared the blood on his lips.

That was the way of it. They always wanted more.

And for the Dracule, it was a dual-pronged need: the desire for hot, sweet, life-sustaining blood combined inextricably with sexual desire. One fed the other: the dual penetrations, the heat and sensuality, the sleek, pulsing sensations, the intimate tastes and scents. Although it was possible, a Dracule rarely indulged in one without the other. Why bother?

She shifted so that her hips moved against him, little gasps and sighs coming from deep in her throat as he returned to feeding, to drawing the pulsing blood from her throat in the same primitive rhythm of coitus. The girl shuddered, vibrating with desire, her fingers curling into his arms.

Voss fed, drawing deep and hard. He breathed in her heated scent, felt the tremors in her torso and her weight suddenly sag between him and the wall. He knew when to stop, and he pulled away. Reluctantly. His cock raged, needing to finish things off.

In response to the interruption, Voss felt the familiar warning twinge on the back of his shoulder.

The girl looked up at him with vacant eyes and he kissed her parted lips in a brief thank you. Then he bent back to the four little wounds on her neck and licked them delicately, slipping his tongue into and around the little indentations to ensure the spread of his healing saliva. After all, he'd just saved her life. It would be a bit of a kick in the face to let her die so soon after.

Just as he was finishing and setting her weak-kneed body up against the wall, Voss heard a noise behind him.

"What in the bloody hell?"

Eddersley.

"Hell, Dewhurst. Can't keep 'em sheathed for more than a few hours, can you?" His friend tsked. Of course, if it were a handsome, muscled young man in the alley, Eddersley would have been unsheathing his own incisors without delay. He'd even looked Voss's way more than once—but that had been decades ago, when they'd first met at one of Cale's parties in Paris.

Voss smiled, still feeling the pleasure. "When the opportunity presents itself, why not? She enjoyed it as much as I. Or at least, that's how she'll remember it." As she tensed, he curled his fingers around her arm so the girl couldn't run off before he was through with her. "You can still join me."

Eddersley didn't look the least bit tempted. "I just visited Rubey's. I'll wait and see what I can find at the Lundhames' tonight. Blue blood's my preference."

Blue blood in a stiff cock, to be precise. "This was nothing more than a bit of foreplay. I've room for more, later, of course." Voss grinned and dabbed at the corners of his mouth with the handkerchief in case of any errant streaks of blood. The girl was making little gasping noises and he looked down at her. "Now, there, m'dear. It's all over for now and soon you won't recall a thing about it. More's the pity for you."

He turned on his gentle thrall, his eyes glowing full and golden-red, and he stared into the girl's gaze. He felt the moment she released the memory of him and what had just occurred: she gave a little sigh and a jolt and then fear blazed into her face.

Good; she'd remember the attack from the man, but wouldn't have the memory of a handsome tawny-haired vampire to share.

"Go," he commanded. "And stay out of the bloody alleys." He released her and watched as the girl pushed past him, dashing toward the street-end of the alley where a lamp provided the relative safety of illumination.

"I thought you were hell-bent on getting to the Lundhames'," Eddersley said. "Didn't think you had time for such a diversion."

Voss straightened up and brushed the sleeve of his coat. "Indeed. But if I hadn't stopped to intervene, she'd have suffered more than a bit of pleasure and four small puncture wounds. 'Twas only a bit of a delay. The Woodmore chits will still be there, I'm certain."

"Never can pass up a bit of the tip-slip, can you, Dewhurst?" said Brickbank as Voss and Eddersley climbed back into the coach.

"Why should I?" he replied, settling into his seat. He was aware of the sharper ache on the back of his right shoulder as he settled into place.

The discomfort was Lucifer's way of annoying him, of course. Reminding him to whom he belonged. The ache wouldn't be nagging at him if he'd gouged his fangs roughly into that little chit's chest, tearing the virgin flesh and sucking until she collapsed—and then left her. Or if he'd savaged her assailant, draining him of his blood or even simply pulling him apart. Or even if he'd driven on by without stopping to interfere.

Voss adjusted his arm and tried to ignore the dull throb emanating through Lucifer's Mark. He knew what it would look like at this moment: the slender jagged line that started beneath the hair at his nape and spread like roots over the back of his right shoulder would be raised like tiny, dark veinlike welts. Normally the mark remained nearly flat and simply looked like the tattoo of a shattered piece of glass. But at times like this, it filled and swelled and became an annoyance.

It was the physical manifestation of the crack in his soul, the one that had occurred when Lucifer visited him in his dreams more than a century ago: the sign of his family's liaison with the devil, the indication of Voss's immortality and power.

A cracked or damaged soul meant that he could live forever and never face the judgment of God. He could do what he wanted, when he wanted. He had access to resources beyond imagination: power, wealth, even knowledge. He had no one to answer to but Lucifer, and only if the devil ever called him to true service.

Unless, of course, he met a stake through his heart or someone sliced off his head.

And the only way either of those things would happen was if he came face-to-face with the damned hyssop plant and it weakened or paralyzed him. And since Voss had no intention of dying, *ever*, he continued to build up his own arsenal of protection by learning the frailties of others.

He would never again be the scrawny fifteen-year-old kid who'd spent more than two hours in the depths of the privy his first week at Eton—on three different occasions—because his upper classmates thought he was too pretty and spoiled.

Regardless of the fact that it was true: he always had been pretty and spoiled.

Perhaps that was why Lucifer had chosen him to be Dracule.

Not for the first time, Voss was thankful that his Asthenia wasn't something common, like tea leaves or silver. Amman Gilreath, poor bastard, had had an Asthenia of pine needles, which had led to an early end for him, thanks to Chas Woodmore.

The thought of Moldavi steered Voss's mind back to where it should have been, instead of on things he couldn't change. His family's deal with the devil had been made in the fifteenth century. Voss, Dimitri, Eddersley, Giordan Cale—all the members of the Draculia, even Moldavi—were the result of Vlad Tepes's, Count Dracula's, desire to rule Romania with an iron fist.

And centuries later, random members of the broad family tree were still paying the price of an unholy covenant negotiated by Vlad the Impaler.

* * *

"I should like to engage your services, Miss Woodmore."

Angelica turned to the pretty young woman, who'd spoken to her through the leaves of a large potted lemon tree settled in the corner of the Lundhames' ballroom. A bit out of breath from the quadrille she'd just finished with the very energetic Mr. Clayton Beemish, Angelica smiled and edged closer to the large plant, allowing its branches to flutter in front of her—the better to keep the conversation unnoticed.

Fortunately Mr. Beemish had taken himself off to fetch a cup of lemonade for her. It would be a while before he returned, she was certain, and as long as none of the other young men noticed that she was unattended, she would have a few moments to talk to this new acquaintance.

That was, except for Lord Harrington. She hadn't seen the handsome young man yet—and as he always made a point of finding her if he was in attendance, she presumed he either wasn't coming or hadn't arrived yet. But if he did appear, she'd certainly choose the pleasure of dancing with him over a possible business transaction.

"Do you have a reference?" Angelica asked, for she was careful with whom she divulged her ability.

"Chastity Drury told me about you. I'm Gertrude Yarmouth," she whispered. One of the green spikes from the lemon tree had caught in her hair, and she pushed it away as she offered a coin to Angelica, gloved hand meeting gloved hand behind the sturdy tree trunk. "Will this be enough for you to tell me about Baron Framingham?"

Ah. Framingham. The man who laughed too loudly and who seemed to be unable to retain a valet, if his attire was any indication. Angelica looked down at the gold crown that had just been slipped to her and resisted the urge to smile in delight. Her reputation was certainly growing, as was the small pouch of coins in her chamber. As soon as she could slip out of the house without Maia bothering her, she would deliver it to St. Anselm's orphanage, where the ladies who ran the home would put it to good use.

"I must have further information before I agree to take you on as a client," she warned, for the services of Angelica Woodmore weren't for the fainthearted. Nor for the destitute.

"Has Framingham asked for your hand?" she continued, for she hadn't heard, nor read, any announcement of a betrothal. And if the man were betrothed, the engagement certainly hadn't affected his interest in other young women since arriving at the Lundhames' ball. Including Angelica herself.

"Yes, he spoke to my father only today. My father approves of the match."

"Have you accepted him, then? Are you certain you wish to engage my services?" Angelica watched the girl closely.

"I have asked my father to allow me a day to think on it—a request which he granted reluctantly. I knew you were going to be here tonight, and I didn't want to make a decision until I learned what you had to tell me. Chastity said you helped her."

Angelica nodded. Now for the most telling question. "Do you wish to accept Framingham? Are you in love with him?" She would return the coin in a moment if the young woman were. She'd come to accept that the very thing which made her so different, and which burdened her in ways that no one else understood, could also be put to good use. Her "sight" could be intriguing, amusing and profitable for certain charities—but not in every case. She'd learned her lesson after what happened with Belinda Mayhew and no longer blindly accepted clients.

"I hardly know the man," Miss Yarmouth said, her voice rising and her hand buffeting the aromatic lemon leaves. "He is… He's nearly forty, and his teeth are so yellow and crooked and all he speaks of are his hounds. Always, his hounds. But he has over thirty thousand a year, and this is my second Season. Papa is annoyed that I've been out for so long and I've only received one other proposal. If I don't accept him, he won't be pleased."

Definitely not a love match, which would make it easier to deliver unpleasant news if that was what it happened to be. "Very well. Consider this—" she held up the coin "—a down payment. You will owe me another one after I give you the information." The orphans at St. Anselm's seemed to grow out of their frocks and pants weekly. Angelica eyed Miss Yarmouth, who gulped but nodded firmly. Then Angelica tucked the crown into her reticule and, after a glance to determine Mr. Beemish's whereabouts (still across the room, in line for lemonade) continued, "You must provide me with something that Framingham has touched with his bare hand. And you understand there is only one thing I can tell you about him."

"Yes, of course. Chastity explained how you helped her. You can tell me only how he will die," Miss Yarmouth said, her voice pitching so low at the end of her speech that the music fairly drowned it out.

"After a fashion. I can only see a person in a still image at the moment of death. And the only reason I am willing," Angelica said, her voice and expression becoming vehement as she tried to ignore the fact that that was no longer quite true, "is to enable you to make a knowledgeable decision as to whether you wish to accept his hand in marriage."

She ruthlessly pushed away the flash of memory from the grisly dream she'd had last week. It had only happened once. Surely it meant nothing.

Miss Yarmouth's eyes were wide and she nodded fervently. "Yes, of course," she said again.

Despite the other woman's assurances, Angelica launched into her standard lecture. "We of the fairer sex have little to say in regards to our marital matches and our lives. If I can offer a piece of information that might tip the scales a bit in our balance, then I am happy to do so."

"I do wish you'd cease this ridiculous game," a voice suddenly hissed into Angelica's ear. "We've got other things to be concerned with tonight."

Angelica pulled her arm away from her older sister's firm grip. "Stow it, Maia. At least one of us ought to enjoy ourselves," she muttered, "and it best be me. Heaven knows you don't know how. Have you even danced *once* tonight?"

"While our brother is quite possibly lying *dead* somewhere?" Maia pressed her slippered foot down hard onto hers, but her sister was nimble enough to pull her toes out before they were smashed, and without stumbling and making a scene in front of her client.

Angelica slipped a sharp elbow into her sister's side as she turned and smiled at Miss Yarmouth. "I shall meet you in the ladies' retiring room in thirty minutes to examine the item you've retrieved from him. Don't be late."

"Thirty minutes?" Miss Yarmouth's lips opened in shock. "But—"

"Yes. Half past midnight. You'll have to work quickly and intelligently," Angelica told her. "My services do not come cheaply or simply, but they are worth it." Then she turned her back on the lemon tree and her client, and faced her sister.

She opened her mouth to tell Maia that she knew Chas wasn't dead…but then closed it. Even now, even to put her sister out of her obvious misery, she wouldn't go on that path. She couldn't allow herself to do so, to open herself—and her family—up to such a Pandora's box.

Nor did Maia understand why Angelica felt compelled to do what she did, assisting the other young women of the *ton.* Maia was affianced to a handsome, kind man for whom she had great affection, but that was only because she had a forceful way about her and because Chas, for all of his constant traveling, loved and cared for his sisters dearly. There were plenty of other young women who made miserable—or worse—matches with men much older than they were. At least Chas wouldn't force any of them into something they didn't want.

Maia was the eldest of the three of them, not counting their brother. He was older than all of his sisters and, since they had been orphaned for ten years, he was also the head of the family, which, although it wasn't titled, held a lovely county seat in Shropshire and a smaller estate in Derby. This made the Woodmore sisters welcomed in most homes of the *ton,* as well as fine wifely candidates for the bachelors thereof.

Chas was twenty-seven, and Maia was nearly twenty—just ten months older than Angelica. Sonia was only thirteen, and she was currently tucked safely away in a convent school in Scotland.

In addition to their comfortable wealth, the Woodmores were a particularly fertile family. And thanks to Angelica's great-great-grandmother, who, after the death of her older, wealthy husband, had become enamored with a handsome young groom, they also had acquired a bit of Gypsy blood that cropped up every generation or so. Chas and Maia hadn't been blessed (or cursed, depending upon whom one spoke to) with the Sight, but their two younger sisters had.

"And I *have* danced—*twice,*" Maia retorted from between tight lips. "Despite the fact that one of my partners couldn't seem to find a spot on the floor *between* my feet during the entire set."

"So you danced with Flewellington? I warned you about him." Angelica's ire faded quickly, as it often did, and she smiled at her sister in sympathy. It had taken only one set with Baron Flewellington for her to learn the same lesson: avoid the man and his large, clumsy feet at all costs. "At least you didn't sit against the wall like you normally do. And, drat it, Harrington isn't here tonight."

"I haven't seen Corvindale yet, either," Maia said, changing the subject and reaching over to adjust one of her sister's curls. "Hold still. This one is coming undone, Ange."

Angelica obeyed as deft fingers adjusted the little pin that held one of the curls in place at her temple. "I'm not certain I would recognize him even if I saw Corvindale," she said. "Are you certain he's to be here?"

"Everyone who is everyone is here tonight. I think it's disgraceful that he hasn't made any attempt to answer the message I sent him yesterday. We haven't heard from Chas for a fortnight, and I'm only following his directions in contacting the earl. I made that perfectly clear in the letter."

Angelica had no doubt of that. If nothing else, her sister was exceedingly capable of expressing herself and her intentions clearly.

And despite the fact that she *knew* he wasn't dead, Angelica had to push away the pang of worry for her brother. He traveled to the Continent quite often, for purposes that remained unclear to his sisters, but he always made certain to be in touch with them regularly by post or other message. The aunt of a distant cousin, Mrs. Fernfeather, and her husband, as necessary, acted as chaperone in those instances. But Chas's last letter had given an unusually terse command that if they didn't hear from him in two weeks that they were to contact the Earl of Corvindale immediately.

"I'm not certain why the earl needs to be brought into the situation," Maia continued. "Chas knows we can take care of ourselves. Don't we always? Mrs. Ferny lacks much in the way of her chaperone skills. And from what I've heard, Corvindale's a... Well, he's not particularly kind or generous. But Chas trusted him and has always spoken well of the man." She'd finished attending to Angelica's hair and was now standing next to her, shoulder-to-shoulder, back to the wall, clearly scanning the large room and out into the grand foyer. "I recall him being very tall, and so it should be easy to spot him if he were here. But I don't see anything of him at all."

The skirts of their frocks, made of the lightest, frothiest silk imaginable, pooled around each other's slippers in delicate swirling crinkles. While the bodices were tight, tied or gathered just beneath the bosom, the remainder of the fabric fell loosely to the floor, which gave them relative ease of movement. Angelica's gown was spring yellow, in deference to the Gypsyish undertones of her skin and her dark hair and eyes. Maia, who had more of a classic, Roman goddess look to her beauty, had a fairer, peaches-and-cream complexion that looked lovely when she wore pale blue.

"But Corvindale needn't be rude about it all," Maia said. She redonned the glove she'd taken off a moment earlier to fix Angelica's hair and patted the sapphire and pearl earbobs she wore, as if ensuring they were still hanging there.

"If you do see him, you can't simply walk up and start lecturing him, Maia."

Her sister frowned, her pretty heart-shaped face sharpening with determination. "I certainly can. It could be a matter of life and death. And aside of that, I'm betrothed. It's not as if I'm a young debutante in my first Season, looking for a husband."

Angelica opened her mouth to argue, but Maia continued, "I can, but I'll be discreet or subtle about it. But I will if I— Oh. Is that him?"

Angelica looked over toward the threshold of the ballroom, where it met the foyer, and saw three gentlemen standing there. "Isn't Corvindale dark? They aren't…"

Her voice trailed off as coldness curled around her heart. She recognized one of them.

The man from her dream.

2

In Which Miss Yarmouth
and Viscount Dewhurst
are Disappointed

"Corvindale isn't here," Voss observed, stepping into the ballroom ahead of his companions.

He'd taken the opportunity to scan the room whilst standing at the top of the convenient three steps from the grand foyer. The space beyond was a kaleidoscope, filled with swirling gowns of every pastel color imaginable, an aromatic soup of lily and rosewater, lavender pomade, powder and the scent of too much physical exertion, along with the enthusiastic strains from a brass quintet in the corner.

"Damned violin is out of tune," he added over his shoulder to Eddersley and tried to mentally block the discordant strains from his ears.

Brickbank stumbled a bit on the trio of steps and Voss resisted the urge to roll his eyes. Apparently the fifteen-minute drive in the carriage, along with the cool night air, had done nothing to sober the fellow up. Thank Luce they hadn't been drinking blood-whiskey, or he'd be utterly useless.

"Next time I'll have Morose lock the damned cabinet," he muttered to himself, and settled against the wall where he could observe the activity a moment longer.

The crush of people moved about like busy ants: on and off the dance floor, around its perimeter, in and out of the entryway to the foyer and to the rooms beyond. It was a constant buzz of activity, noise, color and, of course, scents.

"Luce's breath, I've been away from London for too damned long, Eddersley," he muttered.

This was where he was originally from, after all. He loved the heavy fog that could descend on a moment's notice, making it easier for one of his nature to move about the dirty, busy streets during the day. Despite the war with France, he presumed it hadn't completely depleted the variety of goods and the city's cultural milieu. And he certainly appreciated the vast array of services here—particularly Rubey's.

And, most of all, rich women who wore gloves. In America the ladies weren't so strict about wearing gloves all the time. But here in London…a peeress without her gloves on might as well be lifting her skirts in the alley. And those slender, silken hand coverings made it so much easier to slip a little fang into a slim, ivory wrist, provide a bit of pleasure to both parties…and then hide the evidence. Wealthy women, too, had purer, sweeter and richer blood than their lower-class counterparts— although Voss had been exposed to peers with thin, foul blood and milkmaids or doxies with sweetness running through their veins.

Voss smiled at a particularly fetching matron in vibrant pink as she approached, allowing his features to soften with charm as their eyes caught…and held. *Later, m'dear,* Voss promised her with his eyes, and then cast his gaze down over her figure.

He appreciated the changes in male garb over the years, but it was the current fashion for females which he truly relished. Gone were the layers of heavy skirts and panniers, the restrictive corsets and the ridiculously high hair and wigs that shed powder all over his own clothing. Now, the gowns were simple and light of weight and flowed loosely from beneath the bustline to the floor. And even the corsets and shifts beneath them (for Voss was well acquainted with such underpinnings) were shorter and simpler.

The woman tilted her head, then slid her gaze over his shoulders and down…farther, as deliberate as a hand closing over his cock…as she walked past, her arm tucked in the crook of another man's elbow. The cloudlike flutter of her rosy skirt trailed over Voss's shoe, along with her personal fragrance, and he couldn't hold back a smile despite the bad violin threatening to ruin the night. Couldn't the Lundhames have afforded musicians who knew what they were doing?

As he followed his future tête-à-tête out of sight with his eyes, Voss's attention moved onto a different figure pushing through the crowd toward them. In spite of himself, in spite of the insistent flow of people around and with him, he stilled, his attention caught by the woman.

Young, was his first thought. Too young for his taste. Not experienced enough. Barely out in Society, perhaps seventeen or eighteen at the outside. But…she moved with grace and flair and determination even through the mad crush.

As she drew closer, Voss realized she seemed to be fixated on something behind him, for she was moving at a steady clip through the same buffet of people that surrounded him. Most women strolled leisurely about a party, often arm-in-arm, intending to see and to be seen. But this girl, with her shining dark hair and eyes, moved with deliberation and speed.

The bright yellow gown made her dusky-rose skin look rich and exotic, and as she drew closer, he could make out the almond shape of her dark, dark eyes. Her breasts caught his attention, of course, as they rose from the square line of her bodice, but it was the curve of her throat and the delicate hollow of her collarbone, the slide of her neck, that made his mouth go dry.

Voss clamped his mouth closed, lest the tips of his upper fangs, which had distended without warning, be revealed. They slid neatly back into place, but he found himself a bit shaken. He loosened his fingers and reminded himself to breathe.

Someone jostled him, forcing his attention from the vision in lemon, and as he turned to snap at Brickbank (for who else would it be?), he found himself face-to-face with Dimitri.

"Corvindale," Voss said coolly, despite the fact that he'd been taken totally unaware—normally an impossibility. "Won't you go over there and put that damned violinist out of his misery? His bloody D-string is flat as a hag's tits."

"What are you doing here?" Dimitri said. His countenance, always forbidding and dark, had settled into one of stone. His admirable attire, in tones of charcoal, steel, ink and a white shirtwaist, was nevertheless just as dour as his expression. Aloof, annoyed and arrogant, the earl nevertheless attracted interested, half-lidded glances from women everywhere he went. Yet, it was that cold demeanor that kept all but the most bold of them away. And even the boldest ones couldn't coax even the faintest bit of warmth from those steel-gray eyes.

Voss shrugged languidly. "Certainly not the same thing you're doing. Come to think of it, I can't imagine what would compel the Earl of Corvindale to make an appearance at a ball. So crowded, so filled with people and, Luce forbid, revelry. Surely you're not in the market for a wife, and you certainly can't be looking for anything else from the array of blue-blooded beauties here tonight." He made certain his feral smile indicated to Dimitri just what he was missing.

The earl's expression didn't change. Instead, hardly moving his lips, he said, "Stay away from the Woodmore girls. Or I'll kill you."

A dart of fury suffused him, leaving Voss momentarily struggling to maintain his insouciance. But he refused to let his easy smile slip, knowing that to keep it in place would only annoy Corvindale further. "You wouldn't be the first to try."

He would have sauntered off, presenting him with his back, but at that moment Voss caught a flash of yellow from the corner of his eye. He'd turned during the exchange with Corvindale, and now, as he caught the sunny frock at the edge of his vision, he pivoted just in time to see that the lovely young woman was approaching him.

No, not him.

Brickbank.

The dark-haired beauty swept past him, Eddersley and even Corvindale and came to a sudden, almost startled, halt in front of Voss's tipsy, ginger-haired friend.

As she breezed past, the air stirred, her curls bounced and her gown flowed and Voss caught her scent.

All of the Draculia members, along with their other eccentricities, had a heightened sense of smell. That was a trial as much as a benefit, for the miasma of aromas, especially in an unfamiliar environment, could often be overpowering. Voss had learned to allow the good, the odd and the putrid to meld together into something palatable. But there were times when something separated from the rest and rose to his notice. It might be a smell that was nauseating or strange, or simply rank.

In this case it was…indescribable. Titillating and… intriguing.

Voss realized with a start that he'd been standing there with his nostrils quite literally, ridiculously, flaring, trying to draw in the unusual aura. Fortunately no one else seemed to notice, for the young woman had done something completely and utterly out of etiquette.

Even though he'd been in the Colonies—gad, now they were called the United States, weren't they?—for much of the past three decades, Voss knew that a proper young woman never approached a man whom she didn't know and began to speak to him. Particularly without a chaperone.

But that was precisely what was occurring to the dumfounded Brickbank, whose nose was still tinged red at its pointed tip.

"—must have a moment to speak with you, my lord," she was saying. He had to give her credit, for despite what she must perceive as urgency, her voice was low and calm.

"I…er…" One could only attribute Brickbank's unusual befuddlement to the breach of etiquette in addition to Voss's best brandy. "But of course, miss...er, mada—my lady?"

"Perhaps we could step aside?" she asked.

Voss had sidled closer. Not, he told himself, so that he could sniff delicately at the fragrance that clung to her—he felt ridiculous even acknowledging the fact that he considered doing so—but so that he could determine the exact color of her hair. And eyes. And discern whether that was indeed a delicate little mole at the back of her neck, just where the base curved into a creamy-rose shoulder, or some sort of smudge.

Corvindale said something and shifted so that he cut into Voss's view, bringing the latter back into the moment as if he'd been shaken awake from a dream.

A very compelling dream.

Now that he'd focused back in on the conversation, he realized that she wasn't merely too inexperienced... but she was also the Earl of Corvindale's new ward.

But, Luce's nails, that just made her all the more enticing. He smiled.

"My name is Angelica Woodmore," she was saying. Her hair was dark, nearly black, but with brown lights that made it rich and interesting. Impatience colored her voice, and despite the fact that she'd fairly barreled into a strange group of gentlemen—and rather fierce, austere-looking ones at that—she seemed more intent on having some sort of communication with Brickbank than anything else.

"Miss Woodmore, I am the Earl of Corvindale," said Dimitri in a pronouncement that Voss was certain was meant to stop the chit in her tracks.

It did, in fact. Miss Woodmore paused and looked at him in surprise. Then her almond-shaped eyes narrowed. "My sister has been looking everywhere for you, my lord. We understood you would be here tonight. You have not responded to her letter."

Voss didn't try very hard to smother his amusement at the girl's set-down. Perhaps she wasn't quite as young as he'd thought, taking the earl to task. He shook his head mentally, wondering what it was about the earl that attracted women. Certainly Miss Woodmore wasn't one of them. He was ridiculously glad that was the case.

Corvindale, of course, rose to the occasion by looking down his long, prominent nose at her. "An earl does not generally respond on command, Miss Woodmore. Particularly to imperious orders from young women."

"Angelica!"

A new voice—a feminine one, laced with shock and annoyance, and barely hissing from between clenched teeth but pitched so as to reach above the dull stew of noise—drew the attention of the entire group. Voss recognized immediately that this was another Woodmore sister and he couldn't help the smile that curled the corners of his mouth.

Corvindale looked as if he'd been stung. Well, perhaps that was an exaggeration. The man stiffened and couldn't quite suppress a flare of something that rose in his austere face, but was quickly submerged. Fascinating. Voss could still sense the man's discomfort as he turned to the sister and gave a sharp, smart bow.

"Miss Woodmore," he said.

"Maia, I've found the earl," said Miss Angelica Woodmore unnecessarily.

"So I see," replied her sister. Still with clenched teeth, but at this point Voss wasn't certain if that was for the benefit of Corvindale or Angelica.

The next portion of the conversation between the earl and the sister was lost on Voss, for the lovely Angelica had turned back to Brickbank. Every time she moved, a new, fresh waft of *her* filtered toward him. Voss sidled nearer, sliding past Eddersley to get closer.

"It's of a personal nature," Miss Woodmore was saying. Her expression and demeanor were of matching earnestness, and for a moment, Voss was overwhelmed by annoyance.

Why wasn't she approaching *him* to speak of something of a personal nature? He was quite certain he could find something personal and natural to interest her.

Why on God's green earth did she have to find Brickbank fascinating?

Then Voss realized it was simply because she hadn't seen him yet, and he edged his way even closer. Women always noticed him. And that was one of the delights of his immortal life. He enjoyed as many of them as he wanted, without the hassle of having to woo or court or be the recipient of their many moods. Let alone spend any significant amount of time with them outside of the bedchamber. Why bother? There was always another one waiting.

None too gently, he elbowed up to Brickbank and turned to bestow his most charming smile on the yellow-gowned chit with the alarmingly enticing neck.

It was swanlike, long and curved just so. Elegant… and Voss realized he was having a hard time swallowing. His incisors teased him, slipping out just enough that his tongue brushed against them in a parody of where they really wanted to be: sliding into that ivory flesh, to feel the flood of hot, heavy blood surging into his mouth, over his tongue…into him.

Sweet. It would be sweet and heady and rich, and she would sigh against him, the pleasure trammeling through her veins, matching his. Their breaths would mingle, their bodies sear against the other....

He blinked, focused and nearly turned away, calling himself every ridiculous name he knew. It had been less than thirty minutes since the girl in the alley...and only yesterday since he'd partaken even more fully of the erotic flesh. He certainly didn't need to pant after a virginal young miss who was about to be taken under the wing of that dead-blooded Corvindale, enticing as she might be. Another trip to Rubey's might be in order. Or a tête-à-tête with that saucy matron in pink. She looked as if she'd be a rough, wild ride.

She might be convinced to allow him to sink into her neck instead of her arm. Or thigh. Plump, sensitive thighs were a lovely treat, but not so much as a sleek, bare neck. He felt the stab of interest shimmer through him, and he found himself eyeing that one belonging to Miss Woodmore.

"I feel the need to warn you," she was saying. Obviously Brickbank wasn't listening any more closely than Voss had been, for his expression seemed quite unfocused, as well.

"Warn me?" he repeated.

"Perhaps I might be of assistance," Voss said, at last, *at last,* drawing the girl's attention to him. He gave a genteel bow and took her hand, bringing it to his lips. Her scent surrounded him and he felt something tug in his belly, followed by a sharp twinge on the back of his right shoulder. His mouth brushed the cotton of her glove and he had an instant fantasy of slipping that glove down to bare a narrow wrist. "I am Dewhurst."

Her eyes met his and he felt a sizzle of warmth at the candid interest in them. Ah. Very good.

"I would very much appreciate it if you would recommend to your friend that he heed my warning," she told him.

"And what warning might that be?" Voss returned.

For the first time, she seemed to hesitate. Drawing herself up as if girding for battle, the hollows of her delicate shoulders catching the light and shadow just so, Miss Woodmore moistened her lips and spoke. "I had a dream in which you died," she blurted out, looking at Brickbank.

Voss blinked. A range of emotions blasted through him, the least of which had to do with the fact that he was on the verge of learning what he'd come to learn. If she dreamed of people she didn't know, she might have the Sight. Which would mean he would have a legitimate reason—or at least a justifiable one—to converse with her. He resisted the urge to smile and instead shifted automatically so that his body blocked them from view of the rest of the room. "Go on."

She was still looking at Brickbank, and Voss watched the steady pumping of the pulse in her throat. "I dreamed that you fell off a bridge. That you died."

Brickbank blinked and glanced at Voss, who lifted his gaze and shrugged. "A dream, you say?" the other man replied, suddenly no longer red-nosed and tipsy. "I was in your dream, and fell off a bridge and died?"

A flash of what might have been irritation crossed Miss Woodmore's face—perhaps she felt her explanation had been clear enough that it didn't bear repeating. "Yes. That is what I said."

Voss shrugged again. Odd enough that she'd had a

dream about Brickbank and had recognized him—which could or could not mean she had metaphysical powers. But the fact was, a Dracule wouldn't die from a fall off a bridge. They couldn't drown, nor would the impact of the water damage them beyond a bit of a headache.

They were never going to die. That was part of the arrangement with Lucifer. It was something that Voss was assured of, as long as he was careful with his weakness to hyssop. Not that either of them would be inclined to explain this to the very earnest, lovely—yes, indeed, quite lovely—young woman bristling with intent. Those of the Draculia, of necessity, hid their immortal afflictions from all but other members and their households. And even then, those household members were carefully selected, well-paid, and well-trained to keep their secrets.

That was, Voss paused for a moment to smirk, certainly one of the reasons Corvindale had been reluctant to take on his responsibility as guardian to the Woodmore girls. He could only imagine the sort of disruption the mortal debutantes would have in the household of a Dracule.

"You have my gratitude, then, Miss Woodmore," Brickbank was saying gravely. "Shall keep myself far from any bridges, and thus if there is any danger, it shan't find me."

The young woman appeared only slightly mollified, and Voss could read the suspicion in her expression. She wasn't certain if she was being condescended to or not. "At least," she said, lifting her chin, "you would do well to stay away from bridges whilst dressed as you are. For, you see, you were wearing that *exact* attire in my dream. When you fell off the bridge."

Voss stilled, a renewed prickle of interest settling over him. Fascinating, yet he could not find it terribly disturbing due to its impossibility. Brickbank seemed just as stunned.

Before either of them could speak, Miss Woodmore gave a nod and said, "Very well, then. I've done my duty. Now, if you'll excuse me, my lords. I have a previous engagement."

And she swept away with much more aplomb than a young woman should have.

"What do you see, Miss Woodmore?"

Angelica opened her eyes and attempted to keep her expression bland. "It takes a moment," she explained to Miss Yarmouth. For the third time. "And great concentration. Even…silence."

Hoping that her inquisitive client would get the hint, Angelica closed her eyes again and fingered Baron Framingham's glove. She didn't know how Miss Yarmouth had extracted the item from her possible fiancé, but that wasn't of any concern.

At last, the familiar prickling sort of buzz descended upon her and Angelica focused on the images evolving. It was rather like that moment between sleep and wakefulness…where one was fully aware of what images scanned over the insides of one's eyelids but had no control over their content.

When she was able to summon it, the vision was always a picture, a static image that, while it didn't change, allowed her the chance to examine all its details. A moment in time, captured, as the last bit of life evaporated.

"He's much older. Perhaps fifty. Bald atop his head, many wrinkles. Lying in bed. Eyes closed." She listed off her impressions as she got them. "The window nearby… there's bright sun and leaves on the tree. Full leaves. Summer perhaps. Alas, I cannot tell if there is anyone with him." That was a bit of a lie, for she did see a woman who looked nothing like Miss Yarmouth.

But that could be anyone—a servant, a nurse, a sister—and she never gave any information that could imply or suggest what the woman's decision could or should be.

"Facial hair?" asked the young woman, her voice hushed. "Is he clean-shaven?"

"No facial hair, nor sideburns. There seems to be no sign of injury, but his face is drawn and gray." Angelica opened her eyes. "I believe he dies of old age, or some malady. And from his aged appearance and the loss of his hair, I should expect it will be a decade or more from now." She looked at Miss Yarmouth. "So you must decide if you can bear to be wed to the man for some time."

The inquisitive, impatient Miss Yarmouth didn't seem to appreciate Angelica's advice. "But you have told me very little. How shall I make a decision about that?"

Angelica tucked the second gold crown a bit deeper into her reticule. "You have more information now with which to make a decision than you did earlier this evening. And more information than anyone else would be able to give you."

With the exception, possibly, of Sonia. But that was unlikely, for Angelica knew that her younger sister had a completely different view of their gift of Sight than she did. While Angelica had not only learned to live with it, but to embrace it, Sonia considered her version of the Sight a curse, and that was why she'd entered a convent school. She felt she needed protection for—or perhaps from—her gift.

Angelica rose from the little stool in the corner of the ladies' retiring room—which she had unceremoniously cleared of both maids and ladies upon her arrival—and looked down at the other woman. "The image I receive is only the moment of death. Unlike today, there are times when it's simple to determine the cause or even the age and time: for instance if someone is hit by a carriage or is shot or tumbles down a flight of stairs."

Or falls off a bridge.

Angelica bit her lip. That dream had been so odd, so unexpected. She'd never experienced anything like it before…for it wasn't like her normal visions. Not only had she dreamed actual events, but the information had come to her unbidden. And the most sobering thing about it was that the man had actually appeared tonight. He was a real person. And he'd been dressed exactly as he had in the dream, down to the tie of his neckcloth.

Which meant that he would likely die tonight.

Her lip throbbed from where she'd bit down, but Angelica ignored it. What else could she do? She'd warned Lord Brickbank, and suffered through the condescending looks from him and the skeptical one from his handsome companion. Who was he?

Oh, yes. Dewhurst.

He hadn't seemed any more interested in her pronouncement and warning than Lord Brickbank had, but Angelica had felt a prickling over her skin when he looked at her. As if he was searching for…something.

"I must go," she told Miss Yarmouth. "I wish you the best regards, and I pray you will make a decision that will make you happy, as well as your father and Baron Framingham."

She gave a little bow and left the young woman, who now looked utterly miserable and a bit lost, sitting on her stool alone in the room.

Beyond the warm, tea rose and lily–infused walls of the ladies' tiring room, Angelica was able to draw in a relatively clean breath. The rooms where the ladies might need to disrobe—to correct frock malfunctions or dragging hems—were kept well-heated for obvious reasons and, along with the powder dusting the air, it made for a cloying environment.

"Ah, Miss Woodmore. How serendipitous."

Angelica turned at the sound of the low, smooth voice and felt her heart give a little lurch. For some absurd reason, her cheeks suddenly felt warm as she met the eyes of none other than Viscount Dewhurst. "Whatever do you mean, my lord?" she asked.

He seemed to have appeared from nowhere, for the corridor down which she'd been walking had been empty when she came out of the chamber. She hadn't heard the sound of a door opening, nor of footsteps. Unless he had been waiting for her…

A little prickle of unease, combined with—yes, she must be honest—intrigue, filtered over her shoulders as she glanced past him to gauge how far out of earshot she was from the party. Yet, though her heart was pounding and her palms dampened beneath their gloves, she didn't feel nervous or threatened.

Just…aware.

Very aware.

He stepped from the narrow shadow given off by a statue on a wide pedestal, which had likely contributed to her not noticing him, moving into the corridor near her. "I had hoped to claim you for a dance, if your card isn't filled," he said, still in that warm voice. "And then you disappeared, and I thought I had lost my chance. But now I have been so fortunate as to find you just when I had given up hope." Any sense of the melodramatic in his words was balanced by the twinkle in his eyes.

As it was, Angelica had forgotten about her dance card, which she'd stuffed into her reticule before meeting Miss Yarmouth. It was filled, of course, and she'd missed at least two dances. She thus expected that the gentlemen in question would be looking for her to claim a different song. Which meant that she was overbooked.

But her mouth moved before she realized what she meant to say, and instead this came out: "Dance card? I do believe mine has gone missing, my lord." She shrugged delicately, her little reticule with its two gold crowns and crumpled dance card dangling from her wrist. "And I cannot recall to whom I've promised this next selection."

"As I said," he replied, his green-gold eyes narrowing with humor, "how serendipitous that I should have come upon you. It would be a shame, to say the least, if you were resigned to standing against the wall because you had lost your card. Instead I shall rescue you from such a fate."

He offered his arm, and Angelica, who was no stranger to curling her fingers around a man's coat sleeve, stepped closer as she did so. At once, she became fully aware of not only his height and breadth, but also how terribly handsome he was. All bronze and honey-colored in hair and skin, but with bright emerald glints sharpening his golden eyes. He had thick brows and lashes, and full lips that made her mouth go dry when she looked at it. As he looked down at her, with a bit of a smile on those mobile lips and his eyes warmly considering her, Angelica's breath became unsteady and her cheeks even a bit warmer.

Shaking off the momentary paralysis, she started toward the revelry. After the merest of hesitations, he came along with her…almost as if he'd been expecting her to go in a different direction. Away from the party.

As if Angelica Woodmore was foolish enough to slip away with a strange gentleman. If she were Maia, she'd sniff in annoyance at the insult—whether it was real or imagined. She wasn't about to make the foolish mistake that Eliza Billingsly had made last Season, getting caught in a compromising position with that stoop-shouldered Mr. Deetson-Waring. They were now wed, and Eliza had never looked unhappier.

"I do hope Corvindale will allow you to waltz," Dewhurst said as they approached the ballroom.

Angelica had a little stumble. "A waltz?" The forbidden dance had recently become popular in Paris after being common for more than a decade in Vienna, but its music was rarely played in London. And even rarer were the young debutantes who were allowed to partake in the scandalous moves.

Then she realized what else he'd said. "Corvindale? He's given little attention to us thus far, my lord. I hardly fear he'll impose his sanctions on me for a simple dance." It occurred to Angelica that, with Chas gone and the earl reluctant to take on the responsibility of her guardianship, she might attain a certain, albeit temporary, latitude in her actions. Not that she would do anything foolish…but a young woman could do with a bit of adventure now and again.

Unless she were Maia Woodmore, then she would sit primly and properly and wonder when her fiancé was going to return from the Continent.

Dewhurst was looking down at Angelica with a smile. "My dear Miss Woodmore, I greatly fear you are wrong about that."

"About the earl?"

"No," he said, the slow smile sending a bolt of warmth into her belly, "about the waltz being a simple dance." His eyes narrowed again as humor lit them. "The waltz is sensual and graceful and smooth…and the steps might be considered simple by one who's never executed them before. But the dance itself…it is quite an experience."

Angelica felt, again, that sort of breathlessness. Yet, she managed to keep her voice even and bright. Mildly flirtatious. "Indeed?"

"And if one is partnered by a good dancer, then, my dear Miss Woodmore, the experience is even more enjoyable. And I must confess…I am an excellent dancer."

"Then I shall count myself fortunate that you have deigned to partner me for my first waltz."

"Your good fortune, but my *infinite* pleasure."

All at once, Angelica remembered their initial conversation, the one which they'd shared with Brickbank. And at the same moment, something flashed into her memory—a detail from the dream. The bridge. She recognized it, and had just remembered.

Compelled by a flood of guilt and determination, she paused just at the juncture of their corridor with another hallway and the foyer leading to the ballroom. Voices and laughter, along with the music, had become loud enough that she needed to turn to fully face Dewhurst in order to ensure he'd hear her.

"My lord," she said, releasing his arm and looking up at him. He'd halted, of course, and now looked down at her with a bemused expression. That wide, squared-off jaw with its cleft and smooth, golden skin, complemented by full lips and unruly hair, combined to create a most attractive image. And it was clear he knew just what sort of effect he had on women.

"Feeling a bit apprehensive about dancing the waltz now, my dear miss?" he asked. "We could always take a stroll on the patio until the next quadrille." Those eyes glinted wickedly.

She drew herself up, even crossing her arms in front of her. "No, that's not it at all. It's about your friend, Lord Brickbank."

The levity evaporated from his expression, and for the first time since he'd approached her after she'd left Miss Yarmouth, Angelica saw that he was grave. "Your warning was quite startling, indeed."

"A warning that I am certain he intends to disregard."

She was pleased when he gave an acknowledging incline of his head. At least he didn't intend to pretend. "I'm certain you can understand his skepticism. Do you often make such warnings to gentlemen you've never met?"

"No, in fact I do not. That is why I am certain that the warning must be heeded. I—" She clamped her lips together. Not necessarily prudent to divulge her secret at this point. But how else to explain it, to make him understand that she wasn't a novice at this sort of thing?

Except that she *was* a bit of a novice when it came

to interpreting dreams. She'd never had one with such shocking clarity…such graphic images.

Angelica shook her head to clear it, to try to pare through the frustration. "I have had dreams before," she said. "But I've never met the person afterward."

"So you truly have no way of knowing whether your dream is a true portent?"

She uncrossed her arms, unable to keep her hands stationary when trying to explain. "My great-grandmother had some of what they call the Sight. After hearing stories about her, I've learned to never disregard anything unusual, despite whether it's unprovable or not."

Her hands gesticulated more wildly than was proper, but she was bent on impressing upon him the seriousness of the situation. "Please, my lord. I feel very strongly that you must ensure that he take my warning seriously. And, as absurd as it might seem, I must beg of you to keep him away from Blackfriars Bridge. Especially tonight. It was that bridge, and his exact attire, that I saw in my dream."

Lord Dewhurst seemed to relax a bit. "Miss Woodmore, if only every person were so intent on protecting one's fellow man." His words seemed not the least bit condescending. "What if I were to tell you that it would be impossible—as improbable as that might sound—for Lord Brickbank to die by falling off a bridge? Would that make you feel any better? And would you then agree to hasten out to the dance floor with me before our waltz is finished?"

"Miss Woodmore will not be hastening anywhere with you, Voss. Most especially not to a waltz."

Angelica swallowed a gasp at the sudden appearance of Lord Corvindale, who looked absolutely thunderous.

He was taller than Dewhurst—Voss?—and with his dark hair and clothing, and olive skin, he seemed more imposing and arrogant.

"Angelica," came that familiar sharp whisper.

Relieved to have somewhere to focus her attention other than the furious earl, Angelica found her sister storming up to them as quickly as she would allow herself to storm, clearly following in Corvindale's wake. It was obvious the earl had rudely left her behind in his haste to get to them.

And she truly wished Maia would not say her name with that particular inflection. It was highly annoying, and even more so that, since her sister's name had only two syllables, Angelica couldn't repay her in kind.

"Maia," she replied in a matching tone as her sister continued her reprimand in a low voice.

"Were you truly going to *waltz* with Viscount Dewhurst? That dance is simply scandalous! Chas would never allow it if he were here, and you know it." Her fingers had curved around Angelica's arm and were digging into its soft underside as she tugged her away from the two men, who were speaking sharply and in short bursts, but too low to be discernable. "The matrons would buzz about it for weeks, Angelica. You simply cannot—"

"Perhaps if Alexander ever returned from the Continent and you actually married him, Chas would allow me to," Angelica said, lifting her nose.

To her surprise, Maia's eyes dampened and the tip of her nose turned pink. "That's just *like* you, Angelica. We don't even know if Chas is all right and you're making horrible jokes."

Immediately, Angelica felt guilty and bumped gently against her sister, nudging her in a sort of armless embrace. She wasn't certain if the mistiness was over worry for Chas or Alexander's absence, but it didn't matter. "I'm sorry. You're right. But…I'm just so sure that Chas is fine. He'll be back."

"Really? Do you *know* that?" Maia had stopped just into the ballroom, and they were back near that same lemon tree from earlier in the evening. She looked sharply into Angelica's eyes, her dark blue ones penetrating and hopeful. Then she sagged, hope fading. "But I know you can't. Not for us, not for people you're close to. I only wish you could…just this once."

Angelica squirmed—literally and figuratively. She did not want to open that box. But Maia didn't understand why she wasn't worried about Chas, and perhaps she could give her something that would alleviate her stress…without opening the whole mess. "I just don't *feel* like he's in danger, Maia. Maybe it's wrong of me not to worry, but I just have a feeling I'd *sense* it if he were gone."

To her surprise, Maia gave a little sniffle and nodded, as if receiving confirmation of something she'd already known. "I think I'm foolish to feel that way, too, especially since I don't have your…gift. But I do. And I confess I'm glad to hear you say it, as well. I just hope it isn't wishful thinking on both our parts. But…we've been so close for so long, the four of us, since Mama and Papa died.… I feel as though we have some sort of spiritual connection. Perhaps it's absurd, but it's the only hope I have."

These last words came out as little more than a murmur and Angelica was forced to watch her sister's lips and try to interpret. A pang of guilt pricked at her—

there *was* a way to put Maia out of her misery. But no. This was enough.

It would all work out in the end and Maia need never know that Angelica had indeed opened visions to the lives—and deaths—of all of her siblings.

That was her burden to carry alone.

3

WHEREIN OUR HERO IS ASSIGNED
A MOST INCONVENIENT TASK

Voss stared at himself in the mirror.

His eyes, rarely fully wide even on a happy night, were past half-mast. And bloodshot. Bleary.

Filled with disbelief and shock.

Impossible.

"How could I have been so bloody foolish?" he demanded of his reflection.

It was the same question he'd pummeled himself with for hours. But it was too late for questions and recriminations. Now he had to decide how to proceed.

After leaving the enticing Miss Woodmore—who'd teased him with her alternately dancing then earnest eyes, tantalized him with her long, graceful neck and beckoning scent—he, Eddersley and Brickbank had gone to Rubey's.

It was either that or descend into a brawl with that bastard Corvindale. Tempting as it might have been, Voss was in no mood to have his shirt crinkled or his clothing torn.

Nor, suddenly, had he felt the urge to tease and coax the pink-frocked matron with whom he'd exchanged glances earlier. No. His need and fury had burrowed deep and fierce.

So he'd allowed his two companions to draw him away and they went to Rubey's.

The original Rubey was long-dead, but her discreet establishment near Charing Cross remained. The current "Rubey"—certainly that wasn't her real name—ran it with the same discriminating business sense as her predecessors. In all, Voss believed there had been more than a dozen Rubeys over the centuries, providing the members of the Draculia with a variety of pleasures of the flesh.

Dracule had discriminating tastes when it came to food, drink and pleasure, and Rubey's catered to all of them. The current proprietress provided an establishment that offered women and men who found it titillating and arousing to be fed upon by vampires, along with other physical pleasures. The best drink, the best food—for even though the Dracule required lifeblood for sustenance, many of them had never lost their taste for the same food mortals consumed. Just as they drank brandy often laced with blood, or wine or ale, they could find pleasure in the texture, scent and taste of food, despite the fact that it provided no real nourishment. As with opium and drink, cooked food was a sensual pleasure but not a necessity.

Some of the most popular of Rubey's women—or men—were ones who shared the taste for blood with a Dracule customer, sipping from a sliced vein and giving that unique pleasure in return as they copulated or did whatever the customer fancied.

Last night, Voss had partaken of a bottle of blood-red Bordeaux and then the very sleek, very accommodating limbs of three young women in a room thick with scented smoke designed to heighten the pleasure of all. They certainly seemed well pleased, indeed, when he was finished.

But he found himself unable to slake his lust; nor, surprisingly, was he all that interested in pursuing that conclusion. He considered engaging the only female Dracule that Rubey had on staff and having a rough, bloody time of it...but even that didn't appeal to him.

Too messy, and then there would be unsightly marks all over his skin.

Things became slow and foggy when he had a goblet of Rubey's special drink. Laced with opium and brandy, it had turned the rest of his night into a long, red, sensual blur.

Yet, despite that blur, he recalled mulling over the fact that Angelica Woodmore was not as young as she'd appeared—at least if one looked in her eyes. There, one most definitely saw not only bright intelligence, but also an innate...*comprehension*—he supposed was the best word—that was missing from most other women. And, to be honest, men.

And Voss had indeed been looking in her cocoa-brown eyes. He'd even tested out his thrall on her, allowing his irises to take on the faintest bit of a glow, an edge of his coaxing tug, in an attempt to draw her away from the party instead of to the dance floor. Just to see what her face would look like, caught up in that sensual moment. Perhaps to see if he could identify any part of her unforgettable scent.

She was young and inexperienced, and he wouldn't need more than a little hint of his power to enthrall her.

But…it hadn't worked. She'd seemed immune to the lure in his eyes.

To be sure, he hadn't intended anything other than to ease her away for a moment. A mere moment, where they might have a chance to speak privately, without being—as they'd been—interrupted by Dimitri. Damn him.

Of course, Dimitri hadn't believed Voss when he'd asserted he had merely been asking for a dance, and, now compelled to honesty by the reflection of his drawn, stubbled face, Voss could admit that, in the same position, he wouldn't have believed himself, either.

Regardless of Voss's intentions last evening, the fact remained that Angelica Woodmore hadn't seemed affected by his compelling gaze. And that, perhaps more than anything else, was what had jammed such a burr up his arse at Rubey's.

In the face of his—albeit gentle—onslaught of charm and glamouring, Miss Angelica Woodmore had simply turned and started off toward the dance floor, fairly towing him in her wake.

Now, Voss shifted away from the mirror and stripped off the mangled neckcloth he'd been wearing since leaving for the Lundhames' ball last night. It was well past noon today, and he hadn't arrived back to his house until the sun was well above the horizon—yet another thing that had gone wrong in a night that had started out so promising and that had turned so hellish. He was normally safely in bed before dawn, sleeping until noon like most other gentlemen.

Fortunately the sun was weak today, shrouded in London fog and fighting through the accompanying mist, so at least Voss hadn't had to content with being sizzled by its rays. An enveloping cloak and a bit of care had kept him from being exposed when the beams did peek out as he climbed into a closed carriage.

His shirt had bloodstains on it and he tossed it onto a chair, knowing that Kimton wouldn't even flicker an eyelash.

Christ-blood. How could it have happened?

They'd left Rubey's an hour or so before dawn and somehow had decided to go to Vauxhall—for them, an easy walk down Whitehall and across the river a bit. Three Dracule on a tear, with nothing to fear from any mortal armed with any weapon who might lurk in the shadows. They were fast, strong and could see throughout the green-tinged night.

There was nothing to fear. Always nothing to fear.

Yet, somehow through the red fog of his frenetic pleasure, Voss remembered Angelica's warning about Brickbank.

I must beg of you to keep him away from Blackfriars Bridge. Especially tonight. It was that bridge, and his exact attire, that I saw in my dream.

But they were going to cross Westminster Bridge, loudly and exuberantly, hopeful of finding some gang of thieves or other group of no-gooders in the Gardens that could be terrorized by a trio of drunk vampires. If not, there were always any number of young dandies and their companions who could be frightened.

It was *Westminster* Bridge, far from Blackfriars, and Voss barely hesitated as they stepped on it.

How could Brickbank die from a fall off a bridge, anyway? There was simply no manner in which he could.

Voss laughed at the absurdity. Laughed, loud and

long, exuberant, his mouth still wide with mirth as it happened.

Whether it was Brickbank's Asthenia (copper, the poor brute) that made him fall or merely that he was clumsy from all the drink, they would never know. None of the details were clear: how had he been so close to the edge, what had happened, *how* could it have happened? But something made the man stumble suddenly, and as he attempted to catch his balance, he fell from the bridge.

Voss stopped laughing and ran to the side, expecting to see his friend bobbing in the water and chuckling about the fact that half of the premonition had come true…but that was not the case.

He was not bobbing in the water. Nor was he chuckling.

A freak accident was the only explanation. Brickbank had somehow landed on an old, rotting piece of dock jutting from the water not far from the shoreline, impaling himself through the chest.

Dead. Instantly. One of the only ways a Dracule could die.

The very thought made Voss's blood run cold. *Brickbank was dead.*

Impossible.

Now, hours later, after the body had been retrieved and he and Eddersley had gone to the secret rooms at White's and shared yet another bottle of something to take the sting away, Voss was home.

Pounding headed, thin-blooded, filled with guilt and self-loathing. He could have prevented it.

And on top of that, his Mark was throbbing.

With a snarl, he rang for Kimton and ordered a bath. Thirty minutes later, despite no sleep, Voss felt mar-

ginally better—and that was only because Kimton had
scrubbed his back (avoiding the Mark) and given him a
shave. At least on the outside, he looked less like a man
who'd allowed his friend to die. Dressing in neat, pressed
clothing helped further, and when he was fully attired,
he agreed with himself that he looked just as magnetic
and attractive as he always did.

For, although it was only late in the afternoon and the
sun was still up, Voss needed to go out. He'd flirted with
the idea all morning, knowing all along that he would
end up deciding to go; that it was merely the details left
to be decided.

He must speak with Miss Angelica Woodmore.

Corvindale would be apoplectic, and Voss's only real
hesitation was in determining whether to call on Angelica (when had he begun to think of her in that way?)
openly, so that the earl would know he had defied his
command, or to do it clandestinely so that they wouldn't
be interrupted.

In the end, he decided to do it openly. Corvindale
would learn about it regardless and think the worst of
him no matter what, and, frankly, Voss wasn't terribly
opposed to dusting a bit of the floor with Dimitri, bloody
Earl of Corvindale. Especially in his current mood.

He wouldn't even care if he got blood on his shirt,
because he needed something else to think about. Something other than what had happened to Brickbank.

When he arrived at the relatively small, but very
elegant, well-kept Woodmore home in Mayfair, Voss
alighted from his closed carriage (a very undashing necessity for daytime transportation) gloved and cloaked.
He also held a wide umbrella low over his hat—ostensi-

bly to protect his perfectly combed and lightly pomaded hair from the faint drizzle.

It occurred to him that the sisters might already have been removed to the safety of the earl's home, so it was to his surprise and delight that the door was answered immediately by a well-mannered butler. He accepted his card, hat and cloak, then admitted him promptly with a gesture toward the parlor. Voss had suspected that after last night, Corvindale would have left strict orders that Voss not be received, and he'd anticipated having to bluff or barrel his way in.

Mildly disappointed, he stepped through the parlor door and realized immediately why Corvindale had apparently not seen fit to do so.

"Voss Arden, Viscount Dewhurst," announced the butler.

No fewer than a dozen faces turned and looked over at him, shock blazoning on all of them. Two were the lovely countenances of the sisters Woodmore—but the vast majority of the others were male.

Of course. Voss was so infrequently out during the daylight, and certainly not familiar with current London Society, that he'd forgotten about the rigid practice of afternoon calls.

"My lord, what an honor for you to join us," said Angelica, who seemed to be wedged between two pansy-faced, juvenile-countenanced gentlemen on the settee. She appeared both surprised and delighted by his presence.

And perhaps there was the faintest tinge of rose on her cheeks. He certainly expected there should be.

"I hope you will take some tea?" she added.

Bloody tea wasn't exactly what he'd come for, particularly since a mixture of brandy and wine still sloshed within his belly today. And he didn't particularly care for the lascivious expression on the face of the good-looking dandy who stood behind Angelica. Likely staring down her bosom, the uncouth fop. Harringford or Harringmede or something like that. He'd seen him at White's.

Voss would never do such a gauche thing openly. In fact, he never had to resort to stealing glances or ogles. His lips twitched in a self-satisfied smirk.

"Lord Dewhurst," said Maia, the older one, drawing his attention. She was a pretty one, too, with lighter coloring and a more petite frame than her sister, and Voss wondered briefly whether, if he'd seen her first last night, he'd be as compelled to speak with her as he was to Angelica. His first instinct was *no.*

Was Angelica the only one with the Sight? Or did the others have it, too?

He nodded to the sisters and ignored the rest of the occupants. Non-Dracule members of Society meant little to him for a variety of reasons, and he'd long become impatient with the strictures of their domain: the farce of rigid politeness on the outer crust, while beneath it, a reality nearly as immoral and corrupt as his own world. He'd long ago come to the conclusion that he had no reason to follow mortal rules and live by mortal standards.

It had been a freeing discovery. And it had given him carte blanche to take and do whatever he desired.

And, he realized as he stood at the edge of the room, he *desired* Angelica Woodmore. Deeply.

It wasn't lost on Voss that Maia Woodmore hadn't made any statement of welcome. He could only assume that Corvindale had already begun to impress upon her all of the reasons Voss should be avoided. Hopefully the earl was still abed like any other sane Dracule would be.

Nevertheless, Voss decided that he had no time to waste.

"I'm terribly sorry to interrupt," he said, actually putting sincerity in his tones, "but I must have a word with you, Miss Woodmore."

He was looking at Angelica, so it was clear to which sister he was speaking, but Maia was the first to respond. "Pray have a seat, then, my lord. We have just been discussing the newest play at Drury Lane."

"I wish I could join you, for I hear the lead actress is devastating," Voss replied, his voice now dripping with innocence. "But I fear that I have only a short time to enjoy your company, and it's imperative that I speak with your sister."

During this exchange, Angelica had risen from the sofa and, with a tempered glare at her sister, managed to navigate between the shod feet and pantalooned legs of the myriad of male callers. She was wearing a pale yellow frock today, trimmed with gold ribbon around the neckline (which was, of course, much higher than last night's), and her hair was pulled into a smooth, neat gather at the back of her head. Only a few wisps of hair fanned her cheeks, giving her the look of an exotic pixie. A slender golden chain rested around the base of her throat, with a tiny, matching cross settling into the hollow there.

Voss swallowed hard and deflected his wayward thoughts as he trained his gaze *up*. To her eyes. Cocoa-brown eyes, wide and dark as night.

"I'm certain we don't wish to keep Dewhurst," Angelica was saying to her sister and the room at large. "If you'll excuse me?"

"Angelica," Maia said, beginning to rise. "I don't—"

"Never fear, Miss Woodmore." This time he clearly spoke to the elder sister. "Despite whatever warnings Corvindale might have given you, I have no plans to corrupt your sister in the few moments I will speak with her in the foyer."

With that, he gave a little bow to Angelica, and gestured her to cross in front of him toward the parlor door. Before he turned to follow her out of the room, inhaling subtly as she swept past, Voss turned and took a moment to memorize the faces of the men in the room.

He locked eyes with each of them in turn until he saw the familiar leap of fear and terror in their eyes. Then, quite pleased with himself, he followed Angelica from the room.

"The library is here," she said. "We'll be able to speak privately there."

Indeed. Voss contained a rush of pleasure. The door would remain open, of course. But—blast! His belly felt prickly and odd as he followed her into the room. And his damned shoulder ached.

He mentally patted himself on the back when he not only left the door open, but much wider than was strictly necessary. *Merely a first step,* he told himself and his Mark. *There will be other opportunities to close it later.*

Then he turned to face her, and for a moment, his thoughts and words scattered. Angelica stood near a tall window across the room from him, and in a sort of irony, the embattled sun had managed to emerge from its blanket of clouds beyond her. It shone through the window, bathing her in its soft glow of warm beams…

warmth and light that Voss hadn't felt or been touched by since he was twenty-eight.

A hundred and twenty years without feeling the sun.

For a moment, the ridiculous thought that Angelica Woodmore would be just as elusive as those golden rays worried at him. But that was absurd on so many levels. Nothing could keep him from what he wanted.

Still. How was it she had positioned herself so perfectly: embalmed in a nimbus of light, which made her dusky skin glow and the edges of her hair seem to light—and yet, she was out of reach. Literally. The pool of light served as more of a deterrent than Corvindale ever could.

"My lord?" she asked, smiling at him. "What did you wish to speak with me about?"

Was it possible she *knew?* Had Corvindale told her how to protect herself from the likes of Voss Arden, Viscount Dewhurst and Dracule?

He eyed her closely, not yet employing his thrall, but trying to read anything in her gaze that might indicate whether she knew exactly what she was doing…but there was nothing in her expression other than curious pleasure. That was a fact which warmed him considerably.

"My lord?" she asked again. "Are you feeling quite all right? You look a bit…weary." Her voice trailed off.

Voss straightened in annoyance. He was perfectly groomed and attired. He looked bloody tantalizing.

"How is your friend Lord Brickbank?" she continued, before he could respond.

And suddenly everything came rushing back to him: the images, the guilt and anger, the reason he was here. A heavy, dark ball settled in his belly.

"In fact," Voss said, realizing to his shock that he

needed to steady his voice, "he is not well at all. That's the reason I wished to speak with you."

Angelica's face drained of color and her eyes widened. "My lord, no." Her fingers curved around the back of a nearby chair as if to provide support, and he wondered briefly if she might faint.

"I'm afraid…yes." His voice was curiously choked and Voss resorted to swallowing twice, hard, in order to continue. "He fell from a bridge last night and would have survived, I'm certain, if he had not impaled himself upon a piece of rotted dock."

She'd lifted her free hand to her mouth, her eyes no longer almond shaped but nearly circular. "I am so sorry, my lord. Apparently even my warning couldn't have prevented such an event."

Voss shifted and tried to decide whether her comment was meant to stab him in the chest with reproach, or if she believed that her warning truly had been in vain. Unable to come to a conclusion, he opted to explain further. "The interesting thing, Miss Woodmore, is that my friend fell not from Blackfriars, but from Westminster. I confess, I didn't fully disregard your warning. We avoided Blackfriars. You did name it as the bridge to be avoided, did you not?"

She moved, a little jolt of surprise, and nearly stepped out of her safe circle of sunlight. Not that it would have made a difference if she had, for Voss was feeling uncomfortably cold at the moment. "Indeed, you are correct. I saw Blackfriars in my dream. It's impossible to mistake it, don't you agree?"

He nodded.

"But what does that mean?" Her voice had dropped to nearly a whisper, and a range of expressions passed over her face: thoughtfulness, confusion, deep concern. "What can it mean?"

"It means, I believe," came a deep voice from behind them, "that regardless of the irresponsibility of his companions, Brickbank was destined to die last night. And no precautions could have changed it."

Luce's dark soul. Was he never to be able to finish a conversation with the chit without being interrupted?

Voss didn't bother with a dry, bored comment this time. He merely turned and lifted an eyebrow at Corvindale, who'd stepped into the doorway. The butler stood behind him, holding a hat and cane, obviously having just given the earl entry to the Woodmore home.

"Ah, Voss. What a surprise to see you again. So soon." Corvindale bared his teeth in a definite nonsmile. "I presume Miss Woodmore explained to you that today would be the last day she and her sisters were to receive callers here at Turnbull? I advised them of that earlier today, and they're already in the process of moving to Blackmont Hall until Chas Woodmore returns."

Bloody blasted hell. "I cannot imagine that they would find it very comfortable there," Voss said. "Without a woman to see to things, I can only imagine the drafts, dust and ill illumination they might find. Not to mention skeletons in the closet and—"

"Mirabella," Corvindale interrupted just as blandly, "arrived yesterday morning—along with my dowager Aunt Iliana—and has been preparing for the Woodmore sisters' arrival. I sent for her immediately after you spoke with me at White's." He looked at Angelica. "My sister is in raptures at the thought of having companions her own age living under the roof."

"And so you will be ushering not one, but three young

women throughout Society this Season?" Voss made no attempt to hide his amusement. "Balls, fetes, the theater and of course Almack's. Rides in St. James. Picnics in the country. Presentations at court. And, of course, shopping on Bond. Why, Dimitri, that will be such a departure from your normal, hermitish life. I do look forward to watching the entertainment."

"I don't believe you'll be close enough to observe any of the details, Voss. I've just come from the apartments at White's." This time, Dimitri's smile was genuine. "You've been chosen to see Brickbank's body back to his home. In Romania."

Maia knocked a second time on the door to the earl's study. While she waited for his response, she looked around the corridor, noticing the fine paintings and elegant statues in her temporary (she prayed) home.

They'd been ushered here more quickly than she could have thought possible, arriving early this morning after the visit by Lord Dewhurst yesterday afternoon. Corvindale hadn't even allowed them to pack; their clothing and maids would be arriving later today. Apparently once he'd set his mind to things, they moved very quickly.

Blackmont Hall lived up to its name in some ways, for instead of being bathed in open-windowed light and filled with pintuck and lace pillows and frothy curtains like Turnbull was, the earl's residence had more sober furnishings. The upholstery and wall coverings were of dark colors: midnight-blue, charcoal, wine, forest. The decor was heavy and masculine and gave a sense that its owner preferred to keep his residence without a hint of a woman's touch.

"Yes. Come in," came a very annoyed voice.

Maia pushed the door open and, drawing in a deep breath, stepped in.

Corvindale hadn't bothered to look up. He was reading or studying some sort of massive ledger on his desk, and a pile of pens lay haphazardly next to him instead of in their cup. The ink blots dotting the cloth protecting the desk indicated that he habitually eschewed putting the pens in their holder. The inkwell next to him had a ring of dripped ink around it, as well as several other circles. A sheaf of papers sat neatly at the opposite corner of the desk, held in place by a smooth black stone. And there were books everywhere, on every surface, piled opened, unopened, faceup, facedown…even held to an open spot with another tome acting as a bookmark.

"No bloody need to knock twice," he said in the same welcoming tone as he absently scratched his temple. "I heard you the first time. How—" He looked up at that moment and closed his mouth. "Miss Woodmore. I didn't realize it was you." He rested his pen down on the pile.

"Obviously." She stepped farther into the room, leaving the door wide behind her. She itched to pick up the pens and arrange them in their place and pull the ink-bedabbled cloth for washing. And, heaven above, someone needed to organize the books. "At least, I presume you wouldn't have spoken to me or any of my sisters in that way if you knew."

The windows that flanked his desk were obstructed by long curtains that allowed little light to emerge, but the other windows at the far end of the study were partly uncovered. This gave the chamber an unbalanced look.

"How can you work when it's so dark in here?" she asked, beginning to cross toward the nearest window.

"Leave it," he snapped as she reached for the drapes. He sat up straighter in his chair as her hand fell back to her side. "I have already told Mirabella and Crewston to see to your needs. If you have a complaint about your accommodations, I suggest you speak to my sister." He looked back down, but she noticed that he didn't pick up the pen.

"My lord," Maia said, eyeing the window with a frown. How could he even see the writing on those pages? It was dark and cramped and looked centuries old. "I wanted a moment to speak with you. Things have happened very quickly since the Lundhames' ball and—"

"So at first, I did not respond quickly enough to your peremptory message, and now I have responded too quickly? Devil take it, Miss Woodmore, do make up your mind."

Maia, who had long ceased to be offended by bad language thanks to Chas's undisciplined tongue, merely tightened her jaw and pursed her lips. Her sisters would have recognized that as a clear warning, but of course, the Earl of Corvindale hadn't been thus educated. Yet.

"My lord. I would sincerely appreciate it if you would look at me while I am speaking to you." She was proud that she kept any bit of quaver from her voice.

Corvindale didn't frighten her so much as annoy her. He was certainly imposing, and his brusque manner made him unpleasant to approach. He wasn't boldly handsome in the way Lord Dewhurst was, or her own Alexander, but he was…striking, she supposed. In a hawkish, austere sort of way, with the slender blade of his nose and high, prominent cheekbones.

But a man like him, so overtly angry, didn't frighten her.

It was the people who concealed their darkness and indecency with smiles and charm. They were much more frightening than the brashly annoying ones.

Her brother had always spoken of him with respect and perhaps a bit of reverence. Anyone who could inspire reverence in Chas Woodmore must be very trustworthy indeed. But she'd be lying if she didn't admit her own annoyance with her brother for leaving them in this state.

Now, as she waited in his shadowy study, the earl paused for a moment and then, reluctance in his very being, looked up. Right at her.

For an instant, Maia felt…wobbly. A bit light in the head. And then he shifted, his dark gaze changed, and she was able to draw in air again.

Pie-faced worm. No reason to glare at me like that. "Thank you," she said instead, and folded her hands properly in front of her, tamping down her own annoyance. How many times had Chas gone off to Paris or Vienna or Barcelona for weeks or months without word, and left his sisters and Mrs. Fernfeather to themselves? Why had he been so insistent that Corvindale get involved this time?

Maia was used to taking care of herself and her sisters. She was to be wed soon. She didn't need this stone-faced earl ordering them about, uprooting them from their own home and demanding that they come here to this dark and gloomy one. In one *day.*

"What. Do. You. Want. Miss Woodmore."

"Our chambers are very comfortable," she said in a

rush, feeling her cheeks warm. *Really.* "Mirabella has been exceedingly helpful, and so have Crewston and Mrs. Hunburgh. My sister and I are very appreciative that you've agreed to our brother's request to take on our guardianship." She actually managed to sound sincere. "As I mentioned in my letter, I didn't realize he'd made such arrangements with you until he went missing. We've always had Mrs. Fernfeather and her husband when Chas has been gone. Regardless…I do not wish to impose upon you—your household any longer than is strictly necessary."

"That is one thing on which we are in agreement, Miss Woodmore."

She straightened and her lips pursed again. "And so I wanted to make you aware of our plans to repair to Shropshire as soon as arrangements can be made for the house there to be opened. My fiancé will be arriving from the Continent in short order and once we're wed, you'll no longer be responsible for me, of course. My sisters, including the youngest, will come to live with me and—"

"An odd time to be planning a wedding, with your brother missing, Miss Woodmore. Or are you in such a hurry to marry that you intend to get the deed done before you even learn what has happened to him?"

Maia drew in her breath slowly and with great deliberation. How even to respond to such rudeness? She chose an oblique path. "My fiancé, Mr. Alexander Brad—"

"I am fully aware of the identity of your fiancé, Miss Woodmore." His voice cut in coldly. Corvindale pursed his lips, then continued. "Over the years, your brother has been remarkably conscientious in providing me with whatever information I might need should this occa-

sion—that I am needed to step in as your guardian—
arise. I am only sorry that it has done so."

For the first time, there was a lessening of the chill
in his voice. Or perhaps she was imagining it, for nothing else about him showed any indication of softening.
Of course, his regret was most likely due to the fact that
his life had been inconvenienced and not that Chas had
gone missing.

Well, that made two of them being inconvenienced.
And she was about to put an end to it as expediently as
possible.

Maia looked over at his ink-spotted fingers, the outside of his left palm smeared with black. Too impatient
to let the ink dry fully before writing over it, of course.
Something that she, as a left-handed scribe, had needed
to learn. At that moment, it struck her that she couldn't
recall ever having seen a man's bare hands before, other
than Chas's or her father's. Without gloves, they seemed
so much more powerful and elegant than when encased
in white fabric.

She blinked and looked up, realizing a few moments
of silence had passed. He was looking down at the ledger
again, and Maia drew in a breath of relief that he wasn't
staring at her, waiting for her to speak.

"When Chas went off to Paris on this latest trip," she
said, walking toward the sunny end of the study, "he did
something he'd never done before. He left us instructions of what to do if we didn't hear from him in a fortnight. Almost as if he feared something might happen.
He left a sealed envelope to be opened only if that occurred—which of course it has done. His letter directed
us to contact you immediately after two weeks without
contact from him, my lord."

"So your letter stated, Miss Woodmore. And so you've already—"

"I was hoping that perhaps you might have had word from him. Or…knew something. He never told us anything about why he traveled so much, or what he was doing. I don't even know… I don't even know how you are associated." Maia had to struggle to keep her voice steady. Was she the only one concerned about his disappearance? She brushed her curled fingers over a table as she walked past.

"While I have not heard word from him directly," Corvindale said from the desk behind her, "I assure you that I have begun my own investigation into his disappearance." His voice was smooth and low.

"You have?" She turned in surprise, a great gust of relief in her breath.

"Indeed." He was yet again examining what must be the most fascinating ledger in the history of the world. "I fear that I have nothing to report as of yet, but, Miss Woodmore, I will find out what happened to him." He looked up at that. "Your brother is a valued business associate of mine. I don't wish anything to happen to him, either, Miss Woodmore."

The certainty and underlying threat in his words gave Maia the first sense of relief since she'd realized Chas had disappeared. "Thank you, my lord," she said, for once allowing emotion to color her voice. "And I vow to remove myself and my sisters from your care as soon as I am able."

"Do not be too hasty, Miss Woodmore." He glanced toward the open door, then briefly back at her. "Mirabella will be quite disappointed if you should leave so soon after arriving. She has been looking forward to what she thinks of as a proper Season this year."

Maia nodded. That had become quite clear during her conversations with the pretty redheaded girl, who had just turned eighteen and looked nothing like her elder brother. She actually smiled and laughed. "She mentioned that she hadn't seen you for years, my lord, and that she'd given up on ever getting a proper come-out. She hasn't even been presented yet at court."

In fact, while Mirabella seemed more than capable in the ways of organizing and maintaining a household—according to her, she'd had much to do since being summoned from the small estate in the north to prepare for the Woodmore sisters' arrival at Blackmont—she seemed woefully hesitant in the ways of the *ton*. Since the girl hadn't been to London in more than seven years, Maia wasn't surprised at her lack of confidence.

"Indeed." Corvindale's response was noncommittal. "I understand you three are to attend some event tomorrow night?" He was back at the ledger again, but this time he'd picked up one of the pens. Apparently the audience—such as it was—was over.

"The Midsummer's Masquerade Ball at Sterlinghouse's," Maia explained. "Though your sister hasn't debuted yet, she can attend incognito. She is quite…" Her voice trailed off. She knew when she was being dismissed. "Thank you for setting my mind at ease, my lord. I pray you will have news of my brother soon."

"I will," he replied and stabbed the inkpen into its well, then commenced to writing.

The scratching of pen against paper filled the silence, pausing only as she passed by and fluttered the papers on his desk when she quit the room.

4

MISS WOODMORE WALTZES

"Do try to behave with *some* decorum tonight, Angelica," Maia said in a low voice as they prepared to disembark from the coach at Sterlinghouse. "Put on a good example for Mirabella."

Angelica ignored her, moving farther away on the seat they shared so that her sister couldn't squeeze her arm to emphasize her command.

They sat across from Mirabella and her Aunt Iliana, a nice enough woman who seemed to be forty or fifty years old. Angelica wasn't certain if she was relieved or disappointed that their chaperone wasn't one of those vacant-eyed, gossip-mongering old maids or widows often relegated to seeing to the safety and virtue of their charges. Like their own Mrs. Fernfeather.

In fact, she suspected Aunt Iliana might prove to be entertaining and interesting, if the intelligent glint in her bright blue eyes was any indication.

"I don't believe you have cause for worry tonight," Angelica whispered back to her sister. "No one will recognize me until we remove our masks, and so until then, all of my behaviors will be anonymous." She smiled and held up the black velvet mask trimmed with a gold and silver lace fall that would offer only teasing glimpses of her cheeks and mouth. The rest of the mask completely covered her from nose to brow. "You shall have no scandal by association. Even you could do something scandalous, Cleopatra," she added saucily.

"I certainly would not," Maia hissed back. "And how many times do I have to tell you, I'm Hatshepsut, not Cleopatra."

Angelica rolled her eyes. Her sister was such a pedant. "Who cares about Hatshep-whoever? No one could tell the difference anyway."

But Maia wouldn't leave it alone. "There's no asp on my staff," she replied—as if that explained everything.

Angelica was delighted that Mirabella managed to interrupt. "We're to don our masks before entering?" There was excitement in her voice, for this was to be her first London event, even though she hadn't yet been presented at court and her wardrobe needed to be brought up-to-date. Her mask was of ivory silk, completely covered in lace that fell beyond the section around her eyes to her jaw, and rose up to be a stiff fringe higher than her normal hairline. In this case, it didn't matter, for she wore a wig of white that towered above her crown.

"Yes. We'll be announced, but not with our real identities," Maia explained before Aunt Iliana could open her mouth. She held her gold mask in hand, and the royal staff that went with her costume rested across her lap. "Only by our character or costumes."

Angelica saw the older woman pause, then close her lips and settle back in her seat as if to give free reign to the elder Woodmore girl. She seemed, if not grateful, at least accepting of Maia's bossy tendencies. Angelica appreciated that, for despite her sister's overbearing attitude, she loved and admired her and would have felt badly if there was friction between her and the older woman.

"Everyone is to be unmasked at midnight," Maia continued. "Although last year, the unmasking was much later. No one was ready until nearly one o'clock."

"We're here," Angelica said as she heard the voices of the driver and footman. She moved her flowing skirts out of the way of the other passengers' feet.

At that moment, the door swung open and the three young women and one older one were helped down.

There was an angel in white lace and an elaborate white wig.

Behind her came a petite bejeweled and bangled Egyptian queen in gold, balancing her staff in hand. She was followed by a ruff-necked Elizabeth in a wide, ungainly gown that took some effort to make it fit through the carriage door.

Last came Atropos, carrying her fateful shears and a skein of sparkling gold thread. Her gold-shot black gown draped in a modified Greek fashion in two swaths, from shoulder to waist, then wrapped around and draped again from waist to foot. The effect was a combination of elegance and sensuality, with the light, glinting cloth molding to the shape of her bosom and hips, yet falling freely to obscure her figure at any given moment.

Her arms were bare but for long black gloves, and she carried a dainty golden reticule for her skein and shears. The gown had camellias fashioned of gold fabric marching along the tops of the gathered shoulders, at the waist where the fabric was caught up, and along the generous hem where it trailed along the ground like a ripple of water. A row of gold flowers also lined the gloves from elbow to knuckle. And, her dark hair had been separated into a multitude of sections, twisted with thick gold cord and pinned high at the crown of her head so that gold and walnut-brown curls cascaded down to her neck.

It didn't take Angelica long to discover that the lace which made up the lower half of her mask tickled her cheeks and upper lip, and she considered tearing the fringe off. But after she entered the masquerade ball, she decided against it.

Tonight, she wished to remain as anonymous as possible. Something like expectancy prickled her, and she felt daring and unencumbered. She didn't want to be approached by any young brides-to-be, asking for her to prophesy about their future husbands.

Part of the reason was that Angelica still felt unsettled when she recalled the conversation with Dewhurst—no, she would think of him as Voss, as Corvindale called him. That name suited him more than something that bespoke of early morning meadows. Despite his toffee-colored hair, he was nothing like a sunny morning. More like an afternoon frosted with a soft summer rain: beautiful to look at, yet with a filter of shadow and gloom.

Smiling privately at her own whimsy, Angelica took the opportunity to slip away from Maia when her sister stopped to help Aunt Iliana adjust Mirabella's wings. Angelica had worn the angel costume to one masque last Season and learned that wings made for a difficult evening. They came askew when dancing, they bumped and caught against people whenever moving through the crush and the harness that kept them in place felt rather like an old-fashioned long corset. Last year, Angelica realized too late that her sister had suggested that costume for just such a reason and resolved to pick her own costumes without Maia's help in the future.

The free-flowing fabric and simplicity of her attire made it easy for Angelica to slip between a Romeo and a woodland faerie, who happened to have her own set of ungainly wings, and lose herself in the crush.

Tonight, there were no dance cards. No introductions. No matrons (or sisters) glaring from the walls, taking note of any scandalous behavior.

It was no wonder the Sterlinghouse's annual masque was so popular.

The theme tonight was Ancient Babylon, and Lady Sterlinghouse had outdone herself. Plants hung from high on the walls, blossoming tendrils falling like Rapunzel's hair and releasing floral scents into the air. Fountains rumbled, adding to the low hum of noise from conversation and music, masking everything but nearby sounds. The servants were dressed as ancient Babylonians in long, geometrically patterned robes, and carried trays laden with food and drink.

Angelica was standing near a fountain, wondering where the water came from that spilled down several levels and lightly sprayed into the air, when a dashing knight approached. Fortunately he wasn't wearing real chain mail, just tooled leather over a jerkin and hose.

"I do hope you don't intend to use those on me," he said, gesturing to the shears in her hand.

It was difficult to tell if she knew his voice, muted as it was by the fountain and other sounds, but he seemed familiar. So Angelica smiled and unraveled a hank of the golden thread. Holding it up, pretending to measure him, she tried to see through his mask. But it was shadowy and dark, and she couldn't get a good look. "No, I do not believe your time has yet come, sir knight. You'll live to joust for another day."

He laughed, and she recognized him then. The young and eligible Viscount Harrington, with whom she'd danced at several parties and even once strolled out on a patio, arm in arm. Did he recognize her? Had he sought her out?

"Perhaps you might offer a boon to this lowly man at arms," he suggested. "It would be my honor to wear your favor into battle next."

Angelica smiled and snipped off a generous piece of her golden cord. "I vow this is nothing more than a maiden's favor, not the work of Atropos this night," she told him, wrapping it around his forearm and tying it lightly.

"It is you," he said then, smiling beneath his leather mask. "I was nearly certain, Miss Woodmore. It was your hair and the way you move. But now it is confirmed. Along with your favor, might I also request the next dance?"

"Of course. It would be my pleasure," she replied, replacing her shears and skein in the bag, carefully so that the tips pointed down into a corner of the small satchel. Then she took his arm and allowed him to guide her through the people toward the dance floor.

"It's a waltz," he commented as the musicians began the new song. "May I?" he asked again, turning to face her at the edge of the dance floor.

A thrill of the forbidden tripped through Angelica, and she gave a little curtsy. "Yes, my lord."

Her first waltz.

Angelica's heart beat a bit more rapidly as Harrington

eased her into the unfamiliar position of the dance, nearly *embracing* her. She was hardly able to contain a nervous smile. They stepped into the rhythm of the music with a bit of hesitation and a slight scuff of her slipper as she learned the step.

They made their way around the room in the three-beat rhythm, making small circles with the triangular step. Angelica enjoyed the freedom of the dance—so different from the line dances and quadrilles where every movement was choreographed and a slight change could disrupt the flow.

But while she had always found Harrington to be very charming and quite handsome, she realized now that she'd come face-to-face with him—quite intimately, in fact—that his shoulders weren't as broad as she might have thought. And while he moved with ease, an underlying grace and confidence was missing.

Conversation, she found, was much easier with a waltz than when dancing the traditional dances. Instead of constantly separating and then coming back together, she and her partner had the opportunity for uninterrupted repartee. Harrington suggested they ride in the park someday—an invitation which she accepted—and asked about her sisters. Then he said he'd heard about Corvindale taking them in as his wards.

"Yes, that's true," Angelica told him. "It's only been since yesterday and I'm not certain how long we'll be at Blackmont."

"You didn't mention anything about leaving when I came to call two days ago," he commented, reminding her that, yes, indeed, he had been in her parlor on that day.

The day Dewhurst—Voss—had come and told her about Lord Brickbank.

Suddenly a bit of her pleasure waned.

Brickbank was dead, and, apparently, there was nothing she or anyone could have done to prevent it. The fact had poked at her incessantly, bothering her in a way she hadn't been bothered since the first time she realized her gift—if one could call it that. This incident had disturbed her, perhaps because it had been so unwelcome. The dream had come upon her with no warning, unlike the other times when she had to concentrate and summon the vision or image to make her prophecy.

Angelica prayed she'd have no more odd dreams like that, for it was one thing when she called on her Sight to help a woman make a decision about her future…but this had been so different. So unexpected.

She hadn't known Brickbank, but she'd come to know Voss enough in those brief moments that his loss had affected her more deeply than she'd anticipated. He was likely halfway to Romania by now, taking his friend with him back to be buried in his family plot. How long did it take to travel to Romania?

And back?

And why did it even *matter* to her?

Just as Harrington spun her in a less-than-smooth circle, Angelica saw the figure standing near the fountain she'd been examining only moments before. He seemed to be watching them, and a little frisson sizzled through her at the intensity of his stare.

The shadows embraced him, and the black mask he wore hid all but the lower third of his face. A wide-brimmed hat covered his head and a heavy dark cloak offered more concealment. But he was watching her.

Her heartbeat quickened, and as the dance ended and
Harrington escorted her off the floor, Angelica glanced
back quickly. He was still looking after her, and as their
eyes connected across the space, he gave a bow of acknowledgment. Then, a person moved in the space between them, obstructing the view, and then another, and
when Angelica looked again, he was gone.

It took her a moment for her heart to settle to normal,
and her breathing to steady. Was it possible Voss was
here? That he hadn't left for Romania? It had to be him,
watching her so boldly.

Her belly tingled at the thought and she had to restrain
herself from looking back again as her dance partner—
whose name she had nearly forgotten—drew her through
the clusters of people: a highwayman, a king, an archer,
a Hamlet and Ophelia, a Diana and a butterfly.

"Miss Woodmore?"

She looked up at Harrington and realized he'd been
trying to gain her attention for some time. "I'm terribly parched," she said with a smile, utilizing the excuse
Maia had taught her to free oneself—either permanently
or temporarily—from a companion.

"May I fetch you something to drink?" he asked,
leaning close. He smelled pleasant—a woodsy scent.
"So you don't have to wait in line?"

"Yes, indeed. I understand there is some effervescent
drink with lemon in it. It sounds lovely." Because the
mask obscured her face, she couldn't bat her eyelashes,
but she did look up at him with a smile.

As Harrington rushed off, Angelica realized that,
ironically, she'd used a similar excuse to extricate herself from a different dance partner so that she could
speak with Harrington himself some time ago. Maia,

who'd been very clever at managing her many beaux before settling on Alexander Bradington, would be proud of her sister's expertise.

"Do you care to dance?" came a low voice behind her.

Angelica barely managed to keep from clapping a startled hand to her bosom and instead merely straightened. How had he gotten over here so quickly? "Of course," she replied, turning. Her heart was pounding, and beneath her gloves, her palms had gone damp.

He was there, perhaps not as tall as she'd remembered, but darker and more forbidding thanks to his unrelieved black garb and shadowing hat. The full cloak covered him from shoulder nearly to the floor, and the mask obscured him from temple to upper lip. That left only a bit of jaw and cheek uncovered, but they too were shadowed by a high, white Elizabethan neck ruff.

"Or would you prefer to take in some air beneath the stars?" he added.

His face and eyes were in shadow, and he spoke so low and so near to her ear that, although she could understand what he was saying, and his breath was warm against her, she wasn't able to recognize his voice.

Much as she would like to walk beneath the stars with Lord Dewhurst…Voss…until she was certain it was he, Angelica wouldn't do anything so scandalous.

Although…she was in a mask. No one would recognize her except her sister. "Perhaps after the dance some fresh air would be in order," she said prudently. That would give her time.

"Come then," he said and drew her toward the dance floor.

The music had already begun: another waltz. Only at a masquerade ball would there be so many of the scandalous dances in a row, and Angelica felt a prickle of naughtiness as she allowed him to twirl her into position.

"Have you received any word from your brother?" he murmured.

It *was* Voss, then. Angelica's heart lightened and she smiled up at him, allowing her pleasure to show in her eyes. "I have not," she replied. "But I am surprised to see you here. I thought you would be well on your way to Romania."

There was a pause as he executed some unfamiliar step, half turning her away so that they could pass by another couple. "Ah, yes. I've been delayed."

"Corvindale won't be pleased, I'm certain," Angelica said.

"You've spoken to him?"

"Of course. He avoids us all as much as possible, but of course it is difficult to completely ignore the man whose house we are living in." She was aware of the solidness of his arms, the warmth of his body near hers.

Voss looked down at her, his eyes seeming to almost glow behind the shadow of his mask. "Living in Corvindale's home must be most unpleasant."

She felt a little shiver run over the back of her shoulders. He sounded angry, almost malicious. "I know there is little love lost between the two of you, but he hasn't been unkind to us," she said. There was no reason that she should allow his dislike of the earl to color her own opinion.

Again, a pause as they stepped through several more paces, and Angelica realized that Voss had maneuvered them toward the edge of the dance floor. Beyond the clusters of people and the dangling vines from the Babylonian plants, the doors to the gardens were open. Two sets of tall double doors had been flung wide, allowing easy access to the torchlit pathways several steps below the balcony.

As they drew nearer, a vibrant breeze brushed over her warm skin and Angelica was grateful when Voss eased her off the dance floor. She had begun to feel warm from the dancing and the fresh night air would be a glad change. Especially since she would be with Voss.

Would he try to kiss her? Her belly flipped at the thought and her cheeks warmed. She suspected a kiss from Voss would be very different from the one Harrington had brushed over her lips at the Farbers' fete.

Sliding a firm arm around her waist, he kept her close as they walked through the doors. Angelica had a moment's bit of nervousness and looked behind her to make certain Maia wasn't watching their almost intimate pose—the side of her body was caught up next to his taller one and his arm was tight. He wasn't about to let her go.

"This way," he murmured, leading her past the rushing fountain in the center of the massive balcony and toward the darkest set of stairs. The burned-out torch hung uselessly at the top, and for the first time, Angelica felt a niggle of unease.

"Perhaps we should stay here. It's a lovely view." She paused at the top of the steps, gesturing up at the stars.

The garden lay before them and the sounds of the party loud at their backs. Other couples were out, walking on the balcony. And she could hear the laughter of people below, in the gardens, muted by the rushing fountain. Some of her nervousness lessened.

"There's naught to fear, Miss Woodmore," he said,

tugging at her firmly. "Let us walk and smell the roses. I am looking forward to showing them to you."

Angelica felt a renewed prickle of nerves as he declined to release her, and she glanced back over her shoulder, undecided. She could pull away and make a scene, and then everyone would know she'd been out on the balcony with Dewhurst—somehow she'd stopped thinking of him as Voss—and Maia would be furious.

She stepped hesitantly forward, her foot finding the top step. She didn't want to make a scene. And there were people below; it wasn't as if they were going to be outside alone. Still…

He looked down at her, his eyes piercing and holding hers. There was something wrong. Angelica felt a low, deep tug in her belly, insidious and insistent. Unpleasant. When he urged her forward, she didn't have the energy to protest, although she felt as if she should.

Down another step, and another. The lights from the balcony above became blocked by the fountain and the railing, and they were in near darkness. Angelica blinked and stopped on the steps, a real frisson of fear descending over her.

She shook her head as if she'd just awakened, and when Dewhurst turned back toward her…his eyes were *glowing*. Reddish, piercing, there in the dark.

Angelica stifled a scream and he responded with a guttural sound of surprise and fury, his neck ruff going askew. She saw a smooth, undimpled chin clearly for the first time, and suddenly realized: this wasn't Voss.

The next thing she knew, Angelica's mask was yanked down over her face, covering her eyes. She felt herself tripping and falling, and a strong arm catching her, gathering her up closely before she landed on the ground, and then he was moving with quick, jolting steps.

She tried to scream, tried to claw the velvet away, but his hand closed over her mouth and the mask with all of its lace ground into her skin and lips, stifling her. Panicked, she kicked and fought, but he smashed her up against him and ran.

Her arm was bent up beneath her, her hand curled between her and her attacker, and suddenly she realized she felt the shape of her reticule wadded up beneath her arm. Trying to focus and to keep the fear from oversetting sense, she managed to grasp the little purse. Through the light fabric, she felt the shears and closed her fingers around the entire bag, then stabbed down into the man's torso.

Hard.

She felt it slice into him, the sickening sense of driving into flesh, and she squeezed her eyes shut despite the fact that she was already blinded. He staggered and her dark world tipped as she screamed, then she stabbed again. Dampness leached into her and she felt his grip loosen. Suddenly she tumbled free and landed on the ground. The sound of him crashing away through the hedge sent a wave of relief through her.

Voices and footsteps came and by the time she'd sat up and readjusted the mask over her eyes, Angelica was surrounded by what would normally be the work of a nightmare or hallucinatory episode. A faerie, a peacock, a sultan and a jester had gathered around.

Her fingers and knees shook and her belly felt as though it were about to erupt, but Angelica managed to stand without assistance once the jester helped her to her feet. She realized she still clutched the reticule and suspected it was soaking with blood, so she allowed it to drop to the ground in the dark.

"What has happened?" they were asking in a variety of manners and tones.

Angelica could barely organize her thoughts, let alone summon the words to respond. And now that the moment of terror was over, she wanted nothing more than to forget about it. To forget her fear, the sudden inability to think, her foolish, *foolish* mistake and the harsh hands gripping and holding her. And the glowing eyes.

Glowing eyes. How could that be?

"I'm fine," she said, forcing her voice to be steady. If Maia found out about this incident, she'd never let her come to another ball, let alone a masquerade. Nor would Corvindale or Chas. "I merely lost my way in the dark and some creature ran over my foot and startled me."

"Did you fall in the fountain? Your gown is wet," said the faerie, and Angelica reached automatically to touch the lower part of her skirts.

"It'll dry," she said, realizing it was blood and thankful that it wouldn't show on the dark fabric as more than a shine.

Her hair sagged heavily near the back of her head, instead of at her crown where it had originally been anchored, and it felt as if a few curls had come undone. But the original arrangement had been a loose, messy one, and she hoped it wasn't noticeably different.

No one asked what she'd been doing in the gardens alone—the anonymity of the masks was still at work—and Angelica thanked the characters for their assistance before pivoting toward the ball.

By the time she climbed the steps back to the balcony, where the party roared above, her stomach had settled and her knees had strengthened. Angelica hadn't finished berating herself, however, for her foolish mistake. Hadn't it been at the Lundhames', two nights ago, that she'd reminded herself of the fate of Miss Eliza Billingsly and her compromising position with Mr. Deetson-Waring?

And here she'd gone and done something nearly as foolish, and dangerous, too, simply because she was wearing a mask. Clearly her companion had been after something more serious than a simple kiss in the dark. Had he meant to ravish her somewhere in the back of the garden? Or…was it possible he'd been trying to abduct her? To force a wedding or engagement?

He'd seemed to know who she was, for he'd asked about her brother, and the Woodmores were known to be a well-established, wealthy family.

A little shiver threatened to weaken her knees again, but Angelica fought it away. She'd come through this incident safely, and now she would forget about it. She'd learned her lesson, thankfully, without serious consequences.

"Miss Woodmore. I have your drink."

Heaven's daisies. It was Harrington, standing there with a little glass cup of something pale.

"Why thank you," she said, and gratefully accepted the drink. She was thirsty. "I do hope you weren't waiting long. I had to—I walked outside for a moment just to see the stars." Her fingers still trembled a bit.

"Not at all," he said. "Perhaps you would like to stroll about on the balcony with me?"

It was fortunate that she was drinking from the effervescent lemonade, for if not, she might have responded too quickly. As it was, as she withdrew the cup from her lips, she looked across the dance floor and saw him leaning against one of the Babylonian columns.

It's him.

Voss.

He was masked, of course, with the lower part of his face covered, and only his eyes and thick, slashing brows showing above. He looked like some sort of Indian or Oriental thief, with a low, square hat half covering his thick hair and a sweeping cloak.

A flush of heat swept her as their gazes connected. There was the space of half the room and throngs of people between them, but it was as if he were standing next to her. She had no doubt this time that it was Voss.

How could she have mistaken that other figure for him? She could hardly credit her previous error.

"I…" Angelica looked back at Harrington. Even from behind his mask, she could see the warmth in his eyes. A week earlier, she would have been taking his arm with alacrity and strolling in the moonlight with him. And perhaps even permitting a second, chaste kiss.

But now… She resisted the urge to glance back over her shoulder in Voss's direction. Just because he was here, and looking at her…well, that really meant nothing. Everyone of the *ton* was here tonight. Perhaps he didn't even recognize that it was Angelica behind this coy mask, and even if he did…well, that didn't mean he'd ask her to dance. Or even approach her.

"Miss Woodmore?" Harrington had tilted his head to look down at her during this space of silence. He made his voice loud enough to be heard over the low buzz of voices and strains of music. "I can only imagine how lovely the moonlight will be, filtering over your dark hair. But I should certainly like to see it for myself."

"Oh." She couldn't help a smile in return. Such a romantic thing to say without being ridiculous, like comparing her eyes to diamonds and her skin to silk or whatnot. Lord Fedderley had done that once and it was all she could do to keep from rolling her so-called diamondlike eyes. She lifted the drink again to give herself more time to determine how to respond, and managed, as she lowered it, to glance back to where Voss was standing.

He was gone.

Angelica wasn't prepared for the stab of disappointment when, as she cast her gaze over the perimeter of the room in what would be the path between where he'd been and where she stood, she didn't see him.

That, she supposed, was that.

She turned. And there he was.

5

IN WHICH A SQUEAKING
CHAIR INTERVENES

Angelica's face flushed hot beneath her mask, and suddenly, her heart was slamming in her chest.

But before she could speak or even gather her composure, Voss had taken matters in hand.

"I do believe you've promised this dance to me, Mistress Fate," he said, smoothly turning and somehow gathering up her arm to slip it around his crooked elbow—all without the slightest hitch. "A waltz," he added, looking down at her.

At last, his eyes said, gleaming with satisfaction from above the cloth tied around his lower face. Between the heavy, slashing brows and the squat, boxy hat—and even with the whimsical curls peeking from beneath—he looked striking and dangerous. Dangerous in a manner that made her belly feel as if it were filled with butterflies, not leaden with stone.

Angelica had a fleeting moment of sympathy for Harrington, who had no opportunity to circumvent the tide of Lord Dewhurst. But no sooner had she bid him a hurried "Please excuse me" than Voss had taken her away and to the floor filled with other dancers.

As if he'd done it a hundred times, he spun her neatly to face him, his strong hand settling just so at her waist, and the other curving around her fingers as he lifted her left hand into position. He pulled her so close that the camellias at her waist nearly brushed the side of his cloak.

Angelica had already waltzed—twice!—that evening, but this was an entirely different matter. It was as if every part of her had awakened and now absorbed the slightest sensation. The swish of her gown flowing against and around his pantalooned legs. The imprint of each finger from the hand at her waist.

She was aware of the gentle tension in her raised and extended arm, and the warmth of his gloved palm against hers. The brush of air over her bare, upper arms as they spun with grace around and between the other dancers. The sleek shift of muscle and tendon in his shoulder beneath her hand. The bounce of her hair, the warmth and breadth of his body *so close*. He smelled foreign and spicy, very unlike the common pine and balsam scent Harrington favored.

Again, she wondered how she could ever have mistaken her attacker as Voss. The reality was so much more…*more*.

It was several moments before she realized that he'd not spoken a word since they stepped into the kaleidoscope of swirling couples, and that they'd made their way efficiently around and between the other dancers. She ventured the question that came to mind.

"Surely you haven't been to Romania and back already? To take your friend's body?"

"I bribed Eddersley to go in my stead." His tone was

clipped, and when he turned toward the edge of the group and slipped Angelica between two couples near the side, she realized he was leading her off the floor.

"What are you doing?" she asked. "The song isn't over."

He glanced down with dark, glittering eyes, and she felt as if he'd turned some great force on her. His hand had closed around her arm as he released her from their dance pose, but instead of leading her toward the balcony, which was on the other side of the large chamber, he was edging them toward the most shadowy corner of the room.

"My lord," she managed to say, but her words were certainly lost in his wake, in the midst of the music and conversation.

He fairly towed her along behind him, toward a shadowy corner where a fountain stood between two potted trees. Dangling vines hung from pots on shelves high on the walls, providing a convenient curtain for those who might wish to dally in corners without being seen.

Voss swept away a handful of the vines, speaking sharply into the corner and scattering leaves and flower petals. Seconds later, Angelica was nearly trampled by a Romeo and a befeathered swan as they stumbled out of the alcove and away. Apparently, Juliet was elsewhere.

The next thing she knew, the wall was behind her and Voss was in front of her, very close, his fingers curved around her upper arms. He'd yanked away the mask covering the lower part of his face, and she could see, even in the low light, the flat line of his mouth and the pinch of his nostrils.

She tried to swallow, and felt a renewed rush of heat behind her mask. She wanted to tear the heavy velvet and lace confection away so she wasn't so stifled, and suddenly, the very thought became reality as he stripped it up and off her head, tossing it aside. None too gently.

"What has happened?" he asked, closing his fingers around one of her wrists. His eyes penetrated hers, and for the first time, she felt a trickle of fear. They were glittering, not with fascination, but with…menace. "Tonight. What happened?"

In the closeness of that dim corner, Angelica felt the rise and fall of his breathing, and the racing pulse beating in her throat. It threatened to choke her.

"I don't know what you mean," she said, trying to keep her voice steady.

His breathing shifted and a delicate tremor rippled through his arms as if he were restraining himself. "I smell blood, Angelica. On you. All *over* you. I want to know where in the damned hell it came from."

His words, uttered from between very tight jaws, nevertheless snapped like a whip between them. She couldn't have said which startled her more—his use of her familiar name, the profanity or the fact that he somehow smelled blood. On her.

She moistened her lips, trying to dispel the sudden dryness in her mouth, and felt his hand tighten reflexively, crushing one of the flowers on the top of her glove. It was at that moment that she realized just how dangerous and powerful this man was.

This man, who blocked her into a corner, who had his body very nearly pressed against hers and whose gaze bored down into her like a weapon.

Her heart pounded so hard she was certain he felt it, too, and she tried to contain her nervousness. Fury rolled off him, but she didn't believe it was directed toward her.

If he meant her harm, he wouldn't drag her into a corner where they could easily be discovered.

"I thought he was you. He asked me to waltz," she replied when his fingers tightened again.

He drew back just a bit, loosened his grip. "You thought he was *me?*" A shaft of light settled on his face, illuminating one eye and half of his nose and chin. The illusion made him appear even more intimidating.

"He behaved as if we'd met, and he asked me about Chas right away. So I thought he was you," she defended herself, feeling more in control now. Had his anger been worry for her, then? But, he'd *smelled blood* on her. Such an odd thing to say.

"And then we went out to walk under the stars and… and…he tried to…" Angelica was still a little breathless—from being trotted so quickly across the room, from reliving the fright of her assault, from the steady, dark gaze that continued to bore into her.

"What did he do?" Voss's fingers tightened and she felt the tension riding along his arms, settling in the space between his brows and drawing them tighter. "Where did the blood come from? It's not… It can't be *yours.*"

She shook her head. "No. He— I stabbed him. With my shears. It's his blood."

His eyes widened and then his entire demeanor changed. The edge eased from what was visible of his expression, and his brows relaxed. He wasn't smiling, but surprise—and perhaps relief—shone there. "Your shears?"

"I'm Atropos. You recognized me earlier, did you not? You called me Mistress Fate."

His shrug was fluid, and now the crinkles at the corners of his eyes belied a near smile. "I didn't know which of the three you were. The gown gave you away, despite the fact that you chose black instead of the common white. It's fortunate for you, apparently, that you were Atropos, for I don't believe a mere length of thread and a measuring rod or spindle would have been much assistance to you."

Relieved that his intensity seemed to have eased, she gave him a demure look. "No, I do believe you are correct, my lord."

But his face darkened again, the crinkles next to his eyes smoothing as the groove between his brows became more pronounced. "And the man who assaulted you? What happened to him?" He hadn't released her, and in fact, she was aware of his shoes brushing hers. Warmth and awareness filled the space between them, and she realized her fingers had curled into the edge of his cloak. She loosened them.

"I don't know. He ran off. He didn't return to the party, I'm certain, for surely all the blood would cause comment."

"The condition of your gown didn't," he reminded her.

"But no one can see it," she said. "I don't know how you noticed. You said you *smelled* blood?" She sniffed, but scented nothing but him. Spicy, masculine and arresting. Very close. She felt a bit light-headed.

His lips flattened. "Does Corvindale know?"

"No one knows but you. The earl isn't here this evening."

Now he smiled, but with that false edge. "As much as I'm certain you believe that, I know better than to assume otherwise. He's here."

"As you wish, my lord," she said, suddenly feeling lighter than she had since arriving at the ball. "I suppose we shall find out when the unmasking takes place." She cast a look beyond his shoulder, through the filter of hanging vines. It was rather cozy back here in this little corner.

"But our unmasking has already occurred," he said. Voss's voice had dropped to a purr, and Angelica flashed a quick look at him. He was looking at her in a very different way than he had only moments before. Much like the way he'd been looking at her when their eyes met across the room.

Her heart pounded, hard, as he lifted a hand to skim a gloved finger along the side of her neck. Little prickles of awareness followed and Angelica found herself hardly able to breathe. She could be affronted at such a liberty, but the touch felt oddly chaste. Yet at the same time, the way he looked at her, leaning in closer, felt very intimate.

"I cannot decide whether to be annoyed or gratified," he said, stroking along beneath her chin, holding her eyes with his.

"What do you mean, my lord?"

He withdrew his hand and adjusted a camellia on her shoulder. "Well, my dear, I could be annoyed and affronted that you mistook another gentleman for me. Apparently I hadn't made enough of an impression upon you. Or I could be gratified that, thinking he was me, you agreed to walk in the moonlight with him. As unpleasant as that occasion might have turned out to be."

A little stab of pleasure startled her. "Such a difficult decision, my lord. I cannot even pretend to assist you." She looked away in all demureness, and realized with a start that she was well and truly, no doubt about it, *flirting* with Viscount Dewhurst. And managing quite well.

Maia would be proud. Or…perhaps not, if she knew it was Dewhurst and not Harrington with whom she was being coy.

"What is it that you thought might happen, walking in the moonlight with me?" he asked. His voice was very near her ear, smooth and low, its very timbre somehow discernable despite the dull roar of music, rushing water, and revelry around them. "Perhaps the experience of your first kiss?"

"Oh," she said, her breath gone again at the dark light in his eyes. Yet, she managed to say, "I've already experienced my first kiss."

Those glittering eyes narrowed with pleasure and he whispered, "I'm rather pleased to hear you say that. Now, let us see about making you forget it."

He moved, his mouth covering hers as the wall reared up behind her. He eased—pushed—her back against it, his somehow gloveless hands settling: one, warm, to cup the back of her head, and the other sliding around her waist.

Angelica couldn't have been prepared for the rush of heat and pleasure from the touch of his lips. Neither tentative nor rapacious, they fit to hers deliberately, without apology—molding and tasting, coaxing…demanding hers to respond. And she did, following his lead, aware of the bare touch of his fingers on the underside of her jaw, of the warm mouth delicious over hers and the heat of his body pressing her into the wall.

An explosion of pleasure rushed through her—warm and bold, tingling low in her belly and down…farther. Angelica needed to breathe but she forgot how, sinking into the sleek, sensual rhythm of mouth sliding against mouth.

His tongue surprised her, slipping briefly along the half-part of her lips in a heated little tease, and then his mouth crushed over hers again as his arm tightened around her waist. Voss's breath buffeted warm against her skin as he shifted away, coming low and unsteady. Along her cheek he smoothed his lips, nibbling, pressing gentle kisses that left tingles in their wake.

She'd tilted her head back, unable to hold it up any longer, and the fountain of hair at the back of her head was smashed against the wall, the pins driving into her scalp. His hands drew her closer, his face buried near her ear, his lips moving along her hairline and down to the curve of her neck.

Angelica gasped and trembled; she was sensitive and a bit ticklish there, and the light movements of his nose and mouth buried in her neck's crook made her want to squirm away at the same time as press him closer. She wanted him to kiss and nibble, to taste as he'd done her mouth—not to feather-lightly touch, and she grabbed on to his cloak, pulling him closer, only half aware of what she was doing. She wanted *more*, something more.

"Voss," she whispered to the ceiling, planting her hands on his chest, curling her fingers into the fabric, not sure what she was asking for. But she needed something to release the tightening inside her.

She became vaguely aware of the activity beyond the curtain of vines behind him, and that the music seemed to have started again. Or perhaps it was that the fountain had been turned off or had run out of water, and now the sounds of the jaunty three-step dance tune more easily reached her ears.

The dull roar of people laughing and talking filled the air, filtering through the music as the two of them stood in the dark corner. Her hands settled on his chest, his covering her upper arms, something stretching and shimmering between them.

Voss drew in a rough breath and pulled away. "Thank the fates," he murmured, more to himself than to her.

Releasing Angelica, he fought to steady his voice, to keep himself from sounding breathless. And to keep his damned fangs from showing. *God and Luce.*

He wasn't certain whom to call on for assistance, and in response, the Mark on his shoulder twinged with pain.

Good. Pain. Distraction.

His incisors retracted and he drew in a breath that sounded embarrassingly ragged.

"For what?" Angelica's eyes were glazed and her swollen, crinkled lips parted. She'd sagged against him and he was certain she had no idea how lazy and beckoning she sounded.

With one side of the gown pushed half off her shoulder and her head collapsed back against the wall, she looked as if she'd been ravaged. He wondered what had kept him from doing just that.

One moment, he was ready to drag the glove from her arm and sink his teeth in—or, hell, right into her bared shoulder, in that soft hollow above her collarbone. Her sweet, ivory skin had been there, beneath his mouth, smooth and warm, sweet and salty against his tongue, her pulse racing madly against his lips…and the next moment, he was pulling away, setting her back from him.

Just as well he hadn't. This wasn't the place. She'd scream, there'd be a mess, he'd be found out.

The fact that Corvindale would not be amused was the least of the considerations. Dimitri could sleep on a wooden stake for all Voss cared.

It took Voss a moment to realize that Angelica was waiting for him to explain, looking up at him with shadowed, bedroom eyes. A delicious expanse of creamy bosom and throat was exposed by the off-kilter V of her Greek gown. He closed his eyes for a moment, focusing on everything else around them: the scent of gardenias attached to the hanging vines, the nearby roar of laughter and the spritely tune from the string quintet. The painful ache at the back of his shoulder and the dull throb of his cock. The pressure of his insistent fangs.

Everything but her.

He tried not to breathe too deeply, not to look at the smooth white skin in front of him. He fought to block out the lingering scent of blood—not hers, but it didn't matter—and to keep his eyes from glowing. Too much.

"That bloody squeaking chair," he said, having collected himself. And he stepped back.

She opened her eyes fully and looked at him. "Pardon me?" she said. "I don't understand."

He resisted the urge to reach over and adjust the shoulder of her gown. "One of the musicians is sitting in a chair that squeaks. I think it's the violist, for his movement seems to match the squeak." That, in part, had been what had dragged him from the depths of red heat and need. That incessant squeaking.

"I hadn't noticed," she told him, and cocked her head as if to listen.

He managed a bemused smile. "Most people don't. It's an affliction of mine. One of many, in fact." He couldn't wait to introduce her to some of the others. Voss held his smile in check.

"Indeed?" she replied, and the look she gave him— an unlikely combination of innocence and sass—made him want to grab her again.

But before he could respond, she said something that turned his body to ice. "Your eyes," she said, looking at him closely. "They were almost glowing, a moment ago. It must be a trick of the light, because his were, too."

He forgot to be reticent and polite. "What? *His?*"

She shrank back a bit, but not as much as she could have. "The man from outside. His eyes looked like they were glowing or burning. It must have been the moon—"

A rush of comprehension blasted through him and he grabbed her by the arms. *Satan's black soul.* "What did he say to you? You said he asked about your brother."

Instinctively Voss turned, reversing their positions so he could see beyond the hanging vines. People were dancing, talking, laughing. The damned chair was still squeaking, the pianist fumbled a note…. "What exactly did he do to you?" he demanded as he scanned the room, looking for anything or anyone that upset his instincts.

A vampire had no way to sense or otherwise iden- tify the presence of another vampire unless one came face-to-face with him, and even then, it was more of a *feeling.* Even among the Dracule, they couldn't always identify each other merely by sight.

There were ways, of course…subtle comments that might be made, or a certain way of looking at one to test the waters, so to speak. It was almost like being able to tell when a man preferred another man in his bed, in- stead of the sweet bundle of female curves.

Angelica's eyes had widened, all trace of sensuality

and teasing gone. Now she looked frightened, and by damn, she should be. Voss flattened his lips, an ugly gnawing in his belly.

"He was insistent on going into the dark part of the garden, and when I hesitated, he pulled my mask down so I couldn't see…then he picked me up—"

A shrill scream from beyond the alcove drew their attention and Voss reacted immediately, shoving Angelica back into the corner and positioning himself in front of her. *Damn and the devil. Already?* Another scream, cut off quickly, and then eerie, strained silence.

How could he have been so distracted? By the stones of hell, he should have taken Angelica out of there as soon as he found her instead of dallying on the dance floor and in the corner. But the blood…the smell had scattered his mind, dangerously diverting him.

Voss could see little beyond the vines, but he didn't dare move them for fear of drawing attention. From between velvety white gardenia petals, he watched a faction gather on what had been the dance floor. Five of them, large and imposing. Eyes burning red. And then he smelled it. Blood. Saw it soaking the front of one of them, thanks to Angelica's shears.

Luce's balls.

Tension settled over Voss and he looked around for a weapon. The gun tucked into the deep pocket of his cloak would do nothing against the vampires. There was nothing else in the corner he could utilize for a weapon, either. He'd been a damned fool to not think Moldavi would move so quickly.

The crowd had edged back from the five menacing figures, but Voss knew they couldn't go far. The doors would be guarded by more Dracule or at least their footmen armed with rifles and bayonets. Everyone was trapped…until the vampires got what—or who—they'd come for. And finished feeding.

One of the vampires swept out a powerful arm and grabbed a Roman emperor, jerking him to the center of the room. When the man attempted to fight back, the Dracule twisted his fist into the throat of his victim's shirt and cloak and yanked tightly, lifting him off the floor as the man struggled to kick free.

Damn. This was going to get bloody messy.

And where the hell was Corvindale? Voss couldn't handle five of Moldavi's men plus their footmen, *and* protect the two Woodmore sisters…*and* the earl's so-called sister, who must be around somewhere. Mira-bella would also be a convenient and lucrative prize for Cezar Moldavi.

Damnation.

The vampire slammed his prisoner to the floor and shoved a heeled boot over the man's windpipe, pinning him on the smooth wooden surface as he choked and gasped. No one moved. No one made a sound.

Then Angelica shifted behind him, just a little shud-dering breath. Voss slammed a hand back, whirling to face her. "Hush," he breathed into her ear. "Be still."

"That's him," she whispered, and Voss saw two Dracule shift toward their hiding place, listening.

He put his face close to hers and lifted a finger, press-ing it sharply against his lips in a fierce command of *Silence!* By Luce, those bastards could hear the slight-est sound. Another benefit, or affliction, vested upon Dracule.

"Miss Woodmore." The strained silence was broken by a low, commanding voice. "Show yourself." Angelica jolted behind Voss, and he was vaguely aware that she'd clutched his arm tightly. He closed his fingers over her arm and shook his head once, briefly.

Be still.

It wasn't Moldavi himself who'd given the order—no, he would be safely back in Paris, licking Bonaparte's arse-crack. But Voss recognized the sibilant tone, and as the speaker moved into view, his identity was confirmed.

Belial, one of Moldavi's makes.

A "made" vampire was a mortal chosen, not directly by Lucifer to fulfill Vlad Tepes' familial bargain, but by a Dracule himself. The Dracule fed, draining the mortal of his blood. Then the Dracule turned the man into a vampire minion himself by allowing the mortal to drink from his blood, thus becoming the new vampire's sire, or master. These "made" or "sired" vampires weren't as strong and powerful as the ones chosen by the devil and personally invited into the covenant of the Draculia. It was a sort of hierarchy—the further removed the "made" vampire was from the original sire, the less powerful he or she was for the simple reason that each made vampire inherited the Asthenia of his or her sire, as well as acquiring their own personal one. And so on down the line.

In this case, Cezar Moldavi had made Belial, and Belial was only one of many who answered to Moldavi in payment for immortality and power. And any vampires that Belial sired would be even less powerful than he, and they ultimately answered to him—or, in his absence or death, to Belial's sire, Moldavi.

Voss had encountered Belial in the past, and the only reason one of them wasn't dead was that the sun had come up on them during a hand-to-hand battle, and they'd had to separate in order to take cover.

"Show yourself, Miss Woodmore. Or..." Belial's voice trailed off as he nodded to one of his companions.

The man, another make who had silver-blond hair in a thick braid, moved with the lightning speed all Dracule enjoyed and snatched a gossamer-winged butterfly from the crowd. She screamed and struggled, but there was no help for her. The wig fell from her head, tumbling onto the man who lay still pinned in place by a boot heel.

Two men in the crowd lunged forward to intervene, but were caught instantly by two vampires and slammed to the floor as if they were gnats. A knife flashed and one of them screamed as he was pinned in place through his shoulder. Bloodheat infused the air. The other tried to roll away, and was kicked into the air, tumbling into the crowd. All during this time, the spectators had remained silent in shock.

"Miss Maia Woodmore," Belial lisped in his eerie voice. "Or Miss Angelica Woodmore. Either of you can put an end to this." He sounded polite and sincere even as he watched the silver-braided vampire put his hands on the butterfly.

Angelica tensed behind him and Voss edged backward to keep her in place, ignoring the flash of a pang in his shoulder. *No.* There was nothing she could do.

The butterfly's gown tore easily, exposing a flimsy shift and white skin, frail shoulders and the delicate tendons of her neck and shoulders. Voss's breathing began to deepen.

The Dracule held the girl's two hands behind her back, and tore at her costume again. The shift fell away, clearly exposing two breasts that jounced and jolted as she struggled. Her pitiful screams were the only sound in the room, and when the vampire grasped her hair and yanked her head back, exposing her throat, Voss felt Angelica gasp behind him.

The fangs flashed briefly before they sank into the terrified girl's shoulder. She choked, her body tightening like a bowstring and Voss felt his own blood rising. His fangs threatened, the scent of hot blood, frightened and desperate, beckoned.

Lucifer made them that way. To crave, to *need* not only the rich, warm life-giving liquid, but to revel in the fear and the fight when taking it. And the intertwined sensuality that came with it. The ache in Voss's shoulder lessened as his breathing quickened and he knew that his eyes would be glowing faintly by now.

He closed them, drew in a deep blood-scented breath and focused on the other smells in the air, the sounds, even the woman behind him. Especially the woman behind him, her body stiff and frozen against his back.

No, that didn't help. His blood pounded harder and he had to open his eyes again to push away the smell, the need. No, *no*. Not now. Not here. He steadied himself, breathed, focused.

When Angelica moved, he grabbed her before she could do something foolish. Yanking her close to him, he put his mouth to her ear and spoke short and low. "You can't stop them. Stay here." His heart thudded hard, his fingers curled around her warm arms. They were so delicate, slender. Smooth. He breathed her, he touched her, her hair curled in his face and smelled like summer.

Soon, my dear. *Soon.* He lifted his face away but didn't yet trust himself to look down at her.

Voss knew from the way she trembled and the dampness she pressed against his cheek that she wouldn't listen to his warning for long. He had to do something before she did, or his chance would be all over.

Where the hell was Corvindale? And Maia Woodmore? He knew she was here, too. She was headstrong enough to answer Belial's summons. Why hadn't she stepped forward?

Voss pulled Angelica close to him and looked down into her face, hoping his eyes wouldn't give him away. "Stay here. Don't move. Don't make a sound. No matter what, until I come back for you."

He waited until she nodded, her face streaked with tears and her eyes wide and shocked. She opened her mouth to speak, but he pressed his hand to her warm lips and shook his head sharply. *No.*

Then he slipped to the side, away from the corner, along the wall behind the fountain that had gone silent. When he'd gotten as far as he could from Angelica without being seen, he stepped out into the room.

"What a damned mess," he said as all eyes turned to him. Steadfastly fighting the alluring smell of blood and fear, he curled his lip in disdain. "By Luce, Belial, can you not teach your dogs some manners?"

Belial turned, his eyes bright and orange, his fangs showing in a flash as he smiled unpleasantly. "Ah, Voss. I cannot imagine what you have found yourself doing here."

As always, that low hiss of a voice made him want to twitch. The man sounded as if he had a too-tight neck-cloth on.

"Looking for the Woodmores are you?" Voss said, strolling unconcernedly toward the cluster of Dracule and their victims. The girl was silent now, not yet dead, but wheezing damply as she hung from the vampire's grip over her shoulder.

The thought of Angelica hiding in the corner enabled him to breathe without acknowledging the bloodscent filling the air. But the other members of the Draculia weren't as in control. As Voss stepped forward, one of them lurched down to the man pinned by the knife to the floor. His fangs flashed then sunk into the man's arm as the victim strained and screamed. Voss was certain he heard a sound behind him, and prayed—so to speak—that Angelica would stay put.

Still feigning ease and indifference, he *tsked* and looked at Belial. "Such animals. Is that how you and that dog Bonaparte train them? No manners."

Belial crossed his arms. "Why are you here?"

"Looking for Woodmore's sisters, just as you are." Voss gave a little shrug. "They're not here. And you're disturbing my evening."

"Disturbing your evening?"

Voss didn't look at the vampire feeding in front of him, blocked the sounds of suction and desperate gulping and choking gasps. He focused on Belial and nothing else. "I do love masquerade balls. They allow much easier access. But I prefer a bit more subtlety when arranging my…er…liaisons." He made an offhand gesture to the scene in front of him, making sure to keep his voice pitched so low that only Belial and his companions could hear him. "Much more enjoyable and less of a mess. My valet hates it when I come home with stains."

"I should believe you that the Woodmore bitches aren't here?"

"You don't have to, of course. You can stay and waste your time, although I suppose you might enjoy the entertainment. But drawing too much attention to your proclivities is not the best means to get what you want." Voss was careful to say "your" instead of "our." "I'm certain you haven't forgotten those harrowing weeks in Copenhagen. You nearly slept on a stake, if I recall correctly." He gave a bland smile.

Belial gave a narrow-eyed smile, his orange hair shining as he pursed his lips. Covered everywhere with a wash of dark freckles, he didn't appear threatening. Until the eyes burned and the fangs came out.

"Dimitri said the same," said the silver-haired vampire as he released the girl from his fangs. She slumped to the floor and one of the other Dracule members swooped down on top of her. "The Woodmores aren't here."

Voss hid his annoyance. If Dimitri was here, what the bloody hell was he doing? Where was he?

"There's no love lost between you and Dimitri," Belial murmured, nodding shrewdly. "No reason for you to lie for him."

None at all, although, Voss had to admit, if he had to ally himself with Cezar Moldavi or the Earl of Corvindale, he supposed he'd more readily suffer the latter's cold self-flagellation over Moldavi's indiscriminating violence. Everyone knew Moldavi was a child-bleeder. But either of them could fry in the sunlight for all he cared.

"I haven't seen Dimitri," Voss said, fanning the uncertainty in the vampire's eyes. "And the chits aren't here if they ever were. I was just about to leave when… well." He gestured to the scene in front of him, exuding disdain. "You interrupted my courting."

"Dimitri is a bit…preoccupied at the moment," Belial said, gesturing vaguely to the front foyer. "We've already spoken."

Despite his antipathy for the earl, Voss didn't like the sound of that. He forced himself to shrug easily. "You can continue here. If Dimitri is otherwise engaged, then I've got other things to do." He sniffed in disdain. "Don't draw too much attention to yourself, Belial. I don't want any damned trouble now that I'm back in London. Been too long in the uncivilized America."

He turned, his senses high, his movements casual, and began to walk away. Doubtful one of them would come after him—there was no reason to do so, and every reason not to. But he wasn't a fool. The back of his shoulders prickled and the only sound was the wheeze of someone's fearful breath and the intense gulping.

There was no more Voss could do to dissuade the vampires from continuing their attack and working their way through the crowd of people, feeding, terrorizing, ravaging. He'd reminded Belial that these sorts of overt events didn't go unnoticed. They often resulted in the spawning of well-equipped, wooden-stake-and-sword-toting mortals who called themselves Vampire Hunters—often to great effect. Chas Woodmore was one of them, and the most successful one in recent times. It was fortunate that he had associated himself with Dimitri and no longer went about arbitrarily staking any member of the Draculia he encountered. Dimitri had forced Woodmore to see that there were many Dracule who offered no threat to the mortal world.

Voss walked through the stunned crowd, noticing that they'd unmasked themselves and that they stepped back as he passed through. Just as he reached the main foyer—where three footmen stood with bayonets—he heard Belial behind him. Voss turned, ready, but the vampires were merely making their way out of the room in his wake. A strong testament to the control the leader had over his companions, and only one reason he was a formidable opponent and favorite of Cezar Moldavi.

"Since Dimitri is otherwise engaged, he won't be there when we pay Blackmont a visit," Belial commented as he passed by Voss. He glanced at the sweeping staircase, an amused smile twitching his thick lips.

Then, with a commanding jerk of his head, he thus gave the order for the footmen to fall in line behind him. "I'm certain the Woodmore bitches will be most happy to leave that black hole and find more comfortable accommodations."

Voss shrugged. *Dark soul of Luce, where the hell is Dimitri? Up there?* He didn't look at the stairs, but suspected he knew the answer.

"Best of luck," he told the vampire-make with great insincerity. Belial would never get into Blackmont Hall. Present or not, Dimitri would make certain of that.

And, regardless, Voss knew that at least Angelica was safe, here with him. He resisted the urge to glance back toward the ballroom. She'd wait. He'd told her to.

One thing he'd learned about Angelica Woodmore: she wasn't a fool.

Belial paused as he passed through the front door, the last to leave. "Do give Dimitri Cezar's best. I regret that I forgot to do so."

As soon as the door closed behind him, Voss took to the stairs. As he flew up, his feet barely touching the treads, he heard the soft rumble of stunned voices begin below and then swell to a loud, shocked pitch. Running feet, slamming doors, general chaos.

He'd only be a moment up here and he hoped Angelica would have the sense to do as he'd warned and stay put. Even as he went after Corvindale, he wondered why the hell he should take the time when he could be getting Angelica out of there.

Perhaps the earl was dead.

It took Voss mere seconds to find the correct room; not because he could somehow recognize Corvindale's presence but because he was quick. Down the hall, up another flight, and then...

"Dark soul of Lucifer," he breathed as he walked into the room.

Corvindale lay on his back on the rumpled carpet in the center of what was a cozy, well-lit parlor or den. He wasn't moving, but Voss could hear his breathing. Long, rough, labored. Bloodscent filled the room, Corvindale's shirt was torn from his shoulders, his coat gone, his gloves missing, one arm crossed over his muscular torso.

"Well," he said, walking over to stand above the man. "What have we here?"

He looked down and Corvindale's gaze, dark and yet clouded, bored into him. Loathing filled his eyes and Voss saw his only movement: a faint twitch of fingers as if he were imagining curling them around his neck.

Or a stake.

It was immediately evident to Voss that Corvindale was paralyzed, in pain and otherwise encumbered. Which meant that—

Ah, there it was.

Voss had almost missed it because the man's shirt was bunched up—but as he bent closer to admire the bastard in his immobilization, he saw it. The solution to the riddle he'd sought to solve a century ago in Vienna had just been handed to him. Draped over Dimitri's neck, against the swarthy skin, was a heavy strand of large rubies set in gold links.

"So it's rubies?" Voss said. "I knew it had to be a gemstone of some sort. But I had suspected emeralds or pearls all these years. Rubies. I do hope you checked the Woodmores' jewel boxes when they moved in."

The loathing burned stronger and hotter in Corvindale's eyes, and those fingers moved again on his chest, trying to inch toward the poison that must be burning into his skin, seeping his energy and life. All it would take was the thrust of a wooden pike into his chest.

Death.

Voss swooped down and yanked the jewelry away, tossing it across the room. With a whoosh of breath and a strangled cough, Dimitri leaped to his feet.

Instead of launching himself at Voss, as he had half expected, Dimitri turned toward the French doors leading to the balcony. White shirt in shreds, flapping from his shoulders, the earl went outside. Before Voss could react, he was back, carrying a struggling figure draped in heavy cloth and followed by an angel carrying her own wings.

Voss would have choked on a derisive laugh at the extent to which Corvindale had gone to keep Maia Woodmore from showing herself and getting captured by Belial if he hadn't noticed the man's back. The destroyed shirt clearly exposed the rear of Corvindale's left shoulder, and the sight of the rootlike pattern similar to that on Voss's skin made his own tighten and ache. For, unlike Voss's Mark, which occasionally throbbed and reminded him to whom he belonged, Corvindale's threads rose in heavy, pulsing welts, shiny with what had to be agonizing pain.

6

In Which the Earl of Corvindale
Runs the Blockade

Angelica did what Voss told her to do: she stayed hidden in the shadowy corner.

Later, she would ask herself why she'd done so. If she'd come forward when the red-haired leader called for her, could she have helped? Could she have saved the life of Felicity Chapman, the butterfly? Could she have prevented the death of Mr. Dudley Hoosman, the Roman emperor?

She'd almost done it. Almost left the confines of the vine-shrouded corner, nearly shouted her presence and brushed past Voss out into the open. Anything to stop the screams and the violence. Anything to put an end to the awful, evil tension.

But when she saw Mr. Hoosman, dragged out into the space by the glowing-eyed, ferocious men, everything slowed. The world stopped, centering into a pinhole of a vision: that of Mr. Hoosman, on the floor, his neck and chest shredded to ribbons, the brooch that had held his toga in place over the shoulder glistening with his blood, the red stain saturating the white cloth and the floor beneath it.

She'd seen that image before, once, after she'd picked up the man's handkerchief he'd dropped.

And only moments later, her mouth open in a silent gasp, she saw the image in reality.

Angelica might have fainted if the wall hadn't been behind her and if Voss hadn't been standing so nearby. She tried to tell him, tried to speak, but the words wouldn't come…and he rounded on her, fierce and dark, grasping her arms so tightly. *Don't move. There is nothing you can do. Stay here until I come for you.*

She listened. Angelica was no fool.

Whatever was happening out there on the dance floor, whatever Voss was doing or saying to the attackers, she didn't know. But the man with the glowing red eyes, the one whom she'd stabbed with her shears, was there, standing next to the leader. Who also had burning eyes.

And then she understood. He was what they called a *vampir.* Creatures who drank blood. Legends, tall tales. The stuff of Granny Grapes's ghost stories.

Or so she'd thought.

But now she knew…they were real. And they were all *vampirs,* all of those animalistic men, dragging people out into the middle of the room and feasting on them, tearing into them with claws and long, pointed teeth. Mauling their flesh and draining them of life. The smell of blood floated heavy in the air, and she remembered what Voss had said earlier, about smelling blood on her.

Was this what he meant?

It could have been her, out in the garden. *It could have been her.*

Chills and nausea took over Angelica in the same way

they had when she had learned her parents were dead. The same empty, awful feeling she'd had the first time she realized what her visions meant. As if life would never be good again. As if she'd never smile again.

The fountain was there, a handy receptacle for the contents of her stomach. She managed to hold it back until the *vampirs* left the room.

They left. They *left*. A miracle?

Somehow, somehow Voss had managed to talk them into leaving. How? How did he know them? What had he said?

Frozen, weak, her throat burning from the vomit and her head weightless, Angelica sagged against the wall, trying to sort through the thoughts and memories, visions and fear that pummeled her.

If she'd seen Mr. Hoosman earlier tonight in his Roman emperor costume, and had recognized he was dressed the way he was when he died in her vision… could she have prevented it? How?

Her head was pounding, her belly felt raw and tight. She tried to pull what she remembered of the vision back into her mind, but it was no use. She couldn't think about that any longer.

Because there was a much more important factor to consider. More terrifying than anything she'd seen, and try as she might to banish it, she couldn't.

What had those men wanted from her and Maia?

And… Oh, God, *where was Maia?*

That thought had Angelica stumbling from her sanctuary at last, tearing through the vines and bumping into the fountain on her way. She had to find her sister.

Blood was slick on the floor, and she vaguely registered reddish-brown footprints on the scuffed wood.

Someone had moved the bodies, and most of the party attendees had fled the room. Masks, canes, reticules and other accessories were scattered about, testament to the confusion of fear and terror.

Angelica didn't even know where to look for Maia, but she didn't get far before a hand reached out from nowhere and clamped on her arm.

She stifled a startled shriek and spun to see Voss. Relief battled with urgency and she tried to pull away. "I have to find Maia," she said. "I have to—"

"She's safe," he told her. "She's all right. Corvindale hid her."

"She's safe?" Angelica said. "I want to—"

"She's safe," he said again, turning her around firmly. "Come. We have to leave, now, before they come back."

Angelica didn't argue. She didn't have the strength, and aside of that, she wanted nothing more than to leave this horrible place, the scene of a terrifying evening. She wanted to be home, safe, and to see for herself that Maia was safe. And being in Voss's company on the way there was even better.

"This way," he said when she would have started toward the main entrance. "The carriage is here." His arm was strong and solid, sliding around her waist in gentle support as he hurried her away from the ballroom and out through the deserted kitchens to a servants' entrance.

It wasn't until they were outside and had walked beyond the drive leading to Sterlinghouse that she realized that the carriage to which he'd led her was not the one she'd arrived in with Maia and the others. Angelica stopped and looked at Voss. "What's this?"

He nodded at her question, stepping back slightly at the vehicle. "It's mine. They won't recognize it and won't know that you're inside." He didn't need to say who "they" were. She knew.

He stood next to the open door, gesturing for his footman to climb into the driver's seat. The interior of the carriage was empty.

She hesitated a moment. Did she trust him?

"Miss Woodmore," he said, urgency in his voice. "Please. The pretense will only be effective if you aren't seen climbing in. Or standing here with me."

It was one thing to waltz with the man, and another to speak privately in the dark corner of an occupied room… but this was beyond the pale. Maia would be furious. Angelica could be ruined if anyone found out.

Although, after the terrifying, chaotic events of tonight…would anyone even know or care? Surely more than one young woman had left the party in horror, seeking safety, without a thought to her reputation.

Angelica was too numb to care. Too exhausted, and still fighting back those images of blood and screams and terror. *It could have been her.*

They'd wanted *her.*

Voss had protected her.

He had saved others, too.

Angelica gathered up her skirts and climbed in, her heart pounding and her palms damp, her knees still weak. She settled on the cushioned seat, unsure whether she ought to tuck herself in the corner so as to put as much distance between herself and Voss as possible in case he sat next to her…or to take up a lot of space on the seat so that he would be compelled to sit across the way.

Yet, if he sat next to her, he'd be large and warm, solid and comforting. He might even put his arm around her.

Or kiss her again.

Angelica swallowed hard, so confused, so unable to control or even organize the storm of thoughts and memories from tonight. Her teeth threatened to chatter and she couldn't get warm, despite the fact that it was a mild summer's eve.

Voss spoke to the driver, then climbed in with the flourish of his cloak and settled on the seat across from her.

And then the door closed and they were alone in the shadow-swathed vehicle.

Even in the faulty light, Voss could see how pale she was. Her lips were bloodless and her eyes deep in shadow, wide and very nearly empty of emotion. She huddled in the corner, a quiet and colorless version of the intriguing woman he'd danced with, bantered with, kissed.

Nevertheless, he wanted her. So much that he could barely draw a breath without being fully immersed in her presence. His veins leaped and pounded as he watched the play of passing illumination on her face, the light slipping over her cheeks, her lips, the hollow of her throat.

It was the close confines of the carriage. The silence, the privacy, the realization that they were alone and he could have her. Just as he'd had any number of women, willing, unwilling, coaxed or convinced, over the decades.

He could slide across and sit next to her, murmur in her ear and tempt her to him. It would be over before she knew it, his incisors buried in her neck, her blood flowing onto his tongue, hands on her skin, their bodies straining and twining. Voss swallowed, considering.

And if his hot-eyed thrall didn't loosen her restraints

and bring her willingly into his arms, so be it…she'd find pleasure. Eventually.

It would be effortless. He could pull her to him, yank her across the space between them, gather her into his arms, find what he wanted.

Yet, he didn't move. His Mark twinged as if to ask why he held himself back, but Voss ignored it. Instead he pulled off his cloak and leaned forward quickly, draping it over Angelica, covering her half-bared shoulders. Then he settled back in his seat to plan his next move.

Angelica murmured her thanks and drew the cloak, which must be warm from his body, closer beneath her chin. Her eyes were so dark in her pale, oval face.

And as he looked over at her, captured by the curve of her cheek and the dark, exotic eyes fastened on him, something shifted inside him. Deep within, like a little mechanism falling into place.

He didn't want to hurt this woman.

"Who were they?" she asked. She trained her gaze on him, still wide and shocked, but with some emotion therein. "What do they want from me and Maia?"

The second question was infinitely easier to answer than her first, and he saw no reason to lie. "They want to use you to get to your brother. As collateral or a ransom."

"Chas? Why? For what?"

"He's taken something that belongs to a man named Cezar Moldavi—there's long been bad blood between his family and that of Corvindale and his associates."

That was the simplest way to explain the two factions, or cartels, which split the Draculia: those who supported Cezar Moldavi and his thirst for power over the mortal world, and those who did not. Voss tended not to ally himself openly with either, but that was because he preferred to remain neutral in the ongoing struggle. It was much less messy—and infinitely less dangerous—to remain above the fray. He wasn't about to get caught in the crossfire, so to speak.

"Moldavi wants the…item your brother took returned to him. Those were Moldavi's men tonight."

"Men? Those weren't men," she said, her voice choked, her eyes flashing suddenly with rage. "They were…" She couldn't seem to find the words, and her voice trailed off. "*Vampirs.* They were *vampirs,* weren't they?"

He could barely hear the low syllables over the rumble of wheels along the cobbled street, but he saw the way her lips moved. He was surprised she was familiar enough with the Hungarian word to apply it to a man, rather than a rotting corpse. But, of course, being Chas Woodmore's sister, she would probably know more than most other young women.

"What do you know about vampires?" he asked, pronouncing it in English. He asked partly from curiosity and partly to take control of the conversation's direction.

Voss would be surprised if Chas had actually divulged to his sisters any details of his relationship with Corvindale and the Draculia. Woodmore was discreet, and well aware of the consequences of betraying those with whom he associated. He'd become a valuable asset to Corvindale in particular, but even Chas Woodmore was expendable if he overstepped his bounds.

And now that he'd been foolish enough to elope with Cezar Moldavi's sister… Voss shook his head. Woodmore had been prudent to arrange for his sisters' safety and guardianship. Too damn bad for Corvindale that the earl didn't realize it would likely be a permanent arrangement. And that Voss had relieved him of the burden of one of his charges—at least temporarily.

He couldn't help but smile at the thought of Corvindale's reaction when he learned that Voss had Angelica Woodmore. The smile was more than a bit complacent. Perhaps then the man's cold facade might crack.

Voss hadn't known Dimitri before entering into his agreement with Lucifer. In fact, none of them knew each other before being turned immortal, for each Dracule came from a different geographic place, and in many cases, even different generations.

They became acquainted by accident, or perhaps by Lucifer's influence—or likely a little of both—but since they tended to congregate and find pleasure, sustenance and entertainment in the darkest, most dangerous and expensive pleasure houses or clubs, it wasn't surprising that they should encounter others of the Draculia in the same places in the largest, most exciting cities of Europe: Paris, Rome, Prague, Barcelona and, of course, London. Their world, after all, was a relatively small one.

Angelica had wrapped the cloak even closer around her throat, and he could see the shapes of her knuckles where they curled into the silk-lined wool. "What did you say to them? How did you get them to leave? Do you *know* them?"

So much for diverting the conversation.

"I've had…dealings with them," Voss replied. Strictly speaking, that was true. He wasn't sure why he hesitated telling her more. This conversation was pointless. He should be showing her his fangs and his glowing eyes, and getting beneath that cloak he'd so foolishly given her to hide under.

But, again, he didn't. The fear lingered in her eyes,

and he knew it would come back in full force if she realized he was of the very same cartel of people who'd just mauled two of her peers.

He didn't want to see terror in her eyes. He wanted the desire, the softness he'd seen earlier...when their gazes had met across the ballroom.

"And my brother? He associates with *vampirs?*"

Voss nodded. Luce's soul, why was he even talking to her? Waste of time. "Cezar Moldavi is a very dangerous...man," he told her. "Not only does he want to use you to destroy your brother, but it's possible he's also found out about your...ability. It's not as if you've kept it a secret. You could be a very valuable asset to him. You could give him information that he'd find useful in dealing with his adversaries."

Her eyes widened into circles, and now he could see the whites, gleaming in a flash of streetlamp.

"That's why," Voss said, leaning toward her, breathing in her essence, curling his fingers into his thigh so that he didn't reach for her, "I'm taking you somewhere safe."

She sat upright in her corner, surprising him with a flash of spirit. Anger. "What do you mean? I presumed you were escorting me home—back to Corvindale's residence."

"It's not safe there," he told her. "And it's not safe for both you and Maia to be together. Corvindale and I agreed that you should be separated to make it more difficult for them to find you."

"Maia?"

"The earl will make certain she and your other sister are well protected. And I," he said, settling back against the squabs in direct opposition to where he really wanted to be, "will take care of you. Now," he added, the words coming out before he could comprehend them, "perhaps you should rest a bit. Close your eyes. Nothing will happen to you when you're with me, Angelica."

Either she made a very unladylike sound in response, or he was hearing things. Voss's attention flashed to her eyes and he decided it was more than possible that she *had,* just then, made a frustrated or disbelieving sort of noise. And what on earth did she mean by it anyway?

How could she know what he was thinking?

But by now, she'd hooded her expression and the glimmer of naughtiness had gone. She closed her eyes, even.

His lips twitched. Not quite the proper young miss after all, was Angelica Woodmore. But of course, he'd already had an indication of that. After all, proper young misses didn't barrel up to men they don't know and announce that they'd been in her dream. And were going to die.

That roundabout thought brought him back to the realization that Brickbank was, despite the impossibility, dead. And the very thought had been squirreling around in the back of his mind for two days, digging and clawing and refusing to let go.

In the last hundred twenty years, Voss hadn't given a lot of thought to what happened after death. In fact, he hadn't thought about it at all. Why should he? That was the deal with Lucifer. Power, strength and immortality—ergo, complete freedom with no consequences for his days on earth and the actions thereof. What more could a man want?

But if an unexpected demise could happen to Brickbank, it could conceivably happen to Voss. Not nearly as easily, of course, so perhaps he oughtn't expend any more energy over it, but...

The image of Dimitri, splayed on the floor, held immobile by a necklet of rubies, settled firmly in Voss's mind. A chill gripped him around the back of the neck.

Had Belial and his cohorts wanted, Dimitri would be dead even now.

The fact that they obviously hadn't wanted it wasn't the reason the image bothered Voss. It was the realization that if it could have happened to a man whom Voss, much as he was loathe to admit it, deemed invincible— it could also happen to Voss.

Voss could die.

He forced himself from those dark, unpleasant thoughts. There were much other more fascinating things to contemplate.

Like the lovely, luscious bit of flesh sitting so innocently across from him.

Her head had tipped to the side and her eyes appeared to be closed, but he wouldn't wager his damaged soul on whether she was actually sleeping or not.

No, Voss wasn't that foolish.

Ahh. Heat, thick and liquid. A world of red pleasure, blazing sensuality, a whirlwind of sweet, floral scent. Lush comfort, smooth silk. And an insistent need.

It pulled, urged.

Voss had no reason to resist. He needed this like a drowning man needed air. He eased into the familiar lull, slid away from the reality that edged, dark and evil, at his consciousness. The prickling subsided as he allowed himself into the pleasure. Slipped in.

She had dark hair, long and thick, and dark eyes...

but her skin wasn't right. It wasn't as smooth, as sweet and rosy and spicy. Her scent cloyed and smothered and although she knew just what to do with her hands…oh, *indeed*…and her mouth….

Voss licked her neck, tasted old perfumed oil, and then his incisors slid long, sweetly, into her flesh. She gasped and tautened against him as the rush of tangy, thick ambrosia filled his mouth. He closed his eyes, drank, touched, battled, slid smooth against her…battled.

The back of his shoulder throbbed angrily, fighting with the passion and release that he must have. He closed his mind to it, fought it away, gulped and shifted and thought of Angelica.

Of his hands on her, his mouth and their skin…to skin. The long, sleek slide and the warmth. The rise, the miraculous light, then…her face, wide-eyed and horrified, burst into the image.

No!

Was it her voice or his own?

A streak of pain arced down his shoulder and red blazed behind his eyes, matching the agony.

Rigid with surprise as much as discomfort, Voss opened his eyes. He saw the woman, the crimson and golden room, the tall, pale candles flickering and casting delicate shadows. Blood trailed sleek against her white skin, still pooled hot in his mouth, the essence on his tongue.

Voss caught his breath, working through the sudden onslaught of pain to steady his breathing. To bring himself back here, where he could find release from what pounded through his veins.

She looked up at him, lust and laziness in her eyes as she reached for his shoulders, wanting to draw him back down. Her eyes weren't right. They weren't catlike, exotic enough. Her mouth…her face…*no.*

He couldn't keep from a quick glance above, knowing that Angelica was there. Two floors higher, safely ensconced here at Rubey's, where no one would think to look for them. She was so very near, but the ceiling hung low and heavy and impenetrable.

He could send for her. Simple. Get it over with.

The pain had lessened slightly. He could breathe. Think. Why did she haunt him so?

"Voss," the girl murmured. Her hand slid lower between them, between their hot, slick bodies. Her eyes were glazed, desperate. She licked her lips, shifted against him, closed her fingers more insistently.

He could do that to Angelica. He could make her cry and moan and want him like he wanted her. Like they all wanted him.

She could help him, and he…he could help her. And have her.

Show her the world of desire and passion.

She was two floors above. Unprotected. Virginal and waiting.

A rush of desire flooded him and Voss's breathing deepened. He could still smell her on his fingers from when they'd buried into her hair during their kiss. He thought of how she would smell, close, naked and writhing against him. Her breast heavy in his hand, her hair clinging to the damp of her skin.

Her eyes, heavy with desire after their kiss, rose in his mind. They beckoned, and then suddenly widened with horror and shock.

Fear.

He'd pulled back by now, enough that the sticky heat

of body against body had lessened. Voss heard his own breathing in a room that had become nearly silent. It rasped unsteadily and he hated the weakness it portended.

The throb at the back of his shoulder pounded harder. Insistent. *Go...go...go.*

Take.

Dull pain turned burning and sharp and reminded him that he had no reason for such deprivation. No reason to resist, to deny himself.

Nothing to fear.

Voss turned back to the woman. Easy, familiar relief.

Not Angelica.

The blaze shocked him and Voss gasped. *Luce's dark soul.* The devil wanted him to do it. To take her.

Angelica.

Not now, he told himself. And his Mark. *Not yet. After I get what I need. After she does what I need.*

Then he would take.

Ignoring the pain, driving it away, he lunged for the softness of the woman, buried himself, his senses, his mind, in the moment as he had done so many times before.

Later, sometime much later, he woke, naked, amid twisted sheets stained with blood. He remembered, vaguely, the dark-haired woman. And the blonde after her and the other brunette. The desperate need, the thirst he'd tried to quench. Over and over.

Then...dark dreams he'd tried to avoid, the face of Brickbank. His impaled body. Even the wisp of his soul, spiraling away in the darkness. Horrifying.

Of Angelica, white and sleek. Dark-eyed, tempting, begging.

And Lucifer.

In his dreams?

Voss sat up, his head pounding as if he'd drank a full bottle of blood whiskey.

Bloody damned hell.

Lucifer had only visited him in his dreams once before. The night he'd come to offer his unholy bargain, the temptation of a lifetime.

Slender and dark of hair, bright blue of eyes, pointed of chin and jaw and angular of body, Lucifer wasn't unpleasant to look at. But nor was looking upon him easy or comfortable. There was too much darkness behind those shocking blue eyes.

Sunlight seeped from behind the heavy shutters and curtains in his room and Voss stared at the shape it cast. The last time he'd touched sunlight had been the morning after Lucifer's nocturnal visit.

He hadn't realized what it would do to him. He hadn't realized the dream, the covenant, had been real.

He hadn't been touched by a sunbeam since.

A cold chill settled over him. Why had Luce appeared in his dream? To remind him of the unholy bargain they'd made?

He could remember nothing but his presence, his spectral face. Smiling that easy, smug smile that said he knew a man's every desire. And that he could fulfill it in every way.

Voss's legs felt weak and when he moved to haul himself out of bed, the skin and muscle beneath his right shoulder protested with pain. As he turned, he saw the Mark in a mirror and paused…trapped by the sight.

Not like Dimitri's, whose Mark was black and so

thick and raised it seemed to visibly throb. But Voss's was certainly more prominent than he'd ever seen it.

The ache was bearable, but insistent and penetrating. He moved his arm gingerly, then reached behind to touch the marks. Normally he felt no difference between the black rootlike insignia and his flesh, but now there was a slight swelling and a bit of warmth there.

Voss turned away from the reflection and rang for a bath. He wouldn't go to Angelica sweaty and dirty from his night of blind pleasure.

But nor did he feel remorse for taking what he needed and craved. It was his right, his compulsion. His compensation from Lucifer: never-ending, unrepentant self-indulgence.

He wouldn't hurt her; he wasn't like Cezar Moldavi who caused pain simply for the sake of it, as a revenge for all of the pain inflicted on him during his mortal years.

No, he wouldn't hurt Angelica. But he would have her.

And he wouldn't wait much longer.

Dimitri was tired and annoyed. Not particularly in that order. Definitely not in that order.

In fact, annoyed wasn't a strong enough word for how he was feeling. Livid. That was it.

He glared down at the figure standing between him and his only chance at a modicum of relief. No.

He felt murderous.

"What is it, Miss Woodmore?" he asked. It was clear that the eldest of his new charges wasn't going to allow him to pass to his study unless she spoke to him. And, from the looks of her stubborn expression, at great length.

She had obviously found the time to change from last night's appalling Hatshepsut costume, and, presumably, to rest a bit. At least, that was what her maid had reported, via Dimitri's valet. Once assured that Angelica was not only safe, but would be returning to Blackmont Hall later that morning, Miss Woodmore had felt able to take a bit of repose. Perhaps even a bath, if the spicy floral scent emanating from her hair was any indication.

But Dimitri had spent the last hours of the night and well into the day (for it was now several hours past noon) attending to everything from Belial and his footpads—and their vain attempt to breach Blackmont Hall—to ensuring that the real story of what happened at the masquerade ball was obscured and stifled. A few hints dropped about a bit of playacting at the masquerade gone awry, a few twists of facts into something believable along with the altering of a number of stubborn memories, and several visits to men's clubs to blank out more memories—and all was taken care of.

And now here stood Miss Woodmore, fresh-faced and accusing.

"It's nearly four o'clock, Corvindale. I would like you to tell me precisely where Angelica is," she told him. "And when she is going to arrive here. But most of all, I require assurance that she is safe."

How could this slip of a woman who smelled like spicy flowers manage to fill the entire corridor? He hadn't a prayer of brushing past and ignoring her insulting insinuations.

No, Miss Woodmore would not be ignored.

"Your sister will arrive here at Blackmont Hall when I am convinced it is safe for her to do so," he told Miss

Woodmore. And when he located the chit and her abductor.

He steeled himself against the rush of anger. He had a variety of reasons for disliking and mistrusting Voss. But now he had reason to kill the man.

Lucifer be damned.

The irony of that thought was not lost on him, but Dimitri had no inclination toward amusement at the moment. He had too many distractions to which he must attend, not to mention that he expected Giordan Cale to arrive at any moment.

"Is that all?" he asked, managing to keep the hope from his voice.

She lifted her pointed little chin and gave him a definite glare. "No, it is not. In fact, I wished to speak with you in regard to your conduct last evening." He realized with a start that she was taller than he'd realized, her head nearly reaching to his chin.

"My conduct?" Dimitri was fully aware that the tone of his voice was such that a less insistent individual would turn tail and run. His head had begun to pound and, on top of that, he noticed a shaft of sunlight pouring into the corridor beyond. Someone had uncovered the windows, blast it.

"Not only was it abhorrent and crude, but you didn't even take the moment to explain or apologize before shoving Mirabella and myself into a carriage and sending us off."

"Indeed."

"There was simply no reason for you to put your hands on me—" her voice dipped a bit as if she were infuriated or overcome "—and toss me out onto the balcony like some sort of—"

Dimitri matched her glare with his own. "In fact, I had sufficient reason for doing so. The least of which was the fact that you would not have obeyed me."

"If you had simply explained—"

"There was no time for explanations, even if I had believed you might have heeded them, Miss Woodmore. You would have ignored them just as you have everything else since arriving here, including keeping the windows in this house shrouded, my library in order, and my preference *not to be bothered*."

She didn't step back, despite the fact that his voice had risen to a near-bellow. "If you had simply explained that we were in danger and there was no time for discussion, I would have heeded your warning."

Dimitri didn't bother to hide his irritation and considered simply walking away, pushing past her and finding sanctuary. But before he could respond, she drew in a deep breath and continued, unfortunately along a vein in which he would have preferred to avoid.

"In addition to an apology, I believe it isn't asking overly much to request an explanation for what happened last evening. I understand that Angelica and I were in danger, but I would like to know why and from whom or what. And how it happened that you arrived in time to prevent whatever the outcome might have been…regardless of the clumsy manner in which you executed it."

Dimitri relaxed slightly. Then she hadn't realized he'd been there all along. He'd taken pains not to be noticed, of course, except for that one foolish indulgence on the dance floor…and after. "Clumsy manner?" he repeated, aggravation superseding his relief.

She made an exasperated sound and an elegant feminine gesture with her gloved hand. She had a very delicate wrist. "You pushed me out onto the balcony, *wrapped up in curtains.* Can you not give me the courtesy of telling me why?"

"Because there were some very bad men who want to take you away," Dimitri told her without moving his jaw. "That is why your blasted brother snared me into being your guardian. Because he knew there was no one else who could keep you safe."

"Please, my lord, you sound like a character in one of those Gothic novels by Mrs. Radcliffe, making all sorts of Byzantine comments and cryptic warnings. If you would cease these ambiguous statements and simply tell me what is happening—"

"What then? You would accept my explanations and my orders without question?"

For a moment he thought her lips quivered—either from humor or, Fate forbid it, from some other emotion. "Certainly not. But at least you wouldn't feel the necessity to wrap me up and throw me onto the balcony."

Would the chit never stop screeching about it?

Dimitri crossed his arms over his sagging, stained waistcoat and glared down at her. "The truth is, Miss Woodmore, your brother has gotten himself into serious danger with a society of ruthless men. By disappearing with the sister of one of them, he has not only put himself in a most injurious position, but also you and your sisters—for they would like nothing better than to use one or any of you to get to Chas."

"Then they are after us as hostages? Ransom?" Her dark blue eyes narrowed as if in thought. "But then that must mean Chas is still alive and hidden somewhere if they are trying to abduct us." Relief washed over her face and for a moment, Dimitri was struck by the beauty and intelligence in that stubborn countenance. "He must still be alive. And safe."

He bowed his head. "Your brother is very cunning and able, and you are likely correct. I'm confident he can take care of himself. But you and your sister must not leave this house or see anyone without my permission. You are completely safe whilst in my custody, but Cezar Moldavi is not only ruthless but also very intelligent. And your brother has betrayed him in a most egregious manner. He will not give up easily."

"Cezar Moldavi?" Her eyes widened.

Now it was Dimitri's turn to be surprised. "You recognize that name, then?" Woodmore must have been much more forthcoming with his sisters than he'd thought—and more than was prudent.

"Rather like yourself, Corvindale, I'm familiar with the name but I have never met the man." She fluttered her hands, this time in more agitation. "I mean to say, now that I've met you—"

Dimitri shifted impatiently. "Yes, yes, Miss Woodmore. Please refrain from stating the obvious. Now, I am expecting Mr. Cale any moment now. What other items must you drag forth and force me to ponder?"

"You still have not tendered an apology," she replied primly, and, he thought, with great bravery. "I have never been handled so—"

"Miss Woodmore," he interrupted. "Do you mean to say that should a man push you from the path of an oncoming carriage he should bow and scrape at your feet in apology for mussing your skirts? Or should he ask permission first, before doing so?"

"Well, I do believe—" She stopped herself this time

and pressed her full lips together. Then she took a deep breath and squared her shoulders. "I did not realize we were in some sort of danger. You made no effort to impress that fact upon me—a fact which you obviously well knew. Perhaps in the future, Lord Corvindale, you might be a bit more forthcoming. Particularly about things that apply to me and my sisters."

"Perhaps," he conceded. Simply to shut her up.

She had the temerity to step closer, followed by a stronger waft of spiced flowers. "There is one more thing, my lord. I require your assurances that my sister's reputation will be intact when she is returned here to your custody—or that you will take the appropriate steps to correct any problems thereof."

Dimitri pressed his lips together. If he ever saw Chas Woodmore alive again, he would kill him for visiting this mess upon him. He and Chas were associates—one could almost consider them friends, as odd as it might be for a Dracule to be friends with a vampire hunter. But this situation with the sisters went beyond the boundaries of friendship and strained the slender bit of honor that Dimitri had.

"You have my assurances that I will do my utmost to protect your sister's reputation, Miss Woodmore," he replied stiffly. "No one—other than perhaps yourself and Chas—is more concerned about it than I am. But you haven't any reason to worry. She is safe from Moldavi and in unblemished company."

Miss Woodmore held his gaze for a bit too long, but Dimitri managed to hide the fact that he was lying from behind his incisors.

Voss was going to be dead the moment Dimitri found

him and slammed a stake through his heart. Lucifer could bugger himself. And then maybe he'd be fortunate enough that the devil would be furious enough to kill Dimitri in retaliation.

That was a compelling possibility.

And then Angelica would have to be married off to someone who would keep his mouth shut, quickly and quietly—

At that moment, he was saved from any further interaction with this woman who seemed to be fearless in his presence and who seemed to have no qualms about making demands that any prudent man would be.

"My lord." Vigniers, his butler, appeared in the corridor. "Mr. Giordan Cale has arrived."

Cale, of course, was right on Vigniers's heels, his hat in hand, his strides confident and unrushed. But his face was haggard and weary and for a moment, Dimitri feared the worst news about Narcise Moldavi.

"Dimitri," Cale said by way of greeting. And then, "Miss Woodmore." He gave a quick bow as she, ever the proper miss, curtsied. Her chestnut hair gleamed with shots of gold and copper as she did so.

It occurred to Dimitri at that moment that she'd not curtsied to him at their first official meeting. He frowned. "If you'll excuse us," he said to the infuriating woman. Then he looked at Cale and gestured down the corridor. "My study."

Cale bowed again to the woman then brushed past her, seemingly without hesitation or even without stirring her skirts.

Dimitri could do nothing but follow him, and was absurdly pleased when Miss Woodmore took the hint and shifted out of the way, spicy essence and elegant wrists and all, as he strode past her into the sanctuary of his study.

At last.

WHEREIN OUR HEROINE'S HORIZONS
ARE GREATLY BROADENED

Angelica opened her eyes.

Sun shone through the window of an unfamiliar room, cascading onto the bed where she slept. The chamber was clearly that of a woman, with floral paper on the wall and little glass bottles on the dressing table. Lace-trimmed curtains hung at the open window and in front of what appeared to be a large dressing room.

It took only a glance over at the blue-lined cloak and the pile of her black Greek gown on a bepillowed chair for her to remember.

All the blood. All the violence.

Angelica sat up and the coverlet fell away, leaving her to see that she'd been dressed in a night-rail. Her hair fell around her shoulders, loose and heavy. She was cold, despite the warmth of late afternoon sun pouring into the chamber.

Voss. She looked around, as if he might be lurking in the corner—which of course he wasn't. And which would be outside of unseemly.

But his presence lingered—there, in the cloak he'd draped over her shoulders. In the clean comfort of the room and even, faintly, in the air.

Before she could decide what to do, a firm knock came at the door and it cracked open.

"Ah, you're awake." The woman came in before Angelica bade her to do so. Her clothing, her demeanor, even her opening the door immediately after the knock, indicated that she wasn't a servant.

"Good morning," Angelica said, examining the new arrival.

She was older, perhaps in her late thirties. Her frock, a daydress that showed enough bosom to qualify for an evening gown, was nevertheless made of good lawn and was at the height of fashion. Large, bright scarlet roses patterned the fabric and wide pink ribbon trimmed the sleeves and hem. Although she didn't wear gloves, her strawberry-blond hair was dressed in a proper chignon and a bit of curl flattered her striking face. One wouldn't consider her beautiful, but she had a pleasing, if not shrewd, countenance with high cheekbones and good skin.

"I'm Rubey," she told her, and then turned to make an abrupt gesture behind.

Another woman, younger and clearly a servant, came in carrying a tray with food and tea, and Angelica instantly realized she was hungry.

"Thank you," she said as the tray was deposited on the bed next to her. The servant left and the two women were alone.

"And I can see you've slept well," Rubey said as she poured tea. It was a clear statement rather than a question. "After a frightening night."

Angelica swallowed a delicious bite of orange scone and immediately wanted another. "Where am I? Lord Dewhurst brought me here."

Rubey nodded and settled into a chair in the corner. Perhaps to watch her eat? "Voss is still abed." Her eyes seemed to glint with humor. "He was in need of a bit of… rest…after the events of the night and into the morn. I believe he intends to speak with you shortly." Although her expression wasn't unkind, it and Rubey's demeanor gave Angelica the impression that she was missing some important information.

"You haven't told me where I am."

"You're safe. That's all you need to know for now."

"I need to get a message to my sister," Angelica said. "She'll be frantic by now. There's no clock in here. Do you know what time it is?"

"It's nearly four o'clock."

Angelica's eyes widened in surprise. She'd been vaguely aware of their arrival here, and that the sun was just beginning to rise, but she could hardly credit having slept so long. Usually, even after a late night of dancing and revelry, she woke before noon.

But last night had been different…in more ways than one.

Rubey continued, "And as for the message, I'm certain Voss has seen to that. But you'll have to ask him."

"Only one of many questions, I'm certain," came a deep voice.

Angelica hadn't noticed the door opening, but then she'd been rather involved with her tea and the plate of cheese and scones. The sight of his figure, well illuminated by the splash of light in her room, made her heartbeat kick and her belly flutter, chasing all thoughts of orange-glazed biscuits from her mind.

In surprising dishabille, he wore no coat over his shirt, trousers and waistcoat, and a neckcloth sagged casually around his neck. She couldn't remember ever seeing a man so handsome, so golden and striking and *delicious*. And whose lips were so full and soft and warm… Her cheeks flushed at the memory and she quickly lifted her teacup to drink. Perhaps to hide her face.

"How do you feel today, Miss Woodmore?" he asked in that same smooth voice, standing in the doorway. He glanced at Rubey, who rose from her seat. "Well rested, I trust?"

"Yes, and also well fed," she replied, gesturing to the remains of her scone. "I'm certain I have you to thank."

Voss inclined his head in polite acknowledgment and stepped just inside the door, leaving it ajar next to him. "In addition, I had already presumed your need to be in contact with the eldest Miss Woodmore and thus, I have sent word to Corvindale that you are with me, and to pledge your continued safety. So you need not worry that your sister is concerned for you."

Rubey had moved to the window. She left the curtains and windowpane open wide, but closed the shutters, leaving only a fraction of the sunshine sliding through the top half of the opening. The room was still well illuminated by the day, but the warmth was gone.

"Oh," Angelica said in dismay, her attention turning to the other woman. "Why did you do that?"

"It's safer," Voss replied, stepping farther into the chamber. "We must take no chances that Moldavi's men might glimpse you through the window."

A spike of fear jolted her. "Do you think they've followed us? Or know where you've taken me?"

"I suspect they haven't, for they didn't know you were with me when we left Sterlinghouse last evening. But I intend to take no chances with you and your safety, Miss Woodmore." His eyes settled on her as he smiled slowly. "Not at all."

Standing by the window, Rubey made a soft sound that could have been mistaken for a snort, but Angelica wasn't certain. The woman eyed Voss with a raised brow, and he merely turned his charming smile onto her. "Now, Rubey," he said. There was affection in his voice—something that Angelica hadn't noticed when he spoke to *her*—and also a bit of warning. "You give me too little credit."

"A lie that is, to be sure. I give you more credit than you deserve," she replied, folding her arms over her middle. For the first time, Angelica noticed a bit of Irish lilt in her voice. "And it lightens my coffers more than I care to admit."

"But, Rubey," he said, his voice still easy. "You know I'm good for it." His voice lowered and Angelica felt a little responsive shiver in her belly.

"That you are, which is why I keep you around. But a little slow on the settling up. After this—" she gestured abruptly at Angelica and moved toward Voss "—I expect your account to be settled *most* generously." Then, to Angelica's shock, she poked him in the chest with her finger, just below the loose neckcloth.

Voss didn't seem to care. "I am always generous," he told her in that low, nearly purring voice that made Angelica vacillate between warmth and annoyance. He was fairly ignoring her and quite clearly flirting with this woman.

She didn't like it at all.

Rubey gave a little huff of laughter that ended on a low note. "Indeed," she added in a more husky tone. "When you are finished here, I'll expect you to see to all of it."

She glanced briefly at Angelica to say, "I'll send clothing up for you shortly. And a maid." And then she left the chamber, closing the door in her wake.

For a moment, Angelica sat stunned and speechless. She was alone in a bedchamber, clothed in little more than a thin shift, *with a man.*

With Voss.

He turned to look at her, but before she could speak, he gave a little smile. "Ah, yes. Propriety." To her relief, he opened the door, leaving it more than halfway ajar.

"Thank you," she said, fumbling her hands over the top of the puckered coverlet. The thing that frightened her the most was that the idea of being alone in the bedchamber with Voss *didn't* frighten her, or concern her. In fact, the thought was more than a bit alluring.

Standing near the door's corner, against the wall, he nevertheless seemed to fill the room, his shoulders wide and solid against feminine wallpaper. Though he remained near the darker side of the room, his skin picked up a hint of the golden glow of sunlight. Thick hair, the color of her old ginger cat, streaked with all shades of bronze and honey caught by the light, had been combed back neatly and rose above his high forehead. Yet, its very color and the hint of untamed waves near his ears and throat suggested something less staid and proper lurking beneath.

The sensual little curl at one side of his mouth contributed to that lack of propriety…along with the fact that his neckcloth hung loosely knotted from the opening of his shirt. The shallow V of golden skin and the hollow of his throat she found fascinating, and more than a bit disturbing as her imagination ran to places it had never been.

"Angelica."

Her gaze flew to his and the expression she saw there made her insides plunge. *Oh.*

"If you keep looking at me like that, I'm going to close the door again," he said in a voice that tempted her to ask him to do so.

Heat rushed to her cheeks and Angelica caught her breath, aware of a sudden, very pleasant tightening in her insides. What if he did? What if he came to sit on the edge of the bed—no. That was outside of proper. She swallowed.

As if to put a distance between himself and that enticement, Voss stepped away from the opening and sat on an upholstered stool in front of a small dressing table. His long legs were bent up a bit and, sitting amid lace and glass, he appeared more out of his element than she'd ever seen him…. Yet, with him there was no real awkwardness. He wore no coat, but the crisp white sleeves of his shirt and the intricate pattern on his waistcoat detracted from the pink and yellow florals surrounding him.

Angelica decided she should be relieved that he'd taken a seat so far from her. "Where are we? And who is Rubey? Is she your…sister?"

Her cheeks warmed when he gave a short little laugh. "No, indeed, Rubey is not my sister."

Angelica drew herself up a bit and pulled the coverlet higher. "I suspected not," she added in what she thought of as her Maia-voice. "I was simply giving you the benefit of the doubt. She is a proprietress of some sort, I suppose. Is this her home?"

A suspicion had begun to form during Voss's exchange with Rubey, wherein Angelica realized she was missing some of the underlying meaning of their words. She didn't know much about the demimonde or the sorts of women who would become a man's mistress, but the way Rubey had looked at Voss and the ease of manner between them—along with the very low line of her bodice—made her wonder. She'd spoken of services and of settling accounts.... Angelica became more suspicious.

"Rubey owns the place," Voss told her. "One of several, in fact. She's agreed to let you stay here until I can make other arrangements."

"Is she your mistress?" Angelica asked. "Or is this a brothel?"

The slight widening of his eyes was the only indication of his surprise. "I didn't believe young, well-bred women knew of such things."

"Am I to presume that is a confirmation?" she asked, trying to decide why she felt so uncomfortable. Right in the pit of her belly.

"You needn't presume anything of the sort," Voss said. "Rubey is merely a woman with many skills and assets—not unlike yourself, Miss Woodmore."

She couldn't help but wonder just exactly what sort of skills and assets Rubey had.

And then she realized that, a moment earlier, he'd called her Angelica. Now it was back to Miss Woodmore.

Angelica frowned and all of her warm thoughts dissipated.

But Voss didn't seem to notice, for he continued. "In fact, I was hoping you might use one of your talents to assist me."

Her attention flew to him, but his expression was neutral. Perhaps even…apprehensive. For the first time, she noticed that despite his easy manner, his eyes held weariness. "What exactly do you mean?" Angelica asked, resisting the urge to ask if he hadn't slept well.

Voss shifted in his seat, his long legs ruffling the lacy tablecloth, causing the glass bottles to clink gently. "You foretold the death of my associate Lord Brickbank. And I understand that you have been able, in the past, to predict or foresee the death of others."

When she would have spoken, something like dismay and perhaps anger bubbling up inside her, he continued. His voice lowered and became…tentative. "I confess, it was more than a bit of a shock to me—that which happened with Brickbank. You'd warned us, you'd foretold it…and yet we couldn't prevent it."

His face seemed to sag in the uneven light. Emotion clouded his eyes, and the bit of annoyance she had with him ebbed. "Perhaps not," she said, but gently. "If you had stayed away from the bridges—"

He looked sharply at her. "But you clearly said which bridge. We went nowhere near it, and he still died in the manner you'd foretold."

Angelica eased back against her pillows, closing her eyes briefly. Yes, that very same realization had settled uncomfortably in her thoughts, as well. It made her fingers grow stiff and icy, despite the mild summer day, and her insides tighten.

There was no escaping fate.

And she was fated to bear its knowledge.

"How do you manage it, Angelica?" he asked suddenly, as if it burst from him. Earnestness and something much deeper blossomed in his gaze. "Seeing death at every turn?"

She sensed that he needed the answer; that it was a need for him as much as an understanding about her. "It's become part of my life," she said. "Since I was very young, I would touch something and sometimes the flash of a vision would rush through my mind. I didn't understand what it was at first."

"The first time you realized it was something more, you must have been quite distraught." His voice had gentled.

"I was perhaps five or six. One of the footmen had dropped a glove and I picked it up. The vision was very strong and it startled me. I had an image of him lying on the floor of the stable. He looked odd, but I couldn't have known it was because his neck and legs were broken. I returned the glove to him and two days later, he fell from the loft of the barn."

Voss's eyes glinted golden-green. "Were you the one to find him?"

Angelica shook her head. "No, I was spared that, at least. But I'd told Maia about the vision, and she had managed a peek into the stable when all of the activity was happening. She wouldn't let *me* look, but she did." Her lips moved in the hint of a smile. "Chas was at Eton or he would surely have taken charge himself."

Voss wondered if Chas had been tossed in the privy his first week at school, or if that sort of tradition had gone away with powdered wigs and knee breeches. Re-

gardless, having encountered Chas more than once, Voss
was inclined to suspect that he'd not been subjected to
such an indignity at that age. He might even have been
one of the ones doing the dunking of pretty but scrawny
underclassmen.

Or, more likely, he allowed reluctantly, the pulling of
them out of the muck.

Removing himself from such circuitous musings, he
asked, "What happened after you made the connection
between the vision and the groom's death?"

She understood what he meant. "Maia, and later,
Chas, knew about it, but I never told my parents. They
were still alive then."

He stilled, arrested in the midst of a movement on the
short stool. "Did you know they would die?"

Angelica focused on her fingers, playing with a loose
thread on the coverlet. "It was another year before it happened again. I was playing with my cousin's coat and
wrapped myself up in it while we were playing hide-and-
seek. In the dark corner under the piano, I was hidden
and had to remain quiet…and that was when my mind—
it was rather like it opened. I saw him in his bed. His
face was pale and his lips and eyelids blue. At the time,
he was nine or thereabouts, but in the image, it was clear
he was some years older."

"He died, then? A few years later?"

She nodded. "I didn't tell anyone about the vision that
time because…well, I didn't really know what it meant.
But later, my old Granny Grapes came to me. She knew
about it. She'd figured it out."

"Granny Grapes?" A smile flickered in his eyes.

Affection swarmed her. "She died five years ago, but
she was the one who inherited the Sight in our family

from her mother. She was part Gypsy." She'd been the one to help Angelica understand, learn to accept and control her gift. If it hadn't been for her wisdom and knowledge—

"How do you live with it? With knowing that everyone you meet will die?" His voice was filled with compassion, but also with need. He needed something…but she didn't understand what it was. "Don't you ever wonder what happens after?"

Angelica looked at him. Their eyes met, but not in the sort of heated, explosive way they'd done at the masquerade ball or even when he came into the chamber just now. Something tugged, soft and deep, inside as she connected her gaze with his. "Everyone dies, my lord."

His handsome face seemed bleak. "Why must they?"

"It's the natural way of things, the cycle of life. To everything there is a season, and a time." She dropped the little thread she'd been curling around her fingers. "If there is one thing I've learned from this gift I have, it's that one cannot fear death. It's rarely pleasant or expected or convenient. Most times it's tragic and painful. But we can't avoid it. And for some, it can even be a relief."

She nibbled on her lip, thinking about how long it had taken for her to become comfortable with her Sight. How many nights of worry and anguish she'd slogged through in darkness—both literal and figurative—before Granny Grapes had taken her under her wing and helped her to understand that death was merely a transition to another part of life.

Voss didn't say anything, and she was struck by what seemed to be deepening shadows beneath his eyes.

"I don't mean to sound nonchalant or uncaring," she

told him when the silence stretched moments too long. "I didn't always feel that way."

"Didn't you try to block it out? Did you not try to keep it away? Or did you revel in the knowledge?"

"Yes, and yes…and, at times, yes." She spread her hands. "I've become comfortable with it now. I've learned to control it, and I'm judicious in my use of the Sight. Careful with how and when I call on it."

Except…she hadn't controlled the image of Lord Brickbank falling to his death. That had been visited upon her in her dreams.

She'd never met the man, never touched any of his belongings.

While she'd had other dreams of death in the past, they'd been just dreams. She'd not seen or met the persons portrayed in them.

And that was what made this incident with Lord Brickbank particularly discomfiting…and frightening. Had those other dreams actually happened, without her realizing it? And why did she dream some deaths, but "see" others by touching a personal item? Angelica had looked away as the reminder of Brickbank came to her thoughts, but now she glanced over at Voss. Strangely silent and contemplative, he sat unmoving. For the first time, she saw him without a coy or charming demeanor. Without a light in his eyes or even the dangerous fury that had been there last night during the attacks.

"My lord," she began…but then her voice trailed off.

He shifted suddenly on the little stool, and then that smile was back…the sensual, smooth one that had sent little prickles down her spine. "Well, then," he said. "I cannot say that I've ever had such a moribund conversation with a woman in a bedchamber."

"I've never had *any* conversation with a man in a bed-chamber," she replied primly. Her heart had begun to beat harder, but despite his light comment, she noticed the glint was missing from his eyes.

Voss stood, suddenly looming over her, and she realized once again that she was dressed only in a night rail. And, she decided, this was not the time to ask if he had been the one to arrange for that event. She sincerely hoped he had not, her cheeks warming at the very idea.

"I should like to dress now," she said. Her throat was dry and her lips felt suddenly very full and warm.

Now his gaze lit with humor. "Indeed. Are you requesting maid service from me?"

"No, indeed!" she said, the flush bursting hotter over her face.

"Very well, then," he said, his voice oozing with exaggerated reluctance. "I shall send for someone."

"V—" she said as he started toward the door, then realized her mistake. "My lord, I mean—"

He turned, his hand still on the knob. "Call me Voss. I like the way you make it sound. Angelica."

She could hardly breathe when their eyes met, and for a moment, the only sound was that of low breathing and the distant thumps and bumps of others in the house. "Dewhurst," she said firmly.

He made an odd sort of movement, as if to step toward her and then halting himself at the last moment. Something like a wince crossed his face, and he turned sharply. "I'll send a maid," he said, and then left the room.

Angelica heard the steady, solid clump of his shoes as he strode down the corridor and then, it seemed, down a flight of stairs. Then it was lost amid the other household noises.

Her heart didn't stop pounding, nor the tingling in her belly cease until several moments later when the first servant arrived with buckets of steaming water for her bath.

Angelica closed her eyes and sank back into the tub, the water swishing over her shoulders. Whatever scented oil the maid had sprinkled into the bath was sweet and citrusy, and its residue sat atop the steaming water like circular rainbows.

"What is it called?" she asked without opening her eyes. "The scent you poured into the water?"

Ella, whose movements were neat and exceedingly efficient, had moved behind Angelica and was brushing out her hair. "It's named neroli," she said as Angelica sighed at the heavenly feel of the bristles over her scalp. "The mistress would give you a small bottle of it if y'like."

"That would be very kind," Angelica said and lifted her head as the young woman tucked a folded towel between her neck and the edge of the metal tub. "It's a lovely and unique scent."

"Comes all the way from It'ly," said Ella. "Or is it Ind-ya? Alack, I don't try to remember it all." She giggled and continued with the brushing.

Angelica had noted that a gown, chemise and under-necessaries were waiting for her on the dressing table and marveled to herself at what comfortable lodgings Rubey provided. If she felt a pang of unease in regards to what other *services* the red-haired woman might offer, Angelica pushed it away with relative ease.

Voss was trying to keep her safe, and so far he'd succeeded. She had made the decision to trust him, and so far he hadn't given her reason to question his motives.

But then, Maia's disapproving expression, complete with wagging finger, popped into Angelica's mind and ruined the relaxation of the bath.

Pickle bumps and fern-dots and blast it all! Her eyes opened and she realized that her mouth had twisted into a frown, all on its own.

She could just hear Maia, like an annoying shriek of conscience: "But you don't know the man, Ange. And you've gone *off* with him without a hesitation! What are you *thinking?*"

What was she thinking, indeed.

She was thinking about his beautiful eyes and the way they made her feel when he looked at her. And the lush kiss he'd coaxed from her, making her knees weak and her body rush with heat.

And she was thinking about the deeply hidden, almost lost expression in his eyes when they'd been speaking only a few moments ago. He needed something from her.

Perhaps he was afraid of dying. Or someone he loved was dying, or had died. Something.

Ella had set aside the brush and had just finished pinning Angelica's hair into a loose knot at the base of her neck. Now she watched as Ella bustled about the chamber, preparing towels that had been warming in a little metal trunk near the fire. Such a luxury she'd never even conceived.

"The mistress says what a terrible night y'had," Ella said, closing the top on the trunk with a quiet thud. "You were s'tired when you came in, I thought I was dressin' a babe for bed. I hope you slept well."

"I did," Angelica said. *Well, there is the answer to that question. Too bad Maia isn't here for the confirmation that her sister's virtue is still, indeed, intact.*

Ella came forward, a renewed wave of neroli wafting from the warm towel, and Angelica rose from the tub. As she stood, she noticed two little marks low on the maid's neck.

They looked like small red dots. Or puncture wounds.

The skin around them was smooth and white, and the circles were neat and each was perhaps the diameter of a tiny pea. As Ella shifted, draping the warm, scented towel around her, two more marks were exposed on the back side of her upper shoulder.

A chill replaced the steamy comfort from Angelica's bath, and she couldn't tear her eyes from the marks on Ella's neck. She was suddenly, uncomfortably certain she knew from where those four wounds had come. If she hadn't been witness to the carnage from the *vampirs* last night, Angelica might have thought little of it. But after seeing it for herself, she knew there was no mistaking bite marks.

The maid tucked the towel around Angelica and moved away, seemingly unaware of the horror that must be shining in her charge's face.

Had she been attacked also? And Voss rescued her as well, bringing her to safety at Rubey's? Try as she might, Angelica could see no other marks or scars on Ella's arms or throat, and she was just about to be bold and rude and ask the maid about the marks when a loud shout erupted from below.

Ella turned, holding a chemise, and they both paused to listen. Loud thumps and thuds reverberated, followed by a scream and more alarmed shouting.

"What in heaven?" Angelica said, but she and Ella had both sprung into action. "Someone is in trouble."

"Stay here," Ella said, thrusting the chemise at her and then dashing to the door to peek out.

The sounds of what was clearly a struggle had become more violent, causing the little glass bottles on the dressing table to clink together as the walls and floor shook. More shouts and another scream, followed by crashes and a loud thud.

As Ella peeked out the door, Angelica struggled to tug the chemise over her damp body. Her fingers shook as she tied the lace at the neckline, and then the door slammed shut as the maid turned toward her with wide eyes. "They're coming. I think we should hide."

Angelica could hear the pounding of footsteps on the stairs and looked around for a weapon. The stool Voss had sat on, the brush and combs on the table, the chamber pot…the fireplace poker. She seized it and swung around, her hair sagging at the back of her neck and the chemise still sticking to her belly and the curve of her rear.

Ella, who had lost every bit of her previous efficiency in favor of stark terror, began to shove at the bed. Angelica recognized her intent and rushed to help her push it against the door. In her haste, she bumped against the flimsy dressing table, sending it and its contents crashing to the floor and against the fireplace brick.

"Blast," she muttered, avoiding the broken glass and heaving at the bed, poker in hand. Now she'd done nothing but draw attention to their presence.

The ominous thuds of footsteps reached the top of the stairs by the time the bed was in place against the heavy door. Angelica whirled toward the shuttered window to see if it offered some possibility of escape. She felt the bite of glass under her heel and then the ball of her foot, but the sounds of violence in the hall beyond their door had other worries on her mind.

"Can we get out here?" she asked as she reached the window.

Ella had frozen in place. "It's them," she whispered, her eyes so wide Angelica was certain they'd pop from her skull. "They're here! In the day!" Then she gasped and pointed down. "You're bleeding!"

Angelica's bloodied foot slipped on the stretch of wooden floor as she worked to unhinge the shutter. "That's the least of our worries," she snapped. "Can you help me?"

Where was Voss? Was he in the midst of the fight? Or was he not even here?

"Oh, lordy, lordy," Ella said, grabbing the towel and thrusting it at Angelica. "Wipe it up! Quick, before they—"

She stopped with a little scream as something slammed into the door. The wooden slats bowed and creaked threateningly.

"Who is it?" Angelica shouted to Ella, who was doing nothing but gaping. The shutter released, opening so hard it rebounded against the wall and then back against her temple. Ignoring the unexpected pain, she yanked on the heavy window frame as she stood in tepid sunshine.

The door protested again under another, more ferocious onslaught, and Angelica gave a brief thought to the possibility that Voss might be the one attempting to gain entrance…but, no—surely if it were him, he'd be shouting at her to let him in.

At last, the window opened, and Angelica stuck her head out into the warm sunshine to look down…and down.

Blast! The street was two levels below, and she couldn't see any way to—

There was a loud splintering sound behind her and Ella screamed again. Angelica turned, her heart in her throat, and reached for the poker. The door sagged and she could see two powerful arms reaching through a ragged hole, and just then, a booted foot smashed through near the bottom.

With no other choice, she rushed toward them, swinging the poker, slamming it at the fingers as they tore, bare-handed, at the iron-bound wood. She smashed the poker against one arm and then used its pointed end to stab at the other, then down at the foot kicking at the large hole.

Nothing seemed to stop the intruders; they kept ramming against the weakening door and Angelica tried to fight them back…but only moments later the pieces of wood fell away and two men burst into the room.

Angelica had the impression of hulking figures, burning eyes and the gleam of feral smiles. For a moment, she lost her breath, freezing in fear. But when one of them grabbed Ella and the other lunged for Angelica, she came back to life and swung her poker.

Her cut foot slipped again and she nearly lost her balance, but the poker met its mark, slamming into the side of the fiery-eyed man who reached for her. The blow didn't seem to affect him, and he shoved the metal rod away as if it were a twig, sending Angelica skidding aside as Ella's screams filled the room.

Somehow, Angelica managed to evade the grasping hands and dive under the bed. She lost the poker in the process, and huddled in the corner, frantically trying to think of an escape. If she could get past him and dash toward the doorway…

Suddenly, the bed rose, lifted straight above her, and then flew against the wall. Wooden pieces and bedding crashed in all directions, raining on her and giving her a moment in the flurry to dash to her feet.

She stepped on glass and tripped over a sheet, staggering against a piece of splintered bed frame. Terror gripped her as she fell and one of her attackers moved, trapping her where she crouched in the corner.

He paused, looking down at her as if to give her fear a chance to build. A tall man with broad shoulders and a long face, he had the glowing eyes she'd come to recognize as belonging to the *vampirs*. His hair was short and thick and curling, and he might have been considered attractive if it weren't for the wildness of his smile, the pointed length of two of his teeth, and the murderousness in his eyes. And what looked like a streak of blood on his jaw.

Oh, God, help me.

Those eyes bored into her as a half smile twitched his lips, and he waited as if trying to lull her. Meanwhile, his chest rose and fell as if his own anticipation was heightened.

Angelica realized at that moment that silence had fallen. Even Ella was quiet. The only noise was her own gasping breaths and a soft, eerie gurgling sound that made the hair on her arms rise.

Something heavy and metallic-scented filled the air, and in that frozen moment, she realized it was blood. Lots of blood.

A horrified gasp escaped her and her fingers groped

for something on the floor—a broken bottle, a piece of the bed, a *pillow*—anything. Her hand slipped through the puddle of blood gathering beneath her foot, roaming over the uneven wooden planks.

"Woodmore," said the vampire. "Art thou Woodmore's sister?" He stepped closer. "Speak now, or meet thy fate."

A flicker of his attention to the opposite side of the room tricked her into looking there, where Ella lay half-sprawled across the tilted dressing table. The other intruder bent over her, his hand curled up into her hair. She'd stopped screaming and fighting, and even in her quick glance, Angelica saw the faint twitching of her feet and one hand. Blood stained the front of her gown and tinged her fingers.

"I am," Angelica whispered, hoping that was the proper thing to say. The answer that would save her life…or gain her some time until Voss arrived.

Where was Voss?

"Chas Woodmore's sister?" the man demanded in a voice that could only be described as disappointed. "The hunter?"

Hunter. Suddenly something snapped in Angelica's mind—a vague memory crystallizing into a surge of hope. Stories from her childhood.

A stake. Right. A wooden one. Where? In the…in the *heart*.

"Yes," she said to him as much as to herself. Yes, that was how the story went. Not the metal poker; that wouldn't help. But wood.

A piece of the bed.

Now she felt blindly on the floor with purpose.

His eyes bored into her and she felt a surge of fear.

He looked as if he wanted to tear her into pieces. His smile revealed two sharp incisors and as his grin widened, she saw that his teeth and gums were stained red.

With blood.

"Methinks you lie," he said. A hand swung down and grabbed at her, but before he could drag her to her feet, an emphatic *No!* erupted from the corner. The grip released and she sagged back onto the floor.

He turned to glower at his companion, who, as Angelica watched, dumped the bloody mess that was Ella onto the ground. It landed in the faint square of sunlight. In the moment of distraction, she found what she sought and her sticky fingers closed around a splinter of wood.

"You are the sister of Chas Woodmore," said the one who was obviously the leader, and who'd saved her life. At least for the moment. He walked toward her, swiping his mouth with a scrap of cloth. A quick, sharp look at his companion had the other one stepping back.

Angelica didn't miss the look of fury he cast the leader, but her attention was caught by this new threat.

"Who are you?" she forced herself to ask. A strange calmness had settled over her—a moment when everything seemed to slow down and become very clear. She would have one chance to try and penetrate his chest with this piece of wood.

Whether it would work—

Suddenly a great, sleek force burst into the chamber. Angelica ducked instinctively, and the next thing she knew, the vampire in front of her was flying through the air. The other one lunged, but too late, and Voss—of course it was him, tall and golden and ferociously cat-like—grabbed him by the back of the neck and lifted him effortlessly.

Angelica gaped as Voss flung—literally *flung*—the man across the room, pitching him through the sunny window like a rag doll.

The sound of agonized screams faded into descent as Voss turned to the leader of the pair, who'd landed next to Ella in the pool of sunlight. The intruder was gasping and writhing as if pinned there by some invisible bondage.

Voss lashed out and snatched him by the leg, then spun him neatly up and out into the full sunlight. This one didn't scream, and a sudden quiet descended.

Angelica stared. It had happened so quickly, within a matter of breaths, that she could hardly credit it. Voss was turned away from her, still staring out the window as if to be certain the invaders wouldn't return.

Through the fog of shock, she nevertheless noticed and admired his shoulders—so wide and solid as they rose and fell—and the thick mass of tawny-golden waves brushing the collar of his coat. One hand hung at his side, veined and powerful. Tightly fisted.

"My lord," she whispered after a moment when he didn't turn.

"Go," he said in a short, tight voice. His breathing was deep and controlled, and she could see it move through his body as if it were being dragged. A little shudder rippled over his shoulders as he added, "Get help."

He made a sharp gesture to Ella as he knelt slowly, reluctance in his very movement.

Angelica had pulled to her feet, her knees shaking, her fingers still closed around the wooden splinter, her other hand curled into the front of her chemise.

"Angelica," Voss said. "Go. *Now.*"

Confused, frightened and sick to the very depths of her being, Angelica obeyed and fled the room.

8

IN WHICH LORD DEWHURST
SUFFERS A POOR VINTAGE

Angelica barely made it down the stairs without falling. Her knees shook, threatening to give way and send
her tumbling, and she felt as if she were about to toss
up her accounts at any moment. Yet, it was concern not
only for Ella but for Voss as well that kept her upright
and intent on finding help.

She got to the bottom step and as she followed the
path of destruction—crooked wall pictures, an upended
vase, a streak of something dark on the wallpaper—
down a short corridor, she met up with Rubey.

The older woman looked a bit disheveled, but not
as if she'd been attacked or fought off intruders. No
blood nor claw or tear marks. Her expression was tight
and shocked, and her first words were, "You're unhurt?
What about Ella?"

Angelica shook her head and peeled her tongue off
the roof of her mouth. "Voss is seeing to her. He sent
me for help."

Just then, the sound of heavy footsteps had Angelica

spinning in alarm. But it was Voss. He filled the corridor, his face just as taut as Rubey's, his stride purposeful.

"There's no help for the maid," he told Rubey without looking at Angelica.

"No," Rubey whispered. "Ella?" Her face loosened with pain and shock. "Damn you, Voss, for bringing this here. Your greed and games."

Voss's expression tightened further and he inclined his head as if in acceptance. Still without acknowledging Angelica, keeping his eyes hooded and on Rubey, he said, "We haven't much time. Where is he?"

Apparently the older woman could decipher his code, for she stepped back and gestured down the hall. "Still in there. Pretending to be injured." Her eyes flashed lightning blue as they met Voss's, once again making Angelica feel as if she were missing something important. "Do what you will."

Before she could ask, Voss glanced at her, his eyes scoring down over what she belatedly realized was a scandalously flimsy shift and then her bare legs and feet. Yet, she couldn't bring herself to truly care.

"If you could dress her, and get that damned foot bound up, I would greatly appreciate it." He was speaking again to Rubey, again as if Angelica wasn't there, and she had to bite her tongue to keep from demanding petulantly that he acknowledge her.

Fool.

Then he brushed past her, the sleeve of his coat dislodging a lock of hair from her shoulder, and disappeared down the hall.

"Come. I'll see to you myself," Rubey said wearily. "You can't stay much longer. And I've got to leave, as well."

Angelica resisted the urge to stare after Voss. A little prickle of nervousness ran up her spine. *Do what you will.*

Whatever Rubey had meant, Angelica suspected it wasn't to the good.

She followed the older woman's brisk pace and realized for the first time that the cuts on her foot were deep and painful. Fortunately the bleeding had slowed to an ooze, and as soon as they reached their destination, Rubey made her sit down. Moments later, she gave a damp cloth to Angelica to wipe away the blood.

As she bathed her cuts, noticing that the one in her heel was split and would likely take some time to mend, she realized that this was an exceedingly well-appointed home. A smallish residence, but furnished richly and with elegance. It dawned on her that this must be where Rubey lived, and that possibly her place of business was elsewhere. The chamber to which they'd come was clearly Rubey's private one, and it was decorated in rich gold and all other shades of yellow.

It also occurred to Angelica, as Rubey dug through a large, polished wardrobe across from a very decadent and well-pillowed bed, that the fact that two *vampirs* had invaded the home and killed a maid didn't seem to shock her hostess. Certainly she was aggrieved at the loss of Ella, but she didn't seem to be as stunned and paralyzed as Angelica felt.

This realization coupled with the fact that Ella had had what most certainly were bite marks on her neck, and Angelica began to feel light-headed again. Light of head, and confused. Were these horrific creatures— which she'd had no idea existed beyond Granny Grapes's imagination until only last night—more common than she could have imagined? Did these violent, rapacious monsters live among them like normal people?

And what was Voss's connection to them?

Rubey moved with the same efficiency and spare movements as Ella had, insisting that Angelica don a clean chemise, and even loaning her one of her corsets. Although she didn't attempt to do anything with the mass of wild hair except pin it up loosely again, Rubey tugged and laced and buttoned Angelica into a pretty pink frock in short order.

Just as Angelica was rolling silk stockings up over her knees and aligning borrowed slippers (which were a bit too large) for her feet, Voss strode into the chamber. Uninvited, and clearly comfortable being there.

"We must go," he said to Angelica. She sensed wildness about him, some restrained energy beneath his movements. "Straight away. We've a carriage waiting."

"What of Edouard?" Rubey asked, her lips pinched together.

"Belial paid him well—and he'd already been made Dracule, Luce take it. How the fool didn't think we'd figure him out, I can't imagine. I threw him outside and he's burning in the sun now. Won't see him again."

Rubey made a sound of distaste and turned away. "Blast it, Voss. Every bloody time you come here, you leave a mess."

"That's why you charge me so much," he replied. But this time, there was no humor in his voice, no lilting charm. "And why I always settle up."

"I cannot charge you enough to make up for this," Rubey said. Her eyes were red now. "Ella was… She was…a friend, as well."

"My sincerest apology," Voss said. He sounded as

if he meant it, and he reached to touch Rubey's arm as if to emphasize. "Truly. I don't know when I'll see you again."

"Never will be soon enough," said their hostess. And she sounded, at that moment, as if she meant it, too.

Voss turned sharply. "Miss Woodmore, we must make haste. You're no longer safe here." Formality and command replaced the empathy in his voice.

Angelica allowed him to lead her from the bedchamber and down the corridor. His strides were long and fast, and she felt awkward trying to keep up with him. But her fingers, gloveless, were clasped in his big bare hand, and he steadied her as they hurried along.

The carriage had been pulled up very near the servants' entrance; to climb in was no more than a step out the door and up into the vehicle. The conveyance was parked in a narrow mews between two tall buildings, which made the space dark and shadowy despite the fact that it was several hours before twilight.

For the second time in less than twenty-four hours, Angelica entered a carriage to ride with Voss. Alone.

"Where are we going this time?" she asked as he stood at the doorway, his hand on the edge of the door, his feet on the stoop of the house.

"Somewhere safer," he said. His eyes seemed to glitter with heat as he looked up at her. "Somewhere where they cannot find us."

There was something about the way he said those words that gave her pause. An odd combination of desire and unease prickled inside her.

"Why do you not take me back to Blackmont Hall? Surely it's safe there," Angelica said, remembering the stone wall that surrounded the small plot of land on which the mansion sat. Maia must be sick with worry, too. And what if there'd been a message from Chas?

"I'll not take you back to Corvindale," Voss said flatly. "Not quite yet."

And then, to her shock and surprise, he slammed the door closed, leaving himself on the outside. The sound of the latch catching solidified the realization that he didn't intend to join her.

Angelica whipped the heavy curtains away from the windows just in time to see Voss—she thought it was him, at any rate—heavily cloaked and with a low-riding hat settle on the small stoop at the back of the barouche where the footman would normally stand.

He was choosing to ride outside of the vehicle instead of inside with her? What did that mean?

The sudden jolt of the vehicle starting off nudged her against the padded wall. Voss hadn't moved, but she could see his gloved hands holding on to the handles next to the window. He looked like a black wraith, his cloak flapping as they went on and his face in shadow, his profile turned away and down.

Angelica, exhausted, still more than a bit horrified at the day's events, and now filled with annoyance, settled into her seat and folded her arms over her middle.

"This is a fine kettle," she said to herself. Locked in a carriage, being taken who knew where.

But she wasn't frightened. At least, not of Voss.

There were much worse threats to her person than the tawny-haired man with the hot gaze.

Perhaps he meant to protect her reputation by not riding about London during the day alone in the carriage with her. Not that anyone could see inside the heavily curtained windows.

Or perhaps he thought it would be safer if he rode outside, where he could watch for other attacks.

Or perhaps he didn't wish to be near her any longer. Now that he'd been with Rubey for the afternoon.

For it had become starkly clear to her that he and Rubey had been otherwise engaged when the invaders had come into the house, and had somehow avoided a direct attack. The thought of what they were doing made her feel suddenly quite ill again.

Miserable, she settled into the corner of the carriage. The plush velvet walls and cushions embraced her, and she rested her head back and tried not to think about what a disaster her life had become.

She had to admit it, then. That she'd come to truly fancy Voss in the few days that she'd known him, in the fleeting moments of conversation and in those moments when their eyes had met… Well, she must admit it. She had believed, *hoped,* that he'd fancied her, too.

Foolish purring kitten, as Granny Grapes would say. And she'd jab her finger at Angelica just as Maia was wont to do. *Yer seeing what yer want to see.*

Voss—she really ought to think of him as Dewhurst again—was merely being gentlemanly in taking care of her and taking her off to safety. Protecting her, or any woman in danger, as any man would do.

Yes, they'd had some compelling conversation. And indeed, when they'd talked just this morning whilst she was still abed, Angelica had felt as if the silken thread of a connection had been strung between them when she looked into his eyes and saw something deeper there.

And, yes, there'd been that kiss…

Angelica's toes curled up inside the too-large slippers

as she remembered that kiss, that melting, mind-shattering kiss. And then she forced her thoughts away from it.

Yes, that kiss. But it hadn't been her first kiss, and certainly not his. A kiss didn't have to mean anything. Just because it made the ground shift beneath her feet didn't mean it did the same to him…and even if it did—there was Rubey.

And thus and so went her thoughts, circular, dark, confused and focused on everything but the fact that her life was in danger and that she'd been attacked for the second time in less than a day.

That was simply too dark and terrifying for her to think about.

Angelica opened her eyes when the carriage made a sharp turn and for the first time, she noticed a glove tucked into the cushion of the seat across from her. Was it Voss's? By all indication, this was his carriage.

Angelica bit her lip, looking at the crushed beige glove. She was tempted. Oh, so tempted…

Before she could consider any repercussions, she slid over to pluck it from its spot. Too large to belong to a woman, as she'd suspected, the glove had small, tight stitches and was soft as butter. When she brought it close to her nose, she found that the scent that reminded her of him clung to the silk lining.

And there on the edge of the underside was a monogram. *VA,* with a large, stylized *D* in between the initials. Voss Arden, Lord Dewhurst.

Angelica glanced guiltily out the window of the carriage. But although his hand still grasped the handle and his dark figure stood steady on its small platform, his face was buried in the dark recesses of his hat and the collar of his cloak.

Angelica looked down at the rich leather.

Did she dare?

Did she even want to know?

But the man fascinated her and she needed something other than fear on which to focus her mind. And so she closed her eyes, crumpled Voss's glove in her hand and opened her thoughts.

Voss shifted with each movement of the carriage so that his face—the only exposed part of his skin—would remain out of the sunlight. An inconvenience at the very least…but much less trying than sitting in that small space with Angelica.

For a moment, he lost his thoughts, sliding back into the red haze that had engulfed him when he entered the chamber to find her being attacked by Trastonio and some other gutter-wipe make. Bloodscent filled the air— that of the destroyed maid, and another, sweeter, much more compelling one. From Angelica.

He'd never forget the image that greeted him, penetrating through that sudden, hot fog of desire. Even now, as his leather-clad fingers gripped the handle protruding from the rear of his carriage, in his mind he saw Angelica—wide-eyed, white-faced, huddled in the corner of the chamber. Terror blazed in her exotic eyes, her hair straggled wild and dark around the sagging neckline of her shift. Two white feet and bare calves beneath the hem, streaked with crimson…and her fingers around a piece of wood, her mouth tight with concentration as she prepared to defend herself.

Lucifer's brittle bones. He'd nearly lost her. And lost his chance.

And then to see, and scent, her blood…a most intimate part of her. The thought of it, the sense of tasting it, hot and heavy on his tongue…her lips parted in pleasured sighs and her lush body opening to him… It made his desire uncontrollable. His fingers had dug into the edge of the window as he sent her away before he lost the ability to curb his actions.

Voss thought they'd have more time at Rubey's. He hadn't expected one of her own footmen to betray them to the likes of Belial—but then, of course, men like Edouard did strange things for the chance to become immortal.

Too bloody bad for the man who was now frying in the deadly sun. Voss was certain Belial hadn't told Edouard about that particular drawback of being a made Dracule.

Just as Lucifer hadn't told Voss about that and a variety of other inconveniences as part of their unholy agreement, including the Mark that now throbbed and ached with the devil's own annoyance. Every twist and turn of the carriage as it avoided street urchins or piles of refuse in the street, dogs or even other vehicles, made his shoulder stretch and caused a renewal of pain. When he'd sent Angelica away from the chamber with the dead maid instead of tearing into her flesh, the agonizing sting from his Mark had left him breathless.

Lucifer was never pleased when one of his Dracule thought of someone other than themselves.

The pain had lessened only a fraction since then, and Voss wasn't certain how much longer he could fight it. Closing his eyes, resting his temple against the sun-baked side of the carriage, he drew in a deep breath of summer afternoon in London: warm, close and filled with the smell of rotting food, human and animal waste,

Paranormal Reading...

TWO BOOKS FREE!

Each of your FREE books will thrill you with dramatic, sensual tales featuring dark, sexy and powerful characters.

We'd like to send you **two free books** to introduce you to the Reader Service. Your two books are worth over $10, but they are yours free! We'll even send you **two exciting surprise gifts**. There's no catch. You're under no obligation to buy anything. We charge nothing – ZERO – for your first shipment. *You can't lose!*

Visit us at
www.ReaderService.com

YOURS FREE!

We'll send you 2 fabulous surprise gifts (worth about $10) just for trying "Paranormal"!

The Editor's "Thank You" Free Gifts include:
- **2 Paranormal books!**
- **2 exciting mystery gifts!**

Yes! I have placed my Editor's **"Free Gifts"** seal in the space provided at right. Please send me 2 free books and 2 fabulous mystery gifts. I understand I am under no obligation to purchase any books, as explained on the back of this card.

PLACE
FREE GIFTS
SEAL HERE

237/337 HDL FNM3

FIRST NAME	LAST NAME

ADDRESS

APT.#	CITY

STATE/PROV.	ZIP/POSTAL CODE

Thank You!

EC3-PAR-12 ▼ DETACH AND MAIL CARD TODAY

The Reader Service — Here's How it Works:

Accepting your 2 free books and 2 free gifts (gifts valued at approximately $10.00) places you under no obligation to buy anything. You may keep the books and gifts and return the shipping statement marked "cancel". If you do not cancel, about a month later we'll send you 4 additional books and bill you just $21.42 in the U.S. or $23.46 in Canada. That's a savings of at least 21% off the cover price of all 4 books! It's quite a bargain! Shipping and handling is just 50¢ per book in the U.S. and 75¢ per book in Canada.* You may cancel at any time, but if you choose to continue, every month we'll send you 4 more books, which you may either purchase at the discount price or return to us and cancel your subscription.

BUSINESS REPLY MAIL

FIRST-CLASS MAIL   PERMIT NO. 717   BUFFALO, NY

POSTAGE WILL BE PAID BY ADDRESSEE

THE READER SERVICE
PO BOX 1867
BUFFALO NY 14240-9952

NO POSTAGE
NECESSARY
IF MAILED
IN THE
UNITED STATES

If offer card is missing write to:
The Reader Service, P.O. Box 1867, Buffalo, NY 14240-1867

choking coal smoke and, faintly, summer lilies. Very faintly.

The unpleasant aromas did little to distract his thoughts from the paralyzing burn at his shoulder. He couldn't understand how Dimitri lived with the pain his inflamed Mark must inflict on him at all times. Surely it wasn't worth the self-denial and he could rid himself of the suffering for a moment at the least. But still Dimitri denied himself, after more than a century…since that night in Vienna.

The evening in question began innocently enough. Dimitri had invested in a private men's club being built in Vienna—a large, Baroque-style home that was one of many in the new architectural fashion since the great Turkish siege had ended—and had invited several acquaintances, most of them Dracule, to visit for an evening of cards and women and other entertainment.

Voss had thought it would be the perfect opportunity to confirm his suspicions about Dimitri's Asthenia and add the information to his book of notes. Having played cards with the stone-faced Dimitri in the past and having observed him carefully on several other social occasions in London and Paris, he'd noticed that the man never accepted jewelry as tokens for bets, nor did he interact with men or women who wore ostentatious accessories.

Thus, in the guise of offering his host a gift, Voss had had a series of a dozen special goblets made. Each one had a different jewel hidden in the bottom of the cup's base. The cups were identical except for the different gems, and the type of gem was identified by a mark on the bottom of the cup and the slot in which it rested in their velvet-lined case.

When Voss arrived at the club, he, along with every

other entrant, was required to leave any weapons—particularly swords or wooden canes that could be sharpened—as well as any valuables, locked in private chests at the front of the club. That, of course, included jewels and other accessories, and served only to enhance Voss's suspicion about Dimitri's weakness.

He managed to bring the goblets in, for they were made of hammered metal and appeared very plain and unassuming, just as he'd intended. When Voss entered, he had the chest of cups with him and found a corner behind a heavy curtain in an alcove in which to secrete it. His plan was to offer one to Dimitri filled with his best blooded-brandy as a gift, and then secretly swap the goblets out one by one throughout the night. That way he could determine which gem affected Dimitri without the other man knowing what he was doing.

This type of elaborate ruse was just the sort of thing Voss reveled in. He enjoyed not only the planning, but the execution as well, and considered that a trap had only been perfectly sprung and a puzzle solved when he managed to do so without the victim realizing what was happening.

But in this case, things did not turn out as he'd intended.

He and Dimitri, along with several other guests—mortal and Dracule alike—sat in the main parlor of the club. Windows dark with heavy curtains allowed only a swatch of moonlight to filter through, and a violinist played in the corner. Lovely women, a rarity in men's clubs at least in London, offered trays of drink and slender ivory wrists or shoulders.

The very essence of the place was hot and lush, stemming not from its colonnaded design but from the scent of warm blood and rich wine, along with the haze of hashish smoke filtering from another chamber. The chamber exuded hedonism, complete with food and drink and the most sensual of furnishings—both of the inanimate and mortal type.

Dimitri had planned his establishment well, and even though Voss meant to use the evening to observe and learn from his host, he found himself lulled by the strains of music and the feminine company—and young, hard males as well, for those who tended toward that preference. He confessed to having tried that once, early on after realizing he was to live forever, and when he was very drunk. But in the end it hadn't appealed, and he returned to the lush flesh of women instead of the hard muscle of men.

The most lovely of the women was named Lerina, and she was clearly Dimitri's current mistress. Her elegant shoulder, bared by a low-bodice gown, bore several sets of bite marks on the right side. Every Dracule in the place recognized Dimitri's scent on the woman, and even if they hadn't, the way she watched him with her pale blue eyes would have indicated her allegiance.

Dimitri accepted the first goblet from Voss, and sipped the brandy as Lerina traced her fingers gently over the back of her lover's neck. His dark eyes scanned the room, as if watching for trouble or merely surveying his domain, and he hardly seemed to notice the woman's touch.

That was where Voss and Dimitri differed, as well. Even if Voss was only planning to bed the woman that night, he plied her with attention and charm. When he was finished with her, he was finished…but until then, she was the recipient of all of his attention.

As he sipped from his own cup, Voss observed his host, who was drinking from the goblet with a garnet in the base. He noticed nothing untoward. He'd added a bit of a favorite of his enhancements to the brandy as well, in hopes that it would lower Dimitri's natural defenses even further. The *salvi* wouldn't weaken Dimitri—although it would drug a mortal to sleep almost instantly—but combined with the brandy and blood, it would increase his intoxication to an even deeper level.

Voss partook of the same drink, with the same enhancement, and divided his attention between his host, the lovely Lerina, who seemed desperate for Dimitri's spare notice, and other amusements in the room. Voss had all night to enjoy himself, and fully intended to do so.

He'd refilled Dimitri's goblet a third time—and had swapped for a third gem, the topaz, which had taken the place of a pearl—when everything went to hell.

It started when one of Dimitri's stewards approached swiftly, carrying a chest. As he came closer, Voss recognized it as the box that held his collection of goblets, along with the *salvi*. Damnation.

"My lord," said the steward, showing Dimitri the chest. "I found these in the front alcove. Hidden behind the curtain."

Voss's stomach sank, but he fixed an insouciant smile on his face as Dimitri glanced at the goblets, lined up in their spots with the chemical symbol for each gem marked on its slot in the box. Of course, one slot was empty—for the one cup he held in his hand. He turned a frigid glare onto Voss, who lifted his own glass in salute.

"A gift for my host," Voss said in an effort to bluff

his way through the situation. "A collection of a dozen of the finest craftsmanship."

"So that's what you've done," said Dimitri. His eyes burned red and his mouth flattened into an unpleasant expression. "I wondered. And you expected to trick me thus?"

Voss noticed that his hand trembled, and that the man's face appeared taut and tense. His breathing altered, slowed.

Voss had been right! It *was* a gemstone. Something in the chest. Something that wasn't large enough to cause him great weakness, although in combination with the *salvi* and blood-brandy it had obviously affected him. But there was no way of knowing which one it was, for all dozen were present.

"I would throttle you but I'm afraid I have more imminent concerns to deal with," Dimitri said flatly, and Voss realized he'd shifted his attention from him to something beyond his shoulder. He had an arrested expression on his face as he looked across the room. "But you are no longer welcome here, Voss. See that he leaves," he added to his steward.

Voss stood, knowing when he'd pushed things too far. He didn't see any reason to cause a fight and muss his clothes, so he gave a short little bow of acquiescence. But Dimitri was no longer paying him any attention.

Instead his focus was on a group of men who'd just entered the room.

Cezar Moldavi and five of his companions.

At that time, Voss knew little about Moldavi except that he didn't care for the man. Perhaps it was the way the vampire carried himself, as if there was a large block on his shoulder that he dared anyone to knock off. Or

perhaps it was the manner in which he spoke to everyone, as if he were better than they. Which was a hard
thing to account for, since Cezar Moldavi wasn't the tall-
est of men, and he wasn't particularly pleasant to look
at. He wasn't even half as rich as Voss. In the company
of other Dracule, what exactly did he think was so special about himself?

"Who allowed that child-bleeder entrance?" Dimitri snarled, seeming to forget about the goblets. "I gave
strict instructions—"

"Dimitri," said Moldavi, sweeping toward them
boldly. Voss could tell immediately that he knew he
wasn't welcome, and that he didn't care. His five companions pushed their way through as if they were the
club's owners, rather than guests. "Your place is quite
accommodating."

"I hardly expected to see you here, Moldavi," Dimitri
replied, looking at him from his chair, as if he couldn't
be bothered to rise. But Voss assumed it had to do with
the fact that the man was weakened by the presence of
some gemstone as well as the *salvi.* "There aren't any
children about."

As the steward escorted him toward the door, he
glanced at Moldavi. The man didn't seem offended by
the comments, and in fact returned Dimitri's expression
with a bold and challenging one.

"More's the pity," said Moldavi. "They have the
sweetest, purest blood."

Even Voss couldn't contain his revulsion at that
point, and despite the way the blood—and *salvi*-laced
brandy—had lulled him while heightening his senses,
he felt his belly lurch. So it was Cezar Moldavi who'd
left the young boy's body in the farm fields. Bled nearly

dry, the boy had been eight and left to die in the sun. All of Vienna had heard about it, and the horror had rushed through the mortal population as well as the Draculian underpinnings.

It was one thing to feed on a mortal, to take sustenance. Even from one who had to be coaxed or otherwise enthralled. But to leave one to die, and a child at that...

"I wouldn't know," Dimitri replied. Despite the fact that he hadn't moved or hardly flickered an eyelash, he looked as if he were about to squash a large gnat. His fangs barely showed, and his eyes had banked the red-orange glow of fury. But the sense of suppressed fury fairly radiated from him, even though the chest of goblets still remained in the vicinity, apparently forgotten. "I don't recall sending you an invitation, Cezar."

The other man smiled unpleasantly. "I was certain it had been an oversight. You've always been so inclusive of all of us. Which is why I brought a gift for you." He stepped aside and revealed a cloaked figure behind him.

It was a woman, Voss saw, and immediately, his blood surged and his breathing quickened as someone drew away her cloak. The most beautiful woman he'd ever seen. She had smooth, ivory skin, startling blue eyes and ink-black hair that fell in long, lush waves over her shoulders. She wore a vibrant purple gown that clung to a tall, slender body in the most unfashionable manner, but that left every curve outlined: her breasts, their erect nipples, the swell of her belly and the bones of her hips and even the swell of her mons.

Her only other adornment was a curious bracelet with a feather dangling from it.

"I have no interest in your leavings, Moldavi," Dimitri said. His attention had barely flickered over the woman.

"Especially your sister. Although," he said as if an afterthought, "she's not precisely your type, is she? You prefer to let others partake while you sniff out other amusements." A bit more of his fangs showed.

Even from a distance near the door, Voss saw and heard the rumble of surprise from Moldavi's companions. Apparently they weren't used to their leader being insulted by the implication that he couldn't bed a woman. And neither was he, if the expression on his face was any indication. Surprise and hatred flashed there, and then it was gone.

Voss turned his attention back to the woman. So this was Cezar Moldavi's vampire sister, Narcise. Even with dull, blank eyes, she was an incredible beauty. Enough to make any man, mortal or Dracule, weak in the knees and hard of the cock. How could Dimitri resist? Voss would have accepted her in a moment, and in fact, if he weren't being so unceremoniously escorted from the place, he would have tried.

But that wasn't going to happen, for he realized belatedly that Narcise Moldavi didn't seem to have any freedom of her own. She didn't speak to anyone, and other than a single, brief flash of life in her eyes, she remained little more than a statue at her brother's side. Clearly under his control.

The same couldn't be said for Moldavi, for after Dimitri's dismissal of Narcise, the man's eyes burned brilliant red. "You dare to insult my family?"

"On the contrary. The insult was directed to you alone," Dimitri replied, clearly bored.

By that time, Voss was at the door and he had no choice but to leave, even though he had a feeling that things were about to get interesting.

He didn't find out until months later what exactly had happened that caused the great loathing between Moldavi and Dimitri to become even deeper and more permanent. According to other witnesses, after Voss left, Moldavi pretended to do the same. But instead, he remained in the club and somehow lured Lerina into a dark corner with him.

When Lerina reappeared with Cezar's marks on her left shoulder and his scent on her, Dimitri had had enough. Intoxicated from the *salvi* and likely still weakened by the presence of his Asthenia, he was obviously impaired. Moldavi pulled out a small wooden stake—which he clearly had not left at the door—and lunged at Dimitri. In their struggle they knocked over a lit candelabra.

No one noticed at first because of the ensuing battle, and the fire started quickly, eating into the lush upholstery and furnishings in the chamber as Dimitri grabbed Cezar by the throat. Fueled by fury, he lifted him into the air, throwing him across the room. Cezar landed in a heap amid his followers, beaten by a vampire who was unarmed, not to mention intoxicated and weakened. Completely and utterly humiliated.

Of course, Voss wasn't there to witness the details of the fight, but it was clear from the stories that were told that that night cemented a hatred between the two men even deeper than the discord he'd invited by bringing the goblets.

To add even more injury to Dimitri's insult, the fire not only destroyed his new club, but it also caused the death of Lerina, who had been unable to escape the fire.

In one dark evening, Dimitri lost his mistress, a valuable piece of property and made himself a lethal enemy by humiliating an immortal madman in front of his peers. And had nearly been tricked into revealing his deepest secret.

It was, Voss reflected grimly as he clung to the back of his carriage, no wonder the man blamed him. If he hadn't put the *salvi* in the brandy, things might not have happened the way they had.

Or perhaps they would have.

After all, as Dimitri had warned Voss after Brickbank's death, which couldn't have been avoided despite Voss's precautions: if one was destined to die, there was nothing that could be done to prevent it.

Voss blinked and rubbed his head against the back of the carriage that held Angelica, bringing himself back from more than a hundred years ago to present-day London.

The carriage had navigated through shoppers and street hawkers on busy Bond Street, then along Piccadilly toward Fleet, and at last turned along Bishopsgate. Now it pulled into a narrow opening between two buildings.

Voss knew they'd reached their destination when the smell of the river and all of its accompanying stench melded with that of vomit and stale ale. The Billingsgate Fish Market was two blocks away, and here in the narrow, crooked streets crowded public houses frequented by the fishermen and mongers. The particular establishment to which he had directed his groom had a sign on the front naming it The Golden Lion, but was known as Black Maude's to those who frequented it.

Now that they'd arrived on the eastern side of town amid close, tall buildings, Voss was able to raise his face without fearing it would be seared by the light of the sun. That heavenly body had sunk lower, which meant that Belial and his forces would be out in full force in short order.

Voss was one of the few Dracule who could go out during the daylight, as long as he kept any direct sunbeams from touching his skin. Even on some rainy, very cloudy days, he could walk about without covering for a short time. Tolerance for the sun varied by each individual, but there were some who dared not venture into sunlit air at all—covered or not. Nevertheless, full and direct exposure would kill any Dracule.

Just as Lucifer lived and thrived in the dark, relying on shadows and night to hide his deeds, so were the Dracule made. Sunlight exposed too much.

Voss considered himself relatively fortunate in this matter, which had made his escape from previous sticky situations much easier. And, in this case, it gave him the freedom to remove Angelica to a safer location.

The carriage had come to a complete stop in the back alley behind Maude's, and Voss released the handle, stepping lightly onto the ground. A sharp glance around confirmed that the shadowy passage was deserted. He moved quickly to unlatch the carriage door, more than a bit apprehensive about Angelica's reaction to being abducted in such a manner.

When he opened the door and looked in, she didn't move except to spear him with a cool gaze.

At least she didn't fly at him in a rage as another of his consorts had done when he'd subjected her to a similar mode of transport. Of course, India had been a fiery-haired and tempered vixen even when she was at rest, and that situation had been markedly different than this one. For one, he'd been abducting her from her husband. For another, he'd already shared her bed on more than one occasion.

His mouth dried and the sheaths around his incisors tightened as he realized how soon he'd be doing the same with this young woman.

"Shall I disembark, or are you planning to join me?" Angelica asked in an even voice. Her hair was still pooled around her shoulders, and her slender hands were settled in her lap. The uneven light spilled over the curves of her collarbones and breasts. Voss's breath deepened as he gripped the door frame. She was so very lovely.

But…her eyes. It was her eyes that captured him: clearly annoyed, beckoning, intelligent. And wise.

It was the wisdom there, the peace, that tugged at him.

"I thought you might wish a bit of refreshment," he said. "We're going to stop for a bit."

"Is it safe?" she asked, and that peace edged away to be replaced by wariness. Worry.

She still trusted him enough to ask.

"I won't allow anything to happen to you, Angelica," he said, offering her his hand. *At least, anything that you won't enjoy.*

She murmured something that sounded annoyed, but she rose from her seat and took his hand with her bare fingers. "Does this belong to you?" she asked, showing him one of his gloves.

"I wondered where it had gotten to," he replied and took it as she alighted from the carriage. "Thank you for finding it."

She merely gave him an inscrutable look and lifted

the hem of Rubey's frock so that it didn't drag on the ground.

Voss, feeling unusually put-off by her reticence and calm (he had expected to be confronted with a harridan when he opened the door), and the odd way she was looking at him, opened the grimy door of the building. No sooner had they stepped inside the back entrance, dark with dirt and soot and sticky with grease, than his carriage rumbled off for a change of horses. The groom would return after and wait for them in the alley.

Inside Black Maude's, Voss led Angelica down the dark passage to the private rooms with which he was well familiar. As was expected, no one greeted them in this rear corridor. It wasn't until he unfastened the latch on the third door (the only one with the red string hanging out, indicating that the chamber was empty) and entered the small chamber that he spoke again.

"Are you hungry?" he asked, turning to lock the door behind them and to pull its red string inside. There was another door on the opposite side of the chamber through which he would communicate with the proprietress.

It was all very discreet but, unlike Rubey's, this particular establishment didn't cater to Dracule members. Most of the patrons here were mortals with very specific tastes that they dared not allow to become public.

Angelica stood in the center of the room, looking as if she were afraid to touch anything. Voss couldn't blame her; for although the bed was neatly made, its cleanliness appeared dubious at best. There were two chairs and a small dining table, along with a screen in the corner and a chamber pot. On the table was an unopened bottle of whiskey along with a collection of glasses. And, to his annoyance, in what sounded like the very next room, a woman was trying to sing to a piano that was ridiculously out of tune.

"Your choice of accommodations seems to be deteriorating," she said, gesturing to the space. But a bit of a smile twitched at the corner of her mouth, taking some of the petulance away.

"The chair is likely the safest place," he said, sweeping off his smothering cloak. He settled it over the nearest chair and indicated for her to sit.

And all of a sudden, he felt awkward. He was in a bedchamber, with a woman he desired.

And he felt awkward.

"Is something amusing?" Angelica asked. Despite the sensual disarray of her hair, she managed to look and sound very proper. Even her bare hands were folded neatly in her lap.

A knock at the door interrupted any reply he might have made, and Voss went to slide open its small, inset panel. He ordered food and drink for Angelica, and then closed the sliding door.

"I neglected to ask earlier," Voss said, resisting the urge to pace, and firmly ignoring the painful nudge at the back of his shoulder, "if you were hurt. Other than your…foot."

"Hurt? No, 'tis only a little ache. But frightened?" She lifted her chin and fastened him with her gaze. "Yes, I am quite frightened, Dewhurst. Frightened and confused."

"I prefer you to call me Voss," he said, taking care to allow a bit of huskiness into his voice.

She merely looked at him, and again, he felt as if the ground was falling away beneath his feet. This was a woman he couldn't quite understand…and couldn't control. She didn't make demands, she didn't throw her delicious body at him—but nor was she a shy and retiring virgin, exactly. And she was a woman who saw, and lived, death every day.

How could she bear it? How could she have such peace in her eyes?

Voss would never understand what made him speak at that moment, to ask the question that suddenly, unexpectedly, jumped into his mind. But he did, and later, he found that he didn't regret it. "Do you know when *you* are to die?"

Her eyes widened a fraction and he heard the subtle intake of her breath. He thought she might ignore the question, as she had done earlier when he asked if she'd known about her parents' death before it happened.

"No," she said softly, rising from the becloaked chair. "I attempted it once, holding one of my gloves and concentrating upon it…but I could see nothing. Perhaps it is for the best." She'd taken a few steps and the hem of her dress dragged on the floor. It pulled the neckline of her gown awry and he couldn't help but notice. "I know enough."

"Did it make your childhood very difficult?" he asked, wondering why he didn't simply grab her and drag her up against him, sink inside her. Everything about her filled the room.

He turned away and opened the whiskey. A quick sniff told him it was only marginally better than the rotgut he'd had during a brief trip to Kentucky, but it was something.

He poured a glass and sipped. No, it was even worse than the Kentuckian drink they called moonshine. He managed another sip and restrained a grimace. Perhaps the wine he'd ordered would be better.

"Granny Grapes wouldn't allow me to dwell on it. She helped me to learn how to set things aside. How to accept." Her slippered toe dug into a hole in the rug braided of rags. "I have no doubt I'd be a different person if it weren't for her wisdom." She hesitated, digging her toe deeper. "May I tell you something I've never told anyone?"

Yes. But…why? Why him? Something inside his chest swelled, warming him. The Mark burned in warning. "I would be honored," he said, ignoring it, "Angelica." He set the glass down.

She gave him that odd look again, a wry sort of expression. "So it *is* back to Angelica once more. What has happened to 'Miss Woodmore'? Or is she about only when we are in the presence of your Cyprians?"

The layers of meaning in her words assaulted him, but Voss was a master at paring through to the core of a woman's speech, whether it be murmured pillow talk or screamed demands. "In truth, I *think* of you as Angelica, regardless of what I might say. Angelica." He said her name, drawing it out slowly like a verbal caress.

"Is that so?" she said. But her voice was rough and he saw that her cheeks were flushed tawny pink. Then she drew herself up and he recognized tension settle over her. "Were you with Rubey when those…*vampirs* attacked us?"

Once again, he understood what she was truly asking. He couldn't find it odd or even flattering that she should assume that he and Rubey had been intimately engaged. Not only was it a logical assumption, even for a sheltered young woman and especially after what she'd been exposed to, but Angelica had already proven she had a facile mind.

"We had left to go to her place of business. To settle my accounts. My pocket is now that much lighter." The light tone he'd adopted faded. And Rubey, whom he had considered a friend, had all but exiled him from her place. "If I'd had a glimmer of suspicion that Belial's men would have found us and attacked in the daylight, I would never have left. But neither Rubey nor I had fathomed she might be betrayed by one of her closest employees."

"The daylight. So that part is true? That they cannot go about in the sun?"

Voss nodded, wishing he'd left out that bit of detail. She seemed to know too much already. "I'm relieved that we returned in time to keep anything worse from happening to you. One of the chambermaids managed to get out of the house and to come after us."

"But you weren't in time to save Ella." There was reproach in her voice, and Voss realized he'd forgotten about the dead girl.

"No," he said. Although it had been more than a century since he'd been the cause of a mortal's death—from reckless feeding—he'd also come to accept that it was a casualty of the Draculia and its need to feed on mortal blood. One could learn to control the blind need and leave the victim alive, as Voss had learned to do early on, but many of the Draculia had no concern about doing so. They had no reason to care any more about the lives of the mortals upon which they feasted than a butcher was concerned with the slaughtering of his cow or pig.

This was by design of Lucifer, of course.

Yet, Ella had been the victim of a particularly vicious

vampir, and Voss had seen tendons and torn muscle beneath the ravaged skin of her shoulders and bosom. And blood, so dark and plentiful that it was nearly purple. The snapped and protruding collarbone and the awkward angle of her neck. He went still.

It could have been Angelica.

"How much longer am I going to be hunted by them?" she said. Her voice was thin. "When will it stop?"

"Moldavi won't rest until he gets his sister back, or until he has revenge on your brother for taking her."

"Chas took a *vampir's* sister? Do you mean he kidnapped her?" The fear was replaced by surprise and confusion. "What on earth do you mean? How many of those creatures are there?" Panic stretched her voice.

"To be quite honest, I'm not certain whether he abducted Narcise…or whether they—er—eloped. It's all conjecture, really, but I do know that Moldavi is looking for your brother because Narcise is with him. Or was last seen with him, in Paris. Moldavi is rather closely associated with Bonaparte and has been staying there for some time. And until he gets Narcise back, or until he finds Woodmore, you are in danger because Moldavi will want to use you as bait or ransom for Narcise's return. And if your brother is dead—"

"He's not dead."

Voss stilled. "You know this?"

But she wasn't listening; it was as if she were having her own conversation. "Are you suggesting that my brother has eloped with a *vampir?* How could you even fathom such a thing? Chas would have nothing to do with monsters like that. Or is she not one of those horrible creatures, but just the sister of one?" Her eyes blazed with shock and accusation.

"Narcise is one of them, yes," he replied, feeling as if he were walking on a very delicate sheet of ice. And once again, he wondered why in Luce's name did he even care if he fell through. At least if he did, there would be no reason to wait any longer. His blood surged at the thought.

"Does she bite people, too? With long teeth and claws? Tear into them like paper dolls?" Tears had gathered in her eyes and as she lifted a hand to her mouth, he saw that her fingers trembled violently. "I cannot fathom such vile creatures who take from other people and *leave them to die.* They drink their *blood.* They *take.*"

Voss reminded himself that she could have no idea that she was sitting in the same room with one of those horrible creatures—who wanted nothing more than to do the same to her, among other things—but for some reason, her words stung. "Angelica," he began.

She swiped a tear away and kept talking. "I thought it was all stories, a legend that my granny told us. But they're *real.* And my brother is all sorted up with them. He could be in danger. He *is* in danger. He's gone into hiding, I'm certain of it."

"Everything I know about your brother says that he knows how to take care of himself," Voss told her. "Did you not just say he isn't dead? Do you know this?"

"I'm sure he's not dead. I—"

A knock at the door interrupted her, and Voss, smothering a curse as she fell silent, walked over. A low opening at the bottom of the door allowed for a tray of wine, cheese and bread to be slid beneath—again, keeping the anonymity of the chamber's occupants intact.

"I cannot eat," Angelica said, holding a hand in front of her belly. "I don't know that I shall ever eat again, with those images in my mind. Poor Ella." She looked even more pale-faced than before, and her eyes seemed to have sunken into their sockets in the last few moments. "I cannot believe it of Chas."

Voss put the tray on the table and poured a glass of the wine. "Perhaps you are thirsty?"

"What is that?" she asked, pointing to his glass, likely forgetting that ladies didn't point. "Whiskey? Brandy? Something else that's meant only for men?"

Some of his discomfort slid away. "If you wish to try it, I won't tell anyone." No indeed.

"There are many things about these last two days that I hope you shall not tell anyone," Angelica said. The look she gave him was not one of a coquette, teasing him for more, but one of a woman very aware of her situation... and it was disconcerting.

She took the glass and drank, then, predictably, began coughing uncontrollably. But despite the fact that her eyes watered, she raised the glass for another taste. This time, she was a bit more cautious and the sip went down much easier. "It tastes terrible."

Voss smiled. "I know. The wine isn't much better quality, but you might prefer it."

"It's warm," she said, drinking again. "I mean to say, I feel warm. It makes me feel warm."

"That is not the only way you'll be feeling if you drink too much of it," he said despite the arc of pain that shot through him. *Let her drink,* the devil told him. *She won't fight it.* He thought it prudent to change the subject. "What were you going to tell me, earlier? Or have you changed your mind?"

She sank down onto the cloak-draped chair, whiskey still in hand. Half the generous dollop he'd poured was gone and her movements were already looser. "I've never told another person this. I'm not altogether certain why I should want to tell you, Dewhurst."

"Voss," he said. "Call me Voss."

Angelica frowned and he wasn't certain if it was because she'd taken another drink or because of his suggestion. "Rubey calls you by your given name. That bespeaks of a very intimate relationship."

"I have just asked you to call me by my given name, as well. Do you and I have an intimate relationship?" The words, practiced and easy, slid from his flirtatious tongue. He brought out his smile, the warm one whose allure never failed, to curve his lips. His sisters, his mistresses, the wife of his mathematics teacher, and so many others… None of them had been able to resist.

The smile that told her just what sort of relationship he wanted.

"No, we do not," she replied primly. Oh, so primly. "But if I don't get back to Blackmont Hall or at least to a chaperone soon, my reputation will be ruined on the grounds of mere suspicion and assumption. 'Tis nothing to take lightly, my lord."

So it was "my lord" now. "And then…?"

"And then I'll never make a good marriage. No respectable gentleman will want to wed me." She sipped again. "Chas has made it very clear that I need to make a match this Season. He has little patience for chaperoning us about."

Yes, there was the concern of Chas being more than annoyed that Voss had ruined his sister. And of course, marriage to a Dracule was out of the question—for a variety of reasons in Chas Woodmore's eyes, the least of which was the immortality issue. Not to mention the pact with the devil. Thus, Chas would be incensed if his sister was ruined by Voss, or any other Dracule.

But Voss was fully confident in his ability to evade the *vampir* hunter. It wouldn't be the first time.

Angelica continued talking, the whiskey having done a nice job of loosening her tongue. "But perhaps after Maia and Mr. Bradington wed, she can be my chaperone and Chas can go about his business. Sonia won't be out for another two years."

"Is there a respectable gentleman whom you wish to wed? Is there one who might have his hopes dashed if you do not return? Or if you return…in a questionable state?" Voss wasn't altogether certain why he pursued this topic, but he didn't seem able to control his tongue. Perhaps he ought to try a sip of the whiskey himself.

No. He had no reason to subject himself to that horror.

"Perhaps. Lord Harrington is quite agreeable." Her expression wasn't one of sly flirtation, but rather as if she'd just realized some simple fact such as that the sky was blue.

Voss thought he recalled the man in question—the slender dandy who'd waltzed with her at the masquerade. The one whom he'd put the fear of the devil into with a mere glance while visiting in Angelica's parlor. He smothered a snort. Harrington was probably the sort who'd been thrown in the privy *and* had had his clothes tossed into the coal pit.

"Agreeable is such a flavorless word. I don't believe I should appreciate being described as merely agreeable by a woman such as yourself," he said, lifting an eyebrow.

"That is no surprise," she replied. "I suspect you

would aspire to descriptors like 'charming' and 'handsome' and 'witty.' And 'wealthy.'"

Voss was enjoying this exchange and, from the glint in her eye that he thought was only partly from the whiskey, she seemed to be, as well. The slender ivory column of her neck shifted in and out of shadow as she moved and drank and teased. "Mmm," he said, his voice rumbly. "Perhaps. Or maybe I should simply like to be considered interesting. Or exciting."

She snorted. Definitely, it was a snort. A ladylike one, but nevertheless. "Why would you need to be any of those things when you are a man, and a rich one at that? And not terribly difficult to look upon, either," she added with a sudden saucy look that took him by surprise. "The choice is yours, and your wealth assures you a vast selection to choose from."

If only it were that simple. Despair—such a foreign emotion that he wasn't even certain he recognized it properly—rushed in. Marriage was something in which Dracule members had no reason or desire to indulge.

But it was something that Angelica and those of her class aspired to. It was the focal point of her life, in fact. Marriage, an heir and one to spare, perhaps a daughter... a household that didn't need to be uprooted every few decades because *nothing bloody changed*.

And yet...everything one knew or cared about was eventually left behind. Aged. Died. Turned to dust.

Voss succumbed and took a drink of the wine, which turned out to be thinner than rainwater. Was it too bloody much to expect that Maude have something palatable, considering the fees she charged?

And couldn't the woman in the next room find a high C without going flat?

"Or perhaps you have no intention of marrying," Angelica said, drawing him back to the moment at hand. Her voice had gone as flat as the singer's.

Voss opened his mouth but found he had no response to that. Instead he replied, "You were going to tell me something you've never told anyone before, Angelica. Have you changed your mind, then?"

She sipped again. Her cheeks were flushed and her almond-shaped eyes bright. "I've told no one of this, Dewhurst."

"You've said that," he replied, unaccountably irked by the fact that she continued to call him by his title.

"If I tell you, you must tell me one of your secrets. Will you?"

He smiled, gave a low, rolling laugh and gestured to himself from head to scuffed-up toe. "But I have no secrets. Whatever it is you see here is all there is to know of Lord Dewhurst." He gave the little flourish of a bow.

But when he rose back to full height, her eyes speared him. "Pardon me, my lord, but I can see that isn't true. It's in your eyes. There's something there—some fear, a horror, some grief or perhaps a memory—that you hide."

He froze and they stared at one another for a moment. Even the insistent burning in his shoulder faded because there was nothing at the moment but Angelica. "There is nothing," he said at last.

She tilted her head as she rested the glass on the scarred table, then took a deep breath. "I don't believe you, my lord. But—"

"Call me Voss." Blast it.

She shrugged, still watching him, and the shadows in the dip of her collarbones shifted temptingly. His gums swelled, ready to push the incisors free and he swore he smelled her blood again. Somehow.

Was it she who was becoming foxed, or he?

She shifted then, pulled her gaze away and spoke suddenly and in a rush. "I know when my sisters and brother will die," she said. "I've read their futures and I know how it will happen…and when."

"You know how your brother will die?"

How could he be so very fortunate? This was a most valuable, serendipitous bit of information. He hadn't even thought to ask for it directly, and now it would be handed to him just as the puzzle of Dimitri's Asthenia had. Voss smiled complacently.

Moldavi would pay handsomely to find out when the feared vampire hunter Chas Woodmore was to die, as would Regeris, who rarely ventured from his beloved Barcelona since Woodmore had staked him in the belly as he tumbled from a tower into the ocean. Two inches higher, and the man would be living with Luce in hell instead of having to swim for miles to safety.

The question would be which of them would pay more—and what a delightful problem to have. And the information would cost Voss nothing to obtain; she was offering it up to him freely. The last bit of hazy sweetness evaporated from him, and he focused on the realization of his goal. "You know how he will die, and when, as well?"

"Yes. I've known for years. I've lied to them and—"

"But he is not dead now. You are certain of it?"

"No, Chas is not meant to die until he's very old," Angelica told him. "That's why I have not been so very worried about his disappearance. But Maia has been pacing the chambers and I found her teary-eyed in the garden two days ago."

"Not until he's very old?" Voss considered the implication. Regeris wouldn't be pleased to hear that the vampire hunter would be searching for him for decades longer, and that anything he might do to destroy Woodmore would be in vain. But Voss couldn't be held accountable for fate. Just for supplying the information, and who would have believed he could have come by that tidbit?

And from such an impeccable source.

He could likely sell the information several times over, in fact. There were more than a few Draculia members who would like to see Woodmore dead—or at least to know how much longer they needed to look over their shoulders and sleep with proper protections. Other than Dimitri, with whom Woodmore had long allied himself for some inconceivable reason, and some of his comrades, their brethren across the Channel weren't quite as friendly with their enemy.

Not that Voss needed the money, of course—he had plenty to spare from his other ventures—but it would be quite fascinating to see how and what sort of remuneration he could cull from the parties interested in his news.

Always the game. It was the game that kept things exciting and challenging.

"And Maia."

He realized she'd been talking as he counted his compensation, and he looked over. Now her eyes were bleary, and one of them glistened with a tear.

"You see?" she said, looking at him, waiting for an answer, her voice high and tight. "You knew he was going to die, and yet you could do nothing."

A chill rushed over Voss as he realized she was speaking of Brickbank. He couldn't reply so he took a drink instead. Brickbank was dead and now he faced whatever judgment awaited.

Judgment.

"How would you feel if you lived with that knowledge, waiting for the day to happen? Knowing that one day, she or he would be wearing the clothes, and look the same, and the season would be right…and you would know it was the day. The day of death."

The day of death.

"I've known for years. And I can't tell them. I won't tell them. Do you see? Do you understand why?" Her tongue was loose and the words spilled forth and Voss could only listen.

A tear rolled down her cheek and she stopped. Her chest heaved from suppressed sobs and she simply looked at him. He sensed that she needed something. From him.

Somehow, through the never-ending pain that numbed his body, he managed to speak. "You're a very strong woman," he said. "To have that knowledge and to keep it to yourself. To live with it."

He thought of the knowledge he had, that he'd tricked and lied and deceived to gain over decades. Longer, even.

How he'd used it. How he'd profited from it.

How he'd hurt with it, ruining marriages and reputations. Pitting man against man. Friend against friend. Making money.

And that was even before he'd turned Dracule.

If there was a strong person in the room, it was not him.

Was that why Luce had chosen him?

"Strong?" She laughed bitterly and surprised him. "No one thinks of me as strong. Maia is strong. She's smart and beautiful and she knows just what she wants, and she has managed to get all of it. And soon, a handsome husband who loves her. And she's still a lady. Everyone likes her even though she's bossy. And me… Well, I am the silly one, the one who cannot be serious. The one who must be told everything to do for I cannot determine it myself. Sonia is sweet and kind and pretty. She's the youngest. But I…I'm nothing but a jest."

"I suspect," Voss said, groping for words, "that if Maia had lived through what you've seen and done in the last day, she would not have fared nearly as well. Did you think I hadn't noticed the wooden stick in your hand earlier today? You meant to defend yourself instead of crying and hiding in the corner."

Angelica smiled, swaying a little, and her lashes swept down over her eyes. For a moment he thought she was going to slump into unconsciousness, but she straightened and gave him such a heavy look that heat exploded in his chest.

"Thank you," she said and rose to her feet. Her movements were slow and deliberate, heavy with whiskey. His blood surged. His mouth dried.

Now.

She looked at Voss suddenly, directly, and drew in her breath. Then she spoke in a rush. "It's odd, being here with you. Alone."

With those innocent, emotional words, full awareness burst over him. Searing pain blasted anew inside his shoulder, radiating down his back and leg and along his arm in stunning agony.

Do it.

He must have gasped, for she moved toward him. "What is it?"

"No." He reacted without thought, turning away to hide the flame in his eyes and the swelling in his mouth. His cock shifted, filling. He imagined her naked, filling his hands with her. Tasting her.

It blazed on him, taking his breath and his voice. Pounded. Squeezed.

"Vo—my lord." Her voice was panicked. "What is it?"

"It's *nothing*," he said, forcing the lie from between clenched teeth with lungs that wouldn't move.

He couldn't breathe, couldn't think. There was nothing but white-hot, searing agony blazing through his body, seizing his mind. *Take, take, take.*

It wasn't the need to feed, to drink. It was her. All of her.

He felt her hand on his back, through the two layers of clothing against his Mark. Spinning away, he stumbled into the chair and table. He heard it fall and the clink of glasses and bottle. The smell of whiskey and wine, of Angelica and the layers of men before them in this room filled his nose, suffocating him.

Now, now, now.

She had her hands on him, she was half sobbing and shaking him, trying to get him to look at her and he knew, somehow, that if she saw his face, his eyes…

Her image filled his mind as his hands grasped the wooden planks of the floor. The pain. The pain was… impossible. Nothing like it.

Have to stop it.

His fangs thrust long and sharp. His cock hard and throbbing. His eyes hot and burning.

He knew. How to stop it.

He knew how to turn the agony into red pleasure.

His lungs worked again, deep and harsh. The floor was there beneath his knees, so close he could see the mouse dung, the dirt filling the cracks, a button, a thread caught on the splinter beneath his palm.

"My lord," she cried again, penetrating his concentration. "Voss."

She tugged at his shoulders, and he nearly snarled in response. His arms trembled with effort.

He had to stop it.

Angelica pulled at his shoulder, feeling the ripple of muscle beneath. "Voss," she said again, using his Christian name in an effort to get through to him. What was wrong? "Where's the pain?"

What sort of fit was this? The whiskey had dulled her senses, slowed her mind, but she pushed through it, sliding her hands over his shoulders, trying to tug him up.

At last, he moved, rolling aside, a forearm covering his face as he staggered to his feet, still half turned. She couldn't see his face, couldn't tell if he was still in pain—

"Angelica," he muttered, and turned, reaching for her.

She went into his arms and they closed around her. Tight, strong, comforting. His coat smelled like him, and she could feel his heart racing beneath the shirt under her cheek. His body overwhelmed her with its height and power, his face pressed into the top of her head. She felt him vibrating beneath her touch, his foot moving between hers, then his leg pushing into her skirts. His chest rising and falling as if he'd been running. His warmth.

Too warm. He felt feverish, and she tried to pull back

to look up into his face, but he wouldn't release her, his hands moving to grip the back of her head.

"Angelica," he said against her temple. His lips moved there, kissing her hair. His hands tightened, fingers curling up into her loose curls. He drew in a deep breath that she felt shudder throughout his body, as if he were preparing himself for some great feat.

"Are you all right?" she whispered. "What was it?"

He muttered something unintelligible, something like *Stop....* The next thing she knew, he was kissing her. His full, warm mouth moved along her temple to her cheek, and then suddenly covered her lips. Not gentle, not tentative, but as strong and certain as he was. The world circled and she clung to him, meeting his mouth and feeling the give of her lips against his, the intimate movement as they fit together and shifted and crushed. Hot and slick, his tongue slipped into her mouth and she allowed it, the rush of heat and sensation surprising her.

This...yes. Yes.

This was what she'd felt, she'd wanted. This was what his hot eyes had promised, this sort of deep, tingling pleasure that shot into her belly and tightened her nipples and spiraled lower. Lower, to where his leg pressed, hard and strong beneath her skirts. The pressure, the shift *there* in that most private of places. She swelled and filled and a soft little gasp escaped, just against his mouth.

Angelica closed her eyes and flattened her hands against his chest, her fingers just over the tops of his shoulders, sliding beneath his coat. The chair bumped behind her legs. She half stumbled, half fell into it, lost in the whirl of sensation. The whiskey and Voss were a potent combination, but she knew what she wanted.

He moved away, surprising her, leaving her in the chair and she sat up, dizzy and confused, and then felt his hands on her. He was standing behind the chair now, his palms sliding down the sides of her face...warm, strong, deliberate.

She tipped her head onto the back of the chair, and found that she looked up at him and the smoke-blackened ceiling. She saw the underside of his chin, long and curving and just becoming dark gold with stubble. A hint of his nose, and the tips of his thick hair, gilded by the low lamplight. He stood behind her, his hands easing to her shoulders, his fingers curving under her chin, his thumbs on the sides of her neck, his face, too, turned to the ceiling.

"Voss," she murmured, wondering why he'd moved away. The kissing had been delicious...but she wanted more. She was cold and bereft and curious about what lay beneath his shirt.

His fingers tightened over her skin and she felt each one of them imprinting on her throat, then they slid down...down over her collarbones and the hollow of her throat...into the bodice of her gown. Angelica gasped and tensed, but she found herself arching her shoulders back, the base of her skull resting on the top of the chair as she pushed up into his elegant hands.

He gave a soft, surprised laugh and bent to her temple, his lips warm and moist, intermingling with her hair as his fingers slipped down inside her corset and shift. They curved around her breasts, the corset tightening around her from behind, a gust of cooler air slipping over her encased flesh. Angelica closed her eyes against the revolving room and let herself *feel*.

One thumb shifted, brushing over a tight nipple and

she gasped and her eyes flew open, but his other hand moved and he gently squeezed her breasts. His fingers, long and sure, slid and caressed, and his thumbs…they moved around and over the very tops of her nipples. Her body tightened beneath his touch, tightened so hard it was nearly painful…yet she couldn't deny the ripples of pleasure that streaked down to her belly, over and over again until she realized she was moaning and sighing there in the chair.

"Voss," she muttered, reaching up to close her hands around his wrists, pressing them against her breasts, wanting *something* else…something *more*.…

His mouth was hot against her cheek and she felt him change, something shift. He muttered something she couldn't understand, something like a curse.

Then, a soft groan, his fingers tightening too much over her flesh, and then swiftly he moved again, yanking free. Suddenly he loomed in front of the chair, over her, dark and wild, his knee shoving into the seat next to her hip.

She looked up at him, saw his beautiful face dark and taut with pain. His hair, rich golden-brown, falling in his face, his lips parted, his eyes…burning.

Glowing.

Angelica gasped, but he surged down, gathering her close, burying his face in her neck, pulling her up by the shoulders with desperate hands. His mouth was hot and insistent, his lips hard, drawing on her flesh in that sensitive spot that made her shift and shudder as waves and ripples of sensation flooded her limbs. She clutched at him, feeling the strength of his leg next to hers, crowding her into the chair, let herself spiral into the lull of intense pleasure and then suddenly…*pain.*

She froze, tightening and bowing beneath him, her hands landing futilely on his powerful shoulders as she tried to twist away.

Like a prick, a smooth slide, and then the burst of heat…. Hot liquid surged from her skin, exploded from her vein. She felt him sigh and settle against her even as she froze, unable to move as he drank from her. A scream strangled in the back of her throat.

No.

She pushed at him, even as the warmth drained from her, tears filling her eyes, horror paralyzing her. Betrayal. Fear.

Not Voss was all she could think. *No.*

Dimly she let herself go and prayed he wouldn't kill her.

9

A Trust Is Betrayed

Voss hardly knew what he was doing until his incisors slid into her sweet, warm skin. And then…a burst of heat and pleasure like the shock of lightning. She flooded his mouth, filled him when he swallowed, and his body loosened.

The agony in his shoulder eased, and he could breathe again. He could almost think.

Relief. Oh, Luce, oh, God, *relief.*

He breathed Angelica, tasted her, touched and smelled the deepest, most intimate essence of her.

She convulsed beneath him, twitched in that way they did, and he felt the shock and horror as it shuttled through her. His eyes closed and he tasted, gulped the thick ambrosia and felt the resistance leave her. She sagged.

He trembled.

Stop.

No.

Enough.

The pain was gone, now that he'd given in, but because he'd begun, he wanted more. Not to feed...but all. He needed her, all of her. His vision still blazed red, his hands shook as they imprinted on her skin...but he turned his head away. Pulled free.

Somehow, somehow he released her, stumbled back, swiping at his mouth as if he were a child.

Blood streaked the back of his hand, the smell filled his nose, and he looked at her, fighting the pull, the tempting urge that threatened to draw him back.

Their eyes met: hers dull with shock and pain.

Voss wiped his mouth again, swallowed the last bit of her that remained on his tongue. He trembled, his knees weak. But he could breathe.

Blood streamed from the four bites on her shoulder, in that delicate, soft spot just above her collarbone. It trailed in two crooked lines down into the pink bodice of her gown.

Voss struggled to clear his thoughts, but the blood—the smell—it filled his mind. Her taste, the soft, smooth flesh under his.

He turned away. The pain in his Mark had eased, but he wanted more.

Silence, and then soft gasping sounds drew his attention. Her unsteady breath, not quite sobs. Holding on to the other chair, Voss turned back to see Angelica unmoving. Sitting, ravaged, her hair yanked to one side, cascading over her unwounded shoulder.

Blood, pumping from the punctures, glistening crimson and beckoning him.

He swallowed. Saliva pooled in his mouth, his cock still throbbed, filling his trousers. He closed his eyes for strength.

He had to…finish.

She reared back, flailing, when he reached for her, but he was too strong and he pulled her out of the chair, yanking her upright, ignoring her struggles.

He must.

She strangled out a scream, kicking, wild, but he trapped her between his legs and the chair, grabbed her head and forced it to the side. Her body heaved against his, soft mewling sobs, and her fingers trembled as they pressed into his shoulders.

He bent to the wounds, holding his breath, forcing himself to think of…something…other than the taste of her blood, the salty citrus of her skin, the feel of her curvy, womanly body struggling against his. The raging of his cock, straining to find her center.

Finish it.

With a deep groan of effort, he fit his mouth over the bites and slipped his tongue over the sleek skin, hot with blood and marred by the punctures. He was holding her too hard, his fingers biting into her skull and her shoulder as he slicked healing saliva over her wounds.

And then, with great effort, he thrust her from him, down into the chair and turned away.

Done.

Voss staggered away, wishing for the whiskey or the wine. Hardly aware of his surroundings, he fumbled with the latch on the door, vaguely remembering to leave the red string inside when he opened it—keep her safe—and then he stumbled out of the chamber.

Out, to freedom.

Angelica sat in the chair, unmoving, long after Voss staggered from the chamber.

She wasn't certain if she was afraid he would return... or afraid that he wouldn't.

The wounds on her neck had ceased to bleed, and although they pounded gently as if to remind her they were still there, she felt no real pain or discomfort. The last vestiges of pleasure and the effects of the whiskey had long fled her body, leaving her with the ugly realization.

Voss was a *vampir*.

Some time later, when the sounds beyond the walls of this small, filthy chamber grew louder and more raucous, she stood and moved to the door through which he'd disappeared. Even through the fog of shock and horror, she knew that beyond this door, in the corridor, was a place no lady should ever be.

Yet another violation he'd visited upon her reputation. It would be God's miracle if she came out of this alive, and without being ruined.

Tears, hot and angry more than pained, rolled from her eyes as she pulled at the latch. She wasn't going to wait for him to return and do whatever he wished. She'd take her chances out there.

Surely someone would help her call for a hack. Or even send a message for assistance.

The latch clunked aside. She opened the door to peer out into the corridor and found herself face-to-face with Voss, who stood directly outside.

Angelica gave a little gasp and reared back.

His eyes went to her neck, where her hand had flown to cover the marks there. "Stay in there," was all he said. "I've sent for Corvindale."

And he shut the door.

Narcise Moldavi stared out the window of the inn, watching the grooms in the stable yard below. The sun still sat upon the horizon, fat and orange and taunting. So slow to go to bed. It would be more than another hour before they could be on the road again. And until then, she would observe the courtyard, watching for any sign of familiar horses or persons.

She gripped the shutter and tried not to think about Cezar and what he would do if he found them. Whether he believed she was dead or alive, or had gone willingly or unwillingly, he wouldn't rest until he found Chas.

For Chas had humiliated him by taking her—his prized possession. And the last thing Cezar would suffer was being humiliated, by anyone. He'd had enough of that in his youth. And now as a Dracule, he had the means and the power to fight back. Unfortunately he took his fury out on the innocent as well as anyone who'd even done an imagined slight to him.

She suspected that, despite having been alive for more than a hundred years, Cezar still couldn't grow beyond the strange, weak boy he'd been.

Thank the Fates she was away from him now.

Her fingers tightened and she leaned her cheek against the edge of the wooden shutter. Chas had risked so much for her. How would she ever repay him?

How could she?

As if her thoughts had beckoned, the door to the room they'd let opened. Heart pounding, Narcise turned, her muscles bunching and ready. She didn't relax until she smelled him and recognized his lean, feline form slipping through the opening. Like a shadow, with his Gypsy skin and hair, and ebony eyes, Chas moved and hid in the night as easily as a Dracule.

"Still watching?" he asked, closing the door. His eyes

met hers and she gave a little shiver of pleasure and anticipation.

What sort of fool was she, a vampire consorting with a vampire hunter?

A very delighted fool, in fact.

She nodded and returned his question, and expression, with a smile of which he would only see a hint in the dim light. The single lamp's low flame flickered in the corner, casting long, sensual golden shadows.

But he would understand the message.

A shout in the courtyard below drew her attention and she turned back, watching with interest as two grooms fought with a high-spirited stallion that apparently didn't wish to be saddled. Narcise found herself more than a bit sympathetic for the beast.

Cezar wouldn't expect her to ever return to England, but even if he did, Chas had assured her that he'd never find them where he was taking her—to a small estate in Wales. He'd recently purchased it anonymously through a man of business. But if Bonaparte did invade, what would happen then?

She felt Chas move behind her, and then his hand was there, smoothing a long lock of her hair away from her face to behind her shoulder. His other hand slid around to her belly and then angled up to cover one of her breasts.

As he bent to kiss the side of her neck, in a place that so many others had known, Narcise sighed and reached behind to touch his thick hair. Her breast lifted into his hand and she felt the gentle massage through the man's shirt she wore.

As the heat rushed through her body, her breathing rose and her fangs slid free. She was aware of the tightening of her nipples, now being pleasured on both sides by Chas's long, skillful fingers. He pressed into her from behind, his muscular arms enclosing her, pulling her back against powerful thighs and an unmistakable hardness.

When she rolled her backside into him, around and against the hard ridge, Chas rumbled a deep laugh into her ear and moved a hand down to press between her legs. The tight riding breeches she wore left little protection from his questing fingers as they slid down and around, cupping her quim. Narcise shifted with a husky little groan, pleasure billowing through her like a tufting cloud. Warm and sleek, she swelled and filled there beneath his hand, her head sagging back against his chest.

Nothing like the countless other times, with digging fangs and rough hands in darkness.

This was hot and red and she finally had enough, turning abruptly in his arms. Their mouths met, clashing fiercely and then subsided into gentle, slick kisses.

When she pulled away, her fangs thrusting, needy, from her mouth, she moved into his arms. His skin was warm and salty, smelled and tasted of wool damp from rain and the smoke of the fireplace below. Her tongue swiped his neck and she slid the outside of her incisors along his skin as she nibbled, not penetrating, not yet.

He shivered, trembling against her and she reached between them for the raging cock. It was hot and heavy in her palm, and he groaned when she pulled it free, stroking the head with its own little drop of pleasure.

The tendons in his neck tightened beneath her lips and she felt the rush of blood in his veins against her tongue. Her gums had swollen, and they hurt, thrusting her teeth so hard, but she didn't sink her fangs into that hot brown skin.

"Narcise," he groaned, pulling her face up to meet his. Their mouths met again, fierce and hungry as he pulled at the flap of her breeches, yanking the square of buttons loose.

Her sharp tooth sliced his lip and warm blood slicked her mouth and his. Rich and lush, just enough to tease and to send desire raging through her, and she kissed him deeper.

He smiled against her mouth and pulled away long enough to murmur, "Tease."

She smiled back and sucked hard on his full, lower lip just as he managed to pull her trousers away, yanking them down past her knees. "That's all I need," she said as they tipped onto the bed.

He gave a soft, pained laugh as she straddled him, her breeches clinging to only one leg. Her hands settled onto his shirt, for he was still fully clothed. Narcise looked down into his hot, focused eyes and slicked her tongue over her lips and the jut of her fangs as she curled her fingers around his erection. Chas tensed and his eyes narrowed in pleasure.

Then she shifted and rose and slipped him inside—the hot, hard length of him. She sighed as he filled her, touching her deep inside in that place…and the tremors of pleasure shook inside her, bursting into heat that flushed through her body. *Ah.*

Chas groaned, tipping his head back, the tendons in his neck and throat taut and inviting. She shifted, moving her hips slowly, purposely out of rhythm, teasing him just as he was teasing her. One of his hands reached up to pull at her loose shirt, closing over one of her breasts, and his thumb found the jut of her nipple. Pleasure panged in her belly and down as he gently twisted and stroked.

Narcise shifted again, moving up and down and around and he opened his eyes. "Damn you," he gasped, looking up with glittering eyes. "Do it."

She smiled and planted her hands on his heaving chest, feeling the slide of muscle there and the power of his lethal hands on her hips as he helped her in the rise and fall, the sleek slide. Long and easy, as if they were out for an evening ride.

She bent forward, her face near his, the blood on his lower lip glistening. His breath puffed into her cheek, his hands solid at her hips, his own hips moving up to meet hers.

"Do it," he whispered, turning his face away.

She shifted, scraping her incisors against the smooth heat of his skin, felt his breathing change as he waited for her to sink in. She licked the salt of his flesh, nibbled at the rise of the taut muscle in his throat, felt him tense everywhere…the shift of his breath as he waited.

"No," she whispered, deep in his ear, and thrust her tongue inside as an apology.

"Narcise," he begged.

"You don't want me to," she told him, tasting his lip again, knowing it was the truth. Knowing how he always hated himself after.

Please. His mouth formed the word against her cheek, but she pulled up and away and yanked off her shirt.

Her breasts were free and high, and his hands closed on them. She bent forward for one more swipe over his bloodied lip and then let herself go…increasing the rhythm, lifting her hands above her head as they shifted and slammed together.

She cried out first, the taste of his blood mingled with her own as she bit her lip, his mouth suddenly fastened onto one of her nipples. Her body tightened around his, and he arched beneath her in a final exertion and heartfelt groan.

"Mmm," he said as she shifted to the side, collapsing next to his warm, still-clothed body. A lean hand stroked along her hip and he turned toward her. "What a fool am I," he murmured in a voice not quite low enough to hide the wryness. "Taking up with a vampire."

She closed her eyes, but stretched like a waking cat beneath his hand. Being touched with gentleness was something she craved more than he could understand. "I'm not certain who is more the fool, Chas. The hunter or the hunted." She heard rather than saw him smile, and sensed the cynicism there.

He shifted next to her and sat up. "There is something I must tell you."

Narcise's heart skipped but she kept her eyes closed, kept her body languid. It had been a matter of self-preservation to learn that skill. "You're going to confess how many Dracule you've killed?"

"I've lost count," he replied, an answering hint of humor there. "But you needn't fear I'll turn on you. I've no energy left after this last bout." His hand had stopped stroking her hip and now he moved it away from where it had rested on her waist. "I'm meeting someone below."

Narcise's eyes flew open. "What?" He'd promised he'd keep their whereabouts secret. Completely secret. That he'd tell no one they were in England, let alone where they were. "Chas, what have you done?"

He sat up fully and looked down at her. "I have three sisters. I have to—"

"But Dimitri is seeing to them—and isn't one in a convent school? Cezar will never get past either Dimitri or the holy walls."

Chas was nodding. "Yes, but I must at least let them know I'm alive. And I need to know that they've been taken care of. I assure you, no one will be the wiser to our presence here. Only one person knows of the meeting, and I trust Cale with my life."

Giordan? Narcise's heart stopped. *No.*

"Perhaps you don't remember Giordan Cale, but he's a confidant of Dimitri. Not titled, but rich as Croesus and—" he gave a gentle laugh "—more than a match for me. I met him when I sneaked in to stake him. Obviously, we both lived."

Narcise found her voice. "Obviously." And just as obviously, one thing Chas didn't know was the history between Cezar and Giordan. And her.

"I can meet him below, but it wouldn't be as private if I asked him up here," Chas was saying. "Less chance of us being seen."

She couldn't swallow. That was the very last thing she wanted or needed: her former lover meeting with her current lover. In this very room, where the smell of their relations permeated the chamber, the sheets, the air.

"No," was all she said.

He measured her with his look. "Very well, Narcise."

And she wondered, then, if after all, he did know.

10

CORVINDALE'S CHAMBERS INVADED

The Earl of Corvindale swept into the chamber like a violent storm.

Angelica leaped up from her seat on the chair—not the chair on which Voss had…oh, God, on which he'd attacked her, but the other one.

Corvindale scanned the room quickly, then looked at her with dark, piercing eyes. "You're unhurt?"

Angelica nodded, catching herself before reaching toward the soreness at her neck. Despite the fact that it was *his,* she'd pulled the cloak Voss had left up and around her shoulders, hiding the bite marks and dried blood.

Without another word, Corvindale gestured to the door through which he'd come and she walked toward it. Her heart felt heavy and her head pounded, and she wished for nothing more than to quit this place.

She was relieved that Voss was nowhere to be found as she stepped into the corridor; not that she'd expected him to be, considering what she knew about his interactions with Corvindale. The back of her throat burned and tears threatened her eyes. *How could he?*

"Angelica!" cried a voice, and the next thing she knew, Maia had enveloped her in a crushing hug.

"Blast it, Miss Woodmore," Corvindale snapped. "I told you to remain in the bloody carriage." Pausing to glare at two dishonorable-looking men who'd appeared from around a corner, he urged them down the narrow, dirty hall and gestured even more sharply than he had in the chamber a moment before. "Can you not listen to reason for one moment?"

"It's *my* sister we've come to retrieve," Maia shot back. Her arm curved tight around Angelica's waist as she propelled her down the corridor ahead of the furious earl. Uncharacteristically, Maia's chestnut-auburn hair was in disarray and she was not only dressed in an old daydress, but she was also *gloveless*. "And leaving that aside, what harm could come to me when you are here, my lord?"

Even through the mix of emotions that whirled in her mind, Angelica heard the dip of sarcasm in Maia's voice.

"This is no place for a lady." Corvindale reached past them to fling the external door open. Only a bit more illumination filtered into the hall, for it was well past twilight now. "Devil take it, Miss Woodmore. Do you have a complete lack of sense?"

Maia sniffed and pushed past him out into the darkness, pulling Angelica with her. In her haste, she narrowly avoided a puddle of something disgusting and climbed into the carriage with her sister's help. Maia settled in the seat next to her.

Corvindale spoke to the groom then joined them inside, taking up nearly the entire seat across from them with his wide shoulders and arms stretched across the back. His long legs were tucked into the space between Maia's skirts and the side of the vehicle. The door closed and with barely a jolt, they started off.

"You're not hurt?" Maia was asking as Angelica tried to bury herself in the corner of the seat, huddling beneath the cloak that smelled of Voss. The scent was both nauseating and familiar. "What happened? Where have you been?"

But Angelica didn't wish to talk. Now that she was safe, all she wanted to do was curl up in a corner and cry.

"Angelica," Maia said, tugging at the cloak as if to draw her attention.

Angelica clutched it tighter, partly because she was chilled and partly because she sensed that it would not bode well if Maia or the earl saw the marks on her neck. There would be more questions, more demands and remonstrations, along with pity and sympathy. None of which she wanted to contend with. "Miss Woodmore," Corvindale broke in icily, "perhaps you might leave your sister to her own thoughts. It's clear, at least to me, that she is in no humor to speak at this time."

Angelica felt Maia's outrage and eyed her sister with interest. It wasn't often that she received a set-down, and even more rare that she would decline to respond in her own bitingly proper way. But to her surprise, she merely turned away from the earl and redoubled her efforts to get Angelica to answer her questions.

The drive to Blackmont Hall took much too long, in Angelica's estimation, but she managed to appease her elder sister's demands by giving brief, vague answers to some of her questions. The night was dark, for clouds filtered across the portion of the moon that was showing, and even the streetlamps gave off weak illumination. She could hardly wait to climb out of the carriage and find the sanctuary of her own chamber—or at least, the one that had been allotted to her during their stay with Corvindale.

The thought brought her brother to mind, and Angelica once again felt confusion and surprise at what Voss had told her about Chas.

But the peace she sought was not to be, for no sooner had they stepped into the foyer of the grand but sober house than the earl turned to her. "Angelica," he said. "A word if I may."

Angelica didn't like the expression on his face. It wasn't frightening so much as fearsome: tight and dark, as if he were about to explode with some great fury. She knew that it wasn't directed at her, but regardless, his countenance gave her pause, made her more than a bit apprehensive. "Of course, my lord," she said, and started down the corridor in the direction he gestured.

"If you'll excuse us, Miss Woodmore," he said behind her.

"But—" Maia's voice, strained and just as furious as his expression, was cut off by the earl.

"I will speak to your sister, my *ward,* in private, Miss Woodmore. Perhaps just this one time, you will accede to my orders."

"I wish to be present. I *will* be present," she replied. "She may be your ward temporarily, but she is my sister. Once Mr. Bradington and I are wed—"

"Maia," said Angelica, strangely relieved that her sister wouldn't be there during the interrogation that was sure to come, "I will come directly to your chamber when Lord Corvindale and I are finished."

"Angelica," Maia said in a heartfelt whisper, "I want to be there with you."

Angelica turned to look at her elder sister, who stood as if a bucket of cold water had been thrown on her. "I'm sorry, but it will be easier if you are not. I promise I will come to you straight away."

Maia met her eyes, and Angelica nearly gave in. Her sister seemed not only shocked and saddened but hurt, as well. And she realized at that moment that somehow, Maia felt as if she'd failed her. Somehow, she felt responsible for what had happened.

"As you like," Maia said at last, and then turned away.

The earl gave Angelica a brief nod of gratitude and opened the door she knew led to his study. Once inside, he closed the door, but not all the way.

This brought a bit of a dark smile to her lips. "I appreciate the attention to propriety, my lord, but it's a bit late to be worried about that now."

His face darkened. "Take off that damned cloak and let me see what he's done."

Angelica shouldn't have been surprised that he knew, but she was. The cloak fell away and the earl leaned closer so that he could see her neck.

"Anywhere else?" he asked, shifting back.

She shook her head.

"Anywhere else?" he asked again, looking both distinctly uncomfortable and darkly furious at the same time.

"No." Then she realized what he was asking. "I am… intact." Her cheeks heated but she ignored it.

"By Fate, I'll kill him if your brother doesn't first," Corvindale said, stalking over to the massive desk. A vase holding a collection of roses and lilies sat there, and he paused, staring at it as if it were some foul object. "But I'll make it quick instead of painful."

"Now that you have introduced the topic…" Angelica said, gathering her courage. Corvindale was intimidating in his demeanor, and there was no reason he wouldn't turn his anger on her if she annoyed him, but she would try.

After all, he hadn't yet beheaded Maia.

"Is it true that Chas has gone off with a vampire woman?"

Corvindale cursed, and didn't even attempt to hide the fact that he said something terribly improper. "What else did he tell you?"

"He told me that Cezar Mol…davi, I believe it is, wants to kill Chas and that's why Maia and I are in danger. He wants to use us as ransom. Cezar is one of those horrid monsters, too."

The earl had picked up the slender vase with the flowers in it and now he stalked over to the other end of the study. With a quiet, forceful clunk, he set the vase on a table near the window. "What he told you is true, surprisingly enough. Dewhurst isn't known for his candor. What else did he tell you?"

"Little else. Is my brother truly in danger?" Despite the fact that she'd foreseen Chas's death many years in the future, after all of the upheaval in the last days, Angelica needed reassurance. It was possible that things could change, wasn't it?

"Your brother is more than capable of taking care of himself," Corvindale replied in the most gentle voice she'd heard him use. Which was to say, it was neither loud, sharp, nor harsh…but it wasn't particularly kind by normal standards. "Did Dewhurst not tell you about him?"

"What do you mean?"

The earl shook his head. "It's best that I keep his confidence. But when next we see him—and I am confident we will—I'll insist he tell you and Miss Woodmore the truth."

"Dewhurst said that he might have eloped with Cezar's sister. He wouldn't—couldn't—*marry* one of those monsters, would he?"

Corvindale's face was a study in stonework. "I cannot say what your brother's intention would be, but I sincerely doubt marriage is a possibility. The thought is absurd." He'd walked back toward the desk, then turned and looked at her once again. "Is there anything else you wish to tell me?"

She took that as an invitation to tell him the details of what happened at Rubey's, and his face grew darker. But he said nothing else, other than, "Anything else?"

As if his demeanor invited confidences. Angelica closed her eyes, suddenly weary and heartsick again. "No. May I be excused now, my lord? I would like nothing better than to lie down."

His expression eased slightly, making him look almost handsome. "Yes, go. Tell Mrs. Hunburgh you are to have a bath sent to your chamber."

Angelica left the study and closed the door behind her. She didn't pause to ring for the housekeeper, nor did she go to her chamber. Instead she found her way to Maia's room and opened the ajar door to find her sister pacing the floor.

"At last," she said, rushing to embrace Angelica again. "My darling, I've been so worried for you."

Taking care to keep her marked neck covered by her hair, Angelica hugged her sister back and then allowed the tears to explode.

The peremptory knocking jolted Dimitri from an uneasy sleep, strewn with images and memories he'd much prefer to forget.

He opened his eyes, wondering where in hell his valet was, and rolled over onto his swollen shoulder, twisting in the already amassed sheets. He was as used to the incessant burning as one could become to white-hot pain, but the added pressure sent a sharp, jagged jolt down his hips and legs and he muttered a curse.

Now he was fully awake. And Lucifer's blade, a line of bright light peeked through the shutters of the far window. It was bloody *midday*. Who in the name of blind Fate was banging on his door and where in the burning hell was Greevely to stop them?

"Corvindale!" The voice was familiar and bossy and feminine and had Dimitri bolting up in bed. "I must speak with you!"

Miss Woodmore. He was so furious he couldn't grasp an appropriate curse and instead bellowed, "Go away."

The door *cracked open*. "Corvindale, I must speak with you. It's nearly two o'clock and I've been waiting all morning—"

He was going to kill Chas Woodmore. There were so many ways to do so to a mortal, and he was going to find the one that took the longest. And if Cezar Moldavi happened to beat him to it, Dimitri was going to stake himself just so he could find Woodmore in the afterlife and murder him again.

"Go away, Miss Woodmore," he said again. She

hadn't yet peeked around the door, but he suspected it wouldn't be long before she did, propriety be damned. "If you must speak with me, you can wait until this evening." After he'd finished his first full day's sleep in more than a week. Even then, he had no intention of allowing Miss Woodmore to keep him from his most pressing task: to find Voss and fling him onto a stake.

The door opened further, but revealed nothing of the irksome woman but her voice. "Corvindale! It's imperative that I speak with you. This is a matter that cannot wait, and if you do not come out then I will come in."

Who in Lucifer's world did she think she was?

Dimitri, who of course slept in nothing but his own skin, flattened his lips and made to rise from the bed. He was no fool; she would make good on her threat and then...

Blast it—why not? Perhaps it would put the fear of God, or something, into the chit. It would serve her right.

"I am abed, Miss Woodmore, and have no intention of leaving it. If you insist upon speaking with me at this time, then don't let something as ridiculous as propriety keep you out."

Arranging the sheets so that they at least covered the bare minimum of his dark, hirsute and scarred body, Dimitri settled back against his pillow and waited. Which would win out for Miss Woodmore, propriety or determination?

Or would mere obstinacy drive her actions?

The door inched open a bit more and her fingers came around its edge. "My lord, I must speak with you regarding Angelica."

A contrary smile curved his lips. "I'm afraid you'll have to come in. I can't hear what you are saying."

The door jerked in her hand, and Dimitri's smile became more pleased. *Now go away and let me sleep.*

Even though he didn't particularly wish to revisit the dream he'd recently grappled with, that would be better than the alternative.

But then the door opened and there in the doorway stood Miss Woodmore. Defiance blazed from her very properly dressed and coiffed person. Her chin was raised and her full lips tight. She glanced at him once, then swiftly looked away, and even from his position half across the chamber, he could see the flush that darkened her cheeks.

"This is exceedingly untoward," she announced.

"What is it, Miss Woodmore?" he couldn't help but taunt. "Surely the sight of a man's torso isn't all that upsetting to a woman who is due to be married in short order." It was, he acknowledged privately and a bit maliciously, a rather fine specimen of a torso—notwithstanding the amount of dark hair covering it.

"You could cover yourself," she said from between unmoving jaws.

Dimitri was nearly enjoying himself. Nearly. But despite her discomfort, this entire situation was the outside of unpleasant, and he wished to end it as soon as he could. Nevertheless, he replied, "I see no reason to do so. Now what is it you must speak with me about?"

Her jaw moved but she steadfastly refused to look at him. "It's Angelica. She has been bitten by a…by one of those creatures that came to the masquerade ball. *Vampires.* And she had horrible nightmares last night, my lord. I held her all night long, and she cried and thrashed."

Luce's filthy stick.

"She won't tell me what happened, but I fear that the worst has been done. Not to mention…"

Was it possible that Miss Woodmore's voice had broken? Had cracked with emotion? Dimitri looked closely at her, wishing she would turn in his direction again. He was certain she'd been peeking from the corner of her eye.

"I'm aware of all that you've told me. And if you find it reassuring, your sister has assured me that…er…there is no reason to demand satisfaction or that Dewhurst come up to snuff. She is intact."

"Up to snuff? I should hope not!" Miss Woodmore exclaimed, forgetting herself and glancing at him. "Even if he did—well…I would *never*… Chas would *never*… allow him to come near her again." The choked-up emotion had left her voice and was now replaced by outrage.

"You seem to have forgotten that *I* am Angelica's guardian at this time," Dimitri said, just because it was strictly true.

His reminder seemed to have the desired effect, for her cheeks flushed even more and her dark eyes flashed. "As I said, my lord, *I* would not allow it."

He shifted purposely, and she looked away again. Her lips were so tight they were probably sheet-white, though he was too far away and it was too dim to see that sort of detail.

"What is my brother doing? How long has he been involved with these creatures? And what is *your* involvement, my lord? Do you associate with them, as well? Did you know that Dewhurst was one of them?"

"Do not concern yourself with me or the other details, Miss Woodmore. All you need know is that you and your sisters are safe under my care, here at Black-

mont Hall and at St. Bridies, too. As for your brother…
When he returns, I'm certain that he will answer at least
some of your questions. And I am hopeful he will do so
in short order. Now, is there anything else, Miss Woodmore? This conversation hardly seems worth interrupting my sleep and threatening your reputation. Or is that
not a concern for you, now that you are off the marriage mart?"

She snapped upright and once again turned to look
at him. This time, she seemed to have somehow girded
herself, for she didn't waver as she met his eyes head-
on. "You are beyond vile, Lord Corvindale."

It was painful, but he managed a smirk. She had no
idea how accurate that statement was.

"I insisted on speaking with you because I felt you
should know all of the information. I had hoped you'd
do the courtesy of telling me what is happening and
why. But apparently you cannot be bothered to do even
that." She drew her shoulders back, which had the effect of thrusting out her rather noticeable bosom, but that
lovely picture was ruined by the glare in her eyes and
the hand on her hip. "I also wanted to speak with you
because it will be of the utmost importance that Angelica is seen out and in Society as soon as possible so as
to combat any rumors or *on dits* that might have begun
since the masquerade. That is the only way to preserve
her reputation."

"And this concerns me, how?"

She didn't move except for an unpleasant twitch of
her lips. "Because you must be seen out and about with
us. Quite a lot. In the next few days. In order to ensure
that Angelica's reputation isn't besmirched, we will need
the presence of an earl."

She turned to go, presenting him with her slender back and long, ivory neck and then paused to look over her shoulder. "I shall determine which invitations we will accept and then give them to your valet so that he can see you are properly dressed for the occasions."

With that, she walked out of his chamber and closed the door with finality.

Voss rolled over and opened his eyes. He found himself lying in a massive bed of twisted sheets next to a great, yellow pool of sunshine. He froze and eased back, wondering who'd left the blasted shutters open. At the same time, he realized that his head pounded and the room was altogether unsteady. His mouth felt as if he'd been sucking on a piece of rag all night.

But by now he'd seen that he wasn't in his own chamber, nor was he at Rubey's, or even anywhere he recognized. The window was wide-open and not only did the sun pour in, but so did fresh summer air. Blasted *birds* chirping outside. A table next to the bed held three bottles—empty, or nearly so, based on the smell of whiskey that permeated the chamber as well as the pain in his temples and the vague wisp of memory.

A pool of dark liquid had dried on the table, and the residue of red-brown lined the bottom of one of the glasses. His stomach shifted alarmingly when he recognized it.

Gingerly Voss settled back down and rolled in the other direction. When he saw the white shoulder rising from amid the blankets, and the pool of dark hair…and the red marks on her neck, he remembered.

For a moment, panic seized him. Was she dead?

He tried to focus, tried to slice through the fog and

remember…. Oh, Luce, it had been a whirlwind of heat and pleasure and feeding laced with horrible wildness. He remembered finding her at Bartholomew Fair, and because she had exotic eyes and wavy dark hair, he'd enticed her away with a pouch of coin.

But the frenzy of feeding…the blood whiskey…the animal that had taken hold of him… It was all dark and hellish. Voss chose to reach for her shoulder instead of the chamber pot when his stomach heaved, and when he touched, not icy flesh but warm skin, he exhaled.

Thank you.

He wasn't certain whom he was thanking. Or why.

She shifted and stirred and he saw more marks on her shoulder, her arm, her throat. By Luce, it was a miracle she wasn't dead.

Nauseated, Voss stumbled from the bed, relegated to climbing over the foot so as to avoid both the deadly sunshine and also the woman next to him.

That was when he realized, with distaste, that he still wore his clothing. A night of debauchery and still fully dressed. His white shirt was bloodstained, his neckcloth crooked and forlorn, but hanging from his throat, his pantaloon flap undone but the waist settled at his hips.

Even his damned boots were still on his feet.

At least he didn't remember any of his dreams.

He looked at the door and around the chamber and realized he was trapped by the sunshine. There was no way to reach the shutters and close them, nor to make his way to the door without walking through a pool of light.

For a moment he thought about doing it anyway, walking into the warmth and allowing it to touch his skin. Could the pain be any worse than what he'd felt yesterday, when he'd been with Angelica?

He'd wanted her so badly. And Lucifer knew it, and had made it impossible for him to resist.

At the memory of her stricken, accusing face, the nausea rushed through him again. The loathing that had been there. The devastation in those bright, wise eyes.

What else could he have done? He'd been in agony. The pain had been so unbearable, he would have gone mad if he'd had to live another moment with it.

Hell, he *had* gone mad. Mad with need and desire.

A glance at his sleeping bed partner reminded him of how easy it had been to entice her. If his thrall had worked with Angelica, she would be the one in his bed right now.

He would have pleasured her, too.

Instead he'd frightened and disgusted her. And she certainly wouldn't be of any willing assistance to him now.

Much as he hated the thought, he'd best leave England straight away. After this, Woodmore and Corvindale would be on his trail, after his heart. Voss preferred to keep his life as free of violence as possible, and if they found him, there was more than a chance he might actually get hurt.

Especially if the two were together.

So he would have to depart London and go somewhere else for civilization and culture. Rome. Lisbon. Perhaps Barcelona, where he could make a deal with Regeris. Definitely not back to the Colonies.

Frowning, his knees weak and his world spinning—not to mention the foul taste in his mouth—Voss snatched up a pillow and, sliding his hands into the case, held it up as a shield and rushed through the sunbeam. It burned where it caught a slice of his wrist and wavered over a segment of his temple, but he made it into the shadows on the other side of the lethal light.

He no longer had his double-lined cloak that worked so well to keep every bit of the sun from him, and now when he left this chamber in the boardinghouse, he'd be vulnerable to the light.

But he had to leave. He wanted to get away from this room, the smell of stale blood and spilled whiskey and sex, and be somewhere else. And the problems between France and England wouldn't keep a Dracule from making his way across the Channel and going where he wished. That was the least of his concerns.

Voss glanced at the woman, who'd begun to snore delicately. Definitely not dead, and for some reason, he was relieved yet again. She had given him a good ride last evening, and been very generous with all of her bodily fluids. Perhaps he hadn't compensated her enough. He jammed his hand into the pocket of his coat and found another guinea.

As he pulled out the coin, his glove came with it and Voss paused, suddenly paralyzed by a thought. A glove.

His glove.

Angelica had been holding his glove when he opened the carriage door for her.

Did she know that he was going to die?

"What are you doing here, Voss?" Rubey's blue eyes peered through the small door panel. They weren't kind nor welcoming in the least. In fact, he'd never seen them so cold.

"Won't you let me in?" Voss wheedled, and allowed a bit of that enticing glow into his eyes. "I just want to talk with you, Rubey, darling." The weight of the sunshine beat down on the hooded cloak he'd stolen from the front closet of the boardinghouse, and although it didn't touch him directly, he could feel it like a heavy hand. "Perhaps a bit of tête-à-tête, too. I know how you like—"

"No," she said, and made to slide the door panel closed.

"Wait, Rubey. Please," he said, panic in his voice, jamming his hand into the slot. "I haven't anywhere else to go, and I need to talk with someone. And the sun—"

"Dimitri was here. He and Giordan. Looking for you. Sure as the sun, they're going to kill you when they find you."

A little prickle skittered down his spine. "Angelica? Is she... Did they say anything about her?"

"So it is about Angelica." The blue eyes narrowed thoughtfully, and the small panel remained half open. Then she shook her head. "No, Voss. The last time I let you sugar-talk me into something I shouldn't have, you know what happened."

"I am sorry about the maid," Voss said, removing his hand so he could adjust the slipping cloak.

"You're only saying that because you want me to change my mind."

Voss paused, then smiled in chagrin. It was true. He hadn't given the maid much thought. "I am sorry," he said again, and this time, he did mean it—especially when he thought that it could have been Angelica there in bloody ribbons. "Please, Rubey. You know how it pains me to beg."

That brought a laugh and a bit of reluctant sparkle to her eyes. "That's not strictly true, Voss, darling. I seem to remember that time you took me to Paris and there was more than a bit of begging going on...on your end."

But even that memory—as pleasant as it was—failed to bring a smile to his lips. "Rubey. As a friend, I ask you to let me in. You're one of the wisest people I know. And I need to talk to a wise person." And it wasn't as if Dimitri was going to have a conversation with him that didn't involve a stake or a sword.

The little slot slammed shut and for a moment Voss thought he'd overdone it, but then the door opened and Rubey was there, gesturing angrily. He stepped into the foyer of her private home, the same place that had been violated by the vampires only yesterday.

Or was it the day before? Lucifer's burning soul, he'd lost track of the time since he and Angelica had been at Black Maude's.

"If they come back, I'm not going to lie," Rubey was saying as she slammed the door shut and locked it. Three locks and a heavy slab of wood across it. "I'll tell them you were here, and gladly, Voss."

He noticed fresh marks on her shoulder. "I see that you've been entertaining Cale."

Rubey tossed him a sidewise look. "Giordan and I have an understanding, and don't try to pretend that it's of any concern to you. If it ever was—of which I have immeasurable doubt—that was ten years ago when we first met."

Voss felt the edges of his eyes crinkle in a smile. He didn't need to make any other reply. She was right and they both knew it.

"As you're risking your life being here, I rather suppose we ought to get on with whatever you needed to speak to me about," Rubey said.

"Did Corvindale say anything about Angelica?" he asked, surprising himself, for that was not what he'd intended to say. His only concern was whether the chit had somehow died. "You never did tell me."

"No, he merely commanded me to tell him where you were."

"Perhaps Cale said something further during your... er...pillow talk?"

Rubey gave him a slow smile. "Now, Voss, you know that there's very little time—or energy—for mere talk when I am thus engaged." Then the smile went away and that shrewdness came back in her eyes. "You are concerned for her, aren't you? Isn't that odd for you, Voss? Or is it merely because you know that if she's dead, Dimitri and Chas will be even more intent on sending you to join your friend Brickbank in hell? I wonder what it's like down there, being with Lucifer all the time. Don't you, Voss? At least—"

"Enough," Voss said, uncertain why her taunting annoyed him so. He showed a bit of fang to let her know he was damned serious.

She sobered and gestured to a chair. "Very well, then. Here I am, the wisest woman you know, at your disposal for whatever it is that's on your conscience." Then she laughed. "Oh, dear. Did I truly say that? When have you—or any of you—ever had a conscience?"

Voss felt his eyes warm with a deeper glow and he didn't bother to retract his incisors. And then, suddenly, his annoyance faded. It was replaced by something he didn't recognize, some odd, empty emotion.

"Voss, I am expecting Giordan again shortly. Perhaps you'd like to conduct this conversation now, before he arrives?"

"You're going to die," he said. Her eyes widened,

and he continued, "Someday. You and everyone you know…except us."

Rubey nodded, eyeing him as if he were a mouse. Voss happened to know that, while she had less than a fondness for rodents, she wasn't particularly frightened of them. Which was probably just about how she felt about him. "Everyone dies," she said in an eerie echo of Angelica. "Except the Draculia. And even then…well, that fierce Chas Woodmore has seen to the demise of more than a few of your brethren."

Voss didn't say anything for a moment. He'd battled his way in here because he needed to talk to someone, and it wasn't possible to talk to Angelica without abducting her again.… But he didn't quite understand what he wanted from Rubey.

But he knew he wanted—needed—something. Direction. Wisdom. Hope?

What was happening to him?

Somehow, she seemed to sense what was on his mind. "You Dracule, you prize your immortality and live for centuries, but I've never understood why. I think I should find it lonely and monotonous after a time." She leaned forward in her chair, affording him a generous view down her bodice, corset *and* shift. But even that delightful sight didn't distract him because she was speaking thoughts he'd always tried to ignore. "Giordan offered to make me Dracule. He suggested that if he did, I could be Rubey's proprietress forever. I told him I didn't want to do anything forever."

"Not even live?"

But what happens when you die?

She shook her head. "It's unnatural, living forever. *Nothing* lives forever. Nothing, Voss. Only the demon who made you this way, made you unnatural. Look at how you must live—by feeding on other living beings. I have often wondered why he would do such a thing, but I've come to believe it's because it ties you more tightly to him. You take from your own race. You must. What sort of creature is he that makes you take life from your brethren to live? It's interesting, and frightening. Like copulating, the very act can be intimate and pleasurable…or it can be a violation. Which way do you think the demon wants it to be? Which way does he make it easier for you?"

He needed a drink. Voss stood and went to the cabinet, helping himself to a finger of brandy. Yet…he didn't tell her to cease speaking.

"I've only known you for a decade, Voss, but I can see the emptiness in your life. Nothing changes, does it? The only relationships you have are with other Dracule, and none of you truly trust the others. Instead of envying you, I pity you. All of you. Each of you has nothing but sameness, emptiness, every day. You've nothing to strive for, nothing to look toward. Your lives—even Giordan's—are filled with debauchery and pleasure and nothing else."

"And Prinny's life, and Byron, and Brummell—none of them are denying themselves pleasure. But they'll grow too old or too poor or they'll die and their days will be over. Ours—mine—goes for eternity. It will never change. I'll never be too old to fuck—"

"Ah, yes, the monotony of it all. But it's the very nature of your existence—the need, the drive for pleasure. Do you *never* get tired of indulgences? Pleasure? And not even the hair on your head turning gray or falling out?" Rubey shrugged. "You remain the same, for eternity—unless you land on a stake. Or a sword separates your head from your shoulders. And then what happens? What has your devil promised you then?"

Voss's mouth went dry. His body turned empty and cold because she had said what he couldn't put out of his mind. The thought had tortured him since yesterday. All he could do was nod.

It didn't matter. The deed was done, the covenant made. This was his life.

Forever, as long as he didn't get himself staked or beheaded. Or burned in the sun.

Rubey wasn't finished with her litany of questions. Ones he didn't want to hear, and yet, ones he could no longer ignore. "Do you ever wonder why he chose you? Why the offer was made to you? What did the demon see in you, Voss, all those decades ago, that made him think you would be worthy?"

He gulped the whiskey, closing his eyes as scenes from his past whirled behind his lids, prodded his memory. He'd heard people describe it: how their life passed before their eyes during a near-death experience. He understood that experience.

And what he saw there, the summary of his hundred forty-eight years, was starkly clear. It was all about him. It always had been, since he was a child.

Petted, fussed over, indulged.

"You'll have to answer for it all someday, Voss."

He opened his eyes. "I don't want to," he said, speaking more honestly than he could ever remember doing. Something hot and raw inside him exploded, and so did the searing pain of his Mark. He felt Lucifer's hate at that moment.

"If you're afraid to answer for what you've done here," Rubey said as she leaned forward and rested her hand on his, "then *change.*"

11

OF SNEAKING INTO BEDCHAMBERS
AND UNEXPECTED REUNIONS

There were many ways to sneak into a woman's bed-chamber, and Voss had tried a good variety of them in the last century, with great success and few disappointments.

Since, after all, there was little danger to him physically should he be found with his hand down (or up) a frilly night rail—being shot, tossed from a window or otherwise attacked were not real threats—Voss had no qualms about taking advantage of the lowered defenses of a slumbering woman. There was something even more attractive and sensual than usual when a woman was tousled with sleep, her face slack and without artifice, her slender arms and delicate shoulders exposed from beneath rumpled sheets, her lashes fanning over pale cheeks.

But most of all, he appreciated the way she would come to consciousness under his touch. Most often, like a cat—stretching and sighing, with a languorous roll. Warm skin and creased cheeks, and, most of all, the soft, hot valley between her breasts…easily accessible when bare of a corset. His gentle strokes and nuzzling lips brought her slowly awake to delicious pleasure, and once she opened her eyes, his own would be there… glowing, coaxing and easing any hesitation.

Sneaking into a woman's chamber in the home of a Dracule, however, was a different challenge. Especially if the Dracule was Dimitri.

Nevertheless, Voss had managed it.

Dimitri would be prepared for Belial and his cohorts to attack by climbing over walls or rushing the doors, using brute force. Or perhaps by hijacking a returning maidservant, groom or carriage, or tricking them into coming out—all after the sun was setting, of course… but Voss had a simpler way. It required more patience and planning than Belial or his ilk would have, but he didn't mind.

The earl's household ran like most other gentrified households in London, despite Dimitri's necessary proclivity for sleeping during the day and moving about during the night. As it was, such a lifestyle was not so different than that of most of the *ton,* particularly the gentlemen—which, as a rule, socialized well past midnight most nights. Thus they slept late in the day, often past noon. Since normal business was conducted during the daylight hours as well, it was simpler for most Dracule to have a household that ran thus.

Voss gained admittance, therefore, when he assisted in delivering the large haunch of pig and various other packages from a butcher shop, just after the servants ate supper. In the confusion in the kitchen as he and the butcher's son carried the wrapped pieces in, Voss slipped away to the servants' quarters.

After that, it was a simple matter to remain hidden until the time was right to find Angelica. Being among the servants would also help him determine who was going out for the evening and who would need to be avoided. The staff was busy throughout the rest of the evening, only coming into their living quarters briefly. When they did, Voss heard and smelled them in plenty of time to hide. He moved more quickly than any mortal and made no noise.

Thus, his plan was simple, but it also required fore-planning and patience.

He must stay out of sight for hours in the same house that Angelica lived in, and far enough away that Dimitri wouldn't scent him. Angelica had left the house shortly after his arrival; he knew this, for her maid was discussing her mistress's choice of gown for the night's engagement. Yet, despite her absence, Angelica's scent somehow rose above every other smell—and there were many of them, not all pleasant—in Blackmont Hall, reminding him that she was near.

Even when two of the upper chambermaids somehow found the opportunity to retreat to their shared attic room shortly after supper, undress and conduct simple ablutions in front of a grainy mirror, Voss was hardly distracted. In the past, he would have considered such an opportunity a gift, and he would have emerged from where he hid beneath a narrow bed complete with glowing eyes and a variety of ideas that involved the three of them.… But he had no desire to bestir himself while he was waiting for Angelica to return. When the chatting maids left, smelling of lye soap and cheap rose petal water, Voss found himself wondering precisely why he had taken the trouble. Why he was here, hiding under a dusty bed on a threadbare rag rug.

Of course, a good portion of the reason was that he enjoyed the challenge. And he had the inexplicable desire to annoy Dimitri. He meant to leave the man a farewell gift of sorts so that he was aware that Voss had breached the house on his way from London to…wherever he was going to go now. Seville? Venice?

Constantinople was appealing.

He'd stop first in Paris to do business with Moldavi— or perhaps in Barcelona to see Regeris—and then be on his way. Despite his disregard for governments—imperial or otherwise—Voss had no desire to remain in a land in the midst of a war.

Yes, there were benefits to it: many women were left lonely and unprotected whilst their men were off fighting, and of course, some Dracule appreciated the smorgasbord of fallen soldiers on a silent battlefield. Voss liked fresher blood than that, but he'd been known to partake when necessary. After all, a vampire really only needed to feed once every few days or so. The other times were merely enhancements to or ways to prolong sexual pleasure. It was difficult—and, really, unnecessary in Voss's mind—to separate a bit of a fang-slip and a taste of lifeblood from other physical pleasure. Why bother to try?

Of Voss's relationship with Moldavi, there was no love lost. Despite what others might think, Voss had never done significant business with him. Just enough to keep the man from being suspicious or offended so that Voss didn't become one of his particular targets as Dimitri had become so long ago in Vienna.

Voss crawled from beneath the bed that was barely

wide enough to hold a child, let alone a woman, and thought he might have to have a word with Dimitri about his servants' quarters. Not that he was terribly concerned for the comfort of servants—who was?—but at least if they slept well, they were more productive during the day or night.

But that bit of advice he would save for later, of course. Decades from now, perhaps a century, when Angelica was long dead and this whole incident was well in the past and forgotten.

Yes. A hundred years from now, all this would be forgotten and Voss would still be visiting Rubey's.

Voss lurked about well into the night, easily evading notice. Aside of the two chambermaids who'd changed earlier, he was also privy to a passionate encounter between one of the young, muscular footmen and a curvaceous blonde kitchen maid. He couldn't help but mentally critique the footman's technique, which could have been more visually attractive—for he knew from experience just how a man and woman looked when they were together against the wall. He'd utilized a mirror more than once to determine the best angles.

Another incident involving a less fortunate groom and a redheaded girl ended with the groom half falling down the back stairs after being rebuffed by the toe of a well-placed slipper.

Smirking to himself, Voss shook his head. The groom's advances had been clumsy and doltish…just as his own had been. One hundred and twenty-five years ago.

Originally Voss had assumed that Angelica would be staying in tonight, after her unpleasant experiences that had begun three days earlier with the masquerade ball. But to his surprise—and perhaps annoyance—his eavesdropping indicated that she had gone to a dinner party. Although he didn't see the frock in question, the discussion between the two upstairs maids about her choice of a periwinkle gown with dark blue ribbons induced an unseen nod of approval from Voss.

She would look lovely in blue, with her dusky rose complexion and dark eyes. Perhaps her hair would be dressed high, leaving the slender column of her neck bare for all to see. The delicate ridge of her clavicles, a bit of a swell of bosom, and perhaps even the hint of a shoulder blade...

A twinge of regret tightened his belly, but he pushed it away. He would see her soon enough, mussed from the pillow and sheets, warm with slumber. A pang tightened his gums, but he kept his fangs sheathed.

How would she have hidden the marks he'd left on her shoulder? It had only been two days; they wouldn't have quite healed yet.

Voss frowned. Perhaps with a well-placed curl and a wide necklet. It might mar the picture, but it would preserve her reputation.

He wondered if her reputation was, indeed, intact. Would she find a suitable groom, a man who either didn't know what had occurred—or didn't care?

Not that anything terribly untoward had happened, at least in Voss's mind. A bit of kissing and a single, abbreviated nibble shouldn't be enough to remove a woman from marriage consideration. And as for his own discomfort...the pain from his Mark, while it hadn't completely dissolved, had at least become bearable. It ached more than it ever had before, and occasionally he got a stubborn streak of fire radiating over his torso, but it wasn't enough to send him gasping for breath as it had before. Feeding on Angelica, for however brief a time, had obviously been the right thing to do to stop it.

It was well past two o'clock before the ladies returned from the dinner party. Corvindale was not with them, and Voss suspected that he was scouring London for none other than himself.

Such an irony that he should be hiding here in Corvindale's home, of all places, whilst the very man was hunting him. He grinned in the dark library, where he'd taken refuge shortly after midnight. None of the servants would be looking for reading material, and the ladies were otherwise occupied. He was reluctantly impressed with the choice of literature lining the walls— a great variety of novels as well as books in languages from Greek to Latin to Spanish and even Egyptian and Aramaic. Apparently studying was what Dimitri did instead of socializing.

Studying, researching. Trying to find a way to break a covenant with the devil. Poor damned sot.

There was no way to break the unholy bargain.

Voss's keen ears heard bits of conversation as the ladies came in, and even as they chattered in and around their chambers. Angelica laughed more than once and she seemed rather gay, considering what had happened to her three days earlier. When Voss heard the word "Harrington," followed by a quickly muffled feminine squeal, he frowned. And then low laughter and murmurs that even he couldn't discern.

It didn't take much for him to realize she had likely seen Lord Harrington tonight.

His frown deepened. How quickly she seemed to find other companionship.

Voss was forced to wait for another hour before he could make his way from the dark library up to the second floor, where the bedchambers were. At last, silence reigned over the household, and he slipped from the dual doors of the library. Angelica's scent led him to her room, and after he opened the door and slipped inside, he stood for a moment, his hand still on the knob.

Her scent, her presence…it overwhelmed him. So familiar and so much what he desired.

A sharp twinge of pain burned over his shoulder as if to urge him on, but Voss ignored it. Yet, he salivated as he smelled the citrusy-floral scent melded with woman and a waft of summer breeze from the open window. His mouth throbbed and he had a difficult time controlling the shoot of his fangs—like a green boy who grew hard at the mere mention of a breast.

What was it about this woman that made him so foolish? So thoughtful?

What was it about this one that put him in so much agony?

Luce's blood, he was a hundred forty-eight years old. He'd had thousands of women and never given one more than a second or third thought. Even Rubey.

Even Giliane, a woman he'd even considered making Dracule. Only for a day, but the thought *had* crossed his mind during one of their energetic bouts, back in 1755. They—she—had survived the horrendous earthquake in Lisbon and were celebrating with wine and cheese, stolen from one of the shops.

Now, as Voss looked down at the woman in the chamber he'd invaded, all thoughts of Giliane and every other of the thousands he'd known faded. A shaft of moonlight rippled over Angelica like the caress of a hand, and the curtains fluttered in a soft breeze. She slept with her face half buried in the pillow, her hair loose and curtaining her cheek. One hand was curled beneath her pillow, and the other tucked beneath her chin.

Voss moved closer to the bed, his heart pounding, suddenly rampant. A violent surge of awareness had taken over, trammeling through his veins, rushing to fill his cock and to thrust his incisors free. His skin flushed hot and his eyes warmed with heat.

Yes.

He turned and silently bolted the door behind him.

Angelica shifted onto her back and sighed, moving the pillow in her sleep.

And then she opened her eyes.

Voss froze and their gazes met in the darkness. He stiffened, preparing himself to clamp a hand over her mouth, but then her eyes closed and she turned her head away. Still asleep.

Why was he so relieved?

He reached to touch her hair, gently sliding his hand over the long tresses in a way he hadn't had the chance to before.

There'd been no gentleness, no caresses, no learning the texture and shape of her.

Before he realized it, Voss had come to sit on the bed next to her. His heart pounded, rampant and apprehensive. Ready, again, to cover her mouth to stifle a scream, he gently lifted a thick lock of hair from her bare shoulder, skimming his fingertips over the smooth warm skin.

He wondered how she'd looked in the periwinkle-blue dress. If Harrington had found an opportunity to coax her into a private corner. If she'd smiled at him with the wise light in her eyes, as if to say all would be well. If she'd talked with him about thoughtful things, like life and death.

If she'd told Harrington the secret she'd told Voss.

He bent, pressing his lips to the curve of her shoulder, resisting the sudden blinding urge to slide his fangs into that sweet muscle. Instead his teeth slid along her skin and he flicked his tongue out to taste her.

She was salty and hot, citrus and musk, and he curled his fingers into the blankets. A wave of pain clashed with the new rush of desire and he kissed her again, squeezing his eyes closed against the battle. Lucifer versus Angelica.

Taking, violating...versus coaxing, seducing. It would be nothing to slide into her. Release that hot flood of rich blood. White light shot down to his hips and burned over his back. *Take.*

She was well asleep.... She would enjoy it. She would moan and her eyes would flutter behind her lids and she might perhaps spread her legs so that he could slip a hand into that warm crook, pleasure her while she dreamed.

And then, suddenly, Voss felt something pushing into him. Poking into his torso.

"Get away."

Her words, cold and low, were unmistakable. And the pressure in his torso could only be...

Voss eased back and saw that, yes, indeed, she had a whittled wooden stick pressing against him. A bit too low for his heart, but too close, nevertheless. She must have pulled it from beneath the covers.

She'd been sleeping with a stake. Expecting him?

He tried to smile, but it felt weak. Surprisingly his

fangs had retracted, although his gums still throbbed a bit.

"Get away from me," she said again, and jabbed him hard enough that he felt a definite point through his shirt, into the soft part of belly below his sternum.

Hands raised in placation, he shifted off the bed. "All right, then. There's no need to be overset."

To his chagrin and delight, Angelica sat up, still holding the stake like a talisman in front of her. Her technique left much to be desired, for it wobbled a bit, and it wasn't quite at the right angle...but Voss was not about to underestimate the sister of a renowned vampire hunter.

"Get out of here," she said from between tight jaws. "Or I'll scream."

"Corvindale isn't here to rush to your assistance," Voss couldn't help but mention.

"Are you certain of that?" she replied steadily.

He relaxed a bit and leaned slightly against the bed with his thigh. "Of course. He's searching the City for yours truly, Angelica. He'd never think to look for me here."

"What do you want?" She obviously couldn't find an argument for that, so she tried a different tact. "To finish what you started? Are you going to bleed me dry and tear me into ribbons of flesh?" Bitterness filled her voice.

Voss's belly tightened. *Never.* "No," he said. "Of course not."

She sniffed and the play of moonlight over her face told him that her jaw tightened.

Angelica could have no idea how enticing she looked at that moment, with the pearly light half illuminating the details of her face, and the dip and curve of her shoulder. The strap of her night rail was nothing but a three-finger-wide pink ribbon, and the eyelet lace that edged the straight neckline gapped a bit. Her lips were gently parted and full, and the cloud of dark waves cascaded over her shoulders and onto the pillows.

The only aspect marring that beautiful image was the loathing burning in her eyes. Even in the ineffective light, he saw it. The smile he'd tried to force wavered.

"What do you want, then?" she said again, still as coldly as before.

This was not as simple as he'd expected it to be. Voss knew he could easily overpower her, remove the stake from her hand and do whatever he wanted. He could take what he needed, and be gone from London within hours.

The sharp, pounding pain radiating over his back urged him to grab those delicate shoulders and drag her to him. *Take.*

"I have something for you," he said, pulling two velvet pouches from the inside of his coat. "And for your sister. An apology. To both of you."

"I don't want anything from you." Her voice was cold, and she didn't even glance at the jewelry bags.

"Nevertheless, I shall leave them. Perhaps your sister will accept them. They are quite valuable." He turned and set them on her dressing table. The gifts were really more for Dimitri's sake than Angelica's.

"Very well, then. You've delivered your apology— unwelcome as it is. Now *leave.*"

"I also came to ask that you use your Sight to give me information."

Her eyes widened in shock, and those delicious lips pruned up like an old maid's. "You came to ask a favor of me? Why in God's name would I do anything for *you?*"

Voss winced at her use of the name of God—or perhaps it was simply the Mark—and he once again tried to adopt a placating smile. "Because if you assist me, I'll leave London and I won't bother you ever again."

Despite her bitterness and loathing, he didn't expect her reaction to be quite as quick and businesslike as it was. "You'd leave London? Is that a vow? Because if it is, I would be most happy to make such a bargain."

Something panged uncomfortably in the vicinity of his heart and even his belly squeezed—like it did in the morning after too much blood whiskey and ale and wine had all mixed up and sloshed around. "You have my word," he said.

Angelica snorted in that ladylike way that had amused him previously. "What is it then?"

Voss pulled out the slender gold chain from a different pocket inside his coat. When he'd first acquired it, he hadn't realized that it would be put to use in this way, but now that he knew Angelica's secret, it made perfect sense.

"It isn't a glove—I know that you prefer gloves," he said, looking at her purposely. He forced himself to say it. "You read death on my glove, didn't you? Will you tell me what you saw?"

"What I saw is not at all to my liking."

Voss stilled. Waited. But she said nothing further. "Angelica?"

"It's not to my liking because I saw nothing. I would that I'd foretold a violent, imminent death for you."

"You saw nothing?" He wasn't certain whether to be alarmed or relieved. Did that mean he wasn't to die? Ever? Something like relief blossomed.

"Are you hard of hearing?" She held out her hand. "Give me the chain and be off with you."

"You will attempt it?"

"Leave it with me, and I'll meditate upon it. I'll send you a message in the morning through Rubey with any information I can cull from the chain." The stake shifted warningly in her hand, its point still aimed at him.

Voss hid his surprise. "But how can I trust that you will follow through on our agreement, Angelica?" He allowed his voice to caress her name the way he had done to her shoulder.

That very same shoulder lifted in a delicate shrug. "You will have to trust me." Her eyes narrowed and she straightened. For a moment, he saw something else besides hatred and anger there. It might have been hurt.

"And how am I to know that you wouldn't send me a message simply so that you can advise Corvindale of my direction?"

Her lips quirked a bit. "A brilliant suggestion. Thank you, Dewhurst. I'm not certain I would have thought of that myself in my haste to rid London of your vile presence. Now, if you please, remove yourself from my chamber. And this house."

He couldn't leave. "Don't you wish to know to whom that watch chain belongs?"

Again, a shrug. His eyes followed the shift of moonlight over the hollow of her shoulder and he swallowed, clenching his teeth. "I couldn't care less about anything in regards to you. Now, Dewhurst, if you please… I should like to return to my slumber. You interrupted a very delightful dream."

"I don't suppose I figured in your nocturnal visions," he said, lowering his voice and allowing his eyes to glow a bit. "But you have appeared in mine. Angelica…" He dug his fingers into his thighs to keep from reaching for her…and to distract himself from the pain.

Her shoulders shifted back and her breasts thrust forward and he nearly lunged for her at that point. "Indeed you have," she said, surprising him again. But her voice had dropped and for the first time, it was unsteady. "You've figured quite vividly—in my darkest nightmares. This is the first night I've slept without Maia since I returned."

Voss couldn't breathe. Every bit of insouciance fled and he felt as if he'd been slammed in the gut. "Angelica," he began, searching for something…something to say that would truly placate her. Something real, something to heal her. His thrall seemed to have no effect on her, leaving him helpless.

Her eyes had become haunted circles. "Go away, Dewhurst. I'll send a message to Rubey's in your care. And I'll return the chain then."

Words failed him.

She truly meant it.

Anger, sudden and inexplicable, flared through him, surging to his hands, down his legs. His fangs shot forth, his eyes flamed hot and the dark room filled with a red haze. Voss's fingers curled, ready to grab at her, to tear into her, and he even jerked toward Angelica—but somehow caught himself, turning before he touched the bed.

Somehow, somehow he fought through it, battling the white fury that ordered him to *take, take, take*….

Something helped him stumble to the window—the cold night air, the smooth slide of moonbeam—and he grasped its sill even as the blast of pain seared in his hands and behind his eyes. Lucifer was intent that he would do his bidding.

Voss held on so that he wouldn't turn back. So he wouldn't tear into her.

"Get out of here," he managed to say. If she would leave… "Go. Now."

In the recesses of his consciousness, he heard the rustle of the bedclothes. He battled needy red fog and the demands of his body, somehow focusing on the sounds of her sliding the door's bolt and then the slide as it closed behind her.

When she was gone, he vaulted through the window and landed easily on the ground three floors below.

Angelica stumbled from her chamber still clutching the stake. Her heart pounded and her knees were weak, and she had one thought: to get away. As she turned to rush down the corridor, she slammed into something—someone—soft and warm.

"Angelica, what is it?" Maia automatically caught her in a comforting embrace.

Angelica's arms went around her sister, but even as she did so, she had the presence of mind to push her down the hall, toward Maia's chamber.

She didn't believe Voss would follow her. He'd ordered her to leave, but she wasn't certain. His face…it had been so terrifying.

Almost as if he'd turned into someone else.

Go. Get away.

No, he wasn't coming after her.

But she wasn't going to go back in that chamber again.

"What's that in your hand?" Maia asked as they went into her room. She caught Angelica's wrist and held it up so she could see the stake. "A stick?" Then her eyes went wide. *"Oh."*

She remembered Granny Grapes's stories, too.

"What are you doing awake?" Angelica asked, sitting on her sister's bed. There was something about being in Maia's chamber, with all of her things cluttering the dressing table, and more pillows than anyone could ever use piled high on her bed and chair, that made her feel comforted and safe.

"I came to check on you," Maia told her. They sat on the bed facing each other. "What's happened?"

Angelica considered whether to tell her sister or not. Maia would be angry and worried for her if she learned that Voss had sneaked into her room, and she'd become even more managing and motherly and smother her to death.

But if she told Maia, then her sister would certainly tell Corvindale—likely in a high-pitched, demanding tone. And she was sure that the earl would make certain it didn't happen again.

And that would make her sleep so much easier.

"I had a dream," she said. Which was strictly the truth. She had been dreaming before he woke her. Perhaps she could weave fact with fiction.... "That—Dewhurst came into my chamber at night."

"Darling, I'm so sorry. How terrifying it must be," Maia said, stroking her arm. "I didn't hear you cry out, although I heard something that sounded like you mumbling in your sleep. Or talking to someone."

"It seemed so real," Angelica said, continuing with the charade. "He..." *He was so gentle. I was sleeping and then I felt him touching me and I wanted him to slide closer and take me in his arms. To be the man he'd been...before.*

She wanted to say that. But she couldn't. She hardly dared *think* those words, let alone confess them to Maia. Her sister would not understand.

Her sister, who did everything so perfectly and who always had the answer and who didn't have to live with the demons of death that Angelica did. How could she comprehend the fact that Angelica was both terrified of Voss...and attracted to him, as well?

Or, at least, she had been attracted to him. Now, when she thought of him, there was little more than that heavy ball in her belly. He'd lied to her, he'd tricked her and he'd attacked her. All under the guise of protecting her.

"Sometimes dreams can be more frightening than reality," Maia said. She sounded so certain, so sure. Just as she always did. Angelica thought it would be nice to be so certain about things. All the time. "And sometimes, they can be so much more...beautiful...than reality."

More than willing to turn the subject from her experience, desperate to think of something other than the way she'd warred internally between wanting Voss to touch her and truly wanting to kill him, Angelica said, "What do you mean?"

Maia smiled in a way that Angelica had never seen before. A rather secret sort of smile, as if she were being coy or discreet. She fancied that if there were more illumination than the glow of a lamp in the corner, and a hint of moonlight outside, she might see the rise of a blush on Maia's cheeks.

"Well." Her sister sat up and pulled one of the two dozen pillows onto her lap, clutching it over her belly. Her face changed, becoming more reserved. "I don't know if I should tell you about it. After all, you're still unwed and—"

"And so are you." Angelica was glad to have the spurt of annoyance to focus on, instead of her fingers that still trembled and the sealike pitching of her belly. *Why had he come?* Just when she was beginning to feel safer, to begin to forget him and think about other men. "You aren't married yet, dear sister, and so you haven't any more experience than I have."

There was that secret smile again—so odd from her prim sister—and Maia looked up at her over the top of the ruffled pillow. "But that isn't true, dear *younger* sister. Alexander and I have... Well, we *are* engaged, and Chas and the lady patrons haven't been as vigilant as they were before our engagement was announced."

Now it was Angelica's turn to sit up straight and grab a pillow. She felt her eyes as if they were about to bug from their sockets. "You and Mr. Bradington have—"

"No, no," Maia said. "Not exactly. Not *precisely*. But...Angelica. It's quite...nice. Flossa and Betty are right. It's very pleasant. And I think it gets nicer." Her lips curved a bit.

"And what does this have to do with dreams being better than the reality? Or did you mean they were more frightening than reality?"

"Well." She looked away, adjusting the pillow in her lap. Hesitating.

"What is it?" Angelica pressed, now morbidly curious, as this was a side of her proper sister she had never before seen—and had assumed didn't even exist. Maia had an odd expression on her face—as if she were bursting to share the confidence, but at the same time, ashamed to do so.

"After your experience with Dewhurst, I had a dream. About…it."

"You dreamed about Dewhurst?" Angelica's voice might have risen, but not enough to be heard outside the chamber. She didn't think. Although the door wasn't shut tightly. She needed to keep her voice down or Mirabella would hear them.

And she was fairly certain that event would lace Maia's mouth closed tighter than her smallest corset.

"*Shhh!* You'll wake Mirabella! No, I didn't dream about *Dewhurst.* It's going to sound horrible to you, Angelica." Now Maia's eyes had lost that secretive look, and she shifted back as if to recant her words. "You'll think me mad."

"Not any more than I already do," Angelica replied with a small smile. "Tell me."

Maia smiled, too, but her fingers were plucking energetically at the fringe of lace on her pillow. "I dreamed that a vampire visited me in my chamber. But it wasn't frightening. It was…like embracing Alexander, and kissing him.… But it wasn't him. This was different. Better. And when the vampire bit me—"

Angelica gasped. "What?"

"In my dream, he bit me. Right…here," Maia said softly, touching the side of her smooth, white neck just above the shoulder. "It didn't hurt, in my dream. In fact, it was… It made me…"

That secretive smile was back, and Angelica could hardly credit her ears. "You *liked* it?"

But Maia's eyes had widened in shock and she straightened up sharply, clutching the pillow to her bosom like a shield. "My *lord.*" Her words were shocked and prim with affront.

Angelica turned to look behind her, but she already knew that Corvindale had appeared there in the open door. Dark and shadowed, he stood like a sentinel. Nevertheless, the moonlight caught him across the eyes, giving them a faint glint along with a white shine on the bridge of his strong nose.

Did he already know that Voss had sneaked into her chamber? Was that why he'd ventured to their floor? Should she tell him?

The earl seemed stiffer than usual, and for a moment, he didn't speak. Then said, "My apologies, Miss Woodmore. Angelica," he said. "I had just arrived home when I heard voices. I came to investigate."

"Now that you've determined all is well, perhaps you would allow us to return to our conversation," Maia said stiffly.

"Indeed," Corvindale said, and then, just as he began to turn, he stilled. Raising a peremptory hand, as if to forestall any further comments from Maia, he tilted his head, and then turned back to them. Now his expression was intense and serious. "Someone is below. Stay here."

And then he was gone, closing the door behind him.

Angelica bolted off the bed and went to the door, opened it and put her ear to the crack. Was Voss still about? Had she been wrong and he hadn't left?

"Angelica," Maia admonished in a low voice. "What are you doing?" But then there she was, crowding behind her. Perhaps the reprimand was meant to get Angelica to move and to give Maia the better spot, but she wasn't about to do that, so her sister was forced to crouch and duck beneath her arm to listen. She was shorter than Angelica anyway, so it was only fair.

As they listened to hear if anything was happening

below, Angelica whispered, "Did you really like it, in your dream? When he bit you?"

Maia stilled, her shoulder pressed into Angelica's side. "I don't want to talk about it," she snapped back. "I wish I'd kept my mouth closed."

They were silent for a moment as a single, soft thud from below reached their ears, then nothing.

"I cannot imagine finding it anything but horrifying," Angelica said, her belly tightening at the memory. She'd tried to forget about that moment of soft, sensual kissing and Voss's hands sliding over her breasts in a reckless but delightful way. She'd been flooded with pleasure and heat, and then suddenly...the pain. The surprise and the pain.

Never one to allow another to have the last word, Maia replied, "Even those stories Granny used to tell us, about the vampires. Even then there were some people who didn't find it...horrible. And it was just a *dream, Angelica.*"

Angelica opened her mouth to reply, but clamped it shut when she heard footsteps on the stairs. Without another word, the two of them spun away from the door and fairly leaped back onto the mattress—just as they had done when they were younger and weren't supposed to be out of bed.

As expected, the footsteps came to their chamber and, since it hadn't been shut completely in their haste, the door swung open. But it wasn't Corvindale who stood there.

"Chas!" exclaimed Angelica as she and Maia bounded off the bed.

"Hush," he said, gathering each of them in with one strong arm. "No one can know I'm here."

Angelica looked up at him, the obvious question forming on her lips, but before she could speak, he added, "Come down to the study with me so we can converse privately."

Quickly Angelica returned to her room to don a robe and slippers. The window was open wider than it had been, the curtains fluttering in the soft breeze. That was how Voss had left, of course.

She paused and found herself sniffing the air. Did she fancy it, or did his scent linger? A tightening in her belly reminded her how much she hated him now, how, despite the way he smelled and held her and had kissed her, how handsome and charming he was…how he had *listened* to her, as if he cared what she thought…despite all of the things that had attracted her to him, she could no longer care for him.

The monster that he was had destroyed any affection she might have had.

The robe skimmed her bare feet, and she decided to disdain slippers. But as she turned to leave the chamber, she noticed the two black velvet pouches on her dressing table—Voss's "apology" as he called it.

She paused, then tucked her curiosity beneath her loathing for the man and her desire to talk with Chas, and she hurried from the room.

Down one flight of stairs to the first floor, Angelica followed the spill of light from beneath the door of Corvindale's study. The murmur of voices was so low that she wouldn't have heard it if she hadn't known they were there.

When she walked in, she saw that there was a fifth person in the chamber. A tall, gaunt-faced man in a wide-brimmed hat stood near the fireplace. A small fire burned therein, giving off unnecessary warmth on this summer night. Its illumination, however, was welcome in the dark room.

Maia must have thought the same, for as Angelica walked in, she saw that her sister was in the process of turning up the gas lamp on the other side of the chamber.

Corvindale sat in an armchair, not behind his desk, but in a shadowed corner near a tall window. He was dressed in only his white shirtsleeves and trousers, the shirt unadorned by a neckcloth, but fastened at the throat nevertheless. His long legs were crossed and one scuffed boot was highlighted by a shaft of moonlight. He held a short glass of something that looked like whiskey, reminding Angelica of her unfortunate experience with that liquor.

Maia, having finished adjusting the light of the room to her preference, selected a seat near the lamp. The soft yellow light made her unbound chestnut hair gleam in a variety of shades of bronze, mahogany and honey. The fact that she hadn't pinned it up surprised Angelica, for her sister was so particular about propriety. Being in the room with two men other than their brother, dressed only in a night rail, robe and slippers was hardly permissible…but to have her hair down, as well?

Chas leaned against the desk littered with papers, a pile of pens and a haphazard stack of books. He looked weary and yet, powerful. Angelica hadn't ever thought of her brother as a particularly strong, virile man…but at that moment, she saw him with new eyes, saw him as being formidable. This was a man who, according to Voss, had somehow outsmarted a very strong, evil vampire to kidnap—or elope with—his sister.

At that moment, he looked every bit as capable as that.

She looked at the other man, standing near the fireplace, and realized that it wasn't a man at all. Simply a woman dressed as a man.

"You must be Narcise Moldavi," she said, looking at her. "The vampire."

The woman swept away the wide-brimmed hat that had shadowed her face, and Angelica saw at once that she had been a fool to believe this woman was a man. She was beautiful—the most beautiful woman Angelica had ever seen.

What she'd originally perceived as gauntness in the harsh shadows was instead a lovely face with high cheekbones and sculpted lips. Her hair, pinned up and yet sagging now with the removal of the hat, was coal-black. Her skin… Angelica had never seen such porcelain skin—smooth and white and delicate. The gaze that swept to fasten on her was startlingly blue.

"I am," Narcise replied in a voice nearly as low as a man's. Now without her hat, and her gender acknowledged, it was obvious that the white shirtwaist and loose coat were meant to hide her shape.

"Are you here so that we can welcome you to the family?" Angelica responded. She didn't try to hide her disdain and disapproval, and the woman noticed. Her eyes flared hot and red for a moment, then subsided to blue.

"I'm here, in fact, endangering my person, only because of you," replied the vampire in an even voice.

Chas shot Angelica a warning look that did nothing to quell the horror that her brother could possibly have fallen in love with a bloodthirsty, violent vampire woman. Seeing Narcise, Angelica couldn't imagine any man *not* falling in love with her. Yet…how could he? She was…unnatural.

At that point, Chas would likely have spoken, but Narcise stepped away from the fireplace and walked over to help herself to a glass of Corvindale's whiskey. As she did so, she spoke. "Your brother learned that Voss had abducted you and he insisted on coming to London, despite the danger to me."

"You know very well you didn't have to come to London with him," came a new voice from the doorway. "Don't blame your own cowardice on the girl, Narcise."

Angelica whirled to see another, vaguely familiar man striding into the study. He was shedding his own hat, which exposed a head of thick, curling dark hair and a handsome, strong-jawed face. The flaps and hem of his coat fluttered behind him as he stalked over to stand near Maia. His expression was blank, but she fancied she saw a fire in his eyes.

Narcise shot the newcomer a violent look, complete with what Angelica was certain was a flash of fangs, then walked over to stand next to Chas. The air in the room tightened and no one spoke. The silence stretched for what seemed like a long time.

"Miss Woodmore, Angelica, meet my friend Mr. Giordan Cale." It was Corvindale who spoke abruptly, at last, from his seat in the corner.

"Chas, what in heaven's name is going on here?" Maia demanded. Angelica could almost hear what she didn't say: *And who are all these people? And why didn't you warn me so I could dress properly?*

"I've been attempting to tell you," Chas replied mildly. "And I will…if we aren't going to have any further interruptions?" He glanced at Narcise, but it wasn't a look of reproach as much as it was one of affection. Angelica pressed her lips together.

"You're taking us home," Maia said. "Tomorrow?"

Narcise shifted, and so did Chas. "I'm afraid that's impossible right now," he said.

"What do you mean? You're back. There's no reason for us to stay here any longer," Maia said. The emphasis on the word *here* was not lost on Angelica, and she couldn't help but glance at Corvindale—who was clearly the cause of that tone.

"Don't disappoint the girl, Chas," the earl said. "Take her home." Then he glanced at Cale. "Or perhaps Giordan would take on governess duties?"

Cale snorted and Angelica saw humor flare in his face. "I wouldn't dream of depriving you, Dimitri." His smile was both feral and filled with humor.

"Gentlemen," Chas said, holding up his hands. Improperly gloveless, which Angelica was certain Maia would notice. He looked at his sisters, a softness in his eyes that hadn't been there earlier. "I'm sorry, but I cannot take you back home. I cannot even be seen in London, and there can't be any hint or rumor that I've come back. For Narcise's sake. I'm taking a great risk by being here."

"I don't understand," Maia said. "Then why did you come?"

"To get Angelica away from Voss—although that has already occurred—and to kill the bastard."

Maia gasped at the use of profanity, and it was all Angelica could do not to roll her eyes. They were in a chamber, dressed in their nightclothes, with a vampire and two strange men. An off-color word was the least of their worries.

"That's what I do," Chas said, stepping away from

where he'd been leaning on the desk. "I might as well tell you now, so you understand."

Angelica frowned, but before she could speak, her brother continued. "I kill vampires. Some of them, at any rate," he added with a sidewise glance at Narcise and then Corvindale. "Only the ones who endanger humans."

"What are you talking about?" Maia said. Her voice was faint and Angelica felt a little sorry for her. Between the profanity and their casual state of undress, her very proper sister seemed out of her element. No surprise: she wasn't in control. And Maia, for all she might desire it, hadn't been bit by a vampire—or even come in close proximity to one.

Chas gestured toward Angelica. "You were blessed, or cursed, with Granny Grapes's Sight. And so is Sonia. I've discovered my own ability, courtesy of that same Romanian heritage. I can do something vampires can't even do. I can sense the presence of one...identify them, even if I don't know them."

"Oh," was all Angelica could say. And then she realized what he'd said. "You do this *all the time?* You kill vampires? Isn't it—" she glanced at Narcise, who was looking at her as if she were a toad "—dangerous?"

"Of course it's dangerous," Maia put in. "Don't you recall the stories Granny used to tell us? About the vampires, and the men who hunted... Oh." She looked at Chas. "That's how you knew? What to do?"

He nodded. "All my gratitude goes to Granny Grapes. And as soon as I learned from Cale that Voss had abducted Angelica, I came back. Corvindale is your guardian for the foreseeable future," he said, looking at Maia, "but I wasn't going to stand aside and let Voss compromise my sister."

"I'm not compromised," Angelica said.

"We know he was here tonight, Angelica. Whether you invited him or welcomed him or—"

"I certainly didn't invite him," Angelica shot back in horror, her heart pounding. "I wouldn't invite a terrifying creature like him anywhere!" How had they even known he was there?

"It doesn't matter," Chas continued. "Corvindale and Cale are going to help me find him. And then I'm going to kill him."

12

LORD DEWHURST RECEIVES
A MESSAGE

The public house known as the Gray Stag was raucous and crowded, with more than one shadowy corner in which one could hide oneself. Ale and whiskey flowed freely, and although the particular libation that Voss preferred wasn't served here, he didn't mind a decent ale on occasion. Not that the Stag offered that, but there were times when one must adapt.

He chose the dark corner nearest the rear entrance, and sat with his back to the intersection of two smoke-blackened, stained wooden walls. One benefit to facing away from them—aside of the obvious—was that he wouldn't find himself contemplating what had caused said stains. Some of them were blood, which, of course didn't offend his sensibilities in the least—but there were others that, based on the underlying stench in the area, he suspected were caused by more unpleasant casualties.

The whole place, in fact, smelled like any other public house Voss had ever entered: stale, close, smoky and of unwashed humans with a tinge of animal.

He hailed a harried serving girl by showing her a handful of shillings, and was treated to the sight of her long, slender neck from behind as she hurried away. He smiled to himself in admiration, but made no other move.

He wouldn't leave until after the appointed time had come and gone by an hour. After that, well…who knew what sort of pleasure might await the woman with the long neck?

Voss arranged two tankards on his table so that he would be recognized by the messenger he awaited: one upside down and the other next to it, handles touching. A third he reserved for himself, although he doubted he would actually ingest the ale.

Not that he was certain Angelica would even follow through on her agreement. She'd said she'd send word through Rubey, but Voss knew it wasn't safe for him to wait at her establishment anymore. Corvindale and Woodmore were certainly looking for him, so staying out of sight was the safest way to avoid the inconvenience of a stake in the heart, or any other disruption. Rubey had agreed that if she got word from Angelica, she would send a messenger to meet him at the Gray Stag by midnight.

An uncomfortable twinge tightened his belly as it did whenever he realized he would never see Angelica again. It was for the best, of course, but…it made him feel hollow. Unaccountably empty.

Turning his thoughts away from that unhappy thought, Voss scanned the establishment, watching for any sign that all might not be as it seemed. Waiting for someone to approach him. There was a woman in one of the corners who attracted his attention—not because she looked as if she might want to slip into the dark shadows with a man who'd bite her neck, but because she didn't look as if she belonged in a dingy place like this. She sat alone and no one seemed to give her any notice. She had long blond hair and was dressed in a shapeless gown. There was something…different…about her. And familiar, perhaps. Or perhaps it was simply her appearance that attracted his attention.

Once, Voss turned quickly and caught her watching him. She had a faint smile on an otherwise serene face… but she made no move to approach him.

He kept half an eye on her, simply because she seemed so out of place. He wondered if she were some make of Moldavi's who'd managed to track him…or just an odd whore looking for a trick. Or some servant of Angelica's? When she rose from her seat and approached his table, Voss watched in surprise and hope. Was she from Angelica? Could he be that fortunate?

The woman made her way around and between the servants and patrons as if they didn't exist. None of them seemed to acknowledge her, even when she passed close by.

For some reason, his heart beat faster as she came to stand in front of him. It certainly wasn't because he found her attractive. She was lovely to look at in a serene, peaceful sort of motherly way, but not in the way he was accustomed to thinking of women who approached him in a public house. He looked up at her, wondering if she would be amenable to his particular sort of sport.

"Been a while since you've seen a seamstress, hmm, m'dear?" he said, lifting a brow as he scanned her figure. "You really ought to remedy that if you expect to do well in this city." She looked as if she had emerged from some Saxon or Welsh legend, with a pale, shapeless tunic that dragged upon the floor. Her sleeves were long and she showed not a hint of bosom or even the shape of her figure. His Mark twitched and burned, and he looked with interest at the line of her neck, half obstructed by long blond hair. It was a lovely, long neck.

The faint curve of a smile shaped her lips, and he slightly revised his opinion that she wasn't attractive. He could sink into that.

"Aye, Voss. That's what's come to be expected of you. Always the superficial. Always planning your next conquest. Always the game. 'Tis why he chose you, you know."

His mouth went dry as his old wig powder and Voss suddenly felt as if his brain was about to shatter. Pain and light warred in his mind, and he tried to focus, to make sense of what she was saying. *That's why he chose you.* Something dark and heavy settled in his gut.

"Who are you?" he managed to choke out.

She lifted her shoulders delicately and he noticed her pale, elegant hands and the circlet of keys that hung from her woven leather belt. A medieval chatelaine.

"It matters not," she replied. "You aren't yet ready." The peace and serenity that had shone in her eyes wavered into something like sadness. "I'll be here when you are. I pray that it happens before she's gone."

"Who? What are you talking about? Who are you?" He'd found his voice, even through the rage of pain and the whirl of thoughts that he couldn't seem to control.

"I'd hoped—but you don't remember me. We've met before, on several occasions." Her smile was sad. "Mayhap you'll remember me after this time. But I can tell you naught more. Not until you're ready."

"What are you talking about?" he said again.

"Your friend Rubey is very wise. You were right to go to her. Now, if you'd only listen to her."

Voss closed his eyes against the pain of Luce's fury and his own confusion, and when he opened them a moment later, she was gone. Even though it had been a mere breath that he'd done so—or so he thought—when he scanned the pub, he didn't see a hint of long, flowing sleeves or a shapeless pale tunic. Anywhere.

He took a long drink of the abysmal ale and ordered another one from the wench with the long neck. Had he met the blonde woman before? When? Where?

Why didn't he remember her?

I pray that it happens before she's gone.

What did she mean by that? The little wrench stuttered his heart. Could she be speaking of Angelica?

Likely not. He was leaving here, as soon as he heard from her—and even if he didn't, he had to leave London. Things were simply too…uncomfortable and difficult here.

You aren't yet ready. Ready for what? For what?

Ready to change.

He shook his head. It was as if her voice found its way into his mind.

Change? He couldn't change. He didn't *want* to change.

When Belial walked into the Gray Stag some time after midnight, Voss wasn't overly surprised. Annoyed… yes. Surprised. No. Not in his world.

Especially not tonight.

Despite the fact that there were numerous pubs in London, it was simply his misfortune that the cock-biter would also choose this one in which to imbibe. Voss eased further back into the shadows and half turned his face away as the other vampire and his two companions settled at a table across the room. A structural beam partially blocked what would be their view of Voss, and he settled back into his corner. Checked his pocket watch again.

The meeting time had been set at half past eleven; it was nearly half after twelve. He'd been here since before eleven.

Apparently he was waiting in vain. Angelica had not kept her promise; the hope that perhaps the strange blonde woman might have been her messenger had disappeared, for the woman had slipped out a few moments ago. But he hadn't truly expected Angelica would contact him with news about the watch chain. She didn't seem to realize how valuable her Sight could be to someone…someone with nefarious purposes. Had she never thought of how powerful it could make her?

Voss eyed the drink in front of him. No. She didn't think that way. A wise young woman, she was, but also very innocent in many ways.

Had she never realized what a pawn she could be for someone with unsavory intentions?

Not that his own intentions were unsavory. He merely wished to have as much information as he could have. And to fund his travels.

And who knew when such information might come in handy, especially when dealing with Moldavi?

Voss eyed Belial, keeping his lids half lowered to hide the burning there. He didn't often feel the urge for violence—it was too messy, too much effort—but at this moment, something nagged at him. Some dark urge to fling his table away and to tear off its leg and slam its jagged point into the torso of that freckled, snakelike vampire. Watch him die.

Even the thought sent a rage of fire through his shoulder's Mark, although Voss barely shifted. He was becoming used to the incessant pain.

How much worse *could* it get? Last night, when he'd sent Angelica from her own bedchamber… Even now, the thought of that searing, white pain took his breath away. How he'd even formed the words to warn her to leave, Voss didn't know. He didn't remember anything but that white, hot world until his feet landed in the cool, damp grass.

Lucifer didn't approve of his immortalized men killing other Dracule members—mercenaries, as he called them, in his earthly army—and he expressed his anger the way he always did: through the mark of their agreement.

Already, the symbol of Voss's covenant with Lucifer had become slender, brownish-red ropes of agony. For self-preservation purposes, he hadn't been to his London home for more than a week, although he had sent for Kimton (who could travel easily during the daylight) and new clothing. The valet had tried everything including a foul-smelling salve to ease his master…to no avail. Its rage was a constant reminder of Luce's control.

Voss's fangs pressed into the inside of his lower lip and his fingers curled around the edge of the table.… No, there was no point in angering Lucifer any further. He had a better idea, and crooked his finger to the slender-necked serving girl. Obviously remembering the pile of shillings earlier, she hurried to his side. Another slip of coin, a few whispered words into her ear and she was off to do his bidding.

Even as he watched her from his shadowy position, Voss toyed with the idea of attacking Belial anyway, and putting the made vampire out of his misery instead of relying on the serving girl to eavesdrop. The only person who would miss Belial would be Cezar Moldavi, and the bastard could always sire another arse-licker who'd serve him unquestioningly.

That gave Voss food for thought. How did Lucifer feel about Moldavi having makes—minions that answered to *him* and not Luce? Why did the devil even allow it? His mind circled around that for a moment—better to meditate upon that, he supposed, than to contemplate the fact that Angelica hadn't done what she said she would. Far better to mull about Moldavi and his habits than to think about Angelica in that warm, sleepy state…and the alluring scent that clung to her hair and around her shoulders when he'd come into her chamber last night.

That was, he thought, a good enough reason to rid the earth of Belial. Angelica would be safe. His mind fairly made up, Voss felt his lips stretch in a nasty smile. His pulse pounded beneath his skin, his muscles tensed as he prepared to rise…then eased. Moldavi would simply replace Belial and Angelica would be in jeopardy once again. It was best to let the serving girl find out what she could so that Voss could prevent any further attacks.

There was one good thing about Belial appearing at the Gray Stag tonight with his companions: that meant he wasn't attempting to abduct Angelica or her sisters.

Voss's attention had continued its constant sweep of the irregularly shaped room, and now it focused on the figure that had just entered. Standing just inside the door of the pub, tall and slender with dark eyes and wearing the cloak Voss had purposely left at Rubey's, the young man was unfamiliar to him. But he was wearing the red cloak trimmed in gold...and Voss trusted Rubey.

Voss shifted in his seat and waited, smothering his impatience. The tankards were in position. The young man would find him.

He extracted a guinea from his pouch and set it on the table next to the tankards and lifted his own to drink.

Or, rather, to pretend to drink. And to hide his face should anyone look in his direction.

The young man didn't waste any time. In fact, he was more obvious than Voss would have preferred, but Belial didn't seem to notice how the red-cloaked figure made its way around the pub to the corner where Voss sat. He dropped a packet on the table and swiped up the guinea, then slipped out the rear entrance.

The packet of paper was heavy, and Voss unfolded it with hands that shook more than he'd care to admit. On the creamy paper, the scent of ink was laced with the smell of Angelica's fingerprints, rising over stale ale and sweat. He breathed. A pang, unfamiliar and surprising in its intensity, sizzled through him—a pang different from the constant agony that had become part of his person, radiating from the Mark on his back.

As Bonaparte's watch chain slipped from the packet, cool and snakelike into his palm, Voss reflected that he knew how to make the searing stop—if he chose to.

It would be easy. And very, very pleasurable. And, after all, pleasure was what he lived for...was it not?

It was all he had.

Yet...as he fingered the chain and unfolded the letter with it, he told himself he didn't wish to endanger his own person by going after Angelica—after all, Dimitri and Giordan Cale would be watching even more closely for him now. And he'd heard from Rubey that even Woodmore had chanced a secret appearance in London, looking for Voss. The letter crinkled in his hands.

Her handwriting was feminine, with extra curlicues and sweeping descenders. It fit her, as did the few drips of ink and a smudged fingerprint that bespoke of haste or furtiveness. He found it strangely intimate, seeing a woman's handwriting for the first time. It was rather like touching her bare hand after removing her gloves.

Did you not think I wouldn't know whose it was the moment I touched it? she wrote. *If I weren't so eager to rid London of your presence, I would lie and say I saw nothing, for if this informatio—*Here, she had scratched out the following words, leaving them illegible, then continued: *But I dare not lie, for fear you would use that as an excuse to stay. And you must leave. I do not want to ever see you again, but nor do I wish for your demise. As for the owner of the enclosed item... His death will come, not on a battlefield, not from a coup or other attempt, but in a deathbed, surrounded by only three persons. The chamber is not a great or well-furnished one, but nor is it poor and mean. It feels as if it is some years in the future. The fact that he is alone but for the three, and his body is wasted and his face some years older, suggests that whatever power he now has will at that time be gone or greatly diminished. That is all I can tell you. I bid you* adieu.

She hadn't signed it.

Definitely not the sort of correspondence he was used to receiving from a woman. Not a hint of *amour* anywhere.

Although…she didn't actually wish him dead. That was something.

But then again, he cared little for what she thought.

Voss folded the letter and considered lighting it on the candle sconce behind him, then setting it in one of the tankards to burn—but that was only a brief contemplation. Instead he tucked it into his breast pocket.

Right, then. Woodmore had come back to London, at least temporarily. Not that it was the first time the vampire hunter had been out for Voss's heart…but he thought it best not to tempt the Fates. Now that he'd received the chain back from Angelica, with her valuable knowledge, he was going to leave London and make his way to…St. Petersburg, he decided impulsively. He pursed his lips, suffered through another sip of the thin, pale-as-piss ale and decided he'd send Angelica a brief correspondence to thank her, and to let her know he was leaving. And assuage the bit of conscience that dared niggle at him in the process.

On his way to St. Petersburg, there'd be a quick stop in Paris to meet Moldavi. He'd sell a select portion of the information to the bastard, and then—flush with even more blunt—he'd be putting himself far away from Angelica Woodmore.

Surely, then, the pain would stop.

"Angelica, I neglected to tell you how much I adore your frock," said Mirabella as they settled in the carriage. "That rose hue is too bold for me, I think, but on you, it looks perfect."

Angelica had to force herself to smile at the younger woman. The compliment was sincere, and Lord Corvindale's sister was a delightful change from her own bossy sibling, but Angelica didn't feel terribly cheery this evening. Her unpleasant mood had begun this morning, when she awoke from the disturbing dream that, hours later, still clung to the remnants of her consciousness.

"Thank you," she said to Mirabella as she arranged her skirts to make room for Maia on the bench next to her.

"I wasn't certain I approved of the fabric when you selected it, but I confess, you made the right choice. That pale pink I favored would have made you look too pale," Maia said, settling neatly beside her.

Angelica smiled with more genuine feeling. Maia, admitting she was wrong? How refreshing. "Thank you, dear," she said, wondering if her sister had received a new letter from Mr. Bradington. Perhaps he was to return to London in short order and that was why she seemed less rigid than usual.

Angelica pulled the hem of her whisper-thin wrap from where it had become caught between herself and Maia and reflected that, yes indeed, the gown was the perfect choice for tonight's birthday party. She had loved the rosy-pink sateen the first moment she'd laid eyes on it at Madame Clovis's, and with the pink, green and white sash and trims, it had turned out to be one of her favorite evening frocks.

The party, which wasn't a formal ball but a small, intimate fete, was being given for Lord Harrington. And, based on his insistence that she attend, Angelica suspected that he might not be the only recipient of something pleasant that evening. He'd made a broad hint about their future only yesterday, when they went riding in the sunny park, leaving her to wonder if she might become engaged by the end of the evening. Or, at least, if he might ask.

The very thought made her stomach alternately squirm and flutter. Harrington would be an excellent match.

"The rubies are a nice touch," Maia was saying, and touched her own matching earbobs. "I declare, if I hadn't found those little pouches on your dressing table, Angelica, they might have been forgotten for weeks, or, more likely, knocked down behind the mirror."

If you hadn't been so nosy, poking about my dressing table, I wouldn't have been forced to open them. Angelica's smile had frozen and she adjusted the seam on her left glove. The weight of the robin's egg-size rubies hanging from her ears was only part of the reason for her deteriorating mood. Another part was the horrifying dream she had had the night before, and yet another part was the letter she'd received earlier that day.

"Where did you say you got them from, Angelica?" Maia asked. "I don't recall ever seeing two pairs of ruby earbobs before."

"They're part of Granny Grapes's collection. Surely you remember when we used to try them on when we played lady dress-up," Angelica said in a blatant lie for which she felt no remorse. "I declare, Maia, you seem more fuzzy-brained than usual."

Her elder sister sniffed and frowned, obviously trying to recall an event that had never happened. Angelica hid a smile. Eventually she'd figure out it was a fabrication, but for now, it felt good to have fooled her. Perhaps one day, she'd feel right about telling Maia the truth.

Years from now, after they were both wed.

And as for the letters they'd received earlier... Maia

might have had a correspondence that improved her cheer, but Angelica had not. The seal on the snowy paper clearly indicated that the message was from Voss, and the fact that he'd been so bold as to simply write *Angelica* on it in heavy, masculine ink instead of addressing it properly was just another indication of his lack of propriety.

As with the little black velvet pouches, Angelica intended to leave the letter unopened. She had no desire to read anything he'd written to her; she'd done her part, given him all the information she gleaned from the watch chain, and she didn't want to read any further excuses or requests.

She hadn't had the chance to burn the missive because Maia had come in to snoop around, but that would be rectified as soon as she returned tonight. Instead she'd stuffed it into the drawer with her other stationery before her sister could see it and demand to know all of the pertinent details.

But for some reason, the sight of her name, written so confidently and boldly—such a simple image—on the heavy paper, was burned into her memory and would not be dislodged. No man had ever sent her a letter before, and she couldn't ever recall seeing her name written in a man's hand.

And then there was the dream, still niggling at her. Stark and clear as a garden in the afternoon sun, but far from pleasant. But surely since he'd sent the letter, the dream hadn't come true.… He wasn't yet dead.

Perhaps she ought to open the letter before she burned it.

Perhaps she ought to warn him.

But no. Angelica didn't warn people when she saw

their demise. It did no good—and Lord Brickbank was proof of that.

It was a burden she bore on her own. Knowledge that she must carry in secret.

But in a dream. Another dream. Why could she not read his future by holding his glove? But that it was foisted upon her in a dream…just as his friend's had done. It made no sense.

I wish Granny Grapes was here to help me understand.

She bit her lip and moved the curtain to glance out the carriage window. The moon wasn't quite full, but it cast a strong-willed light that filtered through heavy gray clouds.

"Shall we close the door?" Maia said, leaning forward to latch the half-open thing. "Or is Aunt Iliana feeling well enough to join us after all? We shall be late if we don't leave soon."

"She isn't coming," Mirabella said, "but Corvindale is going to join us in her stead."

"Here? In the carriage?" Maia froze and Angelica felt rather than saw the tension rise as if someone were filling her sister with something unpleasant. "Why does he not meet us there as he usually does?"

"A shocking concept for the earl to ride with us, I agree, but he insisted," Mirabella replied. She seemed delighted about the possibility of riding to the fete with her brother. "I believe he's concerned that we might be waylaid by those horrible men again. Although in another breath, he urges me to have no worries about being in danger."

"I don't see why he has to ride—" Maia snapped her lips closed as the carriage door opened.

Corvindale loomed in the doorway, then climbed in swiftly, and so gracefully that he brushed nary a hem nor bumped a slipper as he settled next to his sister. Nevertheless, the generous space shrunk to a much smaller one with addition of his large, gruff presence. The closeness made the mixture of rose water aroma and Angelica's lily of the valley scent mesh with something sharp and masculine, along with wool and smoke. Dressed in a dark coat, topped with a matching hat and giving the glimpse of a brilliant white shirt and a neckcloth of muted colors, the earl was more formally attired than Angelica could recall ever having seen him, except the first night they'd all met. Apparently he took his chaperonage duties seriously—if not reluctantly.

"Good evening, my lord," Angelica said. "How kind of you to join us. Maia was just commenting on that event and how gratified she is that you've taken our safety so seriously that you'd deign to ride with us."

Maia wasn't very subtle as she knocked her pointed slipper into Angelica's ankle, but the latter had been expecting such a reaction and adjusted her foot appropriately. But any further commentary waned as she glanced over at Corvindale.

The coach had started off with a little jerk, but the man was sitting there with an oddly arrested expression on his face. He seemed frozen, his harsh features even more stony than usual. Dark hair gleamed in the low moonlight, brushed neatly away from his temples, but rough and shaggy around the edges of his collar.

Maia, who had turned up her slender, pretty nose and her face toward the small, curtained window, was pointedly not looking at him. And Mirabella, who seemed to have lost her chattiness the moment her elder brother entered the scene, had succumbed to picking at the embroidery on the back of her glove.

Angelica realized that Corvindale seemed to be staring at her—no, at her ears, and that he appeared to be having difficulty breathing. Had he somehow recognized that her earbobs were from Voss? Was he working to control his fury?

Rather than anger in his face, however, she thought the emotion there was more akin to shock. Or pain?

"My lord?" she asked, tipping slightly into Maia as the coach turned a sharp corner. He didn't respond.

The light in the carriage flickered as they passed by streetlamps, leaving her with the impression that Corvindale had blinked or given some other dismissive sort of gesture. His fingers curled over the front of his knees, one hand curved around a walking stick that she suspected wasn't used for ambulatory purposes as much as for weaponry. At least, she hoped it wasn't.

Apparently despite his intention to protect them from whatever dangers the vampires might have planned, the earl was in no mood to talk. Good. Nor was Angelica.

She turned to look out the window, shoving the curtain aside.

But something bothered her: the uncomfortable silence among them, the sound of harsh, rushed breathing rising just above the rumble of carriage wheels, the fact that she could see no other streetlamps amid the shadows of buildings…and that odd expression on his face.

Angelica turned back to the earl and had the impression in the odd light that his eyelids were fluttering. His lips had drawn back in something clearly like pain and he seemed unable to move.

"Lord Corvindale!" she exclaimed, standing abruptly.

Her head brushed the top of the carriage, and she bumped against the wall. Her shrill voice penetrated Maia's self-imposed pout, and her sister turned back toward them. "Are you ill?"

"What is it?" Maia asked. Any trace of pique had left her voice and she, too, was leaning toward Corvindale.

But the earl seemed to shrink back in the seat, his eyes flashing darkly. *"A...way."*

His lips moved; Angelica was certain that was what he'd said, although it had come out in more of a gasp-like whisper.

"Corvindale, what is it?" Mirabella had come to life as well. Sitting next to her brother, she was the obvious one to pluck at his arm, which did nothing but flop lifelessly. "My lord!" She grasped his shoulders with her small hands and tried to shake him, but the man was too large and solid for her to do more than jolt him a bit.

He made a noise that sounded like a groan, or a frustrated gasp, and although his eyes flashed angrily in the dark, he seemed unable to speak further.

Angelica lifted her hand to pound on the roof of the carriage, but just before she did, the vehicle stopped abruptly. She tumbled back into her rear-facing seat, landing in Maia's lap. Someone shouted outside and the vehicle gave a great jolt, as if something had slammed into the side of it.

Another shout, and then the sound of something like a pistol.

Angelica, trying to disengage herself from Maia's lap, looked over at Corvindale, whose eyes had become more wild and his mouth even more flattened. He seemed to be struggling against some invisible bonds, trying to breathe, eyes bulging. The walking stick shifted slightly in his fingers, but didn't rise.

The door opened and fresh summer air wafted in, followed by a pair of glowing eyes.

Mirabella screamed and cowered next to her brother. Angelica stifled a gasp as she saw the flash of fangs. The burning gaze fastened on hers, and then something heavy and dark lunged toward her.

Strong hands closed over her arms and the next thing she knew, she was being dragged from the vehicle.

Maia screamed and tried to pull her back in, and for a moment, Angelica was suspended in midair, being torn in two directions. But with a great jolt, the vampire tore her free.

Whipping Angelica away from the carriage, her captor held her with an immovable grip despite her struggles. The next thing she knew, she was being shoved into another vehicle.

Tumbling to her knees on the small floor space, Angelica clawed the covering wrap from her face and looked up into the burning red eyes of the vampire Belial.

13

THE AFTERMATH OF
A JEST GONE AWRY

"**I** must speak with the Earl of Corvindale," Maia said firmly. She shoved the toe of her slipper between the door and its frame.

The main entrance to the infamous White's—a place she'd heard of but had never even seen before tonight—was on St. James. Its white brick facade was well lit by two lanterns, but this obscure rear door was the one she'd seen the earl employ. Despite the fact that it seemed abandoned and unused, she'd made her way up and rapped on the door.

"It is imperative that I speak with him. I'll not be turned away."

"The individual of whom you speak is not in residence," said the man with a supercilious sneer that was clearly visible in the stream of light coming from inside. "Aside of that, individuals of the feminine persuasion—" and he said this with even more disdain as he raked her with a glance of distaste "—are not allowed admittance into this structure. Ever."

But Maia had dealt with people of every sort, including slick men of business during the times Chas had been absent. She was not cowed, especially when her sister's life was at stake. "As it happens, I saw the earl walk into this structure with my own eyes. I know he's here and it is of great necessity that I speak with him. Now, if you please, you may either find him and relay my message, or I shall do so myself." She pushed at the door with her gloved hands.

"Indeed, madam, I will not—oh, good evening, sir." The sneer evaporated from his face as he looked up and behind Maia. "I do apologize for—"

"What seems to be the problem?" came a deep, smooth voice at her ear.

Maia turned to see Lord Dewhurst looming on the porch behind her. She wasn't certain whether her first reaction should be one of apprehension or of gratitude. After all, yes, he had abducted Angelica and taken her to that horrible place where she and Corvindale had retrieved her...but he also had actually *sent* for them *and* relinquished her sister. Angelica had been unharmed.

Relatively unharmed—except for four little punctures on her neck, Maia amended mentally.

Yet, Angelica had dreamed of him, in nightmares, sobbing and thrashing about...calling his name. *Voss.*

She wondered what more had occurred between the two.

And whether a vampire could ever be trusted.

"There is no problem," the butler was saying. "May I assist you, my lord?"

Dewhurst looked at Maia. "You seek Corvindale? He's within?"

Her eyes narrowed. "Yes. Despite what this *individ-*

ual says, I saw him enter with my own eyes." Only because when he thought he'd left her with Mirabella back at Blackmont Hall after the attack on the carriage, she'd gone to look for him in his study and had been just in time to see him leave.

Of course she'd followed him, the vile man, using her own footman and carriage. How dare he leave without answering her questions and telling her the plan.

"I've been in search of Corvindale, as well," Dewhurst said. "Just as urgently."

This surprised Maia, considering how angry Corvindale was with Dewhurst.

She didn't know what specifically he did to make the butler shift out of their path and open the door, but a few words exchanged between the two men and Maia was inside with Dewhurst.

As was true for any other proper lady, she'd never been in any gentlemen's club before, although of course she'd heard of this famous one, and as Lord Dewhurst gestured for her to precede him down a dark corridor, Maia took it all in with her gaze. Despite the fact that this seemed to be a deserted area of the club—perhaps a servants' entrance—the decor was just what she would have expected of a haven for the male gender.

Heavy, dark paneling rose from floor to ceiling. Intermittent sconces sent small half spheres of light glowing yellow-orange against the oiled, dark wood. And… *heavens!* The painting of a woman dressed in nothing but transparent gauze!

Along with a variety of pictures, the corridor was studded with several doors, and as they passed along she heard masculine voices rise in laughter, argument and other forms of joviality. But they stopped at none of the doors until the hallway turned.

Dewhurst, who'd disdained the butler and left the man behind them, came to the end of the hall—a dead-end—and turned to look at her. For a moment, Maia's heart leaped into her throat as she realized she was here, alone, in an empty corridor at a club where no one knew she'd come, trapped with a vampire who'd attacked her sister. *Foolish, foolish!*

"My apologies, Miss Woodmore," Dewhurst said in a surprisingly gentle voice, "but you'll need to don this hood if you wish to go any further."

Maia's eyes grew wide as he plucked a heavy velvet hood from a set of hooks on the wall. "You're mad," she said. "Why would I trust you?"

He shrugged with easy indolence. "As you wish. But I haven't time to wait for your compliance. Either do as I ask, or you'll wait here until I—or Corvindale—return. And it could be some time. I am under the assumption that Moldavi's men have succeeded in abducting Angelica."

"Which makes this the *second* time she's been abducted," she told him pointedly.

"I warned Corvindale, blast it." His lips twitched slightly, but then flattened and she fancied she saw a flash of anguish there. Or not.

Maia took the hood, fingering its heavy softness and with a huff of annoyance, pulled it over her head. She couldn't imagine what her hair looked like after the attack in the carriage—which had been only an hour ago, hard as it was to believe. She was still wearing her party frock and her slippers were stained with mud and goodness knew what else…but there was no time to waste.

Once the stifling hood was in place, Dewhurst took her arm and led her…she wasn't certain where. If she'd thought she might see down beneath the hood and trace their steps via a peek of the floor beneath it, she was disappointed. The hood had so many folds and was so long that she could see nothing and had to rely fully on the man next to her. The concern that she might be recognized should they encounter any other member of the club was moot, for the hood obscured her identity.

Their rapid journey included turns and the opening and closing of at least two doors that seemed to slide rather than swing open, and there was a set of stairs (stone or brick, unlike the rest of the flooring, which had been carpeted) down which they tread…and then another door.

The loud voices on the other side of the door stopped abruptly, and Maia fancied it was because of her appearance on the threshold of whatever chamber they'd entered.

Some loud and violent noise sounded as if someone stood, shoving away a table or knocking over a chair, and then there was the sharp symphonic clink and clank of, perhaps, glasses or bottles on a table that might have been bumped or moved, and an abbreviated scuffle.

Dewhurst didn't release her arm, and she felt his fingers tighten as if in readiness. "Don't be a fool," he said sharply. She knew he wasn't speaking to her. "Did you think I would be so foolish as to come unprepared?"

Impatient, she yanked off the hood and found herself standing at the entrance to a small, windowless room that boasted less than half a dozen occupants. Before she could identify any of them other than—oh dear—*Chas,* an aggrieved sound drew her attention.

"You." Corvindale, of course. He was half seated at a table with one hand flat on wood shiny with some spilled liquid, and a few glasses. One was on its side. He was staring at her with a mixture of shock, fury and disgust. Chas stood just to his right, and Maia thought she recognized the other gentleman, but it wasn't Mr. Cale. The female vampire Narcise was nowhere in sight; the remaining occupants were men who appeared to be footmen or other servants and they seemed to melt into the shadows as if to remain unnoticed.

Dewhurst tugged Maia closer, her hem brushing his trousers, and she saw that he'd shifted the flaps of his coat. A large ruby winked in the center of his neckcloth. He smiled coolly at Corvindale, who looked as if he were about to fly across the room, but had been halted in midtrajectory.

"Of course I wouldn't come unprotected, knowing just how you feel about me," Dewhurst was saying. He nodded at Chas, who, Maia noticed, was holding a stake in his hand, and then Mr. Cale. "Keep your distance, and no one will get hurt."

"Maia," Chas said, his voice sharp and steely. "Are you all right?"

"Other than worried to illness for the safety of my sister, while the rest of you sit about and visit at your club? Yes, I am fine." She made no effort to hide the bite in her voice. "If it weren't for Lord Dewhurst, I would still be standing at the door, arguing with the butler. It was he who helped me gain entrance."

"How convenient," Corvindale said. He sank back into his chair, but his gaze flashed, burning at the man standing next to Maia, and all at once she lost her breath.

Impossible.

She stared at the earl, her heart pounding hard and her head light. Impossible, but…it rather made sense. His eyes had *burned.* Red.

How could she have been so blind?

It was no wonder he wanted all of the curtains drawn, even in his study. Why his sister hardly knew him, and even in moments of great urgency called him by his formal name. And why he had been chosen by their brother to take care of them in his absence.

Who better to protect his sisters from a vengeful *vampir* than *another vampir?*

"I cannot believe your incompetence, Dimitri. I sent you the warning," Dewhurst was saying as Maia came back to reality. His voice was cold with fury; no longer smooth and rich as it had been before. "And you, Woodmore. Another disappearing and then reappearing act? Are you here to take care of your sisters or not?"

No. She didn't want to believe it. *Couldn't* believe it.

They were the wards of a *vampir?* My word, were they *everywhere?*

And…her brother *worked* for him? A *vampir* hunter was the associate of a *vampir?* Her head began to hurt.

"Oh, aye, I got your message—along with two bloody pairs of ruby earbobs, you sneaky bastard." Corvindale had stood again, and a vein at the side of his temple throbbed so hard she could see it from across the room. He would have lunged if Chas hadn't thrust an arm out in front of him.

Dewhurst shifted a bit, then thrust his chin belligerently and this time Maia saw a flash of—dear God, *fangs?* "It was a jest, nothing more. I warned her not to wear them in your presence."

"Damn your soul to Lucifer, it's your bloody fault

she's been taken," Chas said. "You and your cursed jests and games, Voss." The stake shifted and the next thing Maia knew, the tension in the chamber snapped, and the place was in an uproar.

Something strong and powerful whipped her off her feet, gathering her up and spinning her away as Chas flew toward Dewhurst. The two men tumbled to the floor as Maia fought in vain to pull away from the strong hands that held her.

"Release me, you idiot man," she said, jamming her elbow into the vicinity of Corvindale's belly. She must have missed, for whatever she hit was solid and hard and made her gasp with pain. And he didn't release her, merely holding her firmly away from the fray and muttering vile things under his breath.

Her brother and Dewhurst were on the floor, and then back on their feet, squaring off, facing each other, half crouched and wild-eyed. Chairs flew, crashing onto tables and sending glass flying. Dewhurst's eyes blazed with fire, and Maia could, for the first time, clearly see the jut of his fangs. He seemed to favor his right shoulder, unable to lift his right arm as high as his left, wincing with pain when Chas flung him into the wall, cradling that arm. Dewhurst stumbled and tripped over Corvindale's outthrust foot, somersaulting into the wall.

The stake rose and Chas followed and Maia stifled a gasp as it whipped down toward Dewhurst's torso, hiding her face even as she cried, "Don't! *Chas!*"

There was a loud noise, a scuffle and then…silence. Followed by the sound of a muttered curse. Maia realized suddenly that her face was buried in a broad, cotton-covered chest, warm and solid and very, very wide. It smelled fresh and sharp and like some pungent herb.

A sudden vision of that very same chest, dark and bare and muscular, half covered beneath his bedclothes, rose in her mind.

At just about the same moment as the blast of embarrassed heat rushed over her face, Corvindale said, "I do hope you aren't wiping your nose on my shirt, Miss Woodmore."

The realization that, while she was still clutching him, he was no longer holding her added to her mortification and Maia spun away. She opened her eyes, fully expecting to see the bloodied corpse of a staked vampire on the floor.

Did vampires bleed?

But Dewhurst stood, brushing easily at his own shirt and Chas faced him, menace in his eyes, stake in his hand. Not a drop of blood in sight, and both men panting as if they'd been running.

"Armor?" Chas said, looking chagrined. He shoved the stake into some interior pocket or sling.

"After a fashion," Dewhurst replied. "I warned you I'd come prepared—for all of you. Now, if you would cease attacking me, I would appreciate the opportunity to assist you in retrieving Angelica."

"Your assistance is neither wanted nor needed," Chas told him. "Aside of that, I want you in no vicinity to any of my sisters. A different country would be preferable. Just because you were prepared this time doesn't always mean that you'll escape my stake."

Dewhurst gave a short, biting laugh. "I didn't believe you were that foolish, Woodmore. In fact, I'm the only one who can assist you in saving Angelica."

Corvindale snorted and walked over to stand next

to Chas. He picked up one of the glasses. "Not bloody likely." The earl sipped.

Dewhurst made a sound of great exasperation. "Very well, then." He shrugged and glanced at Maia. "Best of luck to all of you." He turned toward the door.

"Wait!" Furious, Maia stomped her foot. "Are you just going to allow him to leave?" she demanded, glaring at Chas. "Without hearing what he has to say? Angelica's in *danger* and all you care about is…is whatever insults you've given to each other in the past. I vow, the three of you are like little boys fighting over a ball."

"I don't need his help," Chas said, puffing up his chest and giving her a dark, older-brother look. She ignored it and opened her mouth to speak.

"Perhaps the lady is right." The calm voice came from the corner and Maia whirled to see…Mr. Cale. He appeared so comfortable in their presence that she could only assume that he, too, was a vampire. Although he'd remained out of the fray, now he was the recipient of a frigid glance from her brother. "At least hear what the bastard—pardon me, Miss Woodmore—has to say. Then turn him out."

"It's because of me that you even knew they were to attack this evening," Dewhurst said, looking at Corvindale meaningfully. He glanced at Maia and once again, she thought she recognized real concern or even anguish in his eyes as he spoke to her. "I was fortunate enough to cross paths with the vampire Belial, who is the one sent by Cezar Moldavi to find either your brother…or someone else that could be used as hostage. One of the serving girls at the Gray Stag complied with my…request," he added, flashing his burning eyes, "and got him talking and bragging about his plans for tonight. I assumed a warning to you would be sufficient, Corvindale, but apparently not." He cast a brief, pointed glance at the earl and then gestured lazily at Maia. "When I arrived here to find her arguing with the butler, rather than leaving her on the doorstep where she might have been otherwise noticed, I thought it best to bring her within."

"They had ample opportunity to abduct her as well as Mirabella this evening," Corvindale said from between clenched teeth. "They chose not to. It was Angelica they were after."

Dewhurst nodded. "Because they'd already identified her. I'm certain, for by now, Moldavi has heard of her unusual ability. Angelica wasn't very secretive about it, at least among her friends. Not only does Moldavi want to use her to bring her brother into submission, but also to put her to work. He can force her to tell him what she knows about the person who owns any item he brings to her."

"You're wasting time," Chas said. "We've just about finished our plan to search the city and now you've set us back."

"And where exactly were you going to search in the city?" Dewhurst asked. His lean stance was lazy, as Maia had come to expect, and his voice easy—but under it all, she recognized tension simmering. He felt the urgency just as much as she did. Perhaps more. "Because she's no longer in the city. They're taking her to Paris. They're already well ahead of you on a boat going down the Thames."

Paris? How? They were at war, the French were collecting troops just over the Channel. Impossible.

Maia was prepared for the other men to scoff at the viscount, but to her surprise, they remained silent. Mr.

Cale even gave a brief nod as if to instruct Dewhurst to continue, which he did.

"You didn't think Cezar would risk himself to come here, did you? Belial is bringing Angelica to him. The good news is that she'll arrive unharmed—for Cezar will want to use her for everything he can. And Belial won't dare allow anything to happen to her. The bad news is... not one of you could expect to gain entrance to Moldavi's residence in Paris to get to Angelica. Except for me."

"You forget about me. Moldavi will see me," Cale said. His voice was flat and his eyes empty. "I'll go."

"That's not necessary," Dewhurst replied, just as Corvindale snapped, "No, Giordan."

"I'll go," Dewhurst said firmly. "Moldavi will see me. I have acquired some information he wants about Bonaparte. And I'll be able to get her back."

"How are you going to get to Paris? We're at war!" Maia asked. But it was as if she weren't even in the room. "Mrs. Siddington-Graves has been trapped there for a year!" Which was why her husband had become much less discreet about taking his mistress to the theater.

"Why should I trust you?" Chas was saying.

Dewhurst shrugged. "I returned her once before, didn't I?"

"Complete with nightmares, frightening memories, not to mention marks on her skin," her brother responded. "Not quite unharmed."

Dewhurst's jaw moved but he kept his voice steady. "As you well know, I've spent my life collecting information and learning the weaknesses of my associates and enemies alike. I know how to influence Moldavi."

Chas gave a sharp nod. "Very well, then. I'll accompany you to Paris."

"No! Chas! What if Moldavi captures you, too?" Maia interjected as Dewhurst frowned, shaking his head.

Her brother looked at her as if she'd just offered to hold his hand and tuck him into bed. "I am quite able to take care of myself, Maia. I've already evaded him once, and now I know exactly what I'd be walking into." He glanced at Corvindale, then settled on Cale with an unfathomable expression. "Narcise will have to stay here, of course."

"But, Chas…I don't understand. Why are you working *with vampirs* if you *kill* them?" Maia asked. Her head had begun to pound harder now.

Her brother made an impatient gesture. "It's all rather complicated, and I'm not about to explain it all right now. The simple answer is—there are evil vampires and ones that are…well, not so much of a danger to us mortals. I work to rid the world of the evil ones. At any rate, I'm going to Paris with Voss and we'll bring back Angelica. That's all you need to know at this time."

But Dewhurst interrupted. "If you want to jeopardize my chances, then you may come. Otherwise…follow if you will, but some days behind me. There can be no hint to Moldavi that we're working together."

Corvindale snorted again. "Even if he saw the two of you shaking hands, he wouldn't believe it."

Dewhurst shot him a look of pure dislike. "Precisely."

Under normal circumstances, Voss would be delighted with an excuse to visit Paris. Culture, food, wine and the most flamboyant of women made the city one of his favorite places.

But this visit was to a Paris in flux, with its revised imperial government, new emperor, soldiers in uniform everywhere, talk of the war with England and general government upheaval. Voss recognized in the city an unusual aura of disarray—whether it was from preparations for a coronation still months away, or the sense that things had not quite settled since Napoleon Bonaparte managed to manipulate himself from First Consul to Emperor mere weeks earlier.

Aside from that, of course, Voss wasn't in Paris for anything related to pleasure or leisure. Despite the unrelenting pain in his shoulder, he'd traveled quickly—on horseback at night to Dover, and then below deck while crossing the Channel during a ridiculously sunny day—then back on horseback again across the French countryside to Paris. He took care to avoid the camps at Boulogne, where armies prepared for their invasion of England.

The fact that soldiers and armed guards were more prevalent than the last time he'd been to Paris concerned him not at all. Not only did he have no interest nor stake in any political upheaval (why should he?), Voss had speed, night vision and stealth. Plus, he was impervious to bullets.

It was simpler than seducing a whore to get where he needed to go without being intercepted.

Despite his claims to Woodmore and Dimitri, Voss wasn't altogether confident that Angelica would be unharmed when he found her. Certainly Moldavi would want to utilize her Sight…but what exactly would he do to ensure that she complied?

Thus, he'd been in a state of tense urgency since leaving White's with the reluctant approval of the other Draculia members. Remembering the horror in Angelica's face, the loathing when she spoke of vampires, Voss could only hope—for he didn't pray—that she'd be untouched. The small bite, the bare nibble he'd taken from her a week ago was nothing in comparison to Moldavi's and his cronies' proclivities.

Thus, Voss rested little, except while on the sun-drenched boat. As it was the first time in more than a week that he'd slept without being drenched in whiskey, bloodscent and pleasure, he had expected easy slumber.

He was wrong.

Even now, as he strode through the busy arched galleries of Paris's Palais-Royal and its sprawling gardens, Voss couldn't banish the dark images that had swept into his dreams two days ago. An agonized Brickbank. A terrified, and yet sensual, beckoning Angelica.

And Lucifer. Again. Silent, smiling, but his fingers—long, slender, white—curving over Voss's shoulder. Holding him. Invading his dreams and turning them to nightmares.

You cannot change. You are bound to me.

When Voss had dragged himself back into the reality of day, the imprint of the devil's fingers on his shoulder still burned…as if he were with him still. Even now, as the moon rose, no longer quite full, in the starry sky, he felt the weight of those dreams and wondered why Luce had visited him yet again after more than a century of silence.

Moving quickly along the walkway, Voss avoided the eyes of a particularly friendly prostitute—ahh, the French!—and slipped between a group of jovial men and one of the gallery columns. Louder and more contained than Vauxhall, the *jardins* at what had once been the residence of Cardinal Richelieu abounded with shops, brothels, cafés and theaters—anything for the gentry in search of pleasure. The Café des Chartres, where, according to Moldavi, Napoleon and his new empress, Josephine, had been known to tryst, was tucked into a corner of the *palais* and next to it sat a popular wine bar with revelers spilling onto the stone colonnade edged with lilies and lavender.

As he hurried along, a pale, slender figure caught his eye. She was leaning against one of the columns, and when he saw her, Voss nearly stopped in surprise. It couldn't be. Their eyes met and a shiver rushed through him. It was the blonde woman he'd seen at the Gray Stag. Had she trailed him to Paris?

As then, she was wearing a long, outdated gown that looked as if it belonged on a medieval chatelaine rather than a Parisian shopkeeper, or whore, or whatever she was.

Her pale eyes caught his as he walked past, and she gave a little nod. *So you remember me this time.*

He heard the words in his mind, as if she'd whispered them in his ear—but she hadn't moved from her position against the column.

Good, Voss. You give me hope. Are you ready yet?

He paused and looked at her from across the street. *I don't know what you mean,* he thought, sensing that she'd hear him.

She nodded, and revealed a bit of a smile. Even from a distance, he felt warmth. *You'll know when the time comes.*

A mass of people walked between them, and when they passed by, she was gone.

An uneasy feeling settled over his shoulders, and the rage of his Mark reminded him why he was here. He put it out of his mind and prepared himself for what was certain to be a tenuous, if not deadly, meeting with Moldavi.

At last Voss found the shop front he sought. The spicy sage and rosemary scent of Corcellet's renowned sausages didn't have to fight hard to be noticed above the other smells of *patisserie* or cigar smoke, although the sweet and overbearing gillyflower perfume of the whore who stumbled into Voss gave it some competition.

"Pardon, madame," he said, walking past her into the little *epicerie*. The patés and sausages were of little interest to him, of course, although the scent of blood was heavy in the space and his mouth watered a bit.

How long had it been since he'd fed?

The thought hadn't occurred to him until now, startling Voss as he pushed through the crowded little shop. For it was rare that he went more than a day or two without at least a bit of pleasurable sucking, drinking and fucking. And along with that, perhaps once a week he needed to find three or four willing participants to completely replenish his fluids.

"Monsieur," said the gentleman behind the counter even as he wrapped a package for one of his customers, and gestured sharply to an employee to assist another. The dull roar of shouted orders and animated conversation muted his greeting.

Voss merely nodded and met the proprietor's eyes over the throng of men. A bit of a glow, a flash of fang, was all Corcellet needed to ascertain Voss's requirement. Despite the claims on his attention, he eased from behind the counter and gestured for Voss to follow him.

Moments later, he slipped a generous handful of *sous* into the man's hand and was given admittance to the presumed cellar. He'd been here several times in the past, but it had been nearly a decade since his last visit.

Nothing had changed, however. The air was cool and dank, and smelled of peat and mold along with the spices from above. The large oaken door still led to stairs that spiraled down into one of the old Roman quarries, now little more than tunnels beneath the city. In some areas, skulls and other human bones now literally covered what had been walls carved into stone—a result of overcrowded cemeteries being emptied in the latter part of the previous century. But no one had yet dared breach Cezar Moldavi's subterranean hideaway with such macabre decor.

Not that it would have bothered Moldavi to have stacks of skulls and femurs lining his walls. It was just that no one but a select few knew of this particular entrance and set of tunnels through Corcellet's.

Voss checked the deep pockets of his coat as he followed the familiar route. The packets were there—flat, odd-smelling items that would seem inconsequential to Cezar Moldavi if he bothered to check. They were his ace in the pocket, and, he hoped they'd be as effective for him as they had been for Chas Woodmore. If he had a chance to use them.

He strode quickly, passing three other doorways, until it swept up to a higher level and at last ended in a fourth door. Behind that door, he knew, was a space set just below the ground. Narrow windows, placed right at ground level, offered natural illumination that was sketchy enough to be safe for even the most sun-sensitive of vampires and kept the chamber from being dark and gloomy.

Draculia members spent much of their effort looking for ways out of dark and gloom. With the exception of Dimitri.

Voss paused when the guard sitting in the shadows moved into better view. Hmm. He didn't recall there being one the last time—but then again, he'd been drunk on blood-whiskey and a variety of other influences, and some of the details had been lost. But...a guard. With a sword, and very, very wide shoulders.

"Voss Arden, Viscount Dewhurst," he said to the wall-like man, clearly a made vampire—and likely a newly minted one at that, if the way he tried to sneer around his fangs (awkwardly) was any indication. Voss smiled back, easily, without puncturing himself with his own show of fangs, and made his eyes burn. "Tell Moldavi I'm here."

And all at once, Voss smelled *her*.

He had to steady himself. The scent was so rich and so strong, filtering unerringly to his nostrils that he was certain it had to be from blood. Spilled blood.

Please. No.

Until now, he hadn't allowed himself to think too closely about his mission, other than general urgency. Just: *Get there. Get there.*

He hadn't dwelled on what it meant. What he might find. Why he really was there. But now... Suddenly his heart pounded like a cavalry cresting a hill. *Angelica.* "The *voivode* is not to be disturbed," the guard said.

"He'll want to see me. I must insist that you announce my presence," he replied, keeping his voice charming with an effort. A great effort. Angelica was...just there. Behind that door.

"I think not," replied the guard. "You can wait. Until tomorrow. When Voivode Moldavi is finished."

Voss moved quickly, smoothly, and had the guard against the wall before the bloody bollocks-sucker could react. "I'll see Moldavi now." His fingers closed over the man's windpipe even as the guard's sword clanked ineffectively against the wall behind him. "Trust me. He'll want to see me."

Of course, there was no strangling a Dracule—even one not invited directly by Lucifer—but it did weaken the bloke enough to make his point. A quick jerk of Voss's powerful hand slamming flat-palmed over the man's ear and the guard jolted, stunned, head-spinning and half deaf, beneath Voss's fingers.

That was all he needed to wrench the sword from the guard's weak fingers and press the blade against his neck.

"Now," said Voss, "shall I see Moldavi with your assistance, or without?" The wiry, ropelike Mark on his flesh seared hotter in warning, but he ignored it as the blade he held made a thread of blood over the vampire guard's throat.

His bloodscent was thin and immature, filled with fear and a low-class essence. Despite the fact that he hadn't fed for nearly a week, it attracted Voss even less than the ale at the Gray Stag.

"Assistance," the man gurgled.

Voss released him, but kept the sword in his hand and his fangs long and visible. "Very well." He smiled as if he'd just requested a different neckcloth from his valet and had been rewarded with the perfect choice.

The guard stumbled over to the door, opened a small window and spoke within. He turned, looking more cowed than a vampire had the right to be, and asked, "What was yer name again?"

"Dewhurst," Voss said, trying not to inhale the smells coming from that little window. Angelica. Burning coal. Blood. Wine. *Angelica.*

Focus.

Moldavi wasn't a fool, but he wouldn't expect any trickery from Voss, and therefore, he would have no reason to be on his guard. That was the benefit of Voss having cultivated the persona he had: everyone knew that he had no allegiance to anyone but himself, therefore he was of no threat to anyone unless he was threatened first. Above all, he was known for being a well-compensated informant who sold his information to the highest bidder, regardless of who they were, and a man who enjoyed his pleasures with whoever cared to share them with him.

And that was precisely why he had been the best person to come to rescue Angelica. Moldavi would never suspect him of bestirring himself for anyone else.

Voss was gratified when the pronouncement of his name gained him immediate access, and he resisted the urge to ram the sword into the guard's belly simply because he could. Instead he returned the weapon to the man knowing that Moldavi wouldn't allow it in the chamber, and relying on the fact that the guard would likely employ it to keep any others from interrupting what was to follow.

And he walked in.

Into a veil of bloodscent. Angelica. His fingers curled into the edge of his coat.

The room, the chamber: Voss focused on that immediately after glancing at Moldavi. He had to take it all in before allowing himself to look at Angelica.

For he saw her out of the corner of his eye; the impression, the essence of her. In the corner. Unmoving.

The chamber. Moldavi. He focused again even as he strode in and said, "Right, Cezar, I see you've changed things up a bit since my last visit. Being in the emperor's pocket has been a boon for you, no?"

Swathed in royal blue and emerald-green silk, the primitive stone walls shimmered in firelight coming from a large enclosure—a necessary evil for a subterranean chamber, even on a summer's evening. Two other doors stood at opposite ends of the chamber. Paintings made shadows and wrinkles in the fabric wall coverings. A strip of moonlight beamed through one of the high, narrow windows. Lamps lit every corner of the square chamber, and the chairs and chaises were upholstered in dark brown and blue, with heavy walnut tables.

Beneath his feet were furs. In that breath of a moment, Voss identified a Siberian tiger, white with black stripes, and two others that he supposed were from India—yellowish-orange and black. A brown bear, and a large number of minks stitched together to make a quiltlike rug in front of the chair on which Moldavi sat. A bit too exotic for Voss, but other than that, Moldavi's taste wasn't terribly ostentatious.

The man in question laughed at Voss's comment. "Being in the emperor's pocket? I'm not certain whose pocket is carrying whom." Like his servant, his voice was slightly sibilant and, though it had been centuries, still carried a bit of Transylvania in its accents. Voss knew—because it was his business to know such things—that part of the reason for the faint hiss was that Moldavi's jaw had been broken when he was young, and his teeth hadn't grown back in properly.

Still taking care not to look overtly at Angelica, despite the fact that his very being pulled in that direction, Voss strolled in and slid the toe of his boot across one of the furs as if in admiration. He used the opportunity to glance sidewise over toward the corner and caught the impression of continued stillness. His nostrils twitched, the scent of blood strong and sweet and of Angelica filling them.

In here, he had no need to keep his fangs sheathed, and allowed them to touch his lower lip as he pushed his needs away. Something burned over his shoulder. The fingers of the devil.

"If I had to wager," Voss said, "I should guess that each of you find the other useful…after a fashion. For one, the emperor's propensity for battle and casualties has certainly kept you well fed, and easily so."

"I have been known to sample the convenient buffet of a battlefield, to be sure. You are correct that we both serve the needs of the other."

Voss's expression remained bland. Moldavi's Asthenia happened to be something so common in the world of mortals that he would forever be limited in his own power. Otherwise, Napoleon Bonaparte would be merely a note in the realm of Cezar Moldavi instead of an associate. "Indeed," he replied. "The new emperor is fortunate to have your skills and brilliance."

And if Voss actually knew what Moldavi's weakness was—other than the fact that it kept him fairly sheltered from the mortal world for fear of being accosted by it (silver? gold? paper? ink? an apple?)—he would have a greater chance of extricating both himself and Angelica without it getting messy. As it was, thanks in part to Chas Woodmore, he had a better than average chance of making it anyway.

"Well, then, Voss, what brings you here? Belial claims you were in London only days past."

"I was, but it's such a bore. With the trade cut off, there's not a decent bottle of champagne or Armagnac to be found. The women don't waltz. And the fashions are... Well, need I say more?" He gestured to his attire, clothing he'd worn in America and donned for the purpose of this meeting to make his point. "So I thought to come to the source." He smiled and selected a chair near Moldavi, half facing Angelica.

Voss was acutely aware that he'd seen and sensed no movement from the bundle of woman in the corner. While he was pleased that she'd made no reaction to his presence—for it was imperative that he keep their acquaintance secret from Moldavi—the very fact made his skin prickle with fear.

"I did see Belial in London," Voss added, and as Cezar stood to walk over to a large wooden cabinet, he chanced a glance over at Angelica.

She slumped in a chair. Her eyes were closed and neat tendrils of blood trickled from her nose. Her neck, throat, shoulder...all seemed untasted. Her gloveless hands were curled, white, in her lap.

Sleeping. Voss hoped, hoped with such fervor that Lucifer's spectral fingers tightened on his shoulder so that he couldn't contain a gasp, *hoped* that she was sleeping. Peacefully.

The door on the opposite side of the room opened and two men walked in. Dracule, Voss assumed, but one couldn't be certain until one saw fangs or glowing eyes. They could be mortal minions of the emperor. Either way...blast and hell.

The fewer the people in the chamber while he tried to

manipulate Moldavi, the better. He furtively felt for the packet in his pocket, and with the other hand adjusted his coat so that he felt the weight of Bonaparte's watch chain. One or both of them would need to be employed.

"And what was your business in London? Sniffing around the Woodmore sisters, I presume?" Cezar said, bringing a glass bottle back to his seat. "Your timing, as always, is impeccable, Voss."

The bottle was dark purple, the color of eggplant, and had a golden wax seal which broke as Moldavi twisted off the cork. "We were just about to celebrate with a special toast," Cezar said.

"As to my interest in the Woodmore chits—anything to annoy Woodmore, of course," replied Voss easily, even as he felt a wave of…something…odd. "But I hardly saw the girls. Dimitri is keeping them tightly locked up in Blackmont, as I'm certain you're aware."

"Not as tightly as he meant to," said one of the new arrivals with a low laugh. Voss recognized him as one of Belial's companions at the Gray Stag and at the masquerade ball as well. The other man gestured to the corner where Angelica lay.

"Indeed? Is she one of them?" Voss now had permission to look overtly at the girl, and he took the moment to do so. Her chest rose and fell in shuddering breaths, and one of her fingers twitched. An uneasy sleep.

Or an unnatural one.

Fear seized him more tightly as he returned his attention to Moldavi. A horrible thought—one that he'd tried to ignore since London—rose in the front of his mind.… A thought that made all feeling leech from his body.

It would be just like Moldavi to do it.

"Ah…the reason for the celebratory toast, I presume." Voss forced his voice to remain steady. *No.*

What would be the best revenge for Moldavi to have on Chas Woodmore, vampire hunter? The man who'd stolen his own vampire sister from him?

Why…to turn Woodmore's own sister into a replacement for Narcise. And all of the Draculia knew what Narcise was to Moldavi: his sister, his slave, his whore.

To humiliate Chas Woodmore as Chas had humiliated Moldavi.

Voss's fingers were chilled, and he struggled to cut through the burn over his shoulder and the explosion of thoughts…and that odd sensation of helplessness that seemed to be growing. He vaguely noticed Moldavi pouring four drinks from the aubergine-colored bottle and when the man offered him one of the glasses, he took it.

At that moment, he knew. As if he were punched in the gut and his ears were boxed simultaneously. His lungs tightened. Harder to breathe, more difficult to control the grip of his fingers around the glass. *Hyssop.*

Here.

He looked around the wavering room. Where? The other two vampires had drawn nearer. There were no plants, no food seasoned with the herb. Nothing that could explain his sudden weakness.

The room swirled and tipped and Voss felt as if he were sliding into a pool of water, slogging and slow. *Somewhere.*

"A toast," Cezar was saying, lifting his glass. He looked at Voss, who, with difficulty, managed to raise his to just below his shoulder.

Steady. Steady, focus.

He fought the weakness creeping over him, warring

with the pain in his shoulder and his mental capacity.
"What is it?" he asked, finding it nearly impossible to
move his mouth in speech. Slowly he lowered the glass
to the table next to him. *Where is it?*

He needed to get away. His head felt light and the
room tried to spin, but he fought it still.

"Absinthe," Cezar replied. He smiled with genuine
pleasure, showing a fang studded with a tiny sapphire.
"A bottle of the best French absinthe, which I have been
saving for such an occasion."

Absinthe. Not brandy or whiskey.

Lucifer's nails... It was in the drink. Hyssop syrup.
Of course.

"Drink, Voss," Cezar told him. Looking at him oddly.
"You must join us in the toast. I shall at last have the
Woodmore bastard crawling on his knees. And Dimi-
tri to follow." The others had raised their own glasses.

It could kill him. Did Moldavi know? Could he know?

Voss had guarded his secret so closely. It was impossible for the other man to know. No. No one knew.

It was a horrible, awful coincidence.

Moldavi was looking at him strangely now. With suspicion. His eyes dark and piercing, the faintest warning
of red glowing at the rims of his irises.

Voss couldn't allow him to suspect, to question. He
swallowed, tried to wade through the roaring in his ears,
the tunneling of his vision as it narrowed and darkened.
His hand trembled. Even Angelica's alluring scent had
faded.

"*Drink,* Voss," said Moldavi. The glint in his eyes
had gone beyond suspicion to something akin to delight. The fang's sapphire winked and hypnotized and
Voss realized that, for the first time in his life, he had
wholly miscalculated.

14

WHEREIN A STUMBLE CREATES
A GREAT DIVERSION

When she heard a familiar voice, Angelica opened her eyes in narrow slits. At first she thought she was dreaming.

Voss was *here?*

Immediately her heart swelled and a flush of relief and hope washed over her. *Oh, God, thank you.*

But then, just as suddenly, the warmth evaporated, leaving her cold and frightened again. If only Voss were the man he'd been...*before.* The one she'd begun to have feelings for. An actual *man.*

Knowing that, she was filled with trepidation as she watched him settle into a seat with Cezar Moldavi. Much too friendly. Much too companionable. What did he want? Had they been working together all along?

Chas. Where is Chas?

She'd been pretending to be unconscious for some time now. Chas would be after her as soon as he learned what had happened, and her hope had been to stall for time. So far, she'd been successful…but she'd only been here for a day. Perhaps not even that long.

Voss looked over at her and she held herself still, trying to keep her breathing steady. Despite her slitted vision, she could see him clearly and although she hated him, Angelica couldn't deny that he was so handsome it made her heart hurt. And he seemed so capable and confident.

His honey-brown hair was ruffled around the collar and fell in a curling lock over one eyebrow that would have been endearing if she could trust him. Love him. His jaw, so masculine and chiseled, and those lips… and his fangs. This was the first she'd really seen them, fully exposed. They were wicked-looking, long and lethal and in the fog of her weary, frightened mind, she remembered Maia waxing on about how she'd dreamed of being bitten by incisors like that.

If only… She snapped her eyes closed when he seemed to stare more closely at her. *If only.*

Something burned behind her lids and Angelica tried to squeeze them tighter so that the tear wouldn't trickle down and give away the fact that she was conscious. *Oh, Voss.*

As she struggled to control her emotions—and it was no wonder she found it impossible, after what she'd been through in the last few days—Angelica realized that the mood in the chamber had altered.

"Drink, Voss," Moldavi was saying. He was not a large or imposing man, for all of his feared reputation—but it was his eyes that bespoke of the perfidy and malevolence inside him. He had swarthy skin and an abnormally wide, square jaw. His hair was the same dark brown as his thick, straight brows, and he had hands

as large as dinner plates. Large rings flashed on seven of his fingers. Now his eyes blazed red-orange and he was focused on Voss with an intensity that had Angelica opening her eyes fully.

Something was wrong.

Voss seemed...odd. She was across the chamber, and couldn't quite understand it, but he was acting not unlike Corvindale had in the carriage just before they were attacked. As if he were having trouble breathing, and moving.

And then...ice washed over her. She recognized his clothing. Odd, dull and ill-fitting. More out of fashion than anything she'd ever seen Voss wear. Except in her dream.

The dream she'd had the night before she'd been abducted from Lord Corvindale's carriage in London.

The dream in which...he'd died.

Angelica gasped and all eyes turned to her before she could figure out whether she'd done so purposely or not. Burned into her mind was the image of Voss, splayed on the ground in that awful dun-colored coat and purple and red neckcloth. Dead.

"My guest has awakened," Moldavi said. He smiled a hateful smile and Angelica saw the flash of a blue gem in his fang. "Just in time to join us in our toast to her presence."

So far she'd managed to keep him from biting her, although he'd been inordinately interested in the blood that erupted from her nose during her attempt to fight off one of his companions. She shuddered at the memory of him swiping his finger over her upper lip, and pulling it away, glistening with blood and then sliding it into his mouth. Watching her the whole time with glowing yellow eyes.

Angelica shifted, pulling herself up into a more stable position, and allowed herself a glance at Voss. His eyes met hers, and she was shocked by a blaze of awareness when their gazes clashed. *Oh, Voss.*

Her heart felt crushed, her breathing impossible. *Why did you have to betray me?*

She pulled her attention away and found Moldavi looking at her. "Perhaps you would care to join us in a toast, Miss Woodmore?" he asked. "It is in your honor, after all."

The tone of his voice clearly indicated sarcasm, and Angelica wasn't certain what to do. But before she could decide, there was a clatter, and the crash of breaking glass.

Moldavi gave a sharp exclamation and leaped to his feet. Voss did the same, but his movements were sharp and jerky and he seemed to be clutching the side of his chair for support.

The glass that had been in Voss's hand had shattered on the table, and the dark liquid spread in a pool, draining onto the fur rugs below. The other two men in the room had moved immediately to flank Voss, and in spite of herself, Angelica's heart lodged in her throat.

One of them wrenched Voss's arm behind his back and she saw that he had begun to reach into his pocket, but was arrested in midmove.

"Did you not care for my choice of liqueur, then, Voss?" Moldavi said. His face had settled into a complacent smile that bespoke evil. "Absinthe doesn't appeal?"

"Take your hands from me," Voss said to the men. "You're…mussing my coat." His voice sounded weak to

Angelica, and his face still seemed drawn. He'd shifted away from the chair and table during the little melee, moving farther from the furniture where they'd been sitting and nearer to the fireplace.

He looked at Moldavi. "You didn't care to ask for the purpose of my visit," he said. "If you had…you'd know that I come to do you a service. So if your men will take their hands off my person…our discussion can commence. Or…I can see what Regeris is willing to pay to find out when Chas Woodmore will die."

Angelica managed to hold back a gasp of fury. He was *using* her information? Giving it to Moldavi? And then his words penetrated, and she realized that Voss didn't actually know when her brother was going to die—for she hadn't told him. And even if he did know…it was to be decades from now. Her tension eased and she waited to see what would transpire.

Moldavi must have moved or given some sort of signal, for Voss was released—but not until after his pockets were searched. "Indeed?" Moldavi sounded bored.

Voss stood, his fingers still curled onto the back of a different chair, his face still taut as the contents of his pockets were flopped onto the table. A small pouch of coin, two small cloth-wrapped packets tied with string, a pistol and a knife. A handkerchief.

"What, no passport, Lord Dewhurst?" Moldavi said. "No identification papers. What a surprise."

"If you don't mind," Voss said, and began to carefully scoop the items back into his pockets. "Do you wish to know…the purpose of my visit…or do you wish to sit about sipping women's liqueur?" His speech was slow and careful.

"Personally I prefer the…women's liqueur, as you

call it. I rather appreciated the gray expression on your face when you smelled it." Moldavi stood and came toward Voss.

By now, Angelica's heart was beating furiously. Although she couldn't tell what precisely was going on, she knew that something was not as it appeared. Was he hurt? Ill?

Did Moldavi have some sort of power over him?

Other than that brief connection of their gazes, Voss hadn't acknowledged Angelica at all. Surely if he'd come to abduct her—or to save her—he would have at least made reference to her presence.

Moving only his eyes, Voss glanced at Moldavi, then at the other two vampires. His actions were still slow and careful, and he'd tottered backward so near the fireplace that Angelica had a sudden jolt of fear that he'd fall into it. He seemed labored, and Moldavi seemed to be enjoying it.

"Or was it the glass? Cut crystal?" asked Moldavi, turning back to lift his own glass from the table, his rings clinking against its stem. "Perhaps it was this particular sort of cork?" His eyes narrowed in delight, giving Angelica the impression that he was a cat playing with a mouse.

"I am in possession of…information," Voss said. He raised his hand to his forehead as if to wipe it off, then his fingers slid weakly to settle on his chest, curling into his shirt and tucking under the edge of his coat.

Voss. What is it?

"What sort of information?" Moldavi asked lazily. He swirled his glass and looked at the dark purplish liquid inside. "The only thing I want to know about Woodmore is that he *is* dead."

"Then…about your emperor's…future." Voss tripped and Angelica gasped, barely catching herself from leaping out of her chair as he grabbed the edge of the massive fireplace…just missing falling into the blazing flames.

As he did so, and made an awkward little spin, something slipped from the hand behind him. The small packet tumbled into the fire. Then Voss looked directly at Angelica, held her gaze with purpose. His lips moved; he seemed to be counting: *three, two…* Suddenly, with effort, he pushed himself off the edge of the fireplace and rolled along the wall away from the enclosure.

Boom!

Angelica screamed just as an explosion of smoke erupted from the fireplace. The room was enveloped in a billowing, ugly, purple cloud, and the last thing she saw before the space became dark was Voss's silhouette, hugging the wall.

Shouts and curses and coughing filled the air, but over it all, she heard him call out her name.

"Angelica!"

She didn't think about all of the reasons she shouldn't—she simply moved toward where she'd seen him last. Voss was an infinitely better option than Moldavi.

Thick smoke filled her nose and eyes, and she breathed its heavy air that was unlike any smoke she'd ever smelled. Fingers grasped at her in the fog, low and weak, and she knew it was Voss. "Angelica," his voice was near her ear. She grasped at him, felt the hard muscle in his arm and clung to his solid figure. *Voss. Yes.*

The sounds of rage, of furnishings crashing and grunts and exclamations of pain told her that Moldavi and his men were furious and intent on finding them.

Something crashed above—a window breaking to release the smoke.

Someone bumped into her from behind. She stifled a gasp and skittered away, grasping Voss's arm tighter, as he staggered and half ran with her.

He seemed to know where he was going, and pulled her down, jerking her along in a crouching stagger rather than a run. She stumbled after him, with him, tripping, bumping and jolting, and then there was a pause as he slammed an arm into her, shoving her back against the wall. The smoke had lessened enough that she could see his eyes glowing through it. Smoldering red-orange, close to Angelica, intense and frightening…but soft when he turned them on her.

Suddenly they were moving again, out of the smoke and into some other space. She heard the door close behind them, found that they were in a narrow, dark hall. She could see, and breathe, and there was Voss, grabbing her hand with more strength than moments before…and they *ran.*

Angelica stumbled and Voss steadied her. She could tell that whatever had weakened him—if it hadn't all been a ruse—was no longer in effect. He was fast, so *fast,* strong, and she held on to him for dear life. In fact, her feet hardly touched the ground after he slid his arm around her waist.

He navigated them through a twisty corridor, up and down steps and suddenly they were going through doors, slipping into chambers, shops and even a pub. All at once, they were outside, under a dawning sky, bursting from the building onto a street.

No one on the walkway seemed to notice their sudden appearance, and Angelica couldn't have hoped to find her way back through if her life depended on it. Nor did she have any idea where she was, other than a shop-filled *rue* in Paris.

"Quickly," Voss said, when she paused to catch her breath. He let her feet slide to the ground, and released her except to hold her fingers in his warm ones. "The sun is rising."

Right. The sun was no friend to vampires.

Perhaps it was because he didn't wish to draw attention to them, but now Voss walked more slowly along the street. Since it was just beginning to dawn, revelers were stumbling home after a long night, and early shopkeepers and porters were out preparing for the day.

Voss had removed his coat and carried it under his arm and, with a flirtatious smile and a lightning-quick exchange of coin, he induced a tawdry-looking woman to part with her cloak. He draped the heavily sweet, smoke-scented wrap around Angelica's shoulders, covering her tattered evening frock, and hurried her along. She noticed he stayed close to the buildings, obviously trying to avoid direct beams from the emerging sun.

Angelica had no idea what he'd planned, but certainly she hadn't expected to be hustled along to a very proper, very expensive-looking hotel—*La Maison*—as she was. Voss breezed in through the main door as if he weren't dressed in the most outdated trousers and his face wasn't marked with dirt and smoke. Hers likely was as well, Angelica realized, and remembered the blood from her nose. She ducked her head to hide her face, mortification flushing her cheeks. What was he thinking?

Without pause, he directed her up a flight of stairs to a third story, produced a key and flung the door open to a well-furnished chamber. Light from the new sun poured through three tall windows, cascading over two chairs and a chaise, a screened-off corner next to a footed bath-tub and a small fireplace. And a large bed. Her body went cold, and then warm, and then shivery. She did not look at him.

"Blasted chambermaid," Voss muttered, still standing in the entrance. "Told her to keep the curtains drawn." He looked at Angelica almost sidewise, his lips pressed flat as if he were trying to be casual…yet perhaps a bit discomfited. "If you don't mind?"

She walked into the chamber, a bit dazed, but realized with a start that he meant for her to close the drapes so that he could enter. Angelica walked over to do so, open-ing the windows to allow the summer breeze access. One of them was actually a glass door leading to a small bal-cony, and she walked out onto it to look down over the creamy buildings of Paris. Then she came back in, pull-ing the light under-drapes closed and leaving the heavy over-curtains pulled back in their original position. Still, the room was much dimmer than when they'd entered.

It occurred to her at that moment what an awful, dark life a *vampir* must lead.

It also occurred to her that, with the sun rising, they would be safe—at least for the day—from any pursuit by Moldavi's *vampirs*.

She turned to look at Voss, who'd come into the room now that it was safe and closed the door behind him. The *snick* of a bolt told her he'd secured the door, and her heart stopped.

Was he locking someone out, or locking her in?

He stood in the shadowy alcove of the doorway, his dirty white shirt tight over broad shoulders and a V of golden skin showing from where it had come undone at the throat. The purple and red neckcloth she'd recognized from her dream hung loosely around his throat. He was so handsome, a creature of every shade of gold and honey. So warm and rich. Her mouth became dry and she had a flash of the memory of those full lips closing down on hers. He still held the dark bundle of coat in his hands, and she saw him clasp it closer to his belly in a short, quick jerk.

They stared at each other for a moment, their eyes meeting, holding. Even the flare of light in his golden-green ones didn't send a warning bolt rushing through her.

"Angelica." His voice was little more than a breath, yet it sounded as if he were in pain.

"Thank you," she managed to say and broke away from his gaze. What now? What did they do now?

"Are you hurt? At all?" He remained where he was, across the chamber. But his eyes scanned over her as she dropped the cloak, and she felt the weight of them as if they were his hands.

Angelica shivered. *If only...* "I'm not hurt." She remembered her bloodied nose, and knew she had bruises elsewhere on her from the horrible horseback ride and her vain attempts to escape. But she supposed her fate could have been much worse at the hands of Moldavi.

"Well, then. A bath might perhaps be in order," Voss said suddenly, briskly. He turned away, but not before she saw a flash of white at his lips. Fangs.

Angelica swallowed again. Had she left the frying pan and fallen into a blazing fire instead?

But, yet...this was Voss. Hadn't he ordered her away from him when he sneaked into her bedchamber? If he meant to attack her, he could easily have done it then. Nor did he have to send for Corvindale when he took her to Black Maude's, when he stopped his own attack.

No. It was clear that Voss didn't intend to hurt her.

He didn't *intend* to hurt her. But the look in his eyes…

"A bath… Oh, yes, please!" she replied, looking down at the once-beautiful rose-pink gown. She'd been wearing it for nearly a week. Torn, stained, the ruffles and trims flattened… The frock would never be the same. She hadn't had the courage to glance in the mirror, for fear of what she'd see.

"Right," said Voss, pausing as he dug through a satchel. "I was speaking of a bath for myself…but of course, ladies first."

She looked over at him, surprised at his lack of chivalry—and then saw that he was smiling in jest. Her mouth softened. "Thank you," she said again, her voice low. "Truly."

He looked away, and his face settled with what was surely pain. "I shall call for a bath and leave you to your privacy."

"No," Angelica said before she could think. "No, I don't want to be left alone. Please. I'll forgo the bath… if you can stand me unwashed."

Voss laughed this time, and although he moved stiffly, it seemed easier. "Not only do I not wish to 'stand' you unbathed, but I also wouldn't dream of imposing my own unwashed self upon you. I do believe it can be managed with a modicum of propriety, my dear. If you will trust me."

Those last words hung in the air between them and, as if realizing what he'd said, Voss suddenly turned away.

"There is a screen, you know," he said, gesturing to the corner.

"Yes," she replied.

He walked over to a row of four bell pulls, obviously each for different needs, and yanked on the second one.

"What's wrong with your arm?" Angelica asked, noticing that he'd continued to favor his right side. He'd hardly been able to lift it to reach for the bell pull, in fact.

Voss glanced at her. "Of all the questions you might have asked me, that's the one you choose? Not, 'Where did you come from, Voss?' Or 'How did you find me?' 'Why are we here?' Or even 'What are we going to do now, Voss?'"

Angelica smiled in spite of herself. She liked this man. "Ah, but I wouldn't call you Voss," she replied, her voice dropping in a way that made her flush.

Their eyes met again, stopping her heart, making her belly flip and flutter. Making her *want*…something.

His eyes were hot, so hot and so vibrant that she could sense the need from him even across the room. Even from that simple connection of gazes. He took two rapid steps toward her, then halted, spinning half away as if he'd been shot.

"It will be well-nigh impossible for me to remain in the same chamber as you," he said. "Without wanting to… Without wanting…*you*." His voice was low, very low, and not nearly as smooth as she was used to. "It's part of the affliction…the need for blood. We have to have it to survive. But it's not just blood," he continued. "It's you. I'm dying for the need of you, Angelica."

Her breath clogged and she found herself hypnotized, not merely by his gaze, but his words, as well. Her hand crept to her throat, settling there before she realized it, offering nothing but weak protection.

"And so," he said, his voice gravelly, his golden eyes burning hot. She even saw his nose lift a bit, as if scenting the air. He closed his eyes briefly, then reopened them. "I had my valet prepare something for you. To help. To help you trust me."

He gestured to a flat, metal case no larger than the palm of her hand. It sat on the table in the center of the chamber; perhaps he had taken it out earlier, or just now when digging through his satchel.

"What is it?"

"Open it. Wear it," was all he said, and then turned away, bumping into one of the chairs. He paused, his fingers closed around the top of it, whitening as they dug into the upholstery.

She did as he bid, opening the thick silver case. It was lined with lead. Inside, she found a chain intertwined with the stem of a plant. It was a necklace made from some herb, fortified by a gold chain so that it wouldn't break.

"I don't understand," she said, lifting it, smelling the small, oblong leaves that grew in clusters from their stem. They had a faint, minty scent and some of them boasted tiny, fuzzy lavender flowers.

"Wear it and I won't be able to approach you."

Before she could reply, there was a brisk, business-like knock at the door.

"That would be the bath," he said. "Perhaps you'd like to step behind the screen? And take that with you, if you please."

He spoke in French, rapidly and yet with his customary charm, to the maids. It took some time, but the bath was moved behind the folding screen and filled with steaming water by a small army of chambermaids. A second, smaller tub was brought in for Voss to use, and Angelica couldn't help but appreciate his consideration.

There was lovely, scented French soap and warm towels, along with a clean robe and shift. One of the servants assisted Angelica in peeling off her filthy, worn clothing. She had taken Voss's suggestion and stepped behind the folding screen, and now she slid gratefully into the tub. The chokerlike necklace settled around her neck, plastering to her throat and dipping into its hollow.

"Take these filthy ones," Voss directed from beyond the screen, still in French but much more fluidly than Angelica could speak, "and bring back some clean clothing for the lady."

She thought briefly about arguing—Maia certainly would. It wasn't proper for a woman to accept gifts from a man, especially something as intimate as clothing. But how ridiculous it would be not to accept something so practical, and even more so to posture about it. Sometimes, propriety was so illogical.

So she said nothing, humming to herself to cover up the sounds of his own bath as she washed quickly. After, a maid assisted her in dressing in a loose lawn shift and long peignoir.

Her damp hair pinned up loosely, dripping occasionally down her neck or onto her shoulder, Angelica emerged from behind the screen to find that Voss had also finished his ablutions. Her humming stopped.

All at once, the maids were gone, and they were alone—now in a far more intimate environment of warm, damp skin that had recently been bare, the scents of lavender, lemon and orange in the air, and fewer layers of clothing.

"Explain this," Angelica said, sitting on one of the chairs. She hooked a finger under the necklace and lifted it from her skin. Her fingers trembled but she kept her voice calm. Her belly was in knots.

Voss gave her a crooked smile. "Again with the irrelevant questions, my dear. All you need know is that it is a great deterrent to me."

"To you? Not to anyone else?"

"I'm afraid not." He turned away and Angelica gasped. The shirt he'd donned was not only worn so thin that it was nearly transparent, but the fact that his skin was damp and caused the fabric to cling made it easy for her to see the ugly, dark lines through it.

"My God, Dewhurst…what is that?"

He looked back, frowning. "What?"

But she'd already risen from her chair, moving toward him automatically, reaching for the shoulder where she'd seen something that looked like horrible scarring. Twisting black lines radiating from the back of his shoulder and along his arm, down past where the shirt no longer stuck to his skin. It was no wonder he could hardly move.

"Don't," he said, but it was too late…she'd already moved close enough to touch him.

Remembering the necklace, she stopped and stepped back a pace. "Does it pain you?" she asked, once again lifting the leaf-entwined chain, smelling its mint, now damp from her bath.

His face drawn, his lips flat, Voss nodded, then gave a shrug. "A bit."

She stepped back again and saw that his chest moved

in an easier breath. Odd, fascinating…and a bit frightening.

Angelica sat in a chair across from him, leaving what she judged was space enough for his comfort. "Is it the proximity? The smell? The sight? I thought it was silver that repelled vampires. That was the way Granny Grapes told us."

Voss smiled and moved carefully to sit at the edge of the bed, leaving more space between them. "Your grandmother sounds like a fascinating woman. I wonder how she knew so much about the Draculia. That," he added, "is what we call ourselves."

"Her grandmother was my great-great-grandmother, the Baroness Beatrice Neddelfield, whose much-older husband died when she was merely twenty. The baroness fell in love with a blacksmith, who happened to be the son of a Gypsy from Romania. The way Granny tells it, they fell in love at first sight and Beatrice would have no one but Vinio for her husband. Since she was a widow, she no longer cared what Society thought, and they wed—living happily ever after." Angelica shrugged, thinking, as she had done many times in the past, about the way some people seemed to find a strong, intimate connection to another person so quickly and easily without any explanation or logic. And how, for others, it was something that seeded, rooted and eventually blossomed.

And how some people seemed empty and remote for all of their lives.

"That explains it, then," Voss said. "The Gypsy blood, the Romanian heritage…the first of the Draculia was Vlad Tepes, Count Dracula of Transylvania. And the rest of us are all descendants of his. For obvious reasons, if they choose to do so, Dracule tend to make very good marriages—albeit temporary ones, due to the immortality factor. Many of our antecedents wed titled members of European aristocracy. But the choice to become Dracule is only offered to some of us."

"Such were my granny's bedtime stories," Angelica agreed. "Not of the variety commonly told to English children, however."

"Thank the Fates for that, or how many more of them would grow up wishing to be like your brother."

"You didn't answer my question."

Voss shifted. "Because you aren't asking the ones you ought to, Angelica." His eyes glittered and she felt warm and flushed again.

But no longer apprehensive.

"I'm certain I'll learn the answers in good time. You obviously can't leave the hotel during the daylight, so we are here for some time. And for now, I want to understand how this plant...whatever it is...affects you."

He sighed. "It's not something one discusses, Angelica. It's of a personal nature. Incidentally," he added with a bit of a rueful smile, "that's precisely the reason Corvindale and Cale, and even your brother, are displeased with me. Because I make a point of learning about their...weaknesses. So to speak."

"Lord Corvindale is one, too?" Angelica gasped. "And Mr. Cale?"

"Ah. Yes, indeed. I'm sorry to shatter your illusions. They are also Dracule."

"And my brother...Chas works with Lord Corvindale? How can he work with the man he hunts?"

Voss shrugged. "I don't know the details of the history between them, but as I told you before, there is bad blood between two Draculean factions—those of Corvindale and Moldavi. Aside of the fact that Corvindale has his own reasons for disliking me, I confess, I admire his situation. Having a vampire hunter on one's side is a smart move on Corvindale's part."

"What about Mirabella? She can't be a *vampir*, can she? For…well, she's gone shopping with us."

"No, it's my understanding that Dimitri found her as a babe and raised her as his sister. I don't believe she knows the truth of her origin, either."

"How many of you *are* there?" She couldn't help the distaste in her tone, and from the expression on his face, she saw that he noticed. His features flattened just a bit, just enough to let her know she'd insulted him.

"Not so many as it would seem," he said. "We don't generally reproduce."

Silence reigned for a moment, and Angelica found that she couldn't keep her eyes from him. The necklace gave her an unfamiliar, heady sort of power. Courage and even boldness. She no longer feared him.

And the fact that he'd thought to prepare such a talisman for her—to offer her a way to protect herself—gave her much to think about.

"Have you always been…like this?" she asked, rising to her feet. Her heart was pounding and her palms had begun to dampen.

Voss shook his head, his hair gleaming rich and bronze. His hand was splayed wide on the bed next to him, pressing deeply into a thick coverlet. She couldn't help but notice the length and fine shape of his fingers.

"No, one isn't born Dracule," he replied. "One is… invited."

Angelica raised her brows in question and realized she'd taken a step toward him.

"You wouldn't believe me…. Well, perhaps you would," he amended with a rueful smile. "You who have the Sight, and know that extraordinary things do exist. It was Lucifer. He came to me in a dream."

"The preferred method angels use for communication," Angelica said lightly, after a moment of shock. "Fallen from grace or otherwise."

His lips quirked. "Apparently so. He offered power, strength and immortality. I was twenty-eight, at the prime of my manhood. It was a dream; it wasn't real, but it was tempting. Of course I accepted." Now his mouth flattened. "And neglected to ask what he expected in return."

"Or perhaps the state of being in a dream wouldn't have allowed you to do so." Angelica had come to recognize his expressions by now, and what she saw was grief and pain. And yet…bravado. He would soldier on. Perhaps make light of it. "What did he expect in return?"

"Allegiance…not overt fealty, but he has ways of influencing one's actions. And there is the understanding that, if bidden, a Dracule is meant to do Luce's work, to be called up to arms, so to speak, if the day comes when we're needed."

Horror had begun to filter through Angelica as his words sank in. "The devil's earthly army? To be called up at his whim?"

"I didn't understand that part of it, or really, any of it, at that time," he replied. His voice was testy and sharp. "If I had…"

What sort of a person would agree to such a thing? Angelica couldn't speak. The knowledge that she sat here, with a man who'd sold his soul to Lucifer, was inconceivable. Chilling.

Worse yet was that she wasn't frightened of him, and in fact…she felt connected to him. They, like Beatrice and Vinio, had had that instant, compelling connection.

She liked him—at least when he wasn't driving his incisors into her neck.

"I woke up the next morning, the dream lingering like a nightmare. The first thing I saw when I opened my eyes was a drawing on the wall of my father's study— that was where I'd fallen asleep after too much drinking the night before. He had hung a collection of botanical watercolors, and the one I noticed was a picture of hyssop." He gestured faintly toward her and she understood that was the name of the plant she wore around her neck. "To this day, I'm unaccountably grateful that it wasn't the drawing of grapes that caught my attention first."

He paused, ran a hand through his hair and looked straight at her. "It feels odd to talk about such things. I never have."

"It's a great burden you've borne for… How long has it been?"

"Since 1684."

Angelica couldn't speak for a moment. He was one hundred and…forty-three? Forty-two? Forty-*five* years old?

His bright smile had an edge to it. "Yes, I'm one hundred and forty-eight years old."

Angelica had never been very good at arithmetic. "I find it inconceivable. Yet, I believe you. After all, I've seen…evidence of it." She strolled around the edge of the small round table between the two chairs, trailing her finger on it, feeling herself wanting to move toward him. Despite all of it. "Recall that I, too, have told you my deepest secret. My own burden."

"I was—am—very flattered. You carry a great strength about you, Angelica."

Something unfurled in her chest. He made her feel something that no one else did. Important, worthy… She said, "You awoke, you saw the picture and how did you know that this…whatever it is…had happened?"

"When I walked outside that morning, into the sunlight…after realizing I wasn't hungry for the eggs and ham that had been served. That was the last time I've been in the sun. Those brief moments I spent there were agony."

"But you look as if you belong there," she said, the words coming out before she could stop them. So she continued. "Your skin is so golden. And warm."

Angelica. His lips moved silently and his eyes heated to pure gold. Her heart thumped and she took a step closer, leaving the table behind. His fingers moved on the coverlet next to him.

What am I doing?

He can't hurt you. He's said it himself. You've seen the proof.

"Does it hurt?" she asked, walking closer. "I don't wish to hurt you, my lord. But…"

"It's no great pain…just…as if I cannot breathe. I grow weaker, the closer you come."

She stopped, took a step back, gauging his expression. "I don't seem to be able to stay away." Again, the words came without her permission.

"It's no great thing.… I find I cannot breathe around you regardless."

This made her want to smile and cry at the same time. "If I wear this, I can come close to you, safely… but you're hurting."

"The pain is only too great if the plant touches me. Take care."

Take care.

Was he giving her permission to come to him? To touch him?

The answer was clear in his eyes.

Angelica's palms were damp, her heart raced. *What am I doing?* His shoulders were so wide, and the shirt damp from his hair.

His breathing shifted, lowered and became rough. But his eyes focused on her, pulled, lured…

"What of the way vampires can hypnotize?" she asked, stopping suddenly, remembering more from Granny's stories. Was that all this was? His manipulation? Was he tricking her, just as Lucifer had tricked him? "Are you *tricking* me?"

Voss managed a sharp laugh. "The Fates, *no*." He drew in a breath. "Yes, the thrall—my thrall—is real. And very effective. Except with you. You seem…impervious to it."

Angelica straightened and looked at him with interest. She was perhaps five paces from him, from the bed on which he sat like a rigid soldier. The corners of his mouth were tight.

"I? Impervious?" she asked.

He made a frustrated sound. "Blast it, Angelica, if you weren't…well, you'd likely be able to call me Voss. And you wouldn't be wearing that damned necklet." He looked at her hotly, and the bottom dropped out of her belly. "You wouldn't want to. I promise you that."

The tips of his fangs were showing now, just beneath his upper lip, and the burning in his eyes shone like red-gold flames.

"What is that on your back?" she asked again. "May I tend to it?"

Again, a short, sharp laugh. "There is naught you can do."

She was close enough that if she reached out, she could touch his face. Or shoulder. His breathing was rough, and she realized hers had become unsteady as well.

"If I come closer—"

"Please," he said in a soft groan. *Please,* his lips moved silently.

She did. Empowered by the talisman around her neck, compelled by desire and curiosity, reassured by his need, she went to him.

His shoulders trembled as she rested her hands on them, lightly, taking care that he wouldn't be in pain. She felt him vibrating beneath her touch, and understood that he was fighting, struggling against something.

Under her palms, Voss was warm, hot even. Solid. Broad. The ends of his hair brushed the tops of her fingers and she could smell the citrus and rosemary from his bath. His shoulders rose and fell in little jagged movements.

She looked down and saw his fingers curled up into the coverlet, wrinkling and gathering it into great bunches. His shirt gapped away from his strong, golden neck and she could see down into the back of it…the heavy black tendrils of scarring there on bronze skin.

"My God," she breathed, and without thinking, she pulled the neckcloth away, pulled aside the opening of the shirt so she could see more of it. "What is it?"

They were like little purplish-black ropes, and seemed to pulse and throb as she looked down at them. Shiny, coursing…the pain must be beyond comprehension. They grew like roots from beneath the hair he kept long at the nape, down over the right side of his back, concentrated at the shoulder but spreading like cracks in his flesh past his rib cage.

"Mark…of Luce…ifer," he managed to say. A trickle of sweat ran down his temple, and she saw that his skin had gone shiny and damp. "Please…Angel…ica…"

She thought he meant for her to move back, to give him relief, but when she began to shift away, he made a sound of negation. *No.*

Her hands trembled, and she was hot and shivery all over. Something fluttered in her stomach and Angelica felt something deep inside her curling, unfurling, swelling.

Take care.

She remembered his warning, so when she leaned forward, she bent carefully, holding the necklace tight to her skin so that it wouldn't fall against him, her other hand on his uninjured shoulder. And she lowered her lips to his.

15

An Unfortunate Slip

Voss's world was a war of agony and relief. When her soft lips touched his, half parted and sweet, he nearly cried out from the pleasure, then gasped against her at the sudden, searing pain that followed, driving him to take *more. Oh. God.*

The hyssop, small amount that it was, was so close that he could barely lift a hand, could barely uncurl his fingers from the bedding beneath him. The delicate curve of her throat was right in front of him, the V of her robe, the golden necklace, there…so close. Yet he couldn't move to touch her. He felt his muscles slowing, becoming heavy, even as the rush of desire surged through his veins.

And all the while Angelica's mouth tasted his, and his fought to taste hers back, the Mark on his skin twisted and throbbed, knifing beneath his skin, tempting him… *Take, take, take.*

Slick and full, her lips molded over his, nibbling and licking as her body strained closer. Her breasts, right there, free and loose just beyond his reach. Her nipple strained against the thin material. The druglike mix of lavender and orange and Angelica, warm and sweet and sensual.

Her hands brushed over his hot skin and he felt the flesh on his face tighten beneath her fingers. He lifted his chin and her touch slipped to cup his jaw. More, *more*...he wanted more. His lungs no longer worked and he felt as if he were drowning, spiraling into a vortex of pain-matched pleasure.

Her hip pressed against his torso, the fabric of her robe slid along his thigh. His fangs thrust hard and sharp, his gums swollen with the same need that filled his cock. Voss tried to say her name, but he couldn't drag his thoughts together enough to take the breath.

The next thing he knew, she was lifting his shirt, pulling it from his trousers. The cooler air was good against his damp skin, and her hands were there...over his shoulders, his chest, along the tops of his arms. Tentative, so tentative and light that he wanted to groan with frustration.

She gasped in horror when she brushed over his Mark, and it leaped and pulsed beneath her touch, shooting dark, evil pain through him. "Oh, God, Dewhurst..." Angelica breathed.

Voss. Call me Voss.

He didn't know why it was so important to him, but he wanted it. He wanted her. Deep within, his body strained and writhed with so many battling demands, weak and on fire.

Voss closed his eyes, tried desperately to block out the agony, to gather the strength to touch her. If he didn't, he would die.

"Dewhurst," she said, her voice penetrating the blaze of pain. She was close, her words warm on his desperate skin. He managed to lift a hand, though it felt like a hundredweight, and touch her face. "I'm going to take this off." She lifted the necklace.

Yes, yes, yes. Oh, Luce. Oh, God, please, yes.

Voss drew in his breath as she closed her fingers around the chain. He struggled, his back was on fire, his body wouldn't work…yet it strained and throbbed and *needed*.

No. He moved his lips. *No.*

He tasted blood—his own blood, and knew in a moment, if she pulled on that chain, if she yanked it away, it would be her blood. In his mouth. Her skin, her blood. Hot and sweet, so thick and filled with *her*…sliding down his throat, warming his belly, filling him. *Yes, yes.*

Voss was shaking as he fought it. Squeezed his eyes closed. *No,* he whispered. "No." A single breath was all he could manage.

Angelica stepped away, taking her warmth, and he opened his eyes. Her fingers were still closed over the chain. Her dark, velvet-brown gaze covered him, wide and hot with pleasure. Beckoning. Her lips, full and well kissed, half parted. Her chest and breasts, nipples outlined, straining against the robe, rose and fell. Thick waves of her hair had come undone, half tumbled over her shoulders, a strand caught against her damp neck.

If he'd been able to breathe, he would have groaned at the pure beauty of her.

"If I remove some of the leaves…some of it?" she asked, and began to pluck at them. "Will it be…better?"

Voss swallowed. He couldn't speak; he could formulate nothing. He managed a short nod and wondered, *what next?*

How long could he live through this torture?

Angelica felt the smooth leaves beneath her fingers, and watching Voss, breathless from the expression on his face, she pulled some away. Careful to gather them in her palm so they could be disposed of, she picked from the necklace.

Three, four clumps. A quick glance in the mirror showed her that more than half of the original remained. It also showed her a woman there, with unbound hair and flushed, rosy skin and parted lips. Nothing beneath her robe and shift but skin. Unbound, her breasts felt full and ready, and the place between her legs hot and damp.

Turning away from the alluring image, Angelica took the small handful of leaves and put them into the small metal case in which they'd come. And then she turned back to Voss.

His eyes hadn't left her. Dull, glassy with pain, yet hot and wild with desire, they followed her. The edges of his lips were white and he remained on the bed, half sprawled against a mound of pillows. The discarded shirt was a crumpled white heap on the floor; the awful neck-cloth that predicted his death a snake on the rug.

And his chest, golden and broad, with sleek, hard muscles so different from her own soft and curvy torso. Hair grew there.... She'd never imagined hair on a man's chest, a generous patch of gold and bronze over slabs of muscle. His shoulders, square and smooth, the skin soft and hot, called her back to his side. So beautiful.

What am I doing? she asked herself again.

But she closed her mind to the worries, the concerns, the propriety. Let herself feel.

She was in control. Safe. And she wanted to touch him, taste him. He wanted her to. His eyes begged her to, yet his face drew tight with pain. White near his lips, his skin shiny and damp from struggle.

This time when she came to him, he moved a bit, as if some of the restraint was eased. It had worked, then, she thought dimly as she bent to kiss him again. The necklace flipped forward, and he jolted when it hit his skin. His body whipped taut beneath her hands, bowing sharply. Angelica pulled away, slamming her hand over the plant stem, smashing it against her chest.

"I'm sorry, I'm sorry," she breathed, horrified at the red mark that now appeared across his throat. Like a burn.

"Kiss…me," he managed to say, his fingers trying to close around her arm. "Just…kiss…me…. Touch…me."

She did. She slid her hands up and over the flat planes of his chest, into his hair, kissed the salty warmth of his skin. It trembled and shook beneath her touch and when his hand moved slowly and awkwardly to cup her breast, Angelica pushed into him.

His finger shifted, finding her nipple, somehow easing its way down beneath the fabric to touch it. She snatched in a breath of surprise and pleasure as he moved, just so slightly, over the very sensitive tip. Little shocks shot down into her belly, down into the heat between her legs where her quim felt full and ready. *Ready.*

Oh, she said silently as he moved his finger, swirling around in delicate circles, his eyes fastened on her. Red-hot. His breath came faster and his face darkened, tightened into a shiny mask. Folding into themselves, his lips disappeared into a grim line. His great effort was evident as he shifted his other hand, moving down her belly, toward the throbbing center of herself.

"Please," she managed, still holding the necklace away from him, tempted to tear it away…but the sight of his fangs, long and sharp, so close to her kept her from doing so, even in that fog of pleasure.

He'd warned her. She wasn't a fool.

Then somehow, his hand found its way between her legs…there, in the hot, swollen place, he slipped and slicked long, elegant fingers. Angelica gasped again in surprised pleasure, and then she couldn't think of anything but the heat building inside her.

Her legs shifted, she half fell against him on the bed, barely remembering to hold the necklace at her throat. His breath came faster and more ragged, as if he were running, his skin heating and dampening against her, his fingers moving in faster and faster strokes.

Angelica couldn't breathe, she closed her eyes, her body swelled and suddenly exploded into something indefinable. Something that set her to trembling and shuddering, billowing and hot and suddenly…softness.

Release, pleasure, a smile settling over her whole body.

Voss's hand fell away from Angelica and her hot, sleek warmth, and he lay there, her sated body collapsed against him, the searing pain from the necklace she'd forgotten about burning into his bicep.

Pain such as he'd never experienced blazed through his body, pounding into his shoulder and beyond, to the very tips of his fingers and toes…hot and sharp, constant, unrelenting agony. His eyes could no longer

focus, sweat trickled from his hair. He was swamped by
the musky, sweet scent of Angelica's pleasure…felt the
sleekness of it on his fingers.

Please, someone, please, God, help me.

I'm ready.

His body burned and radiated with streaks of pain,
his cock was filled to bursting, his mouth swollen with
need. He was weak, breathless but needing desperately
to breathe, *wanting…* He truly thought he would die.
Please…help me.

Angelica shifted next to him, lifting herself after
what seemed like an eternity, blessedly taking the hyssop from his skin. The pain lessened, but barely. He
could hardly focus, but fastened on her eyes, heavy-
lidded and sated, her lips full and lush, half-parted. In-
credibly beautiful.

His heart hurt. Deep inside him, his heart hurt.

"Please," she whispered, and leaned forward, leaned
to brush her lips against his, holding his gaze.

He moved, using his last bit of strength and awareness to lift his face up and taste her, so desperate, needy.
Their lips met, his rough and demanding, *taking…*her
hand settling onto his chest, his heart thumping errati-
cally beneath her palm.

And then it happened. Their mouths and tongues
slipped and slid together, mashing and molding and he
moved too sharply and cut her lip.

Instantly the tang filled his mouth, slid over his lower
lip, the thick, heavy blood. It was just a nick, just a tiny
slice, but the taste of it was as if something exploded
inside him: relief, pain, pleasure, madness. He cried out
against her mouth.

More.

He licked her lip, tasted, sucked, and suddenly she pulled away. Her eyes, moments earlier, had been half-closed and soft...now they looked at him in question. A bit of fear shone in her gaze.

Please...please... The flavor of her was still on his tongue, the scent in his nose. Ambrosia, water to a dying man.

The loud pounding on the door penetrated his consciousness, and set Angelica to stumbling off the bed, away from him.

"Dewhurst!" Something slammed against the door, heavy and strong.

Voss tried to focus, to bring himself out of the depths of dark pain. He could hardly pull himself to a sitting position. *Unlock it,* he wanted to say. He knew full well what awaited him. But he couldn't find the words.

Angelica's eyes were wide with fear and shock now, and as she looked over, the door bowed threateningly. Gathering the robe close over her chest, she moved nearer to Voss just as the doorjamb gave way.

With a loud, fierce splinter, the frame pulled from the wall and the door burst open. A figure burst into the room with a swirl of cloak.

"Chas!" Angelica cried.

Before Voss could react, before Angelica could say another word, Woodmore was there, over him, a stake resting in the center of his bare chest.

Eyes blazing, Woodmore stared down at Voss. "The only reason you aren't already dead," said the vampire hunter softly, "is because you succeeded in getting my sister away from Moldavi."

Voss scrambled to gather his thoughts, what little strength he had left and to rise above the shattering pain. "I should have known…you wouldn't give me… two days."

Woodmore's face darkened further. "You seem to have accomplished enough in the short time you had." He looked over at Angelica, who stared at them with wide eyes. "Are you hurt?"

"No. Chas, I—"

"There's *blood,*" Woodmore said flatly. "And you are barely clothed. Both of you." His voice heavy with distaste and loathing, he turned back to Voss and the stake poked harder. "You truly are a bastard. It's a damned good thing I didn't trust you."

Voss met the man's deathly gaze with his own burning one: straight and fearless. He would not explain himself. *Do it. Put me out of my damn misery. I'll face whatever comes. Judgment. Condemnation.*

Woodmore's muscle flexed and the stake pierced Voss's skin. Blood oozed, dark and red. "I'll take it slow, draw it out a bit. Wouldn't want it to be over too quickly. Make it too easy."

"Chas, *no!*" Angelica had flown to her brother's side, and now curled her slender hands around his stake arm.

Woodmore turned on her, his face dark and angry. "This is not your concern, Angelica. Get back." He turned back to Voss. "What is it with my sisters pleading for your miserable life?"

Very aware of the point being made into his breastbone, Voss merely looked up at his opponent. Boldly. Waiting. He tried to force his lips into the familiar smirk, but couldn't manage more than a twitch. Yet, the feel of wood driving into his skin was hardly more than an annoyance in comparison to the pulsing of his Mark, and the terrible weakness from the hyssop.

It would be a relief when Woodmore shoved it through.

"Chas," Angelica said, pulling at his arm. "Leave him be. He saved me from Moldavi."

"With…the help of your…clever smoke explosions," Voss said, trying not to sound too breathless and weak. He failed miserably. Glancing at Angelica, he managed to add, "That was how…your brother…nearly killed me once before. Took me…by surprise."

Woodmore responded to Angelica as if Voss hadn't spoken. "He might have saved you from Moldavi, but it appears no one saved you from *him*."

"Chas, no. Please. He did nothing." Her voice sounded calm and steady, but her eyes were filled with fear.

Voss could do little but lie recumbent and try to ignore the bloodscent from Angelica that still lingered in the air. The essence was long gone from his tongue, and his fangs had slid back into place. Even his raging erection had eased. But the Mark still writhed and burned white agony through him.

"You cannot call *this* nothing," Woodmore snapped, gesturing to her bloodied lip and the sagging neckline of her robe. "This is a world you do not understand, and a man who is no longer a man…. He hasn't a conscience, Angelica. None of them do. They live only for themselves, for their moment of pleasure. They do nothing but *take*."

"And yet you love one of them yourself. You're one to talk," she responded.

Woodmore blanched as if slapped, then acknowledgment flared in his eyes. "You don't understand. And I'm not about to let you—"

"It's too late, Chas. I—I love him," Angelica said. Her voice was still calm but sad.

"Then all the more reason for me to rid you of him," Chas said. And pushed the point harder. It had gone through flesh and muscle. Blood pooled enough that it ran down the side of Voss's torso onto the bedding. One sharp thrust and it would go through his sternum and into the heart.

"Do it," Voss managed to say.

Their eyes met, his and Woodmore's. He dared not look at Angelica. He just wanted the torture to end.

And he could never really have *her*. Not without fear in her eyes. Not without having to battle the pain and agony and the devil on his back. Not without hyssop and his betrayal and her blood between them.

Suddenly he remembered the blonde woman. The voice in his head. *Are you yet ready?*

Another excruciating wave sliced through him, and his fingers and toes curled against it. *Just end it. I'm letting her go. I haven't taken her. Isn't that enough?*

"Chas," whispered Angelica. "I will *never* forgive you. Please…take me away. Let's go. Leave him here. Please." She gestured to the sun blazing through the thin curtains. "He can't follow us."

"You'll never see him again," Woodmore said, lifting the stake a bit, turning to look at her. It was the first time his voice and expression had softened since he entered the room. "I won't allow it. Get any thought of it out of your head."

Angelica didn't look at Voss. "It's gone. Please. Take me home."

Woodmore turned back to Voss one last time. "I'm doing it for her, not for you."

"If you were doing it for me," Voss managed with every bit of strength he had, "you'd finish it."

"Damn you to hell, Voss," Woodmore said, taking Angelica by the arm and starting toward the splintered doorway.

Already done, Woodmore. Already done.

16

THE ORDEAL

Voss didn't know how long he lay on the bloodstained, Angelica-scented bed after they left. Hazy, dimmed beams of sunlight still streamed through the windows. A gentle breeze ruffled the curtains.

Damned Parisian summer day.

At least Moldavi wouldn't be out, searching for them. Woodmore and Angelica would be safe.

He was forced to stir, to try to move his abused body when a knock came on the sagging door. At his bidding, a chambermaid entered, ironically carrying the new clothing he'd ordered for Angelica.

The pain had eased a bit; enough that he could rise from the bed, holding a pillow to the wound on his chest, and pretend that all was well. Even though it was certainly not. His body felt as if it had been stretched beyond its limit, as if it would never work the same again. The Mark continued to haunt him, to needle and slice. But now that Angelica was gone, Voss thought it might forgive him.

Eventually the pain might ease.

Because Luce would never let him go. He'd been foolish to even think it.

Voss noticed that the small metal case that had held the hyssop necklace while protecting him from its power still rested on the small table. But she'd walked out of the chamber still wearing the necklace. Thank Fate she'd kept it on during their—he stopped his mind, forced the images away—during it all. Or Woodmore would have had all the reason in the world to execute him.

Voss's neckcloth was on the floor, that horribly unfashionable strip of fabric he'd forced himself to wear. He pulled on a clean shirt, but wrapped the neckcloth loosely around his throat, for it was the only one he'd brought. The awful dark coat he'd brought from America was a bit dusty and smelled like smoke, but he donned it anyway. He had traveled very light, and very quickly.

He'd done what he'd come to Paris for. Angelica was safe. Woodmore and Corvindale would see to it that she remained thus, and Giordan Cale, too.

The sun was too bright and strong for him to leave, though he was desperate to quit the room. Leave Paris and put it, and England as well, far behind him. He packed up the meager things he'd brought in his satchel, slowly, still weak.

At first he dismissed the strained cry. But when it was repeated, Voss paused to listen. It was coming from outside the open windows.

He ignored it for a moment, but it became louder. More urgent.

Someone was calling for help. Thin, frightened, young.

Frowning, he went to the wafting curtains, staying

out of the bolt of sunshine. Peering around them, maneuvering in shadow, he looked out and saw nothing but dazzling light and a nearby tree.

Another cry caused him to look up, and then he saw two small feet dangling…from above. Nearly a man's height away, and off to the side.

Luce's dark soul, it was a girl! Hanging from the balcony on the higher floor, holding on by two dainty hands. The balcony wasn't directly above his; the platforms were staggered for privacy. If the girl released her death-grip on the railing, she would fall three stories down.

He glanced around—down, up, behind. There was no one else about. No one to notice.

Odd. So very odd.

Something prickled over his skin. Something happened inside…a burst of *right*.

He hesitated only a moment.

Part of him knew it would kill him as he darted out onto the sunny balcony with its red geranium pots. Another part thought if it didn't, at the least it might take away some of the impact of the swollen Mark, spreading the pain so to speak.

The blaze of sun on his bare skin was instant and excruciating, and it stole the breath from him, weakened him to a stumble. Voss held back a scream of pain as he reached up and over, keeping himself from being paralyzed by it.

Please…

Fire blazing over him, his flesh singeing and tightening, he staggered to the edge of the balcony and reached up. Couldn't reach. Half-blind, unable to force his breath to speak, he grasped the railing of his own porch and steadied himself against the brick wall as he climbed onto the rail somehow sensing his way. As if in a dream.

A nightmare.

When his fingers closed around the ankle of the girl, he couldn't speak to warn her. He couldn't see. He could barely sense what he was doing through the white pain... but somehow guided, he managed a good, hard, yank, and pulled her to him...

She screamed, high and childlike, and they tumbled back off the rail, onto the balcony, Voss miraculously managing to vault her into his arms so she didn't flip face-first into the side when she fell. He felt her warm body, slight and struggling, as he collapsed onto the tile floor. The girl pulled away, babbling something that he couldn't comprehend. But then, their eyes connected for a moment as time seemed to pause, and he was struck by familiarity there.

Peace and serenity in pale blue eyes. He'd seen them before.

And through the door and away, she was gone, suddenly, and he was alone. Paralyzed. Burning in the sun.

His Mark was going to explode.... He felt Lucifer's fury filling, swelling, radiating like it had never done before...and he buried his face into the hard floor, grinding dirt and grit into his cheek and chest.

Stop it...stop...

The sun blazed down and he couldn't move. The slender ropes on his back bulged, teemed with hot pain and he screamed in agony, dirt in his mouth and teeth, his nails digging desperately into the surface on which he lay.

And, at last, with one last silvery-hot blaze, he succumbed to the darkness.

But just before he did…there were those pale blue eyes…and a face.

The face of the blonde woman. She was smiling. *You were ready.*

17

OF MUSICALES, PROPOSALS
AND FAT FINGERS

"I don't want to sit in the first row this time," Angelica hissed, pulling out of Maia's grip. Her sister always made them sit in the front at musicales.

How would you feel if no one sat in the first row or two when you were playing piano? she'd say. *As if they were afraid to get too close?*

Since Angelica didn't play piano—or anything else—she wouldn't have the foggiest notion.

Maia paused in her attempt to direct Angelica to the front row at the Stubblefields', annoyance shining in her pretty face. But then it faded. "All right, then," she replied. "Where do you want to sit?"

Nowhere. But Angelica replied, "The last row. In the corner. That way," she added a bit more firmly, "none of the other young ladies will be trying to engage my fortune-telling services during the performance." Since only a small percentage of the attendees at a musicale were actually there to listen to the daughters of whatever household it was play and sing (the rest were there by obligation and/or to catch the eye of a potential mate), this was a very real possibility.

Maia couldn't argue with her logic, and Angelica congratulated herself on her quick thinking.

It had been two weeks since Chas had brought her back from Paris. To this day, Angelica wasn't quite certain how he'd managed to do so without any delay or problem, especially when so many other Londoners were still detained due to the war. Her abduction and their absence at Harrington's party had been explained as a carriage accident, in which Angelica had been slightly injured, and for the last two weeks her societal obligations had been limited.

Once back at Blackmont Hall, she'd found flowers and notes from half of the *ton,* wishing her good recovery, and she'd taken advantage of the chance to hide away for a bit.

Two days after their return to London, Chas had gone off again, leaving his sisters still in the care of a resigned Corvindale. He, apparently, still had things to settle with the *vampir* Narcise and no one seemed to know when he'd return.

Since her return, Angelica had been patently uninterested in employing her Sight at anyone's whim, particularly in a business transaction.

She had, in fact, been patently uninterested in quite a few things, including eating, sleeping, dancing, gossiping and shopping.

Her sister had had to pester her into attending the musicale tonight, threatening to tell Chas (although she never indicated just how she would get that message to their absent brother) that Angelica was pining over a *vampir* if she did not attend.

And Angelica was certainly, definitely, not pining over a *vampir*. A *man,* perhaps.

But not a *vampir*. And why did she feel so dratted empty when she thought about that?

She didn't even know if he was still alive. He was supposed to have died.

He probably had. "Will this do?" asked Maia, gesturing to a row of chairs near a tall, potted plant with her neatly gloved hand. She looked particularly lovely tonight, with her hair scooped up high at the back of her crown in an intricate braided and curling mass. Depending upon the light, her hair could appear mahogany or chestnut, or even honey-red. Angelica had always been a little envious of her sister's classic beauty, compared to her own Gypsyish looks. Yet, she often told herself that though her sister might have gotten the beauty, she also got the bossy, rigid personality of their mother to go along with it.

"You look so pretty tonight. Is it because Mr. Bradington has returned?" asked Angelica as she smiled at Maia, suddenly feeling a rush of affection for her sister. After her experience with Voss, she understood better what happened between a man and a woman and how beautiful it could be. Now she realized how Maia must have felt all these months with Mr. Bradington absent, waiting for him to return. "You seemed so happy when you were dancing with him at the party last night."

Clearly surprised, Maia smiled. Her creamy cheeks pinkened a little. "I am glad he's returned at last. He is an accomplished dancer."

"And when you danced the waltz, he looked down at you in such a way that it makes me want to blush," Angelica said. "His regard is very evident."

Maia's smile faltered just a bit. "I'm not certain that's proper, to be so overt about it in front of everyone."

"Why would you think such a thing? I know that you are careful about propriety, but you're engaged to be married," Angelica said. "I would be so happy if a man looked at me that way, regardless of whether it was in public or private."

She would not think about Voss.

"Corvindale seemed annoyed that we waltzed, even after I informed him that Chas permitted it. *And* I reminded him that we are to be married in two months." Maia's smile had been replaced by very flat lips.

"Corvindale is always annoyed about something," Angelica replied, getting a surprisingly unladylike snort from her sister.

"I've never heard truer words." Then Maia bumped her with her elbow. "Shhh. Tilla is about to play."

As the smattering of applause greeted the youngest Stubblefield sister, who was taking her seat at the piano, Angelica settled into her seat and tried not to look bored.

She found that the performance and the necessity of sitting quietly gave one an ample opportunity to think…something that she found she'd been doing much of lately. Not always pleasant thoughts, but sometimes they were pleasant.

Sometimes the thoughts…the memories…actually made her blush. And the insides of her tingle.

Other times, they made her want to cry.

And still other times they made her angry.

But threading through all of them was Voss.

They had become, she thought, intimate enough that she could think of him again that way.

If he was even still alive. A little shudder whipped

through her now as she remembered that dream where he'd died. She'd kept Chas from killing him, but for all she knew, he was dead anyway. The same coat, the same neckcloth…the image of him sprawled in the sun: the dream was burned in her brain. She remembered what Corvindale had said about Voss's friend: Brickbank was destined to die that night, and no precautions could have changed it.

She'd never know for certain of Voss's fate, unless Chas chose to tell her. And it certainly shouldn't matter to her. But she couldn't deny that it did.

It felt as if that part of her life was unfinished.

The day after she and Chas had returned from Paris, when she couldn't sleep, Angelica had succumbed and opened the drawer in her bureau. The message that had come from Voss after she sent him the letter telling him what she'd learned from the watch chain was still in the drawer, the seal unbroken. Apparently even nosy Maia hadn't found it…unless she'd discovered a way to lift the seal without breaking it.

Angelica wouldn't put it past her.

By the low light of her bedchamber lamp, she looked at her name, written simply as *Angelica* in a dark, strong script. Her eyes burned. After a moment, she broke the seal and unfolded it to find more of his writing filling half of the page.

Angelica,
I am very grateful for the information you provided me, and because of that, I plan to fulfill my
end of the bargain and leave London. I bid you
farewell, then, and offer you a warning: do not
wear the rubies in the presence of Corvindale, or

even at all while you are under his care. I intended
the earbobs to be a jest that only he would comprehend, but in retrospect, I've reconsidered. Wearing them could only cause you hurt and, whether
or not you believe it, that is the last thing I should
ever wish upon you.

Your servant, Voss

The signature was larger than the remainder of the
text, and had a bold and charming flourish—just like
the man himself. Angelica had smiled at the thought and
read it again, and then a third time.

And then she realized she should be angry...for if
she *had* read the message, she would never have worn
the rubies. And she wouldn't have been abducted and
taken to Paris.

But if she'd never been abducted and taken to Paris,
she would never have seen Voss again. And somehow,
that experience, that time with him superseded the discomfort and terror she'd suffered at the hands of Cezar
Moldavi.

What kind of fool *was* she? To have fallen in love
with a *vampir?*

"I love this violin piece," Maia leaned over to whisper,
pointing to one of the items on the program and pulling
Angelica from her musings. "I hope she doesn't ruin it.
Melanie has fat fingers."

Angelica stifled a laugh and then sobered, for she
was reminded of Voss when the second Stubblefield
sister commenced with playing the violin. He'd com-
plained about a violinist's chair squeaking as if it were
some great annoyance. At least this time, the performer
was standing.

"Harrington has just walked in," Maia said suddenly from the side of her mouth.

Angelica closed her eyes and waited.

No. It didn't happen.

The rush of anticipation, the little thrill wasn't there. She didn't have the urge to slyly turn and look at him, to wonder if he'd find a way to ease them into a dark corner for a delicate kiss.

Or a passionate one.

"He's coming this way, along the back of the room," Maia added. "He looks a bit...determined." She smiled knowingly, giving her sister a sidewise look.

The back of Angelica's neck didn't prickle, despite the fact that she knew her beau was easing along the wall just behind her. Her pulse didn't quicken, nor did anything flutter in her belly.

But that was often the way of it, she knew. Marriage rarely began with the instant and passionate connection that her great-great-grandmother Beatrice and the Gypsy groom Vinio had. It more often began with a general regard, an ability to stand the other's presence—and of course, a good family and sufficient income—and then, if one was fortunate, it grew into companionship and affection. Perhaps even love and respect.

That was how it would be with Lord Harrington, should he propose, and Angelica couldn't be more pleased with it. Truly.

And if she was a bit envious of Maia and her fiancé—that the deep regard and affection shaped itself even before the marriage—Angelica simply told herself that the two had been engaged for nearly a year. The affection and intimacy had had time to grow. His absence might have helped intensify that affection, as well.

"He's been so patient, waiting for you," Maia whispered, again pulling Angelica from her thoughts. Why did her sister have to be so talkative tonight? "I do think his attachment is quite solid."

The fact that Angelica and Maia had never made it to Harrington's birthday fete because of the attack by Belial, and Angelica's subsequent abduction, hadn't seemed to deflate the man's regard for her at all.

"Did you speak with him at the party last night?" Maia asked.

Why was her sister so dratted talkative? "No, he wasn't there," Angelica replied.

Maia smirked. "I'm certain he would have been if he thought you were to attend."

Angelica reminded herself that she was fortunate that a young, dashing, comfortably wealthy peer seemed to have such an attachment to her. She couldn't expect a better match.

A small burst of applause interrupted her private lecture and Harrington took that moment to slip into the chair next to her.

She turned and gave him a modest smile that became a bit frozen when he leaned close and whispered, "I have waited two weeks to speak with you, and I shan't be put off any longer. I should like to call on your guardian tomorrow, Miss Woodmore. With your blessing."

Her throat dried. The only reason he would make such a request was so that he could ask for her hand. It was truly going to happen.

Tomorrow she was going to become engaged.

18

In Which Our Heroine Is
Once Again proven to
Be a Light Sleeper

Old habits die hard, Voss thought as he slipped through the window.

Although, it wasn't quite as easy to sneak into a woman's bedchamber as it used to be. And tonight, for expediency purposes, he'd used the most direct—if not most inconvenient—route.

Fortunately Angelica's chamber had a sturdy oak tree growing near enough to allow him to reach the sill of her window from a thick branch, and with a little luck and some planning, he managed to launch himself over to the ledge with only a soft thump. The earl really ought to keep those branches trimmed. He was going to have to have a word with him about that sort of maintenance when this was all over and he was certain he wouldn't have need of them again.

He wasn't as concerned about Corvindale discovering him as he had been the last time he visited Angelica, for a variety of reasons. And since he'd been lurking about for the past three evenings, waiting for a time in which the earl had gone out for the night without the sisters instead of staying in (why would a vampire stay *in* at night anyway?), his patience was strained enough that he was ready to take the chance even if the earl was at home as well.

The window was open, allowing the summer breeze as well as Voss to enter the room. Once inside, he stood, looking down at the rumpled bed and the woman sprawled in it.

His mouth went dry and his heart rammed hard in his chest. She'd said she loved him…but had she meant it?

What would he do if she didn't?

Voss wasn't certain how long he stood looking down at her, but all at once a clock struck from somewhere in the house. Three. Less than three hours until dawn.

Was that enough time?

Moving closer, he saw more detail in the blue-white light of the full moon shining through her window. The citrusy-sweet spice of Angelica, and feminine smells like powders and creams and fabric teased and assaulted him. Her dark lashes, half-parted lips, the masses of dark hair spread over the pillow. How many times had he dreamed of her thus?

A shoulder protruded from beneath the sheets, and one arm was curled to her throat. Then he saw streaks on her face. Shiny streaks running down her cheeks.

Tears?

Voss moved closer, reaching for her. Without warning she gasped and her eyes shot open. She scrambled into a sitting position, a cloud of hair tangling over the bodice of her night rail and spilling onto the blankets.

"You're not dead," she said.

"You have the ability to focus on the most inane

things," Voss said, reeling a bit from her sudden wake-fulness, along with the enticing vision of her rumpled and sleepy. "Not, 'Why are you here, Voss?' 'How did you get in?' Or, even, as you so bluntly said last time, 'Get out.'"

"I believe it was 'Get away.'" Her lips curved a bit. Just a bit. "I am surprised to see you. Does that help?" The low timbre of her voice could have been from sleepi-ness or some other emotion.

Just then he noticed something glinting at her throat, highlighted by the moonlight. Surely it wasn't... "Is that the necklace I gave you?" When he shifted, he could see the dark leaves of fresh hyssop intertwined with the gold. He faltered. What did it mean that she was still wearing the necklace to ward him off...especially if she thought he could be dead?

"Yes. I had to replace the hyssop because the origi-nal leaves dried up." Her fingers plucked at it gently. It was too dark to tell for sure, but he thought they might have trembled a bit.

Then his attention was caught by the shadow be-tween her breasts, a deep valley that he'd explored only once before...and not nearly well enough. Blood surged through him. He wanted nothing more than to slide into that warm bed with her and line his body along her soft, warm one.

"Why were you crying?" he asked, easing himself to sit at the edge of the bed. If she screamed or called out, it would be that much more difficult to make a get-away this time. Her chamber window was rather high off the ground.

And Corvindale would likely be in no mood to listen to any explanation from Voss.

Angelica looked away. She wiped at what was now a dried rivulet on her cheek. "What are you doing here? If Chas finds out…"

"Your brother," Voss said, his voice steely, "isn't going to find out unless you tell him. He's entirely too involved with Moldavi's sister to pay proper attention to his own. Or hadn't you noticed?" Then he smiled ruefully, although she probably couldn't see it anyway. He sat in shadow while she basked in moonlight. "Not that I should complain, because if he had been paying closer attention, I don't think I'd be here now."

"Please," Angelica said. "Why are you here? If someone finds you, I'll be ruined. And tomorrow—" She stopped and he saw her bite her lip.

"What's happening tomorrow?" he asked lightly. "A ride in the park with Lord Harrington? A picnic with Mr. Revelsworth? Or is it a fete on the arm of Sir Brittonsby?"

"I'm going to become engaged."

Just in time. Just in time.

"Indeed," was all he could say. Surprising how his mouth dried and his brain emptied. "But," he said, forcing his signature smile. "You love *me*. Or was that just a lie, to keep your brother from assassinating me with you as witness? I know you don't care for the sight of blood."

"It wasn't a lie. It…isn't," she said.

"Truly?" he asked, something inside him easing. He moved toward her. The first touch of her warm skin, his fingers over her arm, sent a shaft of *rightness* shuttling through him. *Yes.*

"Truly," she whispered. In the low light, their eyes met and he shifted a bit closer, still taking care not to move too quickly. Women could be skittish, even if they claimed they were in love. "I never thought I'd see you again," she added.

"But…you're wearing that," he said, gesturing to the necklace.

She tipped her head down. "It's the only thing I have from you…except the ruby earbobs. And those weren't really for me, were they?"

He gave a shameful laugh. "No. I was being an ass."

"That is exactly what Chas said. Although I think he used a more vulgar term." She looked back up, still toying with the chain. "And I thought that if a miracle happened, and you ever came to me again, I could do this…" She gave a sharp yank, breaking the chain and scattering hyssop leaves. With a flick of her wrist, she sent the necklace flying through the window. "So that you would *know*."

Voss thought he'd been broken before, lying on that sunny ledge…but now, looking into her sultry, exotic eyes, he knew that had only been the beginning. His insides shifted, unfurled, and the last bit of reticence cracked.

"Angelica," he said, sliding toward her.

She welcomed him, her arms moving around him as he gathered her warm body to his. Sweet, soft, silky. Her scent enveloped him…and that of another, as well.

He pulled away to look into her eyes. "You've been near another. A man."

She tensed a bit. "Lord Harrington and I took a turn about the Stubblefields' garden tonight."

"Am I to presume he is the fortunate gentleman to claim your hand?" Voss reached up to touch her head, unable to resist sliding his hand down her thick hair.

Gorgeous, heavy, warm. He wanted to see her standing, dressed in only these tresses.

"He's calling on Corvindale tomorrow at noon."

"And he kissed you as well, I think, no?"

"He did."

"Was he able to make you forget this?" And he moved in.

Their lips met, hers so soft and sweet that he had to restrain himself from devouring hers. But the little moan, the little clutch of her fingers into his hair, the arch of her body from beneath the coverlet ruined that.

He could think of nothing like restraint—only her, of the smooth slide of lips and the gentle click of teeth, the sleek dance of tongue and the gentle nibbling on top and bottom. His breath gone, his body ready, *ready,* after waiting for her for so long…her shoulders, delicate and soft, and her breasts pushing into him. He felt her legs shifting beneath, pulled aside the strap of her night rail, kissed along her neck, felt her shudder beneath his mouth.

She tensed a bit then, and he pulled back to look down at her, knowing she was waiting for him to thrust into her….

"Was he?" Voss asked.

Angelica had to pull herself free from the sensual fog that came with him, and at first she didn't understand. She looked up at the man looming above her, outlined by moonlight that tipped the waves of his hair silver, but shadowed his face…and then she remembered his question.

"No," she replied softly, reaching up to touch his jaw. "No, he wasn't. I don't believe anyone could."

"Angelica…I love you. I want…you." He'd shifted

and now she could see his eyes in the silvery light. They were dark and hungry and her breath caught.

"I'm going to be engaged tomorrow," she said, trying to keep her voice low and steady. "I—"

"Angelica," he whispered. "I'll take care of everything tomorrow. With Corvindale. If...if you'll have me. If you'll trust me."

She didn't know how he would, knew that Chas would never allow it short of them eloping...but she didn't care. Not at this moment, this moment she didn't think she'd ever have, with the deepest part of her craving him. "I'll have you." *Any way I can.* "I've trusted you all along, haven't I?"

On the little gust of a groan, he gathered her up again, crushing his mouth to hers as a hand slipped to curve around her breast. Her nipples had tightened as they'd kissed, but now, as his fingers found the hard, sensitive tip, she flushed warm everywhere. That surge between her legs, hot and sudden, made her arch up and slide herself against him. *This*...this.

She wanted to touch his skin, had regretted not doing it enough in Paris. Never kissing him on that smooth, golden expanse, not ruffling her fingers through that fascinating patch of hair. He pulled back and tore off his coat and then his shirt, and she rose up to flatten her hands against his torso, riding them up over the smooth slabs of muscle dusted with rough hair, the flat nipples and curve of square shoulders.

He was so solid and firm next to her softness, and before she knew it, he'd tugged the blankets away and was pulling her night rail up and over her head. It might even have torn, but she didn't care.

Angelica was naked, silvery moonlight striping over

her belly as he knelt up, looking down at her. It occurred to her, absurdly, that she'd never sprawled on her bed in this condition before—nude and uncovered and bathed in natural light, a little breeze filtering over her sensitive, waiting skin. It felt delicious.

"I've never seen anything so beautiful," he murmured, "in all my one hundred forty-eight years."

She wouldn't think about that now…not that he was so old, that he had this affliction, that at any moment, he could tear into her and draw all of her blood out. He'd proven over and over that he wouldn't do that to her, and tonight…there was something different. A restraint. That wild glow was gone from his eyes, the heaving, gasping breaths were nowhere in evidence.

"But," she said, later wondering from where such bold words came, "you're still clothed and I am quite curious to see what a hundred-forty-eight-year-old man looks like without them."

He gave a choked sort of gasp. "I do hope," he said, unbuttoning the flap of his trousers with practiced, unhurried motions, "that doesn't mean you know what a twenty-eight-year-old man looks like and want to compare us."

She gave a nervous giggle that stopped in a short gasp when he slid his trousers and drawers down over lean hips. Angelica wasn't naive or innocent about the workings of coitus—she and Maia had traded many conversations with the chambermaids about that very subject. But being confronted with the actual implement was enough to steal her breath.

She reached to touch it and he stilled. She glanced at him and saw his eyes close, his breathing stop, and she pulled her hand away.

His eyes flew open. "Angelica."

"I'm sorry…I didn't know."

"No, no, that's not it.…" His smile wavered and he drew in a breath. "You don't know how long I've waited for you to touch me."

"Oh…" She closed her fingers around his erection, shocked by the rush of pleasure she felt at the taut, velvety skin. "My lord."

"Voss, blast it, Angelica. My name is Voss. Say it," he said in a pained sigh.

"Voss," she replied. "I love you, Voss."

He moved quickly at that point, and the next thing she knew, they were skin to skin, length to length. His hands moved everywhere, and his mouth, soft and demanding, his tongue stroking and probing in places she hadn't even known were sensitive: the hollow of her neck, the soft rise of her belly, the inside of her thigh.

Angelica gasped at that, when he bent between her legs, gently spreading them. She couldn't have moved if she'd tried, but when his sleek, wicked tongue began to stroke her, his lips nibbling and tasting, she had to pull a pillow over her face to stifle her sighs and groans.

That luscious heat filled her to swelling, and as he taunted and teased, with long, slick strokes, fast, short ones, she grasped blindly at his head, sliding her fingers through his hair until it all exploded and she fell into a shuddering, gasping mass of nothing.

"Voss," she whispered as he yanked the pillow away, and she saw the fierce expression on his face.

He bent to her, his mouth musky and hot, and his hands sliding down between them. Their bodies, flesh to sleek flesh, curves sliding against firm muscle, slipped and shifted and when he guided himself to her core, he raised his face from the ferocious kiss.

"Angelica," was all he managed, but she read the question in his eyes.

"Yes," she breathed, "I trust you."

His eyes closed momentarily, and then opened again. Looking down at her, something blazing there that had nothing to do with the devil and everything to do with purity, he shifted and pushed...and filled her.

Angelica's eyes widened at the pure shock of eroticism, a feeling she could never have imagined or described...then with a sharp movement, he went deeper. The pain was lost in a wave of pleasure, and then everything changed from gentle stillness to a hot, fast, building rhythm.

He muffled her mouth with his, or perhaps she was stifling him with hers...she didn't know, and simply gave herself over.

And when he tensed and stopped, arched over her, his fingers sliding between them, she gave a little gasp of surprise, then tipped over once again, exploding into heat and light as he buried his face in her neck, shuddering above her.

"That," he murmured into her neck moments later, "was worth every bit of the wait, my love."

"Shall we do it again?" she asked, finding his lips, loving the taste of herself mingled with his own damp flavor.

Voss smiled against her. "Only if you promise to keep quiet. I don't wish Corvindale to interrupt."

Voss considered remaining intertwined with Angelica until someone came in and found them in the morning.

Then they'd *have* to be married. Then even Corvindale couldn't find a way out of it...and all the explanations would be made.

But in the end he decided there was a better way to do it. A bit more dramatic, and also, he confessed privately, deep in his heart, that he wanted to stick one last pin into Corvindale simply to see the man squirm. To force him to show some emotion, something other than the cold bastard side he showed to the world.

His soul might no longer be cracked and damaged, and he might have found everlasting love, but Voss was still imperfect. Just like every other man in the world.

19

THE EARL OF CORVINDALE
AWAITS HIS VISITOR

The Earl of Corvindale was in his study the day after the musicale at the Stubblefield residence, awake at the inconvenient hour of noon. He had managed to avoid attending the event, although, unbeknownst to his wards, he and Cale had put in precautionary measures in the event that Moldavi had already sent a more competent replacement for Belial back to London.

Yet, in truth, neither he nor Woodmore expected Moldavi to act so expediently. Now that the bastard knew the Woodmore sisters wouldn't be so easily plucked, he'd likely be planning some other way to have his revenge on Woodmore and get Narcise back rather than risking his life and those of his makes by pestering Dimitri. Nevertheless, Dimitri would be prepared in case of such an unlikely event. He was no fool.

Woodmore had gone off again, presumably to ensure Narcise's safety—or at least, that was the excuse he'd given, along with the fact that Blackmont Hall offered more protection for his sisters than their own home.

That was a fact which Dimitri could not argue, to his dismay. If he didn't appreciate Woodmore's years of service and friendship, he would have protested much more loudly long before now.

And now Dimitri had to contend with the flurry of activity around Miss Woodmore's upcoming nuptials to the long-absent, and lately returned Mr. Alexander Bradington. Dress patterns, menus, guest lists, seating arrangements, table dressings and decor, and flowers. On and on and on they babbled, his so-called sister Mirabella just as wide-eyed as the bride-to-be herself. He felt as if he was being driven out of his own home.

If he weren't expecting a visitor at noon, Dimitri would have retreated to his club rather than be about during the feminine planning and machinations that accompanied such events.

He frowned, glancing at his watch. It appeared that, very shortly, he would be thrust into the midst of yet another battle plan for another wedding. He'd been informed late last evening that Lord Harrington wished to call on him today in regard to Angelica.

But the man was late.

Dimitri glanced over at the tall windows that lined the wall of his study and noted that, yet again, the curtains weren't fully drawn. He knew on whom to blame that trespass, and his lips tightened. Tomorrow wouldn't be too soon for Miss Woodmore to have her own household to disrupt.

The sun, bright and hot and taunting, shone through the large gaps between the drapes. At least Miss Woodmore had learned to keep the drapes near his desk closed tightly.

And to keep the flowers from the tables.

A knock at his door had Dimitri glancing at his watch. *A full ten minutes tardy, Lord Harrington.* Just like every other fop in London—inconsiderate of a man's time.

"Enter," he called, and stood behind his desk. Dimitri enjoyed projecting a stance of power, especially to mortals.

"Good morning, Dimitri."

The man who strode confidently into the study was not Lord Harrington. In fact, it was a well-dressed, neatly groomed Voss.

"What in the dark hell are you doing in this house?" Dimitri said, furious at the man's effrontery. "You're more of a fool than I'd thought. Woodmore has left word that you're to be staked on sight."

"I don't see you reaching for your ash pike," Voss replied lazily. "But don't let me stop you."

Dimitri tamped down the annoyance. He was used to dealing with this bastard and his insouciance, and he wouldn't allow the man to needle him. He was stronger, older and infinitely wiser. "I owe you more than an ash stake in your heart," he said coolly. "After your games and *salvi* that night in Vienna."

Even now, nearly a century later, he couldn't think of the night Lerina had died and his business had been destroyed without wanting to do something violent…to someone. Preferably the arse-licker in front of him. Yes, it had all started with him and his games and trickery. Moldavi would never have risked his own humiliation by daring to insult and challenge his host if Dimitri hadn't already been sluggish and intoxicated from Voss's ruse.

To his surprise, chagrin colored Voss's face. "Indeed, you do have cause for anger, Dimitri. I see it now. But

I do hope that after our conversation, you'll be a bit more…tolerant."

Dimitri made a show of glancing at his pocket watch, then glanced again at the windows. Full, hot sun, with nary a cloud in the sky showed from between a narrow opening in the far set of drapes. "In fact, I'm expecting another visitor momentarily. I'm afraid I haven't the time nor the inclination to speak with you. Good day, Voss." *Burn in the sun.*

The other man smiled. "Lord Harrington won't be calling today, I'm afraid. I'm here in his stead. To speak with you about my intentions toward Angelica."

At first Dimitri couldn't react, and then he burst out in hard, derisive laughter. "You're mad. If I don't kill you, Woodmore will."

"May I speak, Dimitri? I hope that you'll change your tack…but if not, please know that I am here because I love Angelica. And she loves me. We intend to wed, with or without Woodmore's—or your—blessing. But I hope to gain your support. You of all people will understand, I believe."

There was something different about Voss, the least of which was his almost placating tone. Dimitri had never known the man to show deference to anyone, nor to speak in a tone without that hint of conceit.

Curious now, yet just as wary, Dimitri scoffed. "I can understand my ward believing she loves you—isn't that your forte, Voss? Wooing and coaxing and seducing? But *you,* love *her*? *You* love anyone besides yourself?"

Voss didn't rise to the bait. "I can certainly see how you might look at it from that perspective. You know that even I would never have touched Lerina—or anyone else one of us was feeding and mating with, but—"

"You fail to understand, Voss, that it wasn't the infidelity or even the loss of Lerina that has created my antipathy toward you. I knew who and what she was, and that's why Moldavi even had the opportunity with her. She was trying to gain my attention, poor wretch. Why do you think I was with her?" Dimitri closed his mouth and clenched down hard. He needn't explain himself. Not to him.

Not to anyone.

But Voss looked surprised. "And all these years, I thought it was because you loved her."

Dimitri kept his face stony. He'd only loved one woman, and she'd left him long ago. "No, I never loved Lerina—just as you never loved the scores of women you've been with. Don't misunderstand—I didn't wish her to die, of course. As for you—it's simple. I don't trust you. I don't like you. I have no interest in interacting with you, Voss, because you aspire only to trick and manipulate, and to take from others for your own gain."

Voss stared at him, and for the first time, Dimitri believed that the man might have actually heard him. "Indeed," he said. And nodded, as if accepting what Dimitri had just said.

Voss took a breath and continued, "In spite of that, perhaps what I'm about to show you will change your mind."

"Show me?"

"I mean to show you proof of my regard and intentions toward Angelica." Voss drew off his coat and folded it neatly onto a chair.

Dimitri watched in morbid fascination as the other man then divested himself of a ridiculously tied neckcloth, which also joined the coat, and then untied the collar of his shirt. "Burning hell, Voss, what the devil do you think you're doing?"

"Showing you this." The man whipped off his crisp white shirt and turned away, giving Corvindale a full view of his back.

For a moment, Dimitri couldn't speak. "Satan's dark soul," he whispered at last.

He stared at the smooth expanse of Voss's back, stunned and disbelieving. A shaft of something dark and unfamiliar stabbed him in the belly.

Impossible.

"Your Mark is gone."

"You have an uncanny knack of speaking the obvious," Voss said, but his voice was filled with warmth. Delight, even. He turned and pulled his shirt back on. "There's nothing of the Draculia in me any longer—with the exception of the fact that I still have an enhanced sense of smell. And could still fling three men across the road should I have the mind to do so, so consider that a warning, Dimitri."

"Luce's *damned soul,*" Dimitri said, still working on comprehension. *Impossible.* "I've studied and searched for decades.… No one's ever done it before.…" He flapped his hand toward the shelves of books, the stacks of papers and manuscripts, the hollow, empty feeling growing in his chest. "*How?* How did you break the covenant?"

Voss looked at him, pity and understanding in his face. "I changed."

Of Miracles, Siblings and a Final Request

Voss turned his face up to the sun, drinking in the warmth from which he'd been banned for more than a century. The prickle of a tear stung the corner of his eye at the beauty of it, the knowledge that he was, again, his own man.

With the woman he loved.

"My greatest fear," he said, clasping Angelica's hand as they strolled through the gardens—in the daylight, when all the flowers were actually open!—at Dewhurst, "was that Moldavi would have made you Dracule. All the way to Paris, I couldn't allow myself to think of anything about why I was going, what I needed to do… because if I did, I would think too hard. And then I would have weakened, and he would have found that weakness."

Angelica looked up at him, sunlight creating a nimbus of gold and bronze around her rich walnut hair. "That worry had occurred to me, as well. Along with the fear that he would just…attack me." She gave a little shudder and he pulled her close against him—something he'd been doing as often as possible in the last week. "So I convinced him that I might lose my Sight if he injured me or changed me in any way. I hoped to at least stall any intentions he might have had until Chas got there to save me. I knew he would come, of course. I didn't expect you, but, my lord...*Voss*—" she smiled "—when I opened my eyes and saw you...that's when I knew. You were the only person I really wanted to see. I loved you."

He dropped a kiss onto her lips, quickly and easily, as a man who is comfortable that he will have ample opportunity to do more than that with the woman he loved, whenever he wanted to. "I think you make it sound easier than it was—and yourself more tolerant than you were—but I wholly understand. I felt the same way, although I didn't quite understand it for a long time."

"What's going to happen now? Will Moldavi come after us again? Now that you aren't a vampire anymore, isn't he more dangerous to you?" Her eyes were worried.

"Moldavi isn't stupid—he knows we're prepared for him. I'm still very strong, and I have something he doesn't: the ability to move about in full daylight. And aside of that, there isn't any way he'd know that I'm no longer Dracule. It's not as if Dimitri is going to tell him, although I'm certain he'll find out about it someday. But yes, there is a possibility he might attempt to come after you and Maia again—although Dimitri, Cale and I think it unlikely. He's not about to risk more lives or resources when he knows we're expecting him and have thus far evaded his attacks. And now that I can move about in the day, that gives me even more of an ability to protect you. Try not to worry, Angelica. I won't let anything happen to you."

She nodded, but he could still see the concern in her eyes. There was nothing he could do to erase it, but what he'd told her was true: he and Dimitri felt no imminent danger from Moldavi—at least for the sisters.

The safety of Chas Woodmore's arse was a different story entirely.

They walked for a while, Angelica identifying the flowers and plants he'd long forgotten. At last she asked, "Do you think Chas will ever come home again? To stay?"

"I don't know," he replied honestly. "I suspect that as soon as he receives the message from Corvindale that we intend to wed, he'll be arriving with a stake in his hand. I never did thank you for saving my life, in fact, darling. It's very precious to me, even though it's no longer immortal."

"It was my pleasure," she said with a smile. "I couldn't read your future from your glove, and I've come to believe that I cannot read the future of a *vampir* that way. I don't know why it is, but it seems that I can only see the future of *vampirs* in my dreams—and that those dreams are as random and unmanageable as Fate itself."

"Perhaps they aren't so random, after all," Voss said, thinking of the mysterious blonde woman. "After all, if you hadn't dreamed of Brickbank's demise, as unpleasant as it was, perhaps we wouldn't have found each other."

Her eyes brightened. "Of course! I hadn't thought of that." She squeezed his hand, bare palm to bare palm. "And even though I *dreamed* that you were going to die, wearing that awful neckcloth and coat—I still don't understand why you chose those clothes—and I was afraid that Corvindale was right and we *can't* change Fate, I wasn't going to stand by and allow it to happen. I'd never been able to change my predictions before, but I *had* to try that time."

"But I did die. You were right, my love. I did die."

"Truly?"

He nodded, finally understanding everything himself. Why the blonde woman—she had to have been an angel—had continued to appear to him. That she'd been waiting for him to be ready.

Ready to change. Ready to put someone else ahead of himself—someone from whom he could not hope to gain anything. Ready to act exactly as Lucifer wouldn't want him to act.

When he woke the next day—or some time later—to find himself no longer in pain, no longer Marked, no longer bound to Lucifer, he realized he'd been given the opportunity for a miracle.

It was the one moment in his life that he'd been truly selfless—risking himself, giving his life for someone he didn't even know. Yes, he'd held back from attacking Angelica, from doing what he wanted to her because he knew it would hurt her…and that had been the start of his metamorphosis. But it wasn't until he'd given everything up for someone with whom he had no attachment that the change had been fully realized.

That gift of self had been enough to break an unbreakable covenant.

He realized that, at Rubey's advice, he'd changed. And that the angel had given him that chance.

Voss wondered how many other chances he'd had in the past that he'd ignored. He had a sense there had been more. *You don't remember me, but we've met before.*

"You never saw that little girl again? The one that

you saved? You never found out what happened?" Angelica asked.

"No."

"How odd. One would expect the parents to look for you, and express their gratitude."

But Voss shook his head, a little smile curving his lips. He would explain it to her, about his visitation from an angel that was *not* fallen…but later. When they were private and had plenty of time to talk about it. "I'm not about to question the event, Angelica."

No, indeed, he wasn't. After all, he'd asked for help, he'd begged and pleaded for it while writhing in agony… and the angel had heard him. She'd known he was ready to change, at last.

Looking down at Angelica, he saw worry in her beautiful face. "What is it?"

"Do you think Chas will ever give us his blessing?"

Voss fully intended to make certain the man did, if he ever saw him again. But instead of saying that, he replied, "Corvindale, albeit reluctantly, has agreed to help make our case. Now that I am no longer Dracule, he has no reason to deny us permission. But regardless, Angelica, we're going to wed, with or without your brother's consent. Now that it's been shortened, I'm not about to live the rest of my life without you."

"Thank you for coming back to me, Voss."

"Thank you for throwing away that necklace, Angelica. But there is one more request I'd like to make of you."

"And what is that?"

"You know I love you, I *adore* you, my dear…but when we were in Paris, and you were bathing…you were humming."

"I was trying to keep from hearing you splashing about and wondering...imagining...what you were doing."

He smiled. "Ah. Well, now that you don't have to imagine any longer, my love...would you mind...not humming so much? You tend to be terribly off-key. Usually flat."

"Is that so?" She smiled, her eyes lighting with humor. "So now I know precisely how to get whatever I want from you. I shall hum, or sing—which I'm even worse at—until you give it to me to silence me."

Voss laughed with deep, filling pleasure. He'd had no idea that his life had been so bleak and dark—but now it was filled with light and humor. "My dear, you don't have to resort to that. I've given everything to have you...and I would give anything *for* you. Just... don't sing."

* * * * *

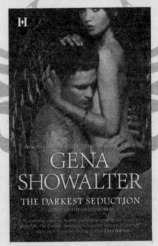

New York Times Bestselling Author

HEATHER GRAHAM

1800s. San Antonio, Texas: At the Longhorn Saloon, a woman was brutally murdered. Her killer was never found.

One year ago: At the same hotel, another woman went missing…but her body was never recovered.

Now: In the past month, San Antonio has become a dumping ground for the battered bodies of long-missing women.

Texas Ranger Logan Raintree has a powerful ability to commune with the dead, and when offered the chance to lead a group of elite paranormal investigators working this case—including Kelsey O'Brien, a U.S. marshal with the ability to "see" the past unfolding in the present—he can't help but accept the challenge.

Only they have the skills to find out whether the spirits of those long-dead Texans are really appearing to the victims before their deaths—or if something more earthly is menacing the city….

THE UNSEEN

Available wherever books are sold.

REQUEST YOUR
FREE BOOKS!

2 FREE NOVELS FROM THE
PARANORMAL ROMANCE COLLECTION
PLUS 2 FREE GIFTS!

YES! Please send me 2 FREE novels from the Paranormal Romance Collection and my 2 FREE gifts (gifts are worth about $10). After receiving them, if I don't wish to receive any more books, I can return the shipping statement marked "cancel." If I don't cancel, I will receive 4 brand-new novels every month and be billed just $21.42 in the U.S. or $23.46 in Canada. That's a saving of at least 21% off the cover price of all 4 books. It's quite a bargain! Shipping and handling is just 50¢ per book in the U.S. and 75¢ per book in Canada.* I understand that accepting the 2 free books and gifts places me under no obligation to buy anything. I can always return a shipment and cancel at any time. Even if I never buy another book, the two free books and gifts are mine to keep forever.

237/337 HDN FEL2

Name	(PLEASE PRINT)

Address	Apt. #

City	State/Prov.	Zip/Postal Code

Signature (if under 18, a parent or guardian must sign)

Mail to the **Reader Service**:
IN U.S.A.: P.O. Box 1867, Buffalo, NY 14240-1867
IN CANADA: P.O. Box 609, Fort Erie, Ontario L2A 5X3

Not valid for current subscribers to the Paranormal Romance Collection
or Harlequin® Nocturne™ books.

Want to try two free books from another line?
Call 1-800-873-8635 or visit www.ReaderService.com.

* Terms and prices subject to change without notice. Prices do not include applicable taxes. Sales tax applicable in N.Y. Canadian residents will be charged applicable taxes. Offer not valid in Quebec. This offer is limited to one order per household. All orders subject to credit approval. Credit or debit balances in a customer's account(s) may be offset by any other outstanding balance owed by or to the customer. Please allow 4 to 6 weeks for delivery. Offer available while quantities last.

Your Privacy—The Reader Service is committed to protecting your privacy. Our Privacy Policy is available online at www.ReaderService.com or upon request from the Reader Service.

We make a portion of our mailing list available to reputable third parties that offer products we believe may interest you. If you prefer that we not exchange your name with third parties, or if you wish to clarify or modify your communication preferences, please visit us at www.ReaderService.com/consumerschoice or write to us at Reader Service Preference Service, P.O. Box 9062, Buffalo, NY 14269. Include your complete name and address.

  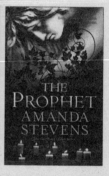

One of the original masters of romance,
***New York Times* bestselling author**

BERTRICE SMALL

invites you to the magical, sensual world of Hetar.

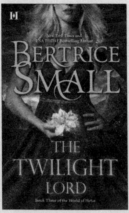

Lara, Domina of Terah, has disappeared, and Magnus Hauk is frantic to find his beloved wife. To do so, he turns to two strong allies—Prince Kaliq of the Shadows and Ilona, the faerie queen. Meanwhile, Kol—the Twilight Lord—revels in his victory. The exquisite Domina is now in his possession, and her powers will soon help him to conquer first Hetar and then Terah. But Lara calls on all her strength—and the passion in her heart—to once again rise to the challenge of her destiny.

Available now!